WORDSWORTH CLASSICS
OF WORLD LITERATURE

General Editor: Tom Griffith

SENTIMENTAL EDUCATION

Gustave Flaubert

Sentimental Education

❖

Translation from the Bouvard Edition,
revised, and with an Introduction,
by Adrianne Tooke

WORDSWORTH CLASSICS
OF WORLD LITERATURE

This edition published 2003 by Wordsworth Editions Limited
8b East Street, Ware, Hertfordshire SG12 9HJ

ISBN 1 84022 121 6

Text © Wordsworth Editions Limited 2003
Introduction © Adrianne Tooke 2003

Wordsworth® is a registered trademark of
Wordsworth Editions Limited

2 4 6 8 10 9 7 5 3 1

Typeset by Antony Gray
Printed and bound in Great Britain by
Mackays of Chatham, Chatham, Kent

INTRODUCTION

When *L'Éducation sentimentale* was published in 1869, after six years in the writing, Flaubert was surprised and disappointed by its reception. Both *Madame Bovary* (1857) and *Salammbô* (1862) had enjoyed immense success, exceeding Flaubert's expectations, despite their formal innovations. But *Sentimental Education* was even more daring, and left most of its readers baffled or hostile or both. Indeed, *Madame Bovary* is still regarded as the most accessible of Flaubert's novels, and *Sentimental Education* still comes as something of a shock. Among the few critics of Flaubert's time who glimpsed what the novel was trying to do were the two major Naturalist novelists, Émile Zola and J.-K. Huysmans. Each made the point, looking back, that it had been the quintessential Naturalist novel, despite Flaubert's own unwillingness to be associated with the doctrines of the Naturalist school. Zola praised the novel for precisely that quality which others had decried as its greatest weakness, namely its structure, which for Zola expressed the essence of modernity and the texture of life itself. *Sentimental Education*, said Zola, in an article of 1875, was 'one of the most original and audacious conceptions, and one of the most difficult to realize which our literature has ever attempted'. 'Gustave Flaubert rejected the idea of a central narrative line. He preferred to give us life as it is lived day by day, with its series of little commonplace incidents, which combine to form a complex, powerful drama. No episodes carefully prepared and melded, but an apparently random collection of facts, an unexceptional sequence of ordinary occurrences, with characters meeting, separating, meeting again, till they have said their last word: merely faces of passers-by jostling each other on a sidewalk [. . .]'.

But *Sentimental Education* is not just a Naturalist novel *avant la lettre*. In his 1920 essay on Flaubert, collected in *Contre Sainte-Beuve*, Proust detected in it something more modern than Naturalism, more universal than the literature of France: 'it is impossible for anyone who has climbed onto this great *Moving Sidewalk* of Flaubert's pages, as they pass along in a continuing, monotonous, indeterminate series, not to see that they are without precedent in literature'. Flaubert himself, in a letter written ten years after publication, conceded that the novel was flawed, technically speaking, but saw that flaw as an effect of the highest artistic integrity: his novel had in a sense outrun even him. 'It's too real and, aesthetically speaking, what's lacking is *the falseness of perspective*. The construction was so carefully thought through that it ceased to be apparent. A work of art must come to a head, to a point, like a pyramid, or else the light must strike on one point of the ball. Now, life isn't like that at all. But then Art isn't Nature. Never mind, I think that nobody has ever taken artistic integrity to such lengths.'

The status of *Sentimental Education* is, happily, no longer in doubt. Readers have caught up with it, thanks in part to later novels which have opened up the domain which Flaubert was the first to explore. Proust's *À la recherche du temps perdu* is itself the most impressive tribute, being Flaubert's novel writ large. *Sentimental Education* is now recognized as the masterpiece it always really was. Readers, critics and poets marvel at the mathematical beauty and precision of its style. Unsparing in its realism, it is also a comic masterpiece. Like all great works, it challenges existing assumptions and certainties. 'There is no Truth!' said Flaubert, in a letter written during the last year of his life, 'there are just ways of seeing'. Flaubert's 'way of seeing' is one of the best: the sharpest, the funniest and at once the most and the least forgiving.

The 1869 *Sentimental Education* is not the first novel by Flaubert of that name. The first, left unpublished by Flaubert, was completed in 1845, when he was twenty-three. The differences between the two are instructive. Both belong to the genre of the *Bildungsroman*, or apprentice-novel, but the first is more formulaic than the second. The first is indebted principally to the first *Bildungsroman* of all, Goethe's *Wilhelm Meisters Lehrjahre* (1795–6), which is about success and failure in the contrasting domains of 'Art' and 'Life'. Wilhelm sets out to become an artist, but after a series of mistakes and wrong turnings discovers his true domain to be that of 'Tätigkeit', a life of bourgeois usefulness and service to society, which he had previously rejected as boring and unworthy. Success and failure are shown to be relative: Goethe compares Wilhelm to Saul, who set out to find his father's asses but found a kingdom instead. The first *Éducation* embodies Goethe's dichotomy between 'Life' and 'Art' in two heroes, who are at first united but whose paths ultimately diverge, one (Jules) opting eventually for Art, and the other (Henry) opting eventually for Life. But Flaubert inverts Goethe's conclusion: Jules's choice is the right one, and investment in 'Life' condemns Henry to a sterile, shallow existence. The idea of 'Tätigkeit' has no place in the France of the 1840s. That point had already been made indeed in two more recent apprentice-novels by Balzac, *Le Père Goriot* (1835) and *Illusions perdues* (1837–1843). Their respective heroes, Eugène de Rastignac and Lucien de Rubempré, are foils to each other, in that the first succeeds where the second fails. But Balzac's France is such a noxious, dangerous place that Rastignac pays a high price for his huge material success in terms of character and peace of mind, while Lucien's failure as an artist has a great deal to do with his trying to be a social and material success as well. So, in the 1845 *Éducation*, true success is not to be found within the social system but out of it. The message of the 1845 *Éducation* is thus clear. It is far less clear in the second.

Love is the principal subject of both *Éducations*. In the first, Henry falls passionately in love with his teacher's wife, Mme Renaud, and eventually succeeds in possessing her. They run away to America, and the love gradually loses its edge in increasing domesticity till it peters out. Jules, on the other hand, loves in vain, and is devastated when he realizes that the faithless Lucinde was two-timing him all along. Love and Art are shown to be somehow connected: Jules's turning to Art is a direct result of disappointment in love, whereas Henry's initial success with Mme Renaud channels his future energies into activities with more short-term profits.

The second *Éducation* takes these elements and reassembles them. Henry's love for Mme Renaud becomes Frédéric's love for Mme Arnoux, but is now unconsummated, like Jules' love for

Lucinde. But the Artist has disappeared. For Flaubert, now, the Artist is a pure abstraction: there is nothing whatever to say about him which his art itself does not say. There are professional artists galore in the second *Éducation*, but we do not see them grappling with their art. The only artist whom we do see behaving in this way is Pellerin, but he does not exactly *grapple* with *Art* as such at all, and that is precisely his problem. Ideas about art still drive the novel, as they drove the first *Éducation*, but they are now worked more subtly into its fabric. Jules-the-Artist is subsumed into the character of Frédéric, who is no artist but who has more to tell us, metaphorically, about the ideal artist than Flaubert felt a practising artist could, as we shall see.

The two novels differ also in scope. Flaubert now extends his field to encompass a whole generation: 'I want to write the moral history of my generation: "sentimental" would be the more accurate term' (letter of 6 October 1864). All the characters – not just Frédéric and Deslauriers – undergo a sentimental education, which readers can assemble for themselves from the fragments which appear in the text. What is more, Flaubert decides to make his novel the story of the 1848 Revolution as well. Indeed, 1848 turned out to be almost too weighty: 'I'm finding it very difficult to slot my characters into the political events of 48! I'm afraid that the background will swamp the foreground. That's the main defect of the genre of the historical novel' (letter of 14 March 1868). Flaubert made things even more difficult for himself by deciding to draw very precise correlations between the individual narratives and the political situation: 'Show that Sentimentalism (as it has developed since 1830) follows Politics and reproduces its phases', as he says in a note to himself. In the event, that sense of history as an awkward, looming presence became one of the novel's strengths, as we shall see; while the link between 'Sentimentalism' and 'Politics' turned out to be less one-way than Flaubert had supposed.

Love and Art

'I want to depict a psychological state – one which really exists,
in my view – which has not yet been described.' (August 1866)

'It's a book about love and passion; but passion in the form in
which it can exist nowadays, that is to say inactive.'

(October 1864)

The love Frédéric feels for Mme Arnoux is Romantic love, a blend
of the worshipful with the sensual, and all the more sensual for
remaining, in the usual sense of the word, chaste. It was drawn
from the life. In 1836, on holiday in Trouville, at the age of fifteen,
Flaubert fell helplessly and possibly one-sidedly in love with Élisa
Schlesinger, the wife of a musical editor, and a woman considerably older than himself. The love lasted for years, unconsummated
(to all intents and purposes, as far as is known), intermittent but
enduring, while other relationships came and went. Flaubert was
always extremely discreet about it but it figures, thinly disguised,
in most of his semi-autobiographical early works, from *Memoirs of
a Madman* (1838) to the first *Sentimental Education*, where the
robust Mme Renaud is a more enterprising and active partner to
Henry than Mme Schlesinger was to Flaubert or Mme Arnoux
will be to Frédéric. In adulthood, Flaubert cultivated imperson-
ality – he is famous for it – but what this means in fact is that he
simply repressed the personal, he did not suppress it entirely; the
author, he said carefully, in a letter of 1852, should be in his work
like God in the universe, present everywhere but nowhere visible.
Among the mass of scenarios, notes and plans he produced for
Sentimental Education is a note which leaves no room for doubt:
'The husband, the wife, the lover, all fond of each other, all
unwilling to take risks . . . Mme Sch. – Mr Sch. me.' This passion
leaves its mark in all Flaubert's works (surviving even in the
relationship between Bouvard and Mme Bordin in *Bouvard et
Pécuchet*). It is responsible for some of his finest writing, and the
love as depicted in *Sentimental Education* will strike a chord in
anyone (not just Romantics) who has ever loved somebody they
cannot 'have'.

However, there is always more than one point of view in
Flaubert, and Frédéric's love for Mme Arnoux is subject to a great
deal of humour and irony. Even Frédéric, bewitched as he is, is

visited with a sense of the absurd from time to time, and then, in a sudden rush of 'healthfulness' and 'egoism' (*sic* p. 119), he vows to shake himself out of his nonsense and ditch this 'bourgeoise', this 'goose' (literally 'turkey'). Romantic love does indeed begin to look out of place in the new consumerist age where nothing is sacred. But the fact that Frédéric's love works against the grain of the times is precisely what gives it its saving grace. Just because it is obliged, for all sorts of reasons, to be 'inactive', it is one of the few activities in the novel to emerge as disinterested. In essence, it is an expression of something which Flaubert never mocks, the aspiration towards the Divine, or some impossible absolute – hence the use from time to time (only half-mocking) of the capitalized 'Elle' to refer to Mme Arnoux, or the frequent evocation of divine figures in relation to her: the Madonna, Diana, or the moon. Though Frédéric is not an artist (Flaubert uses the faintly derogatory term 'poète' to refer to him in his notes), his love for Mme Arnoux brings him close to the artist's disinterested cultivation of the ideal, and in this respect he is a forerunner to Swann, in Proust's *À la recherche du temps perdu*. Thoughts about love in an artist's life are perhaps taken further by Proust, whose Swann fails to make the quantum leap from lover, father, husband to artist, whereas Proust's narrator sees something inadequate in this. Frédéric's position on the fence seems to be sufficient in itself. He is allowed simply simultaneously to listen to dinner-table talk about 'art' and to watch Mme Arnoux's profile and a dimple which comes and goes as she speaks, and to create a miraculous fusion of both in his mind. He is conceived, then, as an ordinary human being rather than as a failed artist. But Flaubert manages to convey a lot about his own view of art, metaphorically, by means of this ordinary human being. Thus, when Frédéric declines Mme Arnoux's (presumed) offer of herself at the end of the novel (III, 6), it is for a mixture of reasons. It is only partly 'so as not to degrade his ideal'; other, more mundane impulses are at work, such as the wish (he is now middle-aged) to avoid complications: 'what a bother it would be!' When he turns on his heel and rolls himself a cigarette, it is, on one level, insulting to Mme Arnoux. And when she then admires his delicacy, it is, on one level, absurd. But this turning away, this refusal to consume, to take and to have, this preference for image over what would conventionally be seen as act, makes his action akin to that of the artist as envisaged by Flaubert: 'ça, c'est le *style*', as a critic of Flaubert observed astutely in 1967, and Mme Arnoux is right.

Sentimentalism, History and Politics

In his short story *Hérodias* (1876) Flaubert takes a story from the New Testament, that of Salome and the beheading of Saint John the Baptist, and turns it inside out, replacing its clear, simple lines and the sense it gives of conforming to a preordained God-given plan with a far more complex narrative, showing events in the making, where nothing is clear and where God's plan, if it exists, looks to be struggling to emerge from a huge muddle. *Sentimental Education*, too, contains an 'alternative version' to the history of the 1848 Revolution. It replaces the authoritative version of an omniscient narrator blessed with the gift of hindsight, and evokes instead the sense of history in the making, steeped in uncertainty and ambiguity (Flaubert's favourite domain). The atmosphere of mystery is heightened, moreover, since events are narrated – as in *Hérodias* – through the consciousness of a necessarily limited observer, usually Frédéric. We see what he sees. If we are canny we see more; but there is no privileged overview, only a 'way of seeing'.

Despite the general atmosphere of fluidity and uncertainty, however, there is also the sense that something inevitable is coming to pass, little by little (history, and the novel, each pursuing its course). This is surely what Proust was thinking of when he used the image of the *moving* sidewalk – the characters are carried along by forces beyond their control. History in this novel plays the role that fate plays in *Madame Bovary*. In each case tremendous sympathy is generated for the characters, who are seen to be caught up in something far greater than themselves, which they can only dimly comprehend, if at all. The way Flaubert manages to combine a sense of randomness, of ebb and flow, with what is in fact a rock-hard infrastructure, supplied by the slowly unfolding events of 1848, is brilliant.

The relationship between 'Sentimentalism' and 'Politics' was in practice less straightforward than Flaubert's original note to himself suggested that it might be. It is not just a case of Sentimentalism 'following' Politics. In the event, each illuminates the other. Telling about 1848 is a way of telling about Frédéric's love for Mme Arnoux, and telling about Frédéric's love for Mme Arnoux is a way of telling about 1848. Thus, a great deal can be implied about each over and above what is actually said. Frédéric's is the primary narrative, certainly, but it is mapped onto the story of 1848. The two sides come together in a masterly series of cross-cuts at two points of the novel, at the end of Part Two (the outbreak of the Revolution), and at the moment of the *coup d'état* (III, 5), and there the connections are unmistakable. But the two central narratives run along together, in parallel and counterpoint, all the way through.

Thus, the novel begins with high hopes, on both sides, with Frédéric's first encounter with Mme Arnoux in Chapter One being balanced by Deslauriers's expressions of faith in a new political future, 'a new 1789', in Chapter Two. Almost immediately, however, the promised action runs into the ground as life takes over, aims are thwarted or forgotten, and side-avenues are followed instead. There *is* action – Frédéric manages eventually to get himself invited to the Arnoux dinners, there is a student demonstration – but only in fits and starts.

In Part Two the sense of purpose reawakens. Chapter One is an echo of the first chapter of Part One: Frédéric is now rich where he was poor, and is now going the right way, that is heading for Paris instead of away from it. He spreads his wings, courting the lively, luscious Rosanette, religiously pursuing the grave, maternal Mme Arnoux, till, in the final chapter of Part Two, he at last persuades Mme Arnoux to agree to a rendezvous with him (on 22 February 1848). Devastated by her failure to appear, then very angry, he settles the next day for Rosanette instead. Part Two ends with his tears and his assurance to Rosanette, only partly mendacious, that 'I'd been wanting you for too long'.

Politically, events also come to a head in Part Two, in a similarly ragged fashion. The Revolution does materialize, against all expectations, and the end of Part Two is as climactic politically as it was for Frédéric in his personal life: after the banning of their reform banquet on 22 February, the people take to the streets on 23rd in an upsurge of animal spirits and rage, which ends with several of them being killed in the incident of the 'shooting of the boulevard des Capucines'. Flaubert's fusion of the two sides here, the personal and the political, is masterly: Rosanette is awoken by the sound of distant rumblings and sees, simultaneously, Frédéric sobbing into his pillow. The rumbling could be anything – thunder, or something from some other genre like a warning from the gods – for Flaubert doesn't explain it, but we see in fact when we turn the page and embark on Part Three that it must have been the noise of the carts trundling through the streets of Paris bearing the dead (which is of course in no way inconsistent with the reader's earlier uninformed guess). Thus, sentimental and political peak and then collapse in unison in this final sequence of Part Two in a most extraordinary and original way.

In Part Three the atmosphere changes, moving swiftly from the initial stages of almost simultaneous achievement and disappointment, triumph and loss, success and failure, through disarray, increasing disillusion and cynicism to ultimate defeat, for the Revolution and for Frédéric in his personal life. Frédéric's attitude, for a while, hardens. He begins to play the system, developing his life-skills as we would now say, and turning his hand now to politics as well, as he prepares to present himself to the people first as a candidate for the Left and then, almost immediately, as a candidate for the Right (a switch which speaks volumes about the ideological disarray of this period). His increasing material-mindedness is reflected in his retaining Rosanette as his mistress and acquiring also the wealthy, aristocratic Mme Dambreuse, while the other two women in his life, the unworldly two, the ones he does not possess, Mme Arnoux and Louise Roque, slip significantly into the background – indeed, Frédéric actually *sees* Mme Arnoux only twice in the whole of Part Three, as she disappears by degrees from his life and from the text, till all that is left are her clothes and effects, flying like ghosts around the sale-room in Chapter Five. And Chapter Five is where, in a dizzying débâcle, Frédéric loses or rejects all four women, and witnesses at first hand the *coup d'état* and the death of his friend Dussardier at the hands of his friend Sénécal. Personal and political are united once more in a dramatic crisis.

The active, fruitful part of the Revolution is confined to just the first chapter of Part Three, which shows how very short-lived it was. By 10 December 1848 (end of Chapter One), it was to all intents and purposes over, just nine months after it had begun – Louis Bonaparte, the future Emperor Napoleon III, is elected President of the Republic and creates a new ministry without a single Republican in it. But the novel shows how Conservative reaction against the new Republic set in almost from the start, giving rise to a series of popular demonstrations all trying vainly to restore the original aims of the Republic. The most important of these is the one always referred to as the 'journées de juin', the June Days of 1848, when the working people were brutally repressed by the very Government they had fought to instal. This was the period when ideological disarray was at its height: Dussardier fights to defend the Republic, so-called, but is tormented by the thought that he should have been fighting on the other side, with the workers. The June Days put paid to any lingering hope the Left might have had that the Republic would survive in anything more than name. With the repression of the June uprising, the Republic became a mere façade, having expelled everything that gave it substance. The next four chapters of Part Three show Conservatism consolidating itself further, till the hard-nosed doctrinaire Republican Sénécal shoots the soft-hearted idealist Republican Dussardier, and the Republican ideal is symbolically destroyed by what it had helped to create.

'Trying to draw conclusions is inept. We're a thread and we want to see the weave.' (Flaubert, in a letter of 1850) But the temptation to do so is irresistible. All *Bildungsromane*, after all, teach the reader something, parodic and ironic though they be. Flaubert certainly felt that there was a lesson to be learned from his, even if he had not *deliberately* worked it in. Flaubert's friend Maxime Du Camp tells a story about Flaubert's reaction to the next revolutionary uprising in France, the Commune of 1870: 'In June 1871, as we were standing together on the terrace beside the Seine, looking at the blackened carcass of the Tuileries [. . .], [Flaubert] said to me: "If people had understood the *Sentimental Education*, none of this would have happened." ' (*Souvenirs littéraires*, chapter 28). What might he have meant by this? The view of 1848 which emerges from *Sentimental Education* coincides with that of Marx, in *The Eighteenth Brumaire of Louis Bonaparte* (1852). When Marx said (quoting Hegel) that history repeats itself as farce, it was 1848 that he had in mind, compared with its illustrious predecessor, 1789. But the *Eighteenth Brumaire* goes on to show that it was a farce with tragic implications. Flaubert seems to have had the same idea: to have let history repeat itself *yet again* in 1870 was to have let things go beyond a joke.

It does not seem as if the Republican ideal *per se* is a farce. Flaubert himself, reflecting that his novel had contrived to offend people of every political persuasion, recognized nonetheless that the Right came off in it worst. There is nothing on the Left to compare with the mindless violence of the anti-Republican Monsieur Roque, firing into the heap of humanity crammed into the tiny prison beneath that self-same terrace on which Flaubert and Du Camp were to walk later by the Seine. And the scene where Frédéric hurls a plate of food at the aristocratic Cisy's silly face is most satisfying to the reader (regardless of the fact that Frédéric's motives were only *metaphorically* political), as is the scene where Frédéric is nauseated by the bland, dishonest platitudes of the Conservatives gathered together in the Dambreuse salon to the point where his control snaps and he tells them all a few home truths – to no effect, of course.

Nonetheless, 'in spite of the most humane legislation that ever existed' in the early days of the new Revolutionary government (a rare authorial comment, p. 314), the gap between the ideal and the realization of that ideal was too great, leading somehow to idiotic sacrifices of the best – Dussardier's death – and encouragement of the worst in man, as when Monsieur Roque, tasting power and fear, blows a man's brains out, just because he can.

It certainly seems as if, in both domains, the ideal is one thing and the reality very much another.

Frédéric's feelings for Mme Arnoux are akin to those of Dussardier for the Republic, a mixture of tenderness and veneration. Neither of them likes the reality which comes to take the place of the ideal. Having traded the ideal of Mme Arnoux for the reality of Rosanette, Frédéric, after the initial euphoria, is full of regrets. Dussardier, similarly, passes from euphoria to a feeling of disgust at the self-seeking he finds once the ideal Republic has given way to the real one: 'I thought, when the Revolution came we would be happy. Do you remember how fine it was? How freely we breathed! But now we've fallen back worse than ever . . . Now, they're killing our Republic . . . But if we only made an effort! If we were only sincere, we might get on together! But no! The workers are no better than the capitalists, you see!' (p 418).

Every reader must be tantalized by the thought of what might have happened if Mme Arnoux *had* turned up at the rendezvous to which Frédéric, greatly daring, invites her at the end of Part Two. Flaubert too allowed himself to toy with that idea in an early scenario: 'she comes to the rendezvous only two or three times – But agitated, in tears – the sex a disaster ('mauvais coup') – disappointment for him'. Most readers would agree with that scenario, I think. The real Mme Arnoux in Frédéric's arms would have been a different person from the ideal Mme Arnoux, so different that she might just as well have been a different woman entirely. She might just as well have been Rosanette. So Flaubert follows that logic to its conclusion and duly embodies the ideal in one woman (Mme Arnoux) and the real in another (Rosanette), thereby demonstrating the Romantic cliché that you never get what you want in a very practical way, as Frédéric tries to cope with an explosive combination of euphoria, sexual delight and bitter disappointment which we guess may have been no different if the woman he had made love to had been Mme Arnoux – at night, as the French say, all cats are grey.

Flaubert's Art

Flaubert left no literary manifesto, deliberately, but his magnificent correspondence is packed with statements of artistic intent and reflections on his writing, particularly in the 1850s when he was writing *Madame Bovary*, and developing and confirming his aesthetic at the same time. He is famous for his cult of style, for the hours and hours he spent writing and re-writing, honing his phrases, working towards an ideal of Beauty in prose which he felt had never yet been reached. Art meant more to him than anything else.

He believed that prose was a new form: poetry in verse had been taken seriously and studied for years, but not prose. In this he was concerned both with overall effect – the novel as a strange and beautiful machine – and with the individual phrase. Proust was the first to draw attention to this in his 1920 essay on Flaubert: in him, he says, grammar comes alive, style is vision – Flaubert is 'a man who by the entirely new and personal use he made of the past definite, of the past indefinite, of the present participle, of certain pronouns and certain propositions, has renewed our vision of things as much as Kant, with his Categories and the theories of Knowledge and the Reality of the external world.' The kind of beauty Flaubert had in mind was not what we mean when we talk about 'fine writing', but a sparer, more taxing kind – and this more awkward kind of prose would be absolutely right for the epic of modern life which *Sentimental Education* turned out to be: 'to give prose the rhythm of poetry (while making sure it remains prose and very much prose) and to write ordinary life as you write history or an epic (without distorting the subject)' (27 March 1853). Flaubert's early texts, with their often beautiful, uncertain, generous rhythms, betray his instinctive love of lyricism and richness. *Madame Bovary* retains something of this exuberance. But Flaubert became more and more ruthless as time went on, paring down his style, and cutting his phrases to the bone: 'Et ce fut tout'; 'Ce fut comme une apparition'; and Proust's favourite: 'Il voyagea.' Flaubert admired what he called a 'muscular' style of writing, the kind he found in a writer like Montesquieu, not beautiful in the conventional sense but with a kind of plastic, architectural beauty.

His medium is everyday language. Words are given all their value, and poetic effects are created even out of clichés. In the final conversation between Frédéric and Mme Arnoux, for instance, the dialogue of the two old lovers is riddled with absurdities, misrepresentation and clichés, and is often very comical; but it is shot through nonetheless with moments of great beauty: the now elderly Mme Arnoux, desperately trying to atone in some measure for the past, ransacks her failing memory for the right words, and can come up with only vague echoes from the stockpot of early Romantic writing which nevertheless exude a rhythmic, faded charm entirely appropriate to the occasion: 'Quelquefois, vos mots me reviennent comme le son d'une cloche, apporté par le vent.' ('Sometimes your words comme back to me like the sound of a bell carried on the wind.') The reader who sees *only* the comedy here, *only* the irony, misses the point as much as the reader who can see neither. 'Irony in no way detracts from pathos. On the contrary, it makes it more intense' (9 October 1852); and humour can be heartbreaking: 'Comedy pushed to extremes, the kind of comedy which doesn't make you laugh, lyricism expressed in humour, is the very essence of writing as far as I'm concerned.' (8 May 1852)

Flaubert's prose creates layers of meaning: 'Prose needs to be crammed with things, *without your noticing them.* But in poetry the *tiniest detail is evident.* So the most discreet comparison in a sentence of prose could produce a whole sonnet. There are many layers of meaning in prose' (30 September 1853, Flaubert's underlining). What is unsaid is often as important as what is said: Flaubert's reader is like Frédéric in Fontainebleau, listening to Rosanette telling the story of her life, and musing over the things she had not said. Flaubert wanted to create the kind of art which produces the effect produced by great natural phenomena: 'What seems to me to be the highest kind of Art (and the most difficult) is not to produce laughter or tears or sexual desire or anger, but to act as nature acts and *make you dream (faire rêver)*' (26 August 1853). As in life, so in the novel, many things are left unclear, never understood completely. This is in part the effect of the device known as Free Indirect Discourse, whereby the characters' feelings or words (spoken or thought) are subsumed by the narrrator in such a way that they are often difficult to distinguish from the narrative itself. Other writers used this technique before Flaubert, but none so consistently as he. Its effect is to add to the uncertainty of interpretation. It is the combination of Free Indirect Discourse and *focalisation* (narration from the point of view of characters) which makes Mme Arnoux's feelings for Frédéric entirely opaque through large tracts of the novel, not only to him but also to the reader. The reader might justifiably hope for more light to be shed in their last conversation together – this is after all what usually happens at the end of a novel – but that conversation raises as many questions as it answers. 'When did you first discover that I loved you?' asks Frédéric. 'When you kissed my wrist between the glove and the cuff', comes the answer. But the reader would search in vain through the pages of the novel to find this gesture and answer the question – the only wrist we will actually have witnessed being kissed was that of Rosanette on her way to the races.

Flaubert complained that nobody understood the end of the

novel. For Frédéric and Deslauriers to conclude that an inconclusive visit to a brothel when Frédéric was fifteen was the 'best time of their lives' seemed to testify only to the most shameless cynicism and desire to shock. There *is* something here of Flaubert's enduring desire to 'astound the bourgeois', certainly, but there is far more to it than that. It could be argued, more positively, that the two friends have now, in later life, attained a certain wisdom, that they can now accept and even value imperfection and incompletion where before they could not. More importantly, the pleasure which they feel and express in this cliché is generated more by *present* circumstances than by what happened in the past. What they are 'really' expressing here is the pleasure of being together at this moment and the pleasure of the act of remembering (however embarrassing or ludicrous the memory itself): 'Hier oder nirgends ist Amerika' as *Wilhelm Meister* puts it – here or nowhere is America. Above all, it expresses the pleasure of narrative itself. As they tell their story together, turn and turn about, egging each other on to fill in the gaps, each acts as author and reader to the other. Most important of all, in Flaubert's book, is the fact that they laugh, as they laughed years ago, in Chapter Two, when we saw them first recalling this incident, thereby echoing the gales of laughter of the prostitutes themselves, at the time, and 'laughter is the most noble way to see life' (letter of 2 March 1854). In all these respects, Frédéric and Deslauriers coincide with their creator, who also knew all about the way language tips, as here, into bathos, making music fit only to make bears dance, as he says in another of his rare authorial comments (this one is from *Madame Bovary*), when you are trying to touch the stars.

Many of the clichés about *Sentimental Education* are correct: it is the novelist's novel; it is the father of the modern novel; it is the novel to end all novels. A man comes to Rosanette's fancy-dress party dressed as a Turk, and his outfit is assembled with such art that there looks to be no art to it at all. It is so exquisitely hideous in its realism that it offends – against the rules of the genre of the fancy-dress ball, against notions of what a Turk should look like, against good taste. There are murmurings. Even the hardened cynics who are Rosanette's guests are somewhat shocked. They are unsure how to react, they are baffled, hostile. Flaubert's realism is equally unsparing, and it too, in bringing a '*real*' Turk to the party, brings with it its own morality and humanity: 'No, we're not very nice. But this ability to assimilate oneself to all kinds of suffering and unhappiness and to suppose oneself to be sharing them is perhaps the only real human charity.' (6 June 1853) Many readers love the novel so much that they read and reread it throughout their lives, and find in it something different every time. When, at the end of Woody Allen's film *Manhattan*, Ike, the hero, lists the things that make life worth living, *Sentimental Education* is one of them. It is not an easy read; but those who stay with it will find that it stays with them.

ADRIANNE TOOKE
Somerville College, Oxford

SUGGESTIONS FOR FURTHER READING

Gustave Flaubert, *Madame Bovary*, 1857

Gustave Flaubert, *Salammbô*, 1862

Marcel Proust, *À la recherche du temps perdu*, 1913–1927

Honoré de Balzac, *Le père Goriot*, 1835

Honoré de Balzac, *Illusions perdues*, 1837–1843

Books and articles about Flaubert

Julian Barnes, *Flaubert's Parrot*, 1984

Benjamin F. Bart, *Flaubert*, 1967

Geneviève Bollème, *Préface à la vie d'écrivain* (selections from Flaubert's correspondence), 1963

Victor Brombert, *The Novels of Flaubert*, 1966

Jonathan Culler, *Flaubert: the uses of uncertainty*, 1974

Alison Fairlie, 'Some patterns of suggestion in *L'Éducation sentimentale*' in *Imagination and Language*, 1981

Jacques Proust, 'Structure et sens de l'*Éducation sentimentale*', *Revue des sciences humaines*, 1967, 67–100

Marcel Proust, 'À propos du "style" de Flaubert', in *Contre Sainte-Beuve*, 1971

Enid Starkie, *Flaubert the Master*, 1971

D. A. Williams, *The Hidden Life at its source: a study of Flaubert's* L'Éducation sentimentale, 1987

SENTIMENTAL
EDUCATION

PART ONE

On the 15th of September, 1840, about six o'clock in the morning, the *Ville de Montereau*, just on the point of starting, was sending forth great whirlwinds of smoke, alongside the Quai St Bernard.

People came rushing on board in breathless haste; circulation was impeded by casks, cables, and baskets of linen; the sailors answered nobody; people jostled one another; between the two paddle boxes there grew up heaps of parcels, and the uproar was drowned in the loud hissing of the steam, which, making its way through plates of sheet iron, enveloped everything in a white cloud, while the bell at the prow kept ringing continuously.

At last, the vessel set out; and the two banks of the river, stocked with warehouses, timberyards, and manufactories, slipped past like two huge ribbons being unrolled.

A young man of eighteen, with long hair, holding an album under his arm, remained near the helm without moving. Through the haze he surveyed steeples, buildings of which he did not know the names; then, with a parting glance, he took in the Ile St Louis, the Cité, Notre-Dame; and presently, as Paris disappeared from his view, he heaved a deep sigh.

Frédéric Moreau, having just matriculated, was returning home to Nogent-sur-Seine, where he was to lead a languishing existence for two months, before going back to *begin his legal studies*. His mother had sent him, with enough to cover his expenses, to Le Havre to see an uncle, from whom she had expectations of his receiving an inheritance; he had returned from there only yesterday; and he made up for not having the opportunity of staying in the capital by taking the longest possible route to reach his own part of the country.

The hubbub had subsided; the passengers had all taken their places; some of them stood warming themselves around the machinery, and the chimney spat forth with a slow, rhythmic rattle its plume of black smoke; little drops of dew trickled over the copper plates; the deck quivered with the slight vibration from within, and the two paddle-wheels, rapidly turning round, lashed the water.

The edges of the river were covered with sand. The vessel passed rafts of wood which began to oscillate under the rippling of the waves, or a boat without sails in which a man sat fishing; then the wandering haze cleared off, the sun appeared, the hill which ran along the course of the Seine to the right subsided by degrees, and another rose nearer on the opposite bank.

It was crowned with trees, which surrounded low built houses, covered with roofs in the Italian style. They had sloping gardens divided by newly built walls, iron railings, lawns, hothouses, and vases of geraniums, laid out regularly on the terraces where one could lean on one's elbow and look out. More than one spectator longed, on beholding those attractive residences which looked so peaceful, to be the owner of one of them, and to dwell there till the end of his days with a good billiard-table, a sailing-boat, a woman or some other such dream. The agreeable novelty of a journey by water made people expansive. Already the wags on board were beginning their jokes. Many began to sing. Gaiety prevailed, and glasses of spirits were poured.

Frédéric was thinking about the room he would occupy in Paris, about the plan of a drama, subjects for pictures, future passions. He found that the happiness merited by the excellence of his soul was slow in arriving. He declaimed some melancholy lines of poetry to himself; he walked with rapid step along the deck; he went on till he reached the end at which the bell was – and, in the centre of a group of passengers and sailors, he saw a gentleman addressing gallant remarks to a countrywoman, while fingering the gold cross which she wore over her breast. He was a jovial-looking man of about forty with frizzy hair. His robust form was encased in a jacket of black velvet, two emeralds sparkled in his cambric shirt, and his wide, white trousers fell over odd-looking red boots of Russian leather set off with blue designs.

The presence of Frédéric did not discompose him. He turned round and winked several times at the young man, as if to draw him in; then he offered cigars to all who were standing around him. But getting tired, no doubt, of their society, he moved away and installed himself further along. Frédéric followed him.

The conversation, at first, turned on the various kinds of tobacco, then quite naturally it glided into a discussion about women. The gentleman in the red boots gave the young man advice; he put forward theories, related anecdotes, referred to himself by way of illustration, and he delivered all this in a paternal tone, with an engaging innocence of corruption.

He was republican in his opinions; he had travelled, he was familiar with the inner life of theatres, restaurants, and newspapers, and knew all the theatrical celebrities, whom he called by their Christian names; Frédéric soon began to confide in him about his projects; and the elder man took an encouraging view of them.

But he stopped talking to take a look at the funnel, then he went mumbling rapidly through a long calculation in order to ascertain 'how much each stroke of the piston at so many times per minute would come to,' etc. – And having found the number he spoke about the scenery, which he admired immensely. He expressed his delight at having got away from business.

Frédéric regarded him with a certain amount of respect, and could not resist the desire to know his name. The stranger, all in one breath, replied:

'Jacques Arnoux, proprietor of L'Art Industriel, Boulevard Montmartre.'

A manservant in a gold-laced cap came up and said:

'Would Monsieur have the kindness to go below? Mademoiselle is crying.'

He vanished.

L'Art Industriel was a hybrid establishment, wherein the functions of an art journal and a picture shop were combined. Frédéric had seen this title several times in the bookseller's window in his native place on big prospectuses, on which the name of Jacques Arnoux displayed itself magisterially.

The sun's rays fell perpendicularly, shedding a glittering light on the iron hoops around the masts, the plates of the bulwarks, and the surface of the water, which, at the prow, was cut into two furrows that spread out as far as the borders of the meadows. At each winding of the river, a screen of pale poplars presented itself with the utmost uniformity. The surrounding country was quite deserted. In the sky there were little white clouds which hung suspended, and the sense of weariness, which vaguely diffused itself over everything, seemed to retard the progress of the steamboat and to add to the insignificant appearance of the passengers.

Putting aside a few persons of good position who were travelling first class, they were workmen or shopkeepers with their wives and children. As it was customary at that time to wear old clothes when travelling, they nearly all had their heads covered with shabby Greek caps or discoloured hats, and wore thin black coats that had become quite threadbare from constant rubbing against writing-desks, or frock-coats with the casings of their buttons loose from continual service in the shop. Here and there some roll-collar waistcoat afforded a glimpse of a calico shirt stained with coffee; pinchbeck pins were stuck into cravats that were all torn; list shoes were kept up by stitched straps; two or three roughs who held in their hands bamboo canes with leathern loops, kept looking furtively at their fellow-passengers, and fathers of families opened their eyes wide while asking questions. People chatted either standing up or squatting over their luggage; some went to sleep in various corners of the vessel; several occupied themselves with eating. The deck was soiled with walnut shells, butt ends of cigars, peelings of pears, and bits and pieces of cold meat, which had been carried wrapped up in paper; three cabinet-makers in smocks had taken up position in front of the drinks counter; a harp-player in rags was resting with his elbows on his instrument; at intervals could be heard the sound of falling coals in the furnace, a shout, or a laugh – and the captain kept walking on the bridge from one paddlebox to the other without stopping for a moment. Frédéric, to get back to his place, pushed forward the grating leading into the part of the vessel reserved for first-class passengers, and in so doing disturbed two sportsmen with their dogs.

What he then saw was like an apparition:

She was seated in the middle of a bench all alone, or, at any rate, he could see no one, dazzled as he was by this vision. At the moment when he was passing, she raised her head; his shoulders bent involuntarily; and, when he had placed himself some distance away, on the same side, he looked at her.

She wore a wide straw hat with pink ribbons which fluttered in the wind, behind her. On either side, her black hair traced the curve of her large eyebrows, descended very low, and seemed amorously to press the oval of her face. Her robe of light muslin spotted with tiny dots spread out in numerous folds. She was in the act of embroidering something; and her straight nose, her chin, her entire person was cut out on the background of the blue sky.

As she remained in the same attitude, he took several turns to the right and to the left to conceal from her his strategy; then he placed himself very close to her parasol which lay against the bench, and pretended to be looking at a sloop on the river.

Never had he seen such lustrous dark skin, such a seductive figure, or such delicately shaped fingers as those through which the sunlight gleamed. He stared with amazement at her work-basket, as if it were something extraordinary. What was her name, her place of residence, her life, her past? He longed to become familiar with the furniture of her apartment, all the dresses that she had worn, the people whom she visited; and the desire of physical possession itself yielded to a deeper yearning, a painful curiosity that knew no bounds.

A negress, wearing a silk handkerchief tied round her head, made her appearance, holding by the hand a little girl already tall for her age. The child, whose eyes were swimming with tears, had just awakened. The lady took the little one on her knees. 'Mademoiselle was not a good girl, though she would soon be seven; her mother would not love her any more; she was too often pardoned for being naughty.' And Frédéric heard those things with delight, as if he had made a discovery, an acquisition.

He assumed that she must be of Andalusian descent, perhaps a creole; had she brought this negress across with her from the West Indian Islands?

A long shawl with violet stripes was thrown behind her back over the brass rail. She must have, many a time, wrapped it around her body, in the midst of the waves, in the long damp evenings, drawn it over her feet, gone to sleep in it! But with the sweep of its fringes it was gradually slipping off, and it was on the point of falling into the water when, with a bound, Frédéric secured it. She said to him:

'Thank you, Monsieur.'

Their eyes met.

'Are you ready, my dear?' cried my lord Arnoux, presenting himself at the hood of the companion ladder.

Mademoiselle Marthe ran over to him, and, clinging to his neck, she began pulling at his moustache. The strains of a harp were heard – she wanted to see the music played; and presently the performer on the instrument, led forward by the negress, entered the first-class section. Arnoux recognized in him a man who had formerly been a model and called him 'tu', to the astonishment of the bystanders. At length the harpist, flinging back his long hair over his shoulders, stretched out his arms and began to play.

It was an Oriental ballad all about poniards, flowers, and stars. The man in rags sang it in a penetrating voice; the thudding of the engine broke into the song with its disruptive rhythms; he plucked the strings more vigorously: the chords vibrated, and their metallic sounds seemed to send forth sobs, and, as it were, the plaint of a proud and vanquished love. On both sides of the river, woods bent down to the edge of the water; a cool breeze swept past them, and Madame Arnoux gazed vaguely into the distance. When the music stopped, she blinked several times as if she were starting out of a dream.

The harpist approached them with an air of humility. While Arnoux was searching his pockets for change, Frédéric stretched out towards the cap his closed hand, and then, opening it in a discreet manner, he deposited in it a gold coin. It was not vanity that prompted him to bestow this alms in her presence, but the idea of a blessing in which he thought she might share, an almost religious impulse of the heart.

Arnoux, pointing out the way, cordially invited him to go below. Frédéric declared that he had just lunched; on the contrary, he was nearly dying of hunger; and he had not a single centime in his purse.

After that, it occurred to him that he had a perfect right, as well as anyone else, to be in the dining-room.

Ladies and gentlemen were seated before round tables, eating, while a waiter went about serving; Monsieur and Madame Arnoux were in the far corner to the right; he took a seat on the long bench covered with velvet, having picked up a newspaper which he found there.

They were to take the coach at Montereau for Châlons. Their tour in Switzerland would last a month. Madame Arnoux scolded her husband for his weakness in dealing with his child. He whispered in her ear something agreeable, no doubt, for she smiled. Then, he got up to draw down the window curtain at her back.

Under the low, white ceiling, a crude light filled the cabin. Frédéric, sitting opposite to the place where she sat, could distinguish the shadow of her eyelashes. She just moistened her lips with her glass and broke a little piece of crust between her fingers; the lapis lazuli locket fastened by a little gold chain to her wrist made a ringing sound, every now and then, as it touched her plate. Those present, however, did not appear to notice her.

At intervals one could see, through the small portholes, the side of a boat taking away passengers or putting them on board. Those who sat round the tables stooped towards the openings, and called out the names of the various places they passed along the river.

Arnoux complained of the cooking: he objected strongly to the amount of the bill, and got it reduced. Then, he carried off the young man towards the forecastle to drink a glass of grog with him. But Frédéric speedily came back again to gaze at Madame Arnoux, who had returned to the awning, beneath which she seated herself. She was reading a slim, grey-covered volume. From time to time, the corners of her mouth lifted and a gleam of pleasure lighted up her forehead. He felt jealous of the inventor of those things which appeared to interest her so much. The more he contemplated her, the more he felt that there were yawning abysses between them. He was reflecting that he should very soon lose sight of her irrevocably, without having extracted a few words from her, without leaving her with even a memory!

On the right, a plain stretched out; on the left, a strip of pastureland rose gently to meet a hillock where one could see vineyards, groups of walnut trees, a mill embedded in greenery, and, beyond that, little zig zag paths over the white mass of rocks that reached up towards the clouds. What bliss it would have been to ascend side by side with her, his arm around her waist, while her gown would sweep the yellow leaves, listening to her voice and gazing up into her glowing eyes! The steamboat might stop, and all they would have to do was to step out of it; and yet this thing, simple as it might be, was not less difficult than it would have been to move the sun!

A little further on, a château appeared with pointed roof and square turrets. A flower garden spread out in the foreground; and avenues ran, like dark archways, under the tall linden trees. He pictured her to himself passing along by these groups of trees. At that moment a young lady and a young man showed themselves on the steps in front of the house, between the pots of orange trees. Then the entire scene vanished.

The little girl kept skipping playfully around him. Frédéric tried to give her a kiss. She hid herself behind her nurse; her mother scolded her for not being nice to the gentleman who had rescued her shawl. Was this an indirect overture?

'Is she going to speak to me at last?' he asked himself.

Time was pressing. How was he to get an invitation to the Arnoux's house? And he could think of nothing better than to draw her attention to the autumnal hues, adding:

'We are close to winter, the season of balls and dinner-parties!'

But Arnoux was entirely occupied with his luggage. They had arrived at the point of the river's bank facing Surville, the two bridges drew nearer, they passed a rope factory, then a range of low-built houses, beneath which there were pots of tar and splinters of wood; and lads went running along the sand turning head over heels. Frédéric recognised a man with a sleeved waist-coat, and called out to him:

'Make haste!'

They were at the landing-place. He had difficulty finding Arnoux amongst the crowd of passengers, and Arnoux replied, shaking his hand, 'Till the next time, dear sir!'

When he was on the quay, Frédéric turned around. She was standing beside the helm. He cast a look towards her into which he tried to put his whole soul; she remained motionless, as if he had done nothing. Then, without paying the slightest attention to the obeisances of his manservant:

'Why didn't you bring the trap down here?'

The man made excuses.

'What a clumsy fellow you are! Give me some money!'

And he went off to get something to eat at an inn.

A quarter of an hour later, he felt an inclination to turn into the coach yard, as if by chance. Perhaps he would see her again.

'What's the use of it?' said he to himself.

And the vehicle carried him off. The two horses did not belong to his mother. She had borrowed one from M. Chambrion, the tax-collector, in order to have it yoked alongside of her own. Isidore, having set forth the day before, had taken a rest at Bray until evening, and had slept at Montereau, so that the animals, with restored vigour, were trotting briskly.

Fields on which the crops had been cut stretched out in apparently endless succession. Two rows of trees lined the road, heaps of stones succeeded each other; and by degrees Villeneuve-Saint-Georges, Ablon, Châtillon, Corbeil, and the other places, his entire journey came back to his recollection with such vividness that he could now recall to mind fresh details, more intimate particulars; under the lowest flounce of her gown, her foot showed itself in a dainty silk boot of brown shade; the awning made of ticking formed a wide canopy over her head, and the little red tassels of the edging kept perpetually trembling in the breeze.

She resembled the women of whom he had read in romances. He would have added nothing to her person, and would have taken nothing from her. The universe had suddenly become enlarged. She was the luminous point towards which all things converged – and, rocked by the movement of the vehicle, with half-closed eyelids, and looking up into the clouds, he abandoned himself to a dreamy, infinite joy.

At Bray, he did not wait till the horses had got their oats, he walked on along the road ahead by himself. Arnoux had addressed her as 'Marie'. He now loudly called out the name 'Marie!' His voice pierced the air and was lost in the distance.

The western sky was one great mass of flaming red. Huge stacks of wheat, rising up in the midst of the stubble fields, projected giant shadows. A dog began to bark in a farmhouse in the distance. He shivered, seized with disquietude for which he could assign no cause.

When Isidore had come up with him, he jumped up into the front seat to drive. His fit of weakness was past. Ile had thoroughly made up his mind to effect an introduction somehow into the house of the Arnoux, and to become intimate with them. Their house should be amusing; besides, he liked Arnoux; then, who could tell? Thereupon a wave of blood rushed up to his face: his temples throbbed, he cracked his whip, shook the reins, and set the horses going at such a pace that the old coachman repeatedly exclaimed:

'Easy! Easy now, or they'll get broken-winded!'

Gradually Frédéric calmed down, and he listened to what his servant was saying.

Monsieur's return was impatiently awaited. Mademoiselle Louise had cried in her anxiety to go in the trap to meet him.

'Who, pray, is Mademoiselle Louise?'

'Monsieur Roque's little girl, you know.'

'Ah! I had forgotten,' rejoined Frédéric, carelessly.

Meanwhile, the two horses could keep up the pace no longer. They were both getting lame; and nine o'clock struck at the church of St Laurent when he arrived at the Place d'Armes, at his mother's house. This house of large dimensions, with a garden looking out on the open country, added to the social importance of Madame Moreau, who was the most respected person in the district.

She came of an old family of nobles, of which the male line was now extinct. Her husband, a plebeian whom her parents had forced her to marry, had met his death by a sword-thrust, during her pregnancy, leaving her an estate much encumbered. She received visitors three times a week, and from time to time gave a fashionable dinner. But the number of wax candles was calculated beforehand, and she looked forward with some impatience to the payment of her rents. These pecuniary embarrassments, concealed as if there were some guilt attached to them, imparted a certain gravity to her character. Nevertheless, she displayed no prudery, no sourness, in the practice of her virtue. Her most trifling charities seemed munificent alms. She was consulted about the selection of servants, the education of young girls, and the art of making preserves, and Monseigneur used to stay at her house on the occasion of his episcopal visitations.

Madame Moreau cherished a lofty ambition for her son. Through a sort of prudence grounded on the expectation of favours, she did not care to hear blame cast on the Government. He would need patronage at the start; then, thanks to his own ability, he would become a councillor of State, an ambassador, a minister. His triumphs at the college of Sens warranted this proud anticipation; he had carried off the prize of honour.

When he entered the drawing-room, all present arose with a great racket; he was embraced; and the chairs, large and small, were drawn up in a big semicircle around the fireplace. M. Gamblin immediately asked him what was his opinion about Madame Lafarge. This case, all the rage at the time, did not fail to lead to a violent discussion; Madame Moreau stopped it, to the regret, however, of M. Gamblin; he deemed it serviceable to the young man in his character of a future lawyer, and, nettled at what had occurred, he left the drawing-room.

Nothing should have caused surprise on the part of a friend of Père Roque! The reference to Roque led them to talk of M. Dambreuse, who had just become the owner of the demesne of La Fortelle. But the Tax-collector had drawn Frédéric aside to know what he thought of M. Guizot's latest work. They were all anxious to get some information about his private affairs; and Madame Benoît went cleverly to work with that end in view by inquiring about his uncle. How was that worthy relative? They no longer heard from him. Had he not a distant cousin in America?

The cook announced that Monsieur's soup was served. The guests discreetly retired. Then, as soon as they were alone in the dining-room, his mother said to him in a low tone:

'Well?'

The old man had received him in a very cordial manner, but without disclosing his intentions.

Madame Moreau sighed.

'Where is she now?' was his thought.

The coach was rolling along the road, and, wrapped up in the shawl, no doubt, she was leaning against the cloth of the coupe, her beautiful head nodding asleep.

They were just going up to their bedrooms when a waiter from the *Swan of the Cross* brought him a note.

'What is that, pray?'

'It's Deslauriers, who wants me,' said he.

'Ha! Your chum!' said Madame Moreau, with a contemptuous sneer. 'He certainly chooses his moments!'

Frédéric hesitated. But friendship was stronger. He got his hat.

'At any rate, don't be long!' said his mother to him.

Charles Deslauriers' father, an ex-captain in the line, who had left the service in 1818, had come back to Nogent, where he had married, and with the money from the dowry bought an administrative post as bailiff which brought him barely enough to maintain him. Embittered by a long course of unjust treatment, suffering still from the effects of old wounds, and always regretting the Emperor, he vented on those around him the fits of rage that seemed to choke him. Few children received so many whackings as his son. In spite of blows, however, the boy did not yield. His mother, when she tried to interpose, was also ill-treated. Finally, the Captain planted the boy in his office, and all the day long kept him bent over his desk copying documents, with the result that his right shoulder was noticeably higher than his left.

In 1833, on the invitation of the president, the Captain sold his office. His wife died of cancer. He then went to live in Dijon; after that he started in business in Troyes, where he was connected with the finding of substitute soldiers; and, having obtained a small scholarship for Charles, placed him at the college of Sens, where Frédéric came across him. But one of the pair was twelve years old, while the other was fifteen; besides, a thousand differences of character and origin tended to keep them apart.

Frédéric had in his chest of drawers all sorts of useful things – choice articles, such as a dressing-case. He liked to lie late in bed in the morning, to look at the swallows, and to read plays, and, regretting the comforts of home, he thought college life rough.

To the bailiff's son it seemed pleasant. He worked so hard that at the end of the second year he had got into the third form. However, owing to his poverty or to his quarrelsome disposition, he was regarded with a subdued malevolence. But when on one occasion, in the courtyard where pupils of the middle grade took exercise, an attendant openly called him a beggar's child, he sprang at the fellow's throat, and would have killed him if three of the ushers had not intervened. Frédéric, carried away by admiration, pressed him in his arms. From that day forward they became fast friends. The affection of a *senior* no doubt flattered the vanity of the younger boy, and the other accepted as a piece of good fortune this devotion freely offered to him.

During the holidays Charles's father left him in the college. A translation of Plato which he opened by chance excited his enthusiasm. Then he became smitten with a love of metaphysical studies; and he made rapid progress, for he approached the subject with all the energy of youth and the self-confidence of an intellect finding its feet; Jouffroy, Cousin, Laromiguière, Malebranche, and the Scots metaphysicians – everything that could be found in the library passed through his hands. He had found it necessary to steal the key in order to get books.

Frédéric's intellectual distractions were of a less serious description. He made sketches of the genealogy of Christ carved on a post in the Rue des Trois-Rois, then of the gateway of the cathedral. After a course of mediaeval dramas, he took up memoirs – Froissart, Comines, Pierre de l'Estoile, and Brantôme.

The impressions made on his mind by this kind of reading took such a hold of it that he felt a need within him of reproducing those pictures of bygone days. His ambition was to be, one day, the Walter Scott of France. Deslauriers dreamed of formulating a vast system of philosophy, which might have the most far-reaching applications.

They chatted over all these matters at recreation hours, in the playground, in front of the moral inscription painted under the clock; they whispered about them in the chapel, even with St Louis staring down at them; they dreamed about them in the dormitory, which looked out onto a burial ground. On walking days they took up a position behind the others, and talked without stopping.

They spoke of what they would do later, when they had left college. First of all, they would set out on a long voyage with the money which Frédéric would take out of his own fortune on reaching his majority. Then they would come back to Paris, they would work together, and would never part – and as a relaxation from their labours, they would have love affairs with princesses in boudoirs lined with satin, or dazzling orgies with famous courtesans. Their rapturous expectations were followed by doubts.

After a crisis of verbose gaiety, they would often lapse into profound silence.

On summer evenings, when they had been walking for a long time over stony paths which bordered on vineyards, or on the highroad in the open country, and when they saw the wheat waving in the sunlight, while the air was filled with the fragrance of angelica, a sort of suffocating sensation took possession of them, and they lay down on their backs, dizzy, intoxicated. Meanwhile the other lads, in their shirtsleeves, were playing at base or flying kites. Then the usher called them. They would return, taking paths which led along by gardens watered by brooklets, then they would pass through the boulevards overshadowed by the old city walls; the deserted streets rang under their tread; the iron gate opened, they climbed the stairs; and they were sad as if after great orgies.

The headmaster maintained that they led each other on. Nevertheless, if Frédéric worked in the upper forms, it was through the exhortations of his friend; and, during the vacation in 1837, he brought Deslauriers to his mother's house.

Madame Moreau disliked the young man. He had a terrible appetite, he refused to go to church on Sundays, he was fond of making republican speeches; to crown all, she got it into her head that he had been the means of leading her son into improper places. Their relations towards each other were watched. This only made their friendship grow stronger; and they bade one another adieu with heartfelt pangs when, in the following year, Deslauriers left the college in order to study law in Paris.

Frédéric was counting on joining him there. For two years they had not laid eyes on each other; and, when their embraces were over, they walked over to the bridges to talk more at their ease.

The Captain, who had now set up a billiard-room at Villenauxe, had reddened with anger when his son had asked him for an account of his trusteeship of his mother's fortune, and had even cut off his maintenance payments, just like that. But, as he intended to become a candidate at a later period for a professor's chair at the Ecole, and as he had no money, Deslauriers accepted the post of principal clerk in an attorney's office at Troyes. By dint of sheer privation he would save four thousand francs; and, even if he were not to inherit anything from his mother, he would always have enough to enable him to work freely for three years while he was waiting for a better position. It was necessary, therefore, to abandon their former project of living together in the Capital, at least for the present.

Frédéric hung his head. This was the first of his dreams which had crumbled into dust.

'Cheer up,' said the Captain's son. 'Life is long; we are young. We'll meet again! Think no more about it!'

He shook him warmly by both hands, and, to distract his attention, questioned him about his journey.

Frédéric had nothing much to tell. But, at the recollection of Madame Arnoux, his vexation disappeared. He did not refer to her, restrained by a wish not to be indelicate. He made up for it by expatiating on Arnoux, recalling his talk, his manners, the people he knew; and Deslauriers urged him strongly to cultivate this new acquaintance.

Frédéric had of late written nothing; his literary opinions had changed: passion was now above everything else in his estimation; he was equally enthusiastic about Werther, René, Franck, Lara, Lélia, and other ideal creations of less merit. Sometimes it seemed to him that music alone was capable of giving expression to his internal agitation; then, he dreamed of symphonies; or else the surface of things seized hold of him, and he longed to paint. He had, however, composed some poetry; Deslauriers considered it very beautiful, but did not ask to hear another piece.

As for himself, he had given up metaphysics. Social economy and the French Revolution absorbed all his attention. He was now a tall fellow of twenty-two, thin, with a wide mouth, and a resolute look. On this particular evening, he wore a poor looking overcoat of lasting; and his shoes were white with dust, for he had come all the way from Villenauxe on foot for the express purpose of seeing Frédéric.

Isidore arrived while they were talking. Madame begged of Monsieur to return home, and, for fear of his catching cold, she had sent him his cloak.

'Wait a bit!' said Deslauriers.

And they continued walking from one end to the other of the two bridges which rest on the narrow islet formed by the canal and the river.

When they were walking on the side towards Nogent, they had, exactly in front of them, a block of houses at a slight angle; to the right might be seen the church, behind the wooden windmills, whose sluices were closed; and, to the left, the shrub hedges, along the bank, formed a boundary for the gardens, which could scarcely be distinguished. But on the side towards Paris the high road formed a straight descending line, and meadows lost themselves in the distance under the vapours of the night. The road was silent, and showed as a whitish gleam in the surrounding gloom. Odours of damp leaves rose towards them; the waterfall, where the stream had been diverted from its course a hundred paces further away, murmured away with that deep harmonious sound which water makes at night.

Deslauriers stopped, and said:

'Funny to have these worthy folks sleeping so peacefully! Patience! A new '89 is on the way. People are tired of constitutions, charters, subtleties, lies! Ah, if I had a newspaper, or a platform, how I would stir all that up! But, to undertake anything whatever, you need money! What a curse it is to be a tavern-keeper's son, and to waste one's youth in quest of bread!'

He hung down his head, bit his lips, and shivered under his threadbare overcoat.

Frédéric flung half his cloak over his friend's shoulders. They both wrapped themselves up in it; and, with their arms around each other's waists, they walked along beneath it, side by side.

'How do you think I can live in Paris without you?' said Frédéric. The bitter tone of his friend had brought back his own sadness. 'I would have done something with a woman who loved me . . . What are you laughing at? Love is the feeding-ground, and, as it were, the atmosphere of genius. Extraordinary emotions produce sublime works. As for looking for the one I need, I give that up! Besides, if I ever find her, she'll reject me. I belong to the race of the disinherited, and I shall pass away with a treasure that will be of paste or of diamond – I don't know which.'

Somebody's shadow fell across the road, and at the same time they heard these words:

'Good evening, gentlemen!'

The person who had uttered them was a little man attired in an ample brown frock-coat, and with a cap on his head which under its peak afforded a glimpse of a sharp nose.

'Monsieur Roque?' said Frédéric.

'The very man!' returned the voice.

This local resident explained his presence by stating that he had come back from inspecting the wolf traps in his garden near the waterside.

'And so you are back again in the old place? Very good! I ascertained that fact through my little girl. Your health is still good, I hope? You are not going away again?'

Then he left them, repelled, probably, by Frédéric's reception.

Madame Moreau, indeed, was not on visiting terms with him; Père Roque lived in peculiar relations with his servant-girl, and was held in very slight esteem, although he was the vice-president at elections, and M. Dambreuse's manager.

'The banker who lives in the Rue d'Anjou?' observed Deslauriers. 'Do you know what you ought to do, old man?'

Isidore once more interrupted. His orders were positive, not to go back without Frédéric. Madame was getting uneasy at his absence.

'All right, all right, we're going,' said Deslauriers. 'He's not going to stay out all night.'

And, as soon as the manservant had disappeared:

'You ought to ask that old chap to introduce you to the Dambreuses: there's nothing so useful as to be a visitor at a rich man's house! Since you have a black coat and white gloves, make use of them! You must mix in that set! You can introduce me into it later. Just think! – a man worth millions! Do all you can to make him like you, and his wife, too. Become her lover!'

Frédéric protested.

'But I'm not saying anything new, I think? Remember Rastignac in the *Comédie Humaine*. You will succeed, I have no doubt!'

Frédéric had so much confidence in Deslauriers that he felt his firmness giving way, and forgetting Madame Arnoux, or including her in the prediction made with regard to the other, he could not keep from smiling.

The Clerk added:

'A last piece of advice: pass your examinations! It's always a good thing to have a handle to your name; and, once and for all, give up your Catholic and Satanic poets, whose philosophy is no more advanced than it was in the twelfth century! Your despair is silly.

The very greatest men have had more difficult beginnings, as in the case of Mirabeau, to name but one. Besides, our separation won't be as long as all that. I'll make my old crook of a father cough up. It's time for me to be going back. Goodbye! Have you got a hundred sous to pay for my dinner?'

Frédéric gave him ten francs, what was left of those he had got that morning from Isidore.

Meanwhile, some forty yards away from the bridges, on the left bank, a light shone from the garret window of a low-built house.

Deslauriers noticed it. Then he said emphatically as he took off his hat:

'Your pardon, Venus, Queen of Heaven! But Penury is the mother of Wisdom. Mercy me, weren't we just slandered enough for that!'

This allusion to an adventure in which they had both taken part, put them in high good humour. They laughed loudly as they passed through the streets.

Then, having settled his bill at the inn, Deslauriers walked back with Frédéric as far as the crossway near the Hôtel-Dieu; and after a long embrace, the two friends parted.

Two months later, Frédéric, having alighted one morning in the Rue Coq-Héron, immediately thought of paying his great visit.

Chance had come to his aid. Père Roque had brought him a roll of papers and requested him to deliver them up himself to M. Dambreuse; and he accompanied the package with an open letter of introduction on behalf of his young fellow-countryman.

Madame Moreau appeared surprised at this proceeding. Frédéric concealed the delight that it gave him.

M. Dambreuse's real name was the Count d'Ambreuse; but since 1825, gradually abandoning his title of nobility and his party, he had turned his attention to business; and with his ears open in every office, his hand in every enterprise, on the watch for every opportunity, as subtle as a Greek and as laborious as a native of Auvergne, he had amassed a fortune which was believed to be considerable; furthermore, he was an officer of the Legion of Honour, a member of the General Council of the Aube, a deputy, and one of these days would be a peer of France; also, always willing to please, he wearied the Minister by his continual applications for aid, for crosses, and licences for tobacconists' shops; and his grievances against authority inclined him to the Centre Left. His wife, the pretty Madame Dambreuse, of whom mention was made in the fashion journals, presided at charitable assemblies. By wheedling the duchesses, she appeased the rancours of the aristocratic faubourg and led the residents to believe that M. Dambreuse might yet repent and render them some services.

The young man was agitated when he called on them.

'I should have done better to wear my dress-coat. No doubt they'll give me an invitation to next week's ball. What will they say to me?'

His self-confidence returned when he reflected that M. Dambreuse was only a bourgeois, and he sprang briskly out of the cab on to the pavement of the Rue d'Anjou.

When he had pushed forward one of the two main gates he

crossed the courtyard, mounted the steps in front of the house, and entered a vestibule paved with coloured marble.

A straight double staircase with red carpet, fastened with brass rods, rested against the high walls of shining stucco. At the bottom of the stairs there was a banana tree, whose wide leaves fell down over the velvet of the baluster. From two bronze candelabra hung porcelain globes, suspended from little chains; the atmosphere was heavy with the fumes exhaled by the gaping vent-holes of the hot-air stoves; and all that could be heard was the ticking of a big clock fixed at the other end of the vestibule, under a wall-trophy.

A bell rang; a valet made his appearance, and introduced Frédéric into a little apartment, where one could observe two strong boxes, with pigeonholes filled with box-files. In the centre of it, M. Dambreuse was writing at a roll-top desk.

He ran his eye over Père Roque's letter, cut open the canvas in which the papers had been wrapped, and examined them.

At some distance, he presented the appearance of being still young, owing to his slight figure. But his thin white hair, his feeble limbs, and, above all, the extraordinary pallor of his face, betrayed a shattered constitution. There was an expression of pitiless energy in his sea-green eyes, colder than eyes of glass. His cheekbones projected, and his finger joints were knotted.

At length, he arose and addressed to the young man a few questions with regard to persons of their acquaintance at Nogent and also with regard to his studies; and then dismissed him with a bow. Frédéric went out through another lobby, and found himself at the lower end of the courtyard near the coachhouse.

A blue brougham, to which a black horse was yoked, stood in front of the steps before the house. The carriage door opened, a lady got in, and the vehicle, with a rumbling noise, went rolling along the gravel.

Frédéric came up to the courtyard gate from the other side at the same moment as she did. As there was not room enough to allow him to pass, he was compelled to wait. The young woman, leaning out of the window, talked to the doorkeeper in a very low tone. All he could see was her back, covered with a violet mantle. However, he took a glance into the interior of the carriage, lined with blue rep, with silk lace and fringes. The lady's ample robes filled up the space within; a scent of iris escaped from this little

padded box, and a vague odour of feminine elegance. The coachman slackened the reins, the horse brushed abruptly past the
starting-point, and all disappeared.

Frédéric returned on foot, following the boulevards.

He regretted not having been able to get a proper view of
Madame Dambreuse.

A little higher than the Rue Montmartre, a regular jumble of
vehicles made him turn his head; and on the opposite side, facing
him, he read on a marble plate:

JACQUES ARNOUX

How was it that he had not thought about her sooner? It was
Deslauriers' fault, and he approached the shop, which, however,
he did not enter; he was waiting for Her to appear.

The high, transparent plate-glass windows presented to one's
gaze statuettes, drawings, engravings, catalogues and numbers of
L'Art Industriel, arranged in a skilful fashion; and the fees for
subscription were repeated on the door, which was decorated in
the centre with the publisher's initials. Against the walls could be
seen large pictures whose varnish had a shiny look, then, in the
background, two chests laden with porcelain, bronze, alluring
curiosities; a little staircase separated them, shut off at the top by a
velvet curtain; and a chandelier of old Dresden china, a green
carpet on the floor, with an inlaid table, gave to this interior the
appearance rather of a drawing-room than of a shop.

Frédéric pretended to be examining the drawings. After hesitating
for a long time, he went in.

A clerk lifted the curtain, and in reply to a question, said that
Monsieur would not be 'at the shop' before five o'clock. But if the
message could be conveyed . . .

'No! I'll come back,' Frédéric answered softly.

The following days were spent in searching for lodgings; and he
fixed upon a room on the second floor of a furnished hotel in the
Rue Saint-Hyacinthe.

With a fresh blotting-case under his arm, he set forth to attend
the opening lecture of the course. Three hundred young men,
bareheaded, filled an amphitheatre, where an old man in a red
gown was delivering a discourse in a monotonous voice; quill pens
went scratching over paper. In this hall he found once more the

dusty odour of school, a professorial lectern of similar shape, the same wearisome monotony! For a fortnight he regularly continued his attendance. But he had left off the study of the Civil Code before getting as far as Article 3, and he gave up the Institutes at the *Summa Divisio Personarum*.

The pleasures that he had promised himself did not come to him; and when he had exhausted a circulating library, gone over the collections in the Louvre, and been at the theatre a great many nights in succession, he sank into the lowest depths of idleness.

His depression was increased by a thousand fresh annoyances. He found it necessary to count his linen and to bear with the door keeper, a bore with the figure of a male hospital nurse who came in the morning to make up his bed, smelling of alcohol and grumbling. He did not like his apartment, which was ornamented with an alabaster timepiece. The partitions were thin; he could hear the students making punch, laughing and singing.

Tired of this solitude, he sought out one of his old schoolfellows named Baptiste Martinon; and he discovered him in a middle-class boarding-house in the Rue Saint-Jacques, cramming up legal procedure before a coal fire.

A woman in a print dress sat opposite him darning socks.

Martinon was what people call a fine figure of a man – tall, plump, with regular features, and prominent bluish eyes; his father, an extensive landowner, had destined him for the magistracy – and wishing already to present a grave exterior, he wore his beard cut like a collar round his neck.

As there was no rational foundation for Frédéric's complaints, and as he could not give evidence of any misfortune, Martinon was unable in any way to understand his lamentations about existence. As for him, he went every morning to the Ecole, after that took a walk in the Luxembourg, in the evening swallowed his half-cup of coffee in the café, and with fifteen hundred francs a year, and the love of this working woman, he felt perfectly happy.

'What happiness!' was Frédéric's internal comment.

At the Ecole he had formed another acquaintance, M. de Cisy, a youth of aristocratic family, who on account of his dainty manners seemed like a young lady.

M. de Cisy devoted himself to drawing, and loved the Gothic style. They frequently went together to admire the Sainte-

Chapelle and Notre-Dame. But the young patrician's rank and pretensions covered an intellect of the feeblest order. Everything took him by surprise; he laughed immoderately at the most trifling joke, and displayed such utter simplicity that Frédéric at first took him for a wag, and finally regarded him as a booby.

The young man found it impossible, therefore, to be effusive with anyone, and he was still waiting for an invitation from the Dambreuses.

On New Year's Day, he sent them visiting cards, but received none in return.

He had gone back to the office of *L'Art Industriel*.

A third time he returned to it, and at last saw Arnoux carrying on an argument with five or six persons around him. He scarcely responded to the young man's bow; and Frédéric was wounded by this reception. None the less he cogitated over the best means of finding his way to Her.

His first idea was to come frequently to the shop on the pretext of getting pictures at low prices. Then he conceived the notion of slipping into the letter-box of the journal a few 'very strong' articles, which would lead to friendly relations. Perhaps it would be better to go straight to the mark at once, and declare his love? Acting on this impulse, he wrote a letter covering a dozen pages, full of lyric movements and apostrophes; but he tore it up, and did nothing, attempted nothing – bereft of motive power by his fear of failure.

Above Arnoux's shop, there were, on the first floor, three windows which were lighted up every evening. Shadows might be seen moving about behind them; especially one, this was hers – and he went very far out of his way in order to gaze at these windows and contemplate this shadow.

A negress who crossed his path one day in the Tuileries, holding a little girl by the hand, recalled to his mind Madame Arnoux's negress. She was sure to come there, like other women; every time he passed through the Tuileries, his heart began to beat with the anticipation of meeting her. On sunny days he continued his walk as far as the end of the Champs-Elysées.

Women seated with careless ease in open carriages, and with their veils floating in the wind, filed past close to him, their horses advancing at a steady walking pace, and with a slight seesaw movement that made the varnished leather of the harness crackle. The vehicles became more numerous, and, slackening speed beyond the Rond-Point, they took up the entire track. The horses' manes and the carriage lamps were close to each other; the steel stirrups, the silver curbs and the brass buckles, cast luminous points here and there in the midst of the short breeches, the white gloves, and the furs, falling over the blazonry of the carriage doors. He felt as if he were lost in some far-off world. His eyes wandered along the rows of female heads; and certain vague resemblances brought back Madame Arnoux to his recollection. He pictured her to himself, in the midst of the others, in one of those little broughams like Madame Dambreuse's brougham. But the sun was setting, and the cold wind raised whirling clouds of dust. The coachmen let their chins sink into their neckcloths, the wheels began to revolve more quickly, the road-metal grated and all the equipages descended the long avenue at a quick trot, touching, sweeping past one another, getting out of one another's way; then, on the Place de la Concorde, they went off in different directions. Behind the Tuileries, the sky turned the colour of slate. The trees of the garden formed two enormous masses, violet-hued at their summits. The gas-lamps were lighted; and the Seine, green all over, was torn into strips of silver silk, by the piers of the bridges.

He went to get a dinner for forty-three sous in a restaurant in the Rue de la Harpe.

He glanced disdainfully at the old mahogany counter, the soiled napkins, the dingy silver plate, and the hats hanging up on the wall. Those around him were students like himself. They talked about their professors, and about their mistresses. Much he cared about professors! Had he a mistress? To avoid being a witness of their enjoyment, he came as late as possible. The tables were all strewn with remnants of food. The two waiters, worn out, lay asleep, each in a corner of his own, and an odour of cooking, lamp-oil and tobacco filled the deserted dining-room.

Then he slowly toiled up the streets again. The gas lamps swung to and fro, casting on the mud long yellowish shafts of light. Shadowy forms surmounted by umbrellas glided along the footpaths. The pavement was slippery, the mist began to fall, and it seemed to him that the moist gloom, wrapping him around, descended into the depths of his heart.

He was smitten with a vague remorse. He renewed his attendance at lectures. But as he was entirely ignorant of the matters which formed the subject of explanation, things of the simplest description puzzled him.

He set about writing a novel entitled *Sylvio, the Fisherman's Son*. The scene of the story was Venice. The hero was himself, and Madame Arnoux was the heroine. She was called Antonia – and, to get possession of her, he assassinated a number of noblemen, burned a portion of the city, and sang a serenade under her balcony, where fluttered in the breeze the red damask curtains of the Boulevard Montmartre. The echoes from other writers, far too numerous, which he noticed produced a disheartening effect on him; he went no further with the work, and his idleness redoubled.

After this, he begged Deslauriers to come and share his room. They might make arrangements to live together with the aid of his allowance of two thousand francs; anything would be better than this intolerable existence. Deslauriers could not yet leave Troyes. He urged his friend to find some means of distracting his thoughts, and to call on Sénécal.

Sénécal was a mathematical tutor, a hardheaded man with republican convictions, a future Saint-Just according to the clerk. Frédéric had ascended the five flights, up which he lived, three times in succession without getting a visit from him in return. He did not go back.

He decided to enjoy himself. He attended the balls at the Opéra. These exhibitions of riotous gaiety froze him the moment he had passed the door. Besides, he was restrained by the fear of being subjected to insult on the subject of money, his notion being that a supper with a masked lady entailed considerable expense and was rather a big adventure.

It seemed to him, however, that he deserved to be loved! Sometimes he used to wake up with his heart full of hope, dressed himself carefully as if he were going to keep an appointment, and started on interminable excursions all over Paris. With every woman who walked in front of him, or came in his direction, he would say: 'That's the one!' Every time it was only a fresh disappointment. The idea of Madame Arnoux strengthened these desires. Perhaps he would find her on his way; and he conjured up odd coincidences, extraordinary perils from which he would save her, in order to get near her.

So the days slipped by with the same tiresome experiences, and enslavement to acquired habits. He turned over the pages of pamphlets under the arcades of the Odéon, went to read the *Revue des Deux Mondes* at the café, entered a hall of the Collège de France, and for an hour listened to a lecture on Chinese or political economy. Every week he wrote long letters to Deslauriers, dined from time to time with Martinon, and occasionally saw M. de Cisy.

He hired a piano and composed German waltzes.

One evening at the theatre of the Palais-Royal, he perceived, in one of the stage boxes, Arnoux with a woman by his side. Was it she? The screen of green taffeta, pulled over the side of the box, hid her face. At length, the curtain rose; the screen was drawn aside. She was a tall woman of about thirty, rather faded, and, when she laughed, her thick lips uncovered a row of splendid teeth. She chatted familiarly with Arnoux, giving him, from time to time, taps, with her fan, on the fingers. Then a fair-haired young girl with eyelids a little red, as if she had just been weeping, seated herself between them. Arnoux after that remained stooped over her shoulder, pouring forth a stream of talk to which she listened without replying. Frédéric taxed his ingenuity to find out the social position of these women, modestly attired in gowns of sober hue with flat, turned-down collars.

At the close of the play, he made a dash for the corridors. The crowd of people going out filled them up. Arnoux, just in front of him, was descending the staircase step by step, with a woman on each arm.

Suddenly a gas burner shed its light on him. He wore a black mourning-band on his hat. She was dead, perhaps? This idea tormented Frédéric's mind so much, that he hurried, next day, to the office of *L'Art Industriel* and paying, without a moment's delay, for one of the engravings exposed in the window for sale, he asked the shop assistant how was Monsieur Arnoux.

The shop assistant replied:

'Why, very well!'

Frédéric, growing pale, added:

'And Madame?'

'Madame, too!'

Frédéric forgot to carry off his engraving.

The winter drew to an end. He was less melancholy in the spring time, began to prepare for his examination and, having passed it indifferently, he started immediately afterwards for Nogent.

He refrained from going to Troyes to see his friend, in order to escape his mother's comments. Then, on his return to Paris at the end of the vacation, he left his lodgings, and took two rooms on the Quai Napoléon, which he furnished. He had given up all hope of getting an invitation from the Dambreuses; his great passion for Madame Arnoux was beginning to die out.

One morning, in the month of December, while going to attend a law lecture, he thought he could observe more than ordinary animation in the Rue Saint-Jacques. The students were rushing precipitately out of the cafés, or calling to each other through open windows, from one house to the other; the shop keepers in the middle of the pavement were exchanging anxious glances; window shutters were being closed; and when he reached the Rue Soufflot, he saw a great gathering around the Panthéon.

Young men in uneven groups, numbering from five to a dozen, walked along, arm-in-arm, and accosted the larger groups, which had stationed themselves here and there; at the lower end of the square, near the railings, men in overalls were holding forth, while policemen, with their three-cornered hats drawn over their ears, and their hands behind their backs, prowled up and down beside the walls, making the flags ring under the tread of their heavy boots. All wore a mysterious, wondering look; they were evidently expecting something to happen; each held back a question which was on the edge of his lips.

Frédéric found himself close to a fair-haired young man with a prepossessing face and a moustache and a tuft of beard on his chin, like a dandy of Louis XIII's time. He asked the stranger what was the cause of the disorder.

'I haven't the least idea,' replied the other, 'nor have they, for that matter! It's a habit of theirs just now! What a joke!'

And he burst out laughing.

The petitions for Reform, which the National Guard were being persuaded to sign, together with the Humann census and other events besides, had, for the past six months, led to inexplicable demonstrations in Paris; and so frequently had they broken out anew, that the newspapers had ceased to refer to them.

'This lacks shape and colour,' continued Frédéric's neighbour. 'Methinks, messire, that we have degenerated! In the good old days of Louis XI, and even in those of Benjamin Constant, there was more mutinous spirit amongst the scholars of the town. Verily, I find them pacific as sheep, stupid as asses, and meet only to be grocers, gadzooks! And these are what we call the cream of our youth!'

He held his arms wide apart after the fashion of Frédéric Lemaître in *Robert Macaire*.

'Cream of our youth, I give you my blessing!'

After this, addressing a rag picker, who was searching through a heap of oyster shells up against the wall of a wine-merchant's:

'Are you one of them – the cream of our youth?'

The old man lifted up a hideous countenance in which were distinguishable, in the midst of a grey beard, a red nose and two dull eyes, bloodshot from drink.

'No, you appear to me rather *one of those men of sinister mien whom we see, in various groups, liberally scattering gold.* . . Oh, scatter away, my patriarch, scatter away! Corrupt me with the treasures of Albion! *Are you English*? I do not reject the presents of Artaxerxes! Let us have a little chat about the Customs Union!'

Frédéric felt a hand laid on his shoulder; he turned round. It was Martinon, looking exceedingly pale.

'Well!' said he with a big sigh, 'another riot!'

He was afraid of being compromised, and moaned and groaned. Some of the men in overalls, especially, made him feel uneasy, suggesting a connection with secret societies.

'You mean to say there are secret societies?' said the young man with the moustaches. 'That's an old dodge of the Government, to frighten the middle classes!'

Martinon urged him to speak in a lower tone, for fear of the police.

'You still believe in the police, do you? Come to that, how do you know, Monsieur, that I'm not a police spy myself?'

And he looked at him in such a way, that Martinon, much discomposed, was, at first, unable to see the joke. The crowd was pushing them, and they had all three been compelled to stand on the little staircase which led, by one of the passages, to the new amphitheatre.

Soon, the throng parted of its own accord; many removed their hats; they bowed towards the distinguished Professor Samuel Rondelot, who, wrapped in his big frock-coat, with his silver spectacles held up high in the air, and breathing hard from his asthma, was advancing at an easy pace, on his way to deliver his lecture. This man was one of the judicial glories of the nineteenth century, the rival of men like Zachariaes and Ruhdorff. His new dignity of peer of France had in no way modified his demeanour. He was known to be poor, and was treated with profound respect.

Meanwhile, at the lower end of the square, some persons cried out:

'Down with Guizot!'

'Down with Pritchard!'

'Down with the traitors!'

'Down with Louis-Philippe!'

The crowd swayed to and fro, and, pressing against the gate of the courtyard, which was shut, prevented the professor from going further. He stopped in front of the staircase. He was soon observed on the highest of the three steps. He spoke; the loud murmurs of the throng drowned his voice. Although previously they had loved him, they hated him now, for he was the representative of Authority. Every time he tried to make himself understood, the shouting began again. He made a sweeping gesture, to induce the students to follow him. He was answered by vociferations from all sides. He shrugged his shoulders disdainfully, and plunged into the passage. Martinon had taken advantage of his position to disappear at the same moment.

'What a coward!' said Frédéric.

'He's sensible!' returned the other.

There was an outburst of applause from the crowd. This retreat, on the part of the professor, was a victory for them. From every window, faces, lighted with curiosity, looked out. Some of those in the crowd struck up the 'Marseillaise'; others proposed to go to Béranger's house.

'To Laffitte's house!'

'To Chateaubriand's house!'

'To Voltaire's house!' yelled the young man with the fair moustaches.

The policemen tried to pass around, saying in the mildest tones they could assume:

'Move on, gentlemen! Move on! Off you go!'

Somebody called out:

'Down with the butchers!'

This was a form of insult usual since the troubles of the month of September. Everyone repeated it. The guardians of public order were booed and hissed; they began to grow pale; one of them could endure it no longer, and, seeing a youth approaching too close, laughing in his face, pushed him back so roughly, that he tumbled over on his back some five paces away, in front of the wine merchant's shop. All drew back; but almost immediately afterwards the policeman rolled on the ground himself, felled by a blow from a kind of Hercules, whose hair stood out like a bundle of tow from an oilskin cap.

Having been stopped for some minutes at the corner of the Rue Saint-Jacques, he had very quickly dropped a large case which he had been carrying, in order to make a spring at the policeman, and, holding him prostrate beneath him, punched his face unmercifully. The other policemen rushed to the rescue. The terrible lad was so strong that it took four of them at least to get the better of him. Two of them shook him, while keeping a grip on his collar, two others dragged him by the arms, a fifth gave him digs of the knee in the ribs, and all of them called him 'brigand', 'assassin', 'troublemaker'. With his breast bare, and his clothes in shreds, he protested that he was innocent; he could not have watched a child being beaten and done nothing.

'My name is Dussardier! I'm employed at Messieurs Valinçart Brothers' lace and fancy warehouse in the Rue de Cléry. Where's my case? I want my case!' He kept repeating: 'Dussardier! . . . Rue de Cléry. My case!'

However, he became quiet, and, with a stoical air, allowed himself to be led towards the guardhouse in the Rue Descartes. A flood of people followed him. Frédéric and the young man with the moustaches walked immediately behind, full of admiration for the shop assistant, and incensed at the violence of Power.

As they advanced, the crowd became less thick.

The policemen from time to time turned round, with threatening looks; and the rowdy ones no longer having anything to do and the spectators not having anything to look at, all drifted away by degrees. Passers-by, who met the procession, as they came along, stared at Dussardier, and in loud tones gave vent to abusive remarks about him. One old woman, at her door, even bawled out that he had stolen a loaf of bread; this unjust accusation increased the irritation of the two friends. At length, they reached the guardhouse. Only about twenty persons were now left, and the sight of the soldiers was enough to disperse them.

Frédéric and his companion boldly asked to have the man who had just been imprisoned delivered up. The sentinel threatened, if they persisted, to ram them into jail too. They said they required to see the commander of the guardhouse, and stated their names, and the fact that they were law students, declaring that the prisoner was one also.

They were ushered into a room perfectly bare, in which four benches lined the roughly-plastered, smoke-blackened walls. At the lower end a hatch opened. Then appeared the sturdy face of Dussardier, who, with his hair all tousled, his honest little eyes, and his square-tipped nose, suggested to one's mind in a confused sort of way the physiognomy of a good dog.

'Don't you recognise us?' said Hussonnet.

This was the name of the young man with the moustaches.

'Why . . . ' stammered Dussardier.

'Stop playing the fool,' returned the other. 'They know you're a law student, just like us.'

In spite of their winks, Dussardier failed to understand. He appeared to be collecting his thoughts, then, suddenly:

'Has my case been found?'

Frédéric, discouraged, raised his eyes to the ceiling. Hussonnet, however, said promptly:

'Ha! Your case, in which you keep your lecture notes? Yes, yes, don't worry!'

They made further pantomimic signs with redoubled energy, till Dussardier at last realised that they had come to help him; and he held his tongue, fearing that he might compromise them. Besides, he experienced a kind of shame at seeing himself raised to the social rank of student, and to an equality with these young men who had such white hands.

'Do you wish to send any message to anyone?' asked Frédéric.

'No, thanks, nobody!'

'What about your family?'

He lowered his head without replying; the poor fellow was a bastard. The two friends stood quite astonished at his silence.

'Have you anything to smoke?' was Frédéric's next question.

He felt about, then drew forth from the depths of one of his pockets the remains of a pipe – a beautiful pipe, made of white talc with a shank of blackwood, a silver cover, and an amber mouthpiece.

For the last three years he had been engaged in completing this masterpiece. He had been careful to keep the bowl of it constantly wrapped in a sheath of chamois leather, to smoke it as slowly as possible, without ever letting it lie on any cold stone substance, and to hang it up every evening over the head of his bed. And now he shook out the fragments of it into his hand, the nails of which were covered with blood; and with his chin sunk on his chest, his eyes fixed and staring, he contemplated this wreck of the thing that had yielded him such delight with a glance of unutterable sadness.

'Suppose we give him some cigars, eh?' said Hussonnet in a whisper, making as if to get some out.

Frédéric had already laid down a cigar-holder, filled, on the edge of the hatchway.

'Come, take it! Goodbye! Chin up!'

Dussardier flung himself on the two hands that were held out towards him. He pressed them frantically, his voice choked with sobs.

'What? . . . For me! . . . For me! . . . '

The two friends eluded his gratitude, departed, and went off to lunch together at the Café Tabourey, in front of the Luxembourg.

While cutting up the beefsteak, Hussonnet informed his companion that he did work for the fashion journals, and manufactured advertisements for *L'Art Industriel*.

'Jacques Arnoux's establishment?' said Frédéric.

'Do you know him?'

'Yes! – No! . . . That is to say, I've seen him, I've met him.'

He carelessly asked Hussonnet if he sometimes saw Arnoux's wife.

'From time to time,' the Bohemian replied.

Frédéric did not venture to follow up his enquiries; this man henceforth would fill up a large space in his life; he paid the lunch bill without any protest on the other's part.

There was a bond of mutual sympathy between them; they gave one another their respective addresses, and Hussonnet cordially invited Frédéric to accompany him to the Rue de Fleurus.

They had reached the middle of the garden, when Arnoux's employee, holding his breath, twisted his features into a hideous grimace, and begin to crow like a cock. Thereupon all the cocks in the vicinity responded with prolonged 'cock-a-doodle-doos'.

'It's a signal,' explained Hussonnet.

They stopped close to the Bobino Theatre, in front of a house to which they had to find their way through an alley. In the skylight of a garret, between some nasturtiums and some sweet peas, a young woman showed herself, bareheaded, in her stays, her two arms resting on the edge of the roof-gutter.

'Good day, my angel, good day, my little duck,' said Hussonnet, blowing her kisses.

He kicked the gate open, and disappeared.

Frédéric waited for him all the week. He did not venture to call on him, lest it might look as if he were in a hurry to get a lunch in return for the one he had paid for; but he sought him all over the Latin Quarter. He came across him one evening, and brought him to his room on the Quai Napoléon.

They had a long chat, opening their hearts to each other. Hussonnet yearned after the glory and the gains of the theatre. He collaborated in the writing of vaudevilles which were not accepted, 'had heaps of plans', could turn a couplet; he sang some of them. Then, noticing on one of the shelves a volume of Hugo and another of Lamartine, he broke out into sarcastic criticisms of the romantic school. These poets had neither good sense nor correctness, and, above all, were not French! He prided himself on his knowledge of the language, and analysed the most beautiful phrases with that carping severity, that academic taste which persons of playful disposition exhibit when they are discussing serious art.

Frédéric was wounded in his predilections; he felt a desire to break off the relationship. Why not take the risk at once of uttering the word on which his happiness depended? He asked the budding man of letters whether it would be possible to get an introduction into the Arnoux's house through his agency.

The thing was declared to be easy, and they fixed upon the following day.

Hussonnet failed to keep the appointment; he missed three

others. One Saturday, about four o'clock, he made his appearance. But, taking advantage of the cab, he drew up first in front of the Théâtre Français to get a box ticket; he got down at a tailor's shop, then at a dressmaker's; he wrote notes in concierges' lodges. At last they came to the Boulevard Montmartre. Frédéric passed through the shop, and went up the staircase. Arnoux recognised him in the mirror in front of his desk; and still continuing to write he stretched out his hand over his shoulder.

Five or six persons, standing up, filled the narrow apartment, which was lighted by a single window looking out onto the court yard; a sofa of brown damask wool occupied the interior of an alcove at the end of the room between two door-curtains of similar material. Upon the chimney piece, covered with old papers, there was a bronze Venus; two candelabra, garnished with rose-coloured candles, supported it, one at each side. On the right, near a filing cabinet, a man, seated in an armchair, was reading the newspaper, with his hat on; the walls were hidden from view beneath the array of prints and pictures, precious engravings or sketches by contemporary masters, adorned with dedications testifying the most sincere affection for Jacques Arnoux.

'You're getting on well all this time?' said he turning round to Frédéric.

And, without waiting for an answer, he asked Hussonnet in a low tone:

'What is your friend's name?'

Then, raising his voice:

'Take a cigar out of the box on the filing cabinet.'

L'Art Industriel, situated in a central position in Paris, was a convenient place of resort, a neutral ground wherein rivalries elbowed each other familiarly. On this day could be seen Anténor Braive, who painted portraits of kings; Jules Burrieu, whose sketches were beginning to popularise the wars in Algeria; the caricaturist Sombaz, the sculptor Vourdat, and others, and not a single one of them corresponded with the student's preconceived ideas. Their manners were simple, their talk free and easy. The mystic Lovarias told an obscene story; and the inventor of Oriental landscape, the famous Dittmer, wore a knitted vest under his waistcoat, and went home on the bus.

The first topic that came up was that of a girl named Apollonie, formerly a model, whom Burrieu alleged that he had seen on the boulevard in a carriage. Hussonnet explained this metamorphosis through the succession of her lovers.

'How well this sly dog knows the girls of Paris!' said Arnoux.

'After you, if there are any of them left, sire,' replied the Bohemian, with a military salute, in imitation of the grenadier offering his flask to Napoleon.

Then they talked about some pictures in which Apollonie's head had figured. They criticised absent colleagues, expressing astonishment at the sums paid for their works; and they were all complaining of not being sufficiently remunerated themselves, when the conversation was interrupted by the entrance of a man of middle stature, who had his coat fastened by a single button, and whose eyes glittered with a rather wild expression.

'What a lot of bourgeois you are!' said he. 'God bless my soul! What does that signify? The old boys who turned out masterpieces didn't bother about Correggio, Murillo . . . '

'Add Pellerin,' said Sombaz.

But, without taking the slightest notice of the epigram, he went on talking with such vehemence, that Arnoux was forced to repeat twice to him:

'My wife wants you on Thursday. Don't forget.'

This remark recalled Madame Arnoux to Frédéric's thoughts. No doubt, one got to her through the little room near the sofa? Arnoux had just opened the door leading into it to get a pocket-handkerchief, and Frédéric had seen a washstand at the far end of it. But at this point a kind of muttering sound came from the corner of the chimney-piece; it was caused by the personage who sat in the armchair reading the newspaper. He was a man of five feet nine inches in height, with rather heavy eyelids, a head of grey hair, and an imposing appearance – and his name was Regimbart.

'What's the matter now, citizen?' said Arnoux.

'Another fresh piece of rascalry on the part of the Government!'

The thing that he was referring to was the dismissal of a school-master; Pellerin again took up his parallel between Michelangelo and Shakespeare. Dittmer was taking himself off when Arnoux pulled him back in order to put two bank notes into his hand. Thereupon Hussonnet said, considering this an opportune time:

'Couldn't you give me an advance, my dear master?'

But Arnoux had resumed his seat, and was administering a severe reprimand to an old man of mean aspect, who wore a pair of blue spectacles.

'Ha! A nice fellow you are, Père Isaac! Here are three works denounced, lost for good! Everybody's laughing at me! People know what they are now! What am I supposed to do with them? I'll have to send them off to California . . . to hell with it! Hold your tongue!'

The speciality of this old chap consisted in attaching the signatures of the great masters at the bottom of these pictures. Arnoux refused to pay him, and dismissed him in a brutal fashion. Then, with an entire change of manner, he bowed to a gentleman of affectedly grave demeanour, who wore whiskers and displayed a white tie round his neck and the cross of the Legion of Honour over his breast.

With his elbow resting on the window fastening he kept talking to him for a long time in honeyed tones. At last he burst out:

'Ah, well, I'm not short of jobbers, Count!'

The nobleman gave way, and Arnoux paid him down twenty-five louis. As soon as he had gone out:

'What a plague these great lords are!'

'A lot of wretches!' muttered Regimbart.

As it grew later, Arnoux was much more busily occupied; he classified articles, tore open letters, set out accounts in a row; at the sound of hammering in the warehouse he went out to look after the packing, then he went back to his ordinary work; and, while he kept his steel pen running over the paper, he responded to witticisms. He had an invitation to dine with his lawyer that evening, and was starting next day for Belgium.

The others chatted about the topics of the day: Cherubini's portrait, the hemicycle of the Fine Arts, and the next Exhibition. Pellerin railed at the Institut. Gossip and serious discussion got mixed up together. The apartment with its low ceiling was so full that no one could move; and the light of the rose-coloured candles was obscured in the smoke of their cigars, like the sun's rays in a mist.

The door near the sofa flew open, and a tall, slender woman entered – with abrupt movements which made all the trinkets of her watch rattle on her black taffeta gown.

It was the woman of whom Frédéric had caught a glimpse last summer at the Palais-Royal. Some of those present, addressing her by name, shook hands with her. Hussonnet had at last managed to extract from his employer the sum of fifty francs; the clock struck seven; all rose to go.

Arnoux told Pellerin to remain, and accompanied Mademoiselle Vatnaz into the dressing-room.

Frédéric could not hear what they said; they spoke in whispers. However, the woman's voice was raised:

'I've been waiting ever since the thing was settled six months ago!'

There was a long silence, and then Mademoiselle Vatnaz reappeared. Arnoux had again promised her something.

'Oh! Oh, later, we'll see!'

'Goodbye! Happy man!' said she, as she was going out.

Arnoux quickly re-entered the dressing-room, rubbed some cosmetic over his moustaches, raised his braces to stretch his straps, and, while he was washing his hands:

'I need two panels to go over the door at two hundred and fifty apiece, in Boucher's style. Is that agreed?'

'All right,' said the artist, his face reddening.

'Good! And don't forget my wife!'

Frédéric accompanied Pellerin to the top of the Faubourg Poissonnière, and asked his permission to come to see him sometimes, a favour which was graciously accorded.

Pellerin read every work on æsthetics, in order to find out the true theory of the Beautiful, convinced that, when he had discovered it, he would produce masterpieces. He surrounded himself with every imaginable auxiliary – drawings, plaster casts, models, engravings; and he kept searching about, eating his heart out; he blamed the weather, his nerves, his studio, went out into the street to find inspiration there, quivered with delight at the thought that he had caught it, then abandoned the work in which he was engaged, and dreamed of another which should be finer. Thus, tormented by the desire for glory and wasting his days in discussions, believing in a thousand fooleries, in systems, in criticism, in the importance of a regulation or a reform in the domain of Art, he had at fifty as yet turned out nothing save mere sketches. His robust pride prevented him from experiencing any discouragement, but he was always irritated, and in that state of exaltation, at the same time factitious and natural, which is characteristic of actors.

On entering his studio one's attention was directed towards two large pictures, in which the first tones of colour laid on here and there made on the white canvas patches of brown, red, and blue. A network of lines in chalk stretched over it, like the meshes of a net which had been mended many times; so that it was impossible to make anything of it. Pellerin explained the subject of these two compositions by pointing out with his thumb the portions that were lacking. The first was intended to represent 'The Madness of Nebuchadnezzar', and the second 'The Burning of Rome by Nero'. Frédéric admired them.

He admired academies of women with dishevelled hair, landscapes in which trunks of trees, twisted by the storm, abounded, and, above all, fantastic pen and ink sketches, echoes of Callot, Rembrandt, or Goya, of which he did not know the models. Pellerin no longer set any value on these works of his youth; he was now all in favour of the grand style; he dogmatised eloquently about Phidias and Winckelmann. The objects around him reinforced the power of his language: one saw a death's head on a prie-dieu, some scimitars, a monk's habit; Frédéric put it on.

When he arrived early, he surprised the artist in his wretched folding bed, which was hidden from view by a strip of tapestry; for Pellerin went to bed late, being an assiduous frequenter of the theatres. An old woman in tatters attended on him, he dined in cheap restaurants, and lived without a mistress. His learning, picked up in the most irregular fashion, rendered his paradoxes amusing. His hatred of the vulgar and the 'bourgeois' overflowed in sarcasms, marked by a superb lyricism, and he had such religious reverence for the masters that it raised him almost to their level.

But why did he never speak about Madame Arnoux? As for her husband, at one time he called him a decent fellow, at other times a charlatan. Frédéric was waiting for some disclosures on his part.

One day, while turning over one of the portfolios in the studio, he thought he could trace in the portrait of a gipsy some resemblance to Mademoiselle Vatnaz, and, as he felt interested in this lady, he desired to know what was her exact social position.

She had been, as far as Pellerin could ascertain, originally a schoolmistress in the provinces; she now gave lessons, and tried to write for the minor journals.

According to Frédéric, one would imagine from her manners with Arnoux that she was his mistress.

'Pshaw! He has others!'

Then, turning away his face, which reddened with shame as he realised the baseness of the suggestion, the young man added, with a swaggering air:

'Very likely his wife pays him back in kind?'

'Not at all! She is virtuous!'

Frédéric experienced a feeling of compunction, and his attendance at the office of the art journal became more marked than before.

The big letters which formed the name of Arnoux on the marble plate above the shop seemed to him quite special and pregnant with significance, like some sacred writing. The wide footpath, which sloped towards it, facilitated his approach, the door almost turned of its own accord; and the handle, smooth to the touch, gave him the sensation of a friendly and, as it were, intelligent hand in his. Unconsciously, he became quite as regular in his visits as Regimbart.

Every day Regimbart seated himself in the chimney corner, in his armchair, got hold of the *National*, and kept possession of it, expressing his thoughts by exclamations or by simple shrugs of the shoulders. From time to time he would wipe his forehead with his pocket-handkerchief, rolled up in a ball, which he usually stuck in between two buttons of his green frock-coat. He wore trousers with a crease, half-boots, and a long cravat; and his hat, with its turned-up brim, made him easily recognised, at a distance, in a crowd.

At eight o'clock in the morning he descended from the heights of Montmartre, in order to imbibe white wine in the Rue Notre-Dame-des-Victoires. His lunch, followed by several games of billiards, took him to three o'clock. He then directed his steps towards the Passage des Panoramas, where he had a glass of absinthe. After the session in Arnoux's shop, he entered the Bordelais Tavern, where he swallowed some vermouth; then, instead of returning home to his wife, he often preferred to dine alone in a little café in the Place Gaillon, where he desired them to serve up to him 'home cooking, natural things'! Finally, he made his way to another billiard-room, and remained there till midnight, till one o'clock in the morning, up till the last moment, when, the gas being put out and the window shutters fastened, the master of the establishment, worn out, begged of him to go.

And it was not the love of drinking that attracted Citizen Regimbart to these places, but the inveterate habit of talking politics there; with advancing age, he had lost his vivacity, and now exhibited only a silent moroseness. One would have said, judging from the gravity of his countenance, that he was turning over in his mind the affairs of the whole world. Nothing, however, came from it; and nobody, even amongst his own friends, knew him to have any occupation, although he gave himself out as running a business advisory service.

Arnoux appeared to have a very great esteem for him. One day he said to Frédéric:

'He knows a lot, I assure you! He's an able man!'

On another occasion Regimbart spread over his desk papers relating to some kaolin mines in Brittany; Arnoux set great store by his experience.

Frédéric showed himself more ceremonious towards Regimbart, going so far as to invite him from time to time to take a glass of absinthe; and, although he considered him a stupid man, he often remained a full hour in his company solely because he was Jacques Arnoux's friend.

After pushing forward some contemporary masters in the early portions of their career, the picture-dealer, a man of progressive ideas, had tried, while clinging to his artistic ways, to extend his pecuniary profits. His object was to emancipate the fine arts, to get the sublime at a cheap rate. Over every industry associated with Parisian luxury he exercised an influence which proved fortunate with respect to little things, but fatal with respect to great things. With his mania for pandering to public opinion, he made clever artists swerve from their true path, corrupted the strong, exhausted the weak, and got distinction for those of mediocre talent; he controlled their fates with the assistance of his connections and of his magazine. Young painters were ambitious of seeing their works in his window, and upholsterers came to him for their patterns. Frédéric regarded him, at the same time, as a millionaire, as a *dilettante*, and as a man of action. However, he found many things that filled him with astonishment, for friend Arnoux was rather sly in his commercial transactions.

He received from the depths of Germany or of Italy a picture purchased in Paris for fifteen hundred francs, and, exhibiting an invoice that brought the price up to four thousand, sold it on, as a favour, for three thousand five hundred. One of his usual tricks with painters was to exact as a sweetener a smaller copy of their picture, under the pretence that he would bring out an engraving of it; he always sold the copy and the engraving never appeared. To those who complained that he had taken advantage of them, he would reply by a slap on the stomach. An excellent fellow nonetheless, he squandered money on cigars for his acquaintances, used the 'tu' form to people he did not know, displayed enthusiasm for a work or a man and, when this happened, let nothing stand in his way, spared no expense, and threw himself into visits, correspondence, and advertising. He looked upon himself as very upright, and in his need to confide ingenuously told his friends about his shady acts.

Once, in order to annoy a colleague who was inaugurating another art journal with a big banquet, he asked Frédéric to write, under his own eyes, a little before the hour fixed for the entertainment, letters to the guests recalling the invitations.

'This impugns nobody's honour, you understand?'

And the young man did not dare to refuse him this service.

Next day, on entering with Hussonnet M. Arnoux's office, Frédéric saw through the door (the one opening onto the staircase) the hem of a lady's dress disappearing.

'A thousand pardons!' said Hussonnet. 'If I'd known there were women . . .'

'Oh, that one's mine,' replied Arnoux. 'She just came up to pay me a visit as she was passing.'

'What?' said Frédéric.

'Why, yes! She's on her way home, back to the house.'

The charm of the things around him was suddenly withdrawn. All that had seemed to him to be diffused vaguely throughout the place had now vanished, or rather, it had never been there. He experienced an infinite amazement, and something like the painful sensation of having been betrayed.

Arnoux, rummaging about in his drawer, was smiling. Was he

laughing at him? The clerk laid down a bundle of moist papers on the table.

'Ha! The posters!' exclaimed the picture-dealer. 'I shan't dine early this evening!'

Regimbart took up his hat.

'What, are you leaving me?'

'Seven o'clock!' said Regimbart.

Frédéric followed him.

At the corner of the Rue Montmartre, he turned round; he glanced towards the windows of the first floor; and he laughed internally, pitying himself as he recalled to mind with what love he had so often contemplated them! Where, then, did she live? How was he to meet her now? Once more around the object of his desire a solitude opened more immense than ever!

'Do you feel like having . . . ?' asked Regimbart.

'Having who?'

'An absinthe!'

And, yielding to his cravings, Frédéric allowed himself to be led towards the Bordelais Tavern. Whilst his companion, leaning on his elbow, was staring at the decanter, he was casting his eyes right and left. But he caught a glimpse of Pellerin's profile on the pavement outside; he gave a quick tap at the windowpane, and the painter had scarcely sat down when Regimbart asked him why they no longer saw him at the office of *L'Art Industriel*.

'May I rot if ever I go back there again! The man's a brute, a tradesman, a scoundrel, a downright rogue!'

These insulting words harmonised with Frédéric's present angry mood. Nevertheless, he was wounded, for it seemed to him that they hit at Madame Arnoux more or less.

'Why, what has he done to you?' said Regimbart.

Pellerin's only response was to stamp his foot on the ground and snort.

He had been devoting himself to artistic work of a clandestine nature, such as portraits in charcoal and chalk, or pastiches of the great masters for amateurs of limited knowledge; and, as he felt humiliated by these inferior productions, he preferred to hold his tongue on the subject as a general rule. But 'Arnoux's dirty ways' exasperated him too much. He had to relieve his feelings.

In accordance with an order, which had been given in Frédéric's very presence, he had brought Arnoux two pictures. Thereupon the dealer took the liberty of criticising them! He had found fault with the composition, the colouring, and the drawing, especially the drawing; he would not, in short, take them at any price. But, driven to extremities by a bill falling due, Pellerin had had to give them to the Jew Isaac; and, a fortnight later, Arnoux himself sold them to a Spaniard for two thousand francs.

'Not a penny less! What a filthy trick! And by God, he's done many other things just as bad! We'll see him in the dock one of these days.'

'How you exaggerate!' said Frédéric, in a timid voice.

'Come now, that's a good one! I exaggerate!' exclaimed the artist, giving the table a great blow with his fist.

This violence had the effect of completely restoring the young man's self-command. No doubt he might have acted more nicely; still, if Arnoux found these two pictures . . .

'Bad! Say it out! Have you seen them? Is this your profession? Now, let me tell you, my son, I don't allow this sort of thing from amateurs!'

'Ah! It's not my business!' said Frédéric.

'Then, what interest have you in defending him?' returned Pellerin, coldly.

The young man faltered:

'But . . . because I'm his friend.'

'Go and give him a hug for me! Good evening!'

And the painter rushed away in a rage, and, of course, without mentioning his drink.

Frédéric, whilst defending Arnoux, had convinced himself. In the heat of his eloquence, he was filled with tenderness towards this man, so intelligent and kind, slandered by his friends, and who was only now working all alone, abandoned. He could not resist a strange impulse to go at once and see him again. Ten minutes afterwards he pushed open the door of the shop.

Arnoux was preparing, with the assistance of his clerk, some huge posters for an exhibition of pictures.

'Hallo! What brings you back?'

This question, simple though it was, embarrassed Frédéric; and, at a loss for an answer, he asked whether they had happened to find a notebook of his, a little notebook with a blue leather cover.

'The one you put your love letters in?' said Arnoux.

Frédéric, blushing like a maiden, protested against such an assumption.

'Your poems then?' returned the picture-dealer.

He was handling the pictorial specimens which were spread out around him, discussing their form, colouring, and frames; and Frédéric felt more and more irritated by his air of abstraction, and particularly by the appearance of his hands passing over the posters – large hands, rather soft, with flat nails. At length, Arnoux arose; and saying, 'That's that!' he chucked the young man familiarly under the chin. Frédéric was offended at this liberty, and recoiled a pace or two; then he made for the shop door, and passed out through it, as he imagined, for the last time in his life. Madame Arnoux herself was as if diminished by the vulgarity of her husband.

During the same week he got a letter, informing him that Deslauriers would be in Paris on the following Thursday. Then he flung himself back violently on this affection as one of a more solid and lofty character. A man of this sort was worth all the women in the world. He would no longer have any need of Regimbart, of Pellerin, of Hussonnet, of anyone! In order to provide his friend with as comfortable lodgings as possible, he bought an iron bedstead and a second armchair, and stripped off some of his own bed-covering to garnish this one properly; and on Thursday morning he was dressing himself to go to meet Deslauriers when there was a ring at the door. Arnoux entered.

'Just one word! Yesterday I got a lovely trout from Geneva; we expect you by and by, at seven o'clock sharp . . . The address is Rue de Choiseul 24B. Don't forget!'

Frédéric was obliged to sit down. His knees were tottering under him. He repeated to himself, 'At last! At last!' Then he wrote to his tailor, to his hatter, and to his bootmaker; and he despatched these three notes by three different messengers. The key turned in the lock, and the concierge appeared with a trunk on his shoulder.

Frédéric, on seeing Deslauriers, began to tremble like an adulteress under the glance of her husband.

'What's wrong with you?' said Deslauriers. 'Surely you got my letter?'

Frédéric had not the strength to lie.

He opened his arms, and flung himself on his friend's breast.

Then the Clerk told his story. His father had thought to avoid giving an account of his trusteeship, fancying that the period limited for rendering such accounts was ten years. But, well up in legal procedure, Deslauriers had finally managed to get the share coming to him from his mother into his clutches, seven thousand francs clear, which he had there with him in an old pocketbook.

'It's a reserve fund, in case of misfortune. I must think about investing it, and find quarters for myself tomorrow morning. Today I'm perfectly free, and am entirely at your service, my old friend!'

'Oh! Don't put yourself out!' said Frédéric. 'If you had anything of importance to do this evening . . . '

'Come, now! I'd be a selfish wretch . . . '

This epithet, flung out at random, touched Frédéric to the quick, like an insulting allusion.

The concierge had placed on the table close to the fire some cutlets, cold meat, a lobster, some sweets for dessert, and two bottles of Bordeaux. Deslauriers was touched by this excellent reception.

'My word, you're treating me like a king!'

They talked about their past and about the future; and, from time to time, they grasped each other's hands across the table, gazing at each other tenderly for a moment. But a messenger came with a new hat. Deslauriers, in a loud tone, remarked how shiny the crown was.

Next came the tailor himself to fit on the coat, to which he had given a touch with the iron.

'Anyone would think you were going to be married,' said Deslauriers.

An hour later, a third individual appeared on the scene, and drew forth from a big black bag a pair of shining patent leather boots, splendid objects. While Frédéric was trying them on, the bootmaker observed with a mocking glance the shoes of the country visitor.

'Does Monsieur require anything?'

'No, thank you,' replied the Clerk, tucking under his chair his old shoes fastened with strings.

This humiliating incident annoyed Frédéric. He put off his

confession. At length he exclaimed, as if an idea had just occurred to him:

'Ah! Damn it! I was forgetting!'

'What?'

'I have to dine out this evening!'

'At the Dambreuses'? Why do you never say anything to me about them in your letters?'

It was not at the Dambreuses', but at the Arnoux's.

'You should have let me know before!' said Deslauriers. 'I would have come a day later.'

'Impossible!' returned Frédéric, abruptly. 'I only got the invitation this morning, a little while ago.'

And to redeem his error and distract his friend's mind from the occurrence, he proceeded to unfasten the tangled cords round his trunk, and to arrange all his belongings in the chest of drawers, expressed his willingness to give him his own bed, and offered to sleep himself in the woodstore. Then, as soon as it was four o'clock, he began the preparations for his toilet.

'You have plenty of time!' said the other.

At last he was dressed and off he went.

'How like the rich!' thought Deslauriers.

And he went to dine in the Rue Saint-Jacques, at a little restaurant kept by a man he knew.

Frédéric stopped several times while going up the stairs, so violently did his heart beat. One of his gloves, which was too tight, burst; and while he was fastening back the torn part under his shirt-cuff, Arnoux, who was mounting the stairs behind him, took his arm and led him in.

The anteroom, decorated in the Chinese fashion, had a painted lantern hanging from the ceiling, and bamboos in the corners. As he was passing through the drawing-room, Frédéric stumbled against a tiger's skin. The place had not yet been lighted up, but two lamps were burning in the boudoir at the far end of the room.

Mademoiselle Marthe came to announce that her mamma was dressing. Arnoux raised her as high as his mouth in order to kiss her; then, as he wished to go to the cellar himself to select certain bottles of wine, he left Frédéric with the little girl.

She had grown much larger since the trip in the steamboat. Her dark hair descended in long ringlets, which curled over her bare arms. Her dress, more puffed out than the petticoat of a *danseuse*, allowed her rosy calves to be seen, and her pretty childlike form had all the fresh odour of a bunch of flowers. She received the young gentleman's compliments with a coquettish air, fixed on him her large, thoughtful eyes, then slipping off amid the furniture, disappeared like a cat.

He no longer felt ill at ease. The globes of the lamps, covered with a paper lace-work, sent forth a milky light, softening the colour of the walls, hung with mauve satin. Through the fender bars, as through the slits in a big fan, the coal could be seen in the fireplace; and close beside the clock there was a little chest with silver clasps. Here and there things lay about which gave the place a look of home: a doll in the middle of the sofa, a fichu over the back of a chair, and on the work-table a piece of woollen knitting, from which two ivory needles were hanging with their points downwards. It was altogether a peaceful spot, suggesting the idea of propriety and innocent family life.

Arnoux returned; and Madame Arnoux appeared at the other doorway. As she was enveloped in shadow, the young man could at first distinguish only her head. She wore a black velvet gown, and in her hair she had fastened a long Algerian snood in red silk net, which, coiling round her comb, fell over her left shoulder.

Arnoux introduced Frédéric.

'Oh! I remember Monsieur perfectly well,' she responded.

Then the guests arrived, nearly all at the same time: Dittmer, Lovarias, Burrieu, the composer Rosenwald, the poet Théophile Lorris, two art critics, colleagues of Hussonnet, a paper manufacturer, and in the rear the illustrious Pierre-Paul Meinsius, the last representative of the grand school of painting, who blithely carried along with his glory his eighty years and his big paunch.

When they were passing into the dining-room, Madame Arnoux took his arm. A chair had been left vacant for Pellerin. Arnoux, though he took advantage of him, was fond of him. Besides, he was afraid of his terrible tongue – so much so, that, in order to soften him, he had given a portrait of him in *L'Art Industriel*, accompanied by exaggerated eulogies; and Pellerin, more sensitive about distinction than about money, made his appearance about eight o'clock quite out of breath. Frédéric fancied that they had been a long time reconciled.

He liked the company, the dishes, everything. The dining-room, which resembled a mediæval parlour, was hung with embossed leather; a Dutch whatnot faced a rack for chibouks; and around the table the Bohemian glasses, variously coloured, had, in the midst of the flowers and fruits, the effect of an illumination in a garden.

He had to make his choice between ten sorts of mustard. He ate gaspacho, curry, ginger, Corsican blackbirds, and Roman lasagna; he drank extraordinary wines, liebfraumilch and tokay. Arnoux indeed prided himself on entertaining people in good style. With an eye to the procurement of eatables, he paid court to mail coach drivers, and was in league with cooks of great houses, who communicated to him the secrets of rare sauces.

But Frédéric was particularly amused by the conversation. His taste for travelling was tickled by Dittmer, who talked about the East; he gratified his curiosity about theatrical matters by listening to Rosenwald's chat about the Opéra; and the atrocious existence of Bohemia seemed to him droll when seen through the gaiety of Hussonnet, who related, in a picturesque fashion, how he had spent an entire winter with no food except Dutch cheese. Then, a discussion between Lovarias and Burrieu about the Florentine School revealed masterpieces to him, opened up vistas, and he found difficulty in restraining his enthusiasm when Pellerin exclaimed:

'Don't bother me with your hideous reality! What does it mean, reality? Some see things black, others blue, most see stupid. There's nothing less natural than Michelangelo, nothing more powerful! The anxiety about external truth is a mark of the vulgarity of our times; and art will become, if things go on that way, a sort of poor joke inferior to religion in terms of poetry, and inferior to politics in terms of interest. You'll never reach its end — yes, its end! — which is to cause within us an impersonal exaltation, with small-scale works, in spite of all your fancy execution. Look, for instance, at Bassolier's pictures: they're pretty, neat, sweet, and by no means heavy! You can put them in your pocket, take them with you on your travels! Solicitors will pay twenty thousand francs for them, and there aren't two pennies' worth of ideas in them; but without ideality, there's no grandeur! Without grandeur there's no beauty! Olympus is a mountain! The most fantastic monument will always be the Pyramids. Exuberance is better than taste, the desert is better than a pavement, and a savage is better than a hairdresser!'

Frédéric, as he listened to these words, was watching Madame Arnoux. They sank into his soul like metals falling into a furnace, added to his passion, and turned it into love.

His chair was three seats below hers on the same side. From time to time, she bent forward a little, turning aside her head to address a few words to her little daughter; and as she smiled on these occasions, a dimple took shape in her cheek, giving to her face an expression of kindness more delicate.

As soon as the time came for the gentlemen to take their wine, she disappeared. The conversation became very free and easy; M. Arnoux shone in it, and Frédéric was astonished at the cynicism of these men. However, their preoccupation with woman established between them and him, as it were, an equality, which raised him in his own estimation.

When they had returned to the drawing-room, he took up, to keep himself in countenance, one of the albums which lay about on the table. The great artists of the day had illustrated it with drawings, had written in them snatches of verse or prose, or simply their signatures; in the midst of famous names there were many that he had never heard of before, and original thoughts appeared only underneath a flood of nonsense. All these effusions contained a more or less direct expression of homage towards Madame Arnoux. Frédéric would have been afraid to write a line beside them.

She went into her boudoir to find the little chest with silver clasps which he had noticed on the mantelshelf. It was a present from her husband, a work of the Renaissance. Arnoux's friends complimented him, and his wife thanked him; his tender emotions were aroused, and before all the guests he gave her a kiss.

After this they all chatted in groups here and there; the worthy Meinsius was with Madame Arnoux on an easy chair close beside the fire; she was leaning forward towards his ear, their heads were touching – and Frédéric would have been glad to be deaf, infirm, and ugly, to have an illustrious name and white hair, in short, to possess something which would install him in such intimate asso-ciation with her. He ate out his heart, furious at being so young.

But she came into the corner of the drawing-room in which he stood, asked him whether he was acquainted with any of the guests, whether he was fond of painting, how long he had been a student in Paris. Every word that came out of her mouth seemed to Frédéric something entirely new, an exclusive appendage of her person. He gazed attentively at the tendrils of her hair, the ends of which caressed her bare shoulder; and he was unable to take away his eyes, he plunged his soul into the whiteness of that feminine flesh; and yet he did not venture to raise his eyelids to glance at her higher, face to face.

Rosenwald interrupted them, begging of Madame Arnoux to sing something. He played a prelude, she waited; her lips opened slightly, and a sound, pure, long-continued, silvery, rose into the air.

Frédéric did not understand any of the Italian words.

The song began with a grave measure, something like church music, then in a more animated strain, with a crescendo movement, it broke into repeated bursts of sound, then suddenly subsided; and the melody came back again tenderly, with a wide and easy swing.

She stood beside the keyboard with her arms hanging down and a far-off look on her face. Sometimes, in order to read the music, she lowered her head and blinked for a moment. Her contralto voice took in the low notes a mournful intonation which had a chilling effect on the listener, and then her beautiful head, with those great brows of hers, bent over her shoulder; her bosom swelled, her arms opened, her throat as she trilled fell back as if under aerial kisses; she flung out three sharp notes, came down again, cast forth one higher still, and, after a silence, finished with a prolonged low note.

Rosenwald did not leave the piano. He continued playing, to amuse himself. From time to time a guest stole away. At eleven o'clock, as the last of them were going off, Arnoux went out along with Pellerin, under the pretext of seeing him home. He was one of those people who say that they are ill when they do not 'take a turn' after dinner.

Madame Arnoux had made her way towards the anteroom; Dittmer and Hussonnet were bowing to her; she stretched out her hand to them; she did the same to Frédéric, and he felt as if something were penetrating every particle of his skin.

He left his friends; he needed to be alone. His heart was overflowing. Why had she offered him her hand? Was it a thoughtless act, or an encouragement? 'Come now! I'm mad!' Besides, what did it matter, when he could now visit her entirely at his ease, live in the very atmosphere she breathed.

The streets were deserted. Now and then a heavy wagon would roll past, shaking the paving stones. The houses came one after another with their grey fronts, their closed windows; and he thought with disdain of all those human beings in bed behind those walls who existed without seeing her, and not one of whom dreamed of her existence! He had no consciousness of his surroundings, of space, of anything; and striking the ground with his heel, rapping with his walking stick on the shutters of the shops, he kept walking on continually, aimlessly, in a state of excitement, carried away by his emotions. Suddenly he felt himself surrounded by a circle of damp air, and found that he was on the edge of the quays.

The gas-lamps shone in two straight lines, which ran on endlessly, and long red flames flickered in the depths of the water. The waves were slate-coloured, while the sky, which was of clearer hue, seemed to be supported by the vast masses of shadow that rose on each side of the river. The darkness was intensified by buildings whose outlines the eye could not distinguish. A luminous haze floated above the roofs further on; all the noises of the night had melted into a single monotonous hum; a light wind blew.

He had stopped in the middle of the Pont-Neuf, and, taking off his hat and exposing his chest, he drank in the air. And now he felt as if something that was inexhaustible were rising up from the very depths of his being, a flood of tenderness that enervated him, like the motion of the waves under his eyes. A church clock slowly struck one, like a voice calling out to him.

Then he was seized with one of those shuddering sensations of the soul in which one seems to be transported into a higher world. He felt endowed with some extraordinary faculty, the aim of which he could not determine. He asked himself seriously whether he would be a great painter or a great poet – and he decided in favour of painting, for the exigencies of this profession would bring him into contact with Madame Arnoux. So, then, he had found his vocation! The object of his existence was now perfectly clear, and there could be no mistake about the future.

When he had shut his door, he heard someone snoring in the dark closet near his bedroom. It was his friend. He had forgotten about him.

His own face presented itself to his view in the glass. He thought himself handsome — and for a minute he remained gazing at himself.

Before twelve o'clock next day he had bought himself a box of colours, some paintbrushes, and an easel. Pellerin consented to give him lessons, and Frédéric brought him to his lodgings to see whether anything was wanting among his painting utensils.

Deslauriers had come in, and the second armchair was occupied by a young man. The Clerk said, pointing towards him:

'That's him! There he is! Sénécal!'

Frédéric disliked this young man. His forehead was heightened by the way in which he wore his hair, cut straight like a brush. There was a certain hard, cold look in his grey eyes; and his long black coat, his entire costume, savoured of the pedagogue and the ecclesiastic.

They first discussed topics of the hour, amongst others the *Stabat* of Rossini; Sénécal, in answer to a question, declared that he never went to the theatre. Pellerin opened the box of colours.

'Are these all for you?' said the Clerk.

'Why, certainly!'

'Oh really! Gracious!'

And he leaned over the table, at which the mathematical tutor was turning over the leaves of a volume of Louis Blanc. He had brought it with him, and was reading passages from it in low tones, while Pellerin and Frédéric were examining together the palette, the knife, and the bladders; then the talk came round to the dinner at Arnoux's.

'The picture-dealer, is it?' asked Sénécal. 'A nice gentleman, truly!'

'Why, now?' said Pellerin.

Sénécal replied:

'A man who makes money by political turpitude!'

And he went on to talk about a well-known lithograph, in which all the Royal Family was represented as being engaged in edifying occupations: Louis-Philippe had a copy of the Code in his hand, the Queen had a Catholic prayer book, the Princesses were embroidering, the Duc de Nemours was girding on a sword, M. de Joinville was showing a map to his young brothers; and at the end of the apartment could be seen a bed with two divisions. This picture, which was entitled 'A Good Family', was a source of delight to the bourgeois, but a bane to patriots. Pellerin, in a tone of vexation, as if he had been the producer of this work himself, observed by way of answer that all opinions were equally valid; Sénécal protested. Art should aim exclusively at promoting morality amongst the masses! The only subjects that ought to be reproduced were those which impelled people to virtuous actions; all others were injurious.

'But that depends on the execution!' cried Pellerin. 'I might produce masterpieces!'

'So much the worse for you, then! You have no right . . .'

'What?'

'No, monsieur! You have no right to excite my interest in matters of which I disapprove. What need have we of laborious trifles, from which it is impossible to derive any benefit, those Venuses, for instance, with all your landscapes? I see there no instruction for the people! Show us rather their miseries! Arouse enthusiasm in us for their sacrifices! Ah, my goodness, there's no lack of subjects: the farm, the workshop . . .'

Pellerin was stammering with indignation at this, and, imagining that he had found an argument:

'Molière, do you accept him?'

'Certainly!' said Sénécal. 'I admire him as a precursor of the French Revolution.'

'Ha! The Revolution! What art! Never was there a more pitiable epoch!'

'None greater, Monsieur!'

Pellerin folded his arms, and looking at him straight in the face:

'You look like a real National Guard to me!'

His opponent, accustomed to discussions, responded:

'I'm not, and I detest it just as much as you! But with such principles we corrupt the masses! And this sort of thing plays into the hands of the Government! It wouldn't be so powerful but for the complicity of a lot of rogues like him.'

The painter took up the defence of the picture-dealer, for Sénécal's opinions exasperated him. He even went so far as to maintain that Arnoux was really a man with a heart of gold, devoted to his friends, deeply attached to his wife.

'Oh! Oh! If you offered him a good sum, he wouldn't refuse to let her serve as a model.'

Frédéric turned pale.

'So then, he has done you some great injury, Monsieur?'

'Me? No! I saw him once in a café with a friend. That's all.'

Sénécal had spoken truly. But he had his teeth daily set on edge by the advertisements for *L'Art Industriel*. Arnoux was for him the representative of a world which he considered fatal to democracy. An austere Republican, he suspected that there was something corrupt in every form of elegance, and the more so as he had no needs and was inflexible in his integrity.

They found some difficulty in resuming the conversation. The painter soon recalled to mind his appointment, the tutor his pupils; and, when they had gone, after a long silence, Deslauriers asked a number of questions about Arnoux.

'You will introduce me there sometime, won't you, old man?'

'Certainly,' said Frédéric.

Then they set about planning their life together. Deslauriers had without much trouble obtained the post of second clerk in a solicitor's office, he had also entered his name for the terms at the Law School, and bought the indispensable books – and the life of which they had dreamed so intensely now began.

It was delightful, thanks to the beauty of their youth. As Deslauriers had said nothing as to any pecuniary arrangement, Frédéric did not refer to the subject. He defrayed all the expenses, kept the cupboard well stocked, and looked after all the household requirements; but if it happened to be desirable to give the concierge a blasting, the Clerk took that on his own shoulders, still playing the part, which he had assumed in their college days, of protector and senior.

Separated all day long, they met again in the evening. Each took his place at the fireside and set about his work. But before long it would be interrupted. Then would follow endless confidences, bursts of merriment for no reason, and occasional disputes about the lamp smoking or a book being mislaid, brief quarrels which subsided in laughter.

While in bed they left open the door of the woodstore, and

chattered to each other from a distance.

In the morning they strolled in their shirtsleeves on the terrace; the sun rose, light vapours passed over the river, from the nearby flower-market close shrill voices reached their ears – and the smoke from their pipes whirled round in the clear air, which was refreshing to their eyes still puffed with sleep; as they breathed it in, they had a sense of boundless expectations.

When it was not raining on Sunday they went out together; and, arm-in-arm, they sauntered through the streets. The same reflection nearly always occurred to them at the same time, or else they would go on chatting without noticing anything around them. Deslauriers longed for riches, as a means for gaining power over men. He would have liked to possess an influence over a vast number of people, to make a great noise, to have three secretaries under his command, and to give a big political dinner once a week. Frédéric would have a palace furnished in the Moorish fashion, to spend his life reclining on cashmere divans, to the murmur of a fountain, attended by negro pages – and these things, of which he had only dreamed, became in the end so definite that they made him feel as dejected as if he had lost them.

'What's the use of talking about all these things,' said he, 'when we'll never have them?'

'Who knows?' returned Deslauriers.

In spite of his democratic views, he urged Frédéric to get an introduction into the Dambreuses' house. The other, by way of objection, pointed to the failure of his previous attempts.

'Bah! Go back! They'll give you an invitation!'

Towards the middle of the month of March, they received amongst other bills of a rather awkward description that of the restaurant-keeper who supplied them with dinners. Frédéric, not having the entire amount, borrowed a hundred crowns from Deslauriers; a fortnight afterwards, he renewed the same request, and the Clerk administered a lecture to him on the extravagant habits to which he gave himself up in the Arnoux's society.

Indeed, he put no restraint upon himself in this respect. A view of Venice, a view of Naples, and another of Constantinople occupying the centre of the three walls, equestrian subjects by Alfred de Dreux here and there, a group by Pradier over the mantelpiece, numbers of *L'Art Industriel* lying on the piano, and cardboard folders on the floor in the corners, encumbered the apartment to such an extent that it was hard to find a place to lay a book on, or to find elbow-room. Frédéric maintained that he needed all this for his painting.

He worked in Pellerin's studio. But the latter was often out, being accustomed to attend at every funeral and public event of which an account was given in the newspapers – and so it was that Frédéric spent entire hours all alone in the studio. The quietude of this spacious room, which nothing disturbed save the scampering of the mice, the light falling from the ceiling, and even the rumbling of the stove, made him sink at first into a kind of intellectual wellbeing. Then his eyes, wandering away from the task at which he was engaged, roamed over the peeling walls, around the knick-knacks on the shelves, along the torsos on which the dust that had collected made, as it were, shreds of velvet; and, like a traveller who has lost his way in the middle of a wood, and whom every path brings back to the same spot, continually, he found underlying every idea in his mind the recollection of Madame Arnoux.

He selected days for calling on her; when he had reached the second floor, he would pause on the threshold, hesitating as to whether he ought to ring or not. Steps drew nigh; the door opened, and with the announcement 'Madame is out', a sense of relief would come upon him, as if a weight had been lifted from his heart.

He met her, however. On the first occasion there were three other ladies with her; the next time it was in the afternoon, and Mademoiselle Marthe's writing-master came on the scene. Besides, the men whom Madame Arnoux received did not pay her visits. For the sake of prudence he deemed it better not to call again.

But he did not fail to present himself regularly at the office of *L'Art Industriel* every Wednesday in order to get an invitation to the Thursday dinners; and he remained there after all the others, even longer than Regimbart, up to the last moment, pretending to be looking at an engraving or to be running his eye through a newspaper. At last Arnoux would say to him, 'Shall you be free tomorrow evening?' And, before the sentence was finished, he would accept. Arnoux appeared to have taken a fancy to him. He showed him how to become a good judge of wines, how to make hot punch, and how to prepare a woodcock ragoût; Frédéric followed his advice with docility – feeling an attachment to everything connected with Madame Arnoux, her furniture, her servants, her house, her street.

During these dinners he scarcely uttered a word; he just looked at her. She had a little mole close to her right temple; the hair on each side of her face was darker than the rest of her hair, and seemed always a little moist at the edges; from time to time she stroked it with only two fingers. He knew the shape of each of her nails, he took delight in listening to the rustle of her silk skirt as she swept past doors, he stealthily inhaled the perfume that came from her handkerchief; her comb, her gloves, her rings were for him things of special interest, important as works of art, almost endowed with life like individuals; all took possession of his heart and strengthened his passion.

He had not had the strength to conceal it from Deslauriers. When he came home from Madame Arnoux's, he would wake him up, as if inadvertently, in order to have an opportunity of talking about her.

Deslauriers, who slept in the woodstore, close to where they had their water supply, would give a great yawn. Frédéric seated himself at the foot of his bed. At first, he spoke about the dinner, then he reported a thousand petty details, in which he saw marks of disdain or of affection. On one occasion, for instance, she had refused his arm, in order to take Dittmer's, and Frédéric was in despair.

'Ah! How stupid!'

Or else she had called him her 'dear friend'.

'Get on with it, then!'

'But I daren't,' said Frédéric.

'Well, then, forget it! Good night.'

Deslauriers turned on his side, and fell asleep. He was utterly unable to comprehend this love, which seemed to him a final aberration of adolescence; and, as his society was apparently no longer enough to content Frédéric, he conceived the idea of bringing together, once a week, those whom they both recognised as friends.

They came on Saturday about nine o'clock. The three Algerian cotton curtains were carefully drawn; the lamp and four candles were burning; in the middle of the table the tobacco pot, filled with pipes, displayed itself between the beer bottles, the teapot, a flagon of rum, and some fancy biscuits. They discussed the immortality of the soul, and drew comparisons between the different professors.

One evening Hussonnet introduced a tall young man, attired in a frock-coat too short in the wrists, and with a look of embarrassment on his face. It was the young fellow whom they had gone to release from the guardhouse the year before.

As he had not been able to restore the box of lace which he had lost in the scuffle, his employer had accused him of theft, and threatened to prosecute him; he was now working for a firm of carriers. Hussonnet had come across him that morning at the corner of the street, and brought him along, for Dussardier, in a spirit of gratitude, had expressed a wish to see 'the other one'.

He stretched out towards Frédéric the cigar-holder, still full, which he had religiously preserved, in the hope of being able to give it back. The young men invited him to pay them a second visit; and he did not fail to do so.

They all had sympathies in common. At first, their hatred of the Government reached the height of an unquestionable dogma. Martinon alone attempted to defend Louis-Philippe. They overwhelmed him with the commonplaces to be found in every newspaper – the 'new Bastilles' in Paris, the September laws, Pritchard, Lord Guizot – so thoroughly that Martinon held his tongue for fear of giving offence to somebody. During his seven years in college he had never incurred the penalty of an imposition, and at the Law School he knew how to make himself agreeable to the professors. He usually wore a big frock-coat of the colour of putty, with india-rubber goloshes; but one evening he presented himself arrayed like a bridegroom, in a velvet roll-collar waistcoat, a white tie, and a gold chain.

The astonishment of the other young men was greatly increased when they learned that he had just come away from M. Dambreuse's house. In fact, the banker Dambreuse had just bought a sizeable portion of a wood from Martinon senior; and, when the worthy man introduced his son, the other had invited them both to dinner.

'Were there a lot of truffles?' asked Deslauriers. 'And did you take his wife by the waist between two doors, *sicut decet?*'

Hereupon the conversation turned on women. Pellerin would not accept that there were beautiful women (he preferred tigers); besides, the human female was an inferior creature in the aesthetic hierarchy:

'What fascinates you is just the very thing that degrades her as an idea; I mean her breasts, her hair . . . '

'Nevertheless,' objected Frédéric, 'long black hair and large dark eyes . . . '

'Oh, we know all about that!' cried Hussonnet. 'Enough of Andalusian beauties on the lawn! And classical beauties? No thank you! For the fact is, make no mistake! A fast woman is more fun than the Venus of Milo! Let's be Gallic, in Heaven's name! And Regency, if we can!

'*Flow, generous wines! Ladies, deign to smile!*

'We must pass from the dark to the fair! Is that your opinion, Dussardier, old man?'

Dussardier did not reply. They all pressed him to ascertain what his tastes were.

'Well,' said he, colouring, 'personally, I would like to love the same one, always!'

This was said in such a way that there was a moment of silence, some of them being surprised at this candour, and others finding in his words, perhaps, the secret desire of their hearts.

Sénécal placed his mug of beer on the mantelpiece, and declared dogmatically that, as prostitution was tyrannical and marriage immoral, it was better to practise abstinence. Deslauriers regarded women as a source of amusement, nothing more. M. de Cisy looked upon them with the utmost dread.

Brought up under the eyes of a grandmother who was devout, he found the society of these young men as alluring as a place of ill-repute and as instructive as the Sorbonne. They gave him all the lessons he could want; and so much zeal did he exhibit that he even wanted to smoke in spite of the sickness that upset him every time he made the experiment. Frédéric paid him the greatest attention. He admired the shade of this young gentleman's cravats, the fur on his overcoat, and especially his boots, as thin as gloves, and so very neat and fine that they had a look of insolence about them; his carriage used to wait for him below in the street.

One evening, after his departure, when there was a fall of snow, Sénécal began to pity his driver. He then declaimed against kid-gloved exquisites and the Jockey Club. He had more respect for a workman than for these fine gentlemen.

'I, at least, work for my living! I am poor!'

'That's quite evident,' said Frédéric, at length, losing patience.

The tutor retained a grudge against him for this remark.

But, as Regimbart had said he knew Sénécal a little, Frédéric, wishing to be civil to a friend of Arnoux, asked him to come to the Saturday meetings, and the two patriots were glad to be brought together in this way.

They differed, however.

Sénécal – whose skull came to a point – fixed his attention merely on systems. Regimbart, on the other hand, saw in facts nothing but facts. The thing that chiefly troubled him was the Rhine frontier. He claimed to be an authority on the subject of artillery, and got his clothes made by a tailor of the École Polytechnique.

The first day, when they asked him to take some cakes, he disdainfully shrugged his shoulders, saying that these were women's things; and on the next few occasions his manner was not much more gracious. Whenever speculative ideas had reached a certain high level, he would mutter: 'Oh! No Utopias, no dreams!' On the subject of Art (though he used to visit the studios, where he occasionally consented to give a lesson in fencing) his opinions were not noted for their elevation. He compared the style of M. Marrast to that of Voltaire, and Mademoiselle Vatnaz to Madame de Staël, on account of an ode on Poland 'in which there was some spirit'. In short, Regimbart bored everyone, and especially Deslauriers, for the Citizen was a friend of Arnoux. Now the Clerk was most anxious to become familiar with that household in the hope that he might there make the acquaintance of people who would be an advantage to him. 'How long before you take me there?' he would say. Arnoux was either overburdened with business, or else starting on a journey; then it was not worth while, as the dinners were coming to an end.

If he had been called on to risk his life for his friend, Frédéric would have done so. But, as he was desirous of making as good a figure as possible, and was most careful about his language and manners, and so attentive to his costume that he always presented himself at the office of *L'Art Industriel* irreproachably gloved, he was afraid that Deslauriers, with his shabby black coat, his attorney-like appearance, and his swaggering kind of talk, might make himself disagreeable to Madame Arnoux, and thus compromise him and lower him in her estimation. He did not mind the others, but Deslauriers, precisely, would have caused him far more embarrassment. The Clerk saw that his friend did not wish to keep his promise, and Frédéric's silence seemed to him an aggravation of the insult.

He would have liked to exercise absolute control over him, to see him developing in accordance with the ideal of their youth; and his indolence excited his indignation as a breach of duty and a want of loyalty towards himself. Moreover, Frédéric, with his thoughts full of Madame Arnoux, frequently talked about her husband; and Deslauriers now began an intolerable running joke by repeating the name a hundred times a day, at the end of each remark, like the parrot-cry of an idiot. When there was a knock at the door, he would answer, 'Come in, Arnoux!' At the restaurant he would ask for a Brie cheese 'in imitation of Arnoux'; and at night, pretending to wake up from a bad dream, he would rouse his comrade by howling out, 'Arnoux! Arnoux!' At last Frédéric, exasperated, said to him one day, in a piteous voice:

'Oh, leave me in peace about Arnoux!'

'Never!' replied the clerk.

He always! Everywhere! Burning or icy cold,
The pictured form of Arnoux . . .

'Hold your tongue, I tell you!' exclaimed Frédéric, raising his fist. Then less angrily he added:

'You know very well this is a painful subject to me.'

'Oh! Excuse me, old fellow,' returned Deslauriers with a very low bow. 'From this time forth we will be considerate towards Mademoiselle's nerves! Again, I say, forgive me! A thousand pardons!'

And so the joke came to an end.

But, three weeks later, one evening, Deslauriers said to him:

'Well, I have just seen Madame Arnoux!'

'Where?'

'At the Palais, with Balandard, the solicitor. A dark woman, is she not, of middle height?'

Frédéric made a gesture of assent. He waited for Deslauriers to speak. At the least expression of admiration he would have opened his heart, and would have fairly hugged the other; however, Deslauriers remained silent; at last, unable to contain himself any longer, Frédéric, with assumed indifference, asked him what he thought of her.

Deslauriers considered that she was 'not bad, but nothing out of the ordinary'.

'Ah! Is that so,' said Frédéric.

They soon reached the month of August, the time when he was to present himself for his second examination. According to the prevailing opinion, the subjects could be made up in a fortnight. Frédéric, having full confidence in his own powers, swallowed up in a trice the first four books of the Code of Procedure, the first three of the Penal Code, many bits of the system of Criminal Investigation, and a part of the Civil Code, with the annotations of M. Poncelet. The night before, Deslauriers made him run through the whole course, a process which did not finish till morning; and, in order to take advantage of even the last quarter of an hour, continued questioning him while they walked along the pavement together.

As several examinations were taking place at the same time, there were many persons in the precincts, and amongst others Hussonnet and Cisy; young men never failed to come and watch these ordeals when the fortunes of their comrades were at stake. Frédéric put on the traditional black gown; then, followed by the throng, with three other students, he entered a spacious room, into which the light penetrated through uncurtained windows, and which was garnished with benches ranged along the walls. In the centre, leather chairs were drawn round a table adorned with a green cover. This separated the candidates from the examiners in their red gowns and ermine shoulder-knots, with gold-laced flat caps on their heads.

Frédéric found himself the last but one in the series – an unfortunate place. In answer to the first question, as to the difference between a convention and a contract, he defined the one as if it were the other; and the professor, who was a fair sort of man, said to him, 'Don't be agitated, Monsieur! Compose yourself!' Then, having asked two easy questions, which were answered in a doubtful fashion, he passed on at last to the fourth. This wretched beginning made Frédéric lose confidence. Deslauriers, who was facing him amongst the spectators, made a sign to him to indicate that all was not yet lost; and at the second batch of questions, dealing with criminal law, he came out tolerably well. But, after the third, with reference to the 'mystic will', the examiner having remained impassive the whole time, his mental distress redoubled; for Hussonnet brought his hands together as if to applaud, whilst Deslauriers indulged in liberal shrugs of the shoulders. Finally, the moment was reached when it was necessary to be examined on Procedure! The questions were about third-party opposition. The professor, displeased at listening to theories opposed to his own, asked him in a churlish tone:

'And so is this your view, monsieur? How do you reconcile the principle of article 1351 of the Civil Code with this extraordinary line of attack?'

Frédéric had a great headache from not having slept the night before. A ray of sunlight, penetrating through one of the slits in a Venetian blind, fell on his face. Standing behind his chair, he kept fidgeting about and tugging at his moustache.

'I am still awaiting your answer!' the man with the gold-edged cap observed.

And as Frédéric's movements, no doubt, irritated him:

'You won't find it in that moustache of yours!'

This sarcasm made the spectators laugh; the professor, feeling flattered, relented. He put two more questions with reference to adjournment and summary jurisdiction, then nodded his head by way of approval; the examination was over. Frédéric retired into the vestibule.

While an usher was taking off his gown, to hand it on to some other person immediately afterwards, his friends gathered around him, and succeeded in confusing him with their conflicting opinions as to the result of his examination. Presently the announcement was made in a sonorous voice at the entrance of the hall: 'The third was . . . referred!'

'Ploughed!' said Hussonnet. 'Let's go!'

In front of the concierge's lodge they met Martinon, flushed, excited, with a smile in his eyes and the halo of victory around his brow. He had just passed his final examination without any impediment. All that was left was the thesis. Before a fortnight he would be a graduate. His family enjoyed the acquaintance of a Minister, 'a fine career' was opening before him.

'Say what you like, he's got the better of you,' said Deslauriers.

There is nothing so humiliating as to see blockheads succeed in undertakings in which we fail. Frédéric, filled with vexation, replied that he did not care. He had higher pretensions; and as Hussonnet made a show of leaving, Frédéric took him aside, and said to him:

'Not a word about this to them, mind!'

It was easy to keep it secret, since Arnoux was starting the next morning for Germany.

When he came back in the evening the Clerk found his friend singularly altered: he danced about and whistled; and, the other being astonished at this capricious change of mood, Frédéric declared that he did not intend to go home to his mother, as he meant to spend his holidays working.

At the news of Arnoux's departure, a feeling of joy had taken possession of him. He might present himself at the house whenever he liked without any fear of having his visits broken in upon. The consciousness of absolute security would make him self-confident. Above all he would not forced to leave, he would not be separated from Her! Something more powerful than an iron chain attached him to Paris; a voice from the depths of his heart called out to him to remain.

There were obstacles in his path. These he got over by writing to his mother: he first of all admitted that he had failed to pass, owing to alterations made in the course – a mere mischance, an injustice – besides, all the great advocates (he referred to them by name) had been rejected at their examinations. But he calculated on presenting himself again in the month of November. Now, having no time to lose, he would not go home this year; and he asked, in addition to the quarterly allowance, for two hundred and fifty francs, to get coached in law by a private tutor, which would be of great assistance to him; and he threw around the entire epistle a garland of regrets, condolences, expressions of endearment, and protestations of filial love.

Madame Moreau, who had been expecting him the following day, was doubly grieved. She threw a veil over her son's misadventure, and in answer told him to 'come all the same'. Frédéric would not give way, and the result was a falling out between them. However, at the end of the week, he received the amount of the quarter's allowance together with the sum required for the payment of the private tutor, which served to pay for a pair of pearl-grey trousers, a white felt hat, and a gold-headed cane.

When he had procured all these things he thought:

'Perhaps this is a vulgar idea?'

And a feeling of considerable hesitation took possession of him.

In order to make sure as to whether he ought to call on Madame Arnoux, he tossed three coins into the air in succession. On each occasion luck was in his favour. So then Fate must have ordained it. He hailed a cab and drove to the Rue de Choiseul.

He quickly ascended the staircase and drew the bell-pull, but without effect. He felt as if he were about to faint.

Then, with fierce energy, he shook the heavy red silk tassel. There was a resounding peal which gradually died away till no further sound was heard. Frédéric felt frightened.

He pasted his ear to the door – not a breath! He looked in through the keyhole, and all he saw in the anteroom were two reed-points on the wallpaper in the midst of the designs of flowers. At last, he was on the point of going away when he changed his mind. This time, he gave a timid little ring. The door flew open; and Arnoux himself appeared on the threshold, with his hair all in disorder, his face crimson, and looking surly.

'Hallo! What the deuce brings you here? Come in!'

He led Frédéric, not into the boudoir or into his bedroom, but into the dining-room, where on the table could be seen a bottle of champagne and two glasses; and, in an abrupt tone:

'There's something you want to ask me, my dear friend?'

'No! Nothing! Nothing!' stammered the young man, trying to think of some excuse for his visit.

At length, he said to Arnoux that he had called to have news of him, as Hussonnet had announced that he had gone to Germany.

'Not at all!' returned Arnoux. 'What a feather-headed fellow that boy is to get everything wrong!'

In order to conceal his agitation, Frédéric kept walking from right to left in the dining-room. Colliding with the leg of a chair, he knocked down a parasol which had been laid across it, and the ivory handle broke.

'Good heavens!' he exclaimed. 'How sorry I am for having broken Madame Arnoux's parasol!'

At this remark, the picture-dealer raised his head and smiled in a very peculiar fashion. Frédéric, taking advantage of the opportunity thus offered to talk about her, added shyly:

'Could I not see her?'

She had gone to the country to see her mother, who was ill.

He did not venture to ask any questions as to the length of time that she would be away. He merely enquired what was Madame Arnoux's native place.

'Chartres! Does that surprise you?'

'Surprise me? Oh, no! Why should it? Not in the least!'

After that, they could find absolutely nothing to say to each other. Arnoux, having made a cigarette for himself, was walking round the table, puffing. Frédéric, standing near the stove, stared at the walls, the display shelves, and the floor; and delightful pictures flitted through his memory, or, rather, before his eyes. At last he left.

A piece of newspaper, rolled into a ball, lay on the floor in the anteroom; Arnoux snatched it up; and, raising himself on the tips of his toes, he stuck it into the bell, in order, as he said, that he might be able to continue his interrupted siesta. Then, as he grasped Frédéric's hand:

'Kindly tell the porter that I am not in!'

And he shut the door after him with a bang.

Frédéric descended the staircase step by step. The ill-success of this first attempt discouraged him as to the possible results of those that might follow. Then began three months of absolute boredom. As he had nothing to do, his melancholy was aggravated by the want of occupation.

He spent whole hours gazing from his balcony down at the river as it flowed between the quays, with their bulwarks of grey stone, blackened here and there by the outflow of the sewers, with a pontoon of washerwomen moored close to the bank, where some lads amused themselves sometimes, in the mud, by giving a poodle a bath. His eyes, turning aside from the stone bridge of Notre-Dame and three suspension bridges on the left, continually directed their gaze towards the Quai-aux-Ormes, resting on a group of old trees, resembling the linden trees of the Montereau wharf. The Tour Saint-Jacques, the Hôtel de Ville, Saint-Gervais, Saint-Louis, and Saint-Paul, rose up in front of him amid a confused mass of roofs – and the genius of the July Column glittered in the east like a large gold star, whilst at the other end the dome of the Tuileries showed its outlines against the sky in one great round mass of blue. Madame Arnoux's house must be over there, behind it.

He went back to his room; then, throwing himself on the sofa, he abandoned himself to a confused succession of thoughts: plans for works, schemes for the guidance of his life, dreams for the future. At last, in order to escape from himself, he went out.

He wandered aimlessly up through the Latin Quarter, usually so noisy, but deserted at this time, for the students had gone back to join their families. The great walls of the colleges, which the silence seemed to lengthen, wore a still more melancholy aspect; all sorts of peaceful sounds could be heard, the flapping of wings in cages, the noise made by the turning of a lathe, or the strokes of a cobbler's hammer; and the old-clothes men, standing in the middle of the streets, looked up questioningly at each window, to no avail. In the interior of solitary cafés the barmaid yawned among her full decanters; the newspapers were left undisturbed on the tables of reading-rooms; in the ironing establishments linen quivered in the puffs of warm wind. From time to time he stopped to look at the window of a secondhand bookshop; an omnibus which grazed the footpath as it came rumbling along made him turn round; and, when he found himself at the Luxembourg, he went no further.

Occasionally he was attracted towards the boulevards by the hope of finding some distraction. After dark alleys, exuding fresh moist odours, he reached vast, deserted, open squares, dazzling with light, in which monuments cast at the side of the pavement jagged black shadows. But once more the wagons and the shops appeared, and the crowd had the effect of stunning him – especially on Sunday, when, from the Bastille to the Madeleine, it swayed in one immense flood over the asphalt, in the midst of a cloud of dust, in an incessant clamour; he felt disgusted at the meanness of the faces, the silliness of the talk, and the idiotic self-satisfaction that oozed through these sweating foreheads! However, the consciousness of being superior to these individuals mitigated the weariness which he experienced in gazing at them.

Every day he went to the office of *L'Art Industriel* – and in order to ascertain when Madame Arnoux would be back, he made elaborate enquiries about her mother. Arnoux's answer never varied; 'the change for the better was continuing', his wife, with his little daughter, would be returning the following week. The longer she delayed in coming back, the more uneasiness Frédéric exhibited – so that Arnoux, touched by so much affection, took him five or six times to dine at a restaurant.

In the long talks which they had together on these occasions Frédéric realised that the picture-dealer was not a great mind. Arnoux might, however, take notice of his coolness; and then it was an opportunity to repay, in a small measure, his kind attentions.

So, being anxious to do things on a grand scale, the young man sold all his new clothes to a secondhand clothes-dealer for the sum of eighty francs; and having increased it with a hundred more francs which he had left, he called at Arnoux's house to take him to dinner. Regimbart happened to be there, and all three of them set forth for the Trois-Frères-Provençaux.

The Citizen began by taking off his overcoat, and, knowing that the two others would defer to him, drew up the menu. But in vain did he make his way to the kitchen to speak personally to the chef, go down to the cellar, with every corner of which he was familiar, and send for the master of the establishment, to whom he 'gave a ticking off'; he was not satisfied with the dishes, the wines, or the attendance! At each new dish, at each fresh bottle, as soon as he had swallowed the first mouthful, the first draught, he dropped his fork or thrust his glass away from him; then, leaning with his elbows on the tablecloth and stretching out his arms, he declared loudly that there was nowhere left to dine in Paris! Finally, not knowing what to think of to eat, Regimbart ordered beans dressed with oil, 'quite plain', which, though only a partial success, slightly appeased him. Then he had a talk with the waiter all about the latter's predecessors at the 'Provençaux': 'What had become of Antoine? And a fellow named Eugène? And Théodore, the little fellow who always used to attend downstairs? There was much finer fare in those days, and Burgundy vintages the like of which they would never see again.'

Then there was a discussion as to the value of land in the suburbs, Arnoux having speculated in that way, and looked on it as a safe thing. In the meantime, however, he was losing on the interest. As he did not want to sell at any price, Regimbart would find someone; and these two gentlemen proceeded to make calculations with a pencil till the end of dessert.

They went out to get coffee at a tavern in the Passage du Saumon, upstairs. Frédéric had to remain on his legs while interminable games of billiards were played, washed down with innumerable glasses of beer – and he lingered on there till midnight without knowing why, through want of energy, through sheer stupidity, in the vague expectation that something might happen which would give a favourable turn to his love.

Whenever would he see her again? Frédéric was in despair. But, one evening, towards the close of November, Arnoux said to him:

'My wife came back yesterday, you know!'

Next day, at five o'clock, he was walking through her door.

He began by congratulating her on her mother's recovery from such a serious illness.

'Why, no! Who told you that?'

'Arnoux!'

She gave vent to a slight 'Ah!' then added that she had had grave fears at first, which, however, had now been dispelled.

She was seated close beside the fire in the upholstered easy-chair. He was on the sofa, with his hat between his knees; and the conversation was difficult to carry on, as she kept letting it drop; he could find no opening for expression of his feelings. But, when he began to complain of having to study legal quibbling, she answered, 'Yes . . . I understand . . . business . . . ' and she let her face fall, buried suddenly in her own reflections.

He was eager to know what they were, and could not even think of anything else. The twilight shadows gathered around them.

She rose, having to go out about some shopping, then she reappeared in a velvet hood and a black mantle edged with squirrel fur. He plucked up courage and offered to accompany her.

It was now so dark that one could scarcely see; the weather was cold, and had an unpleasant odour, owing to a heavy fog, which

partially blotted out the fronts of the houses. Frédéric inhaled it
with delight; for he could feel through the wadding of her coat the
form of her arm; and her hand, cased in a chamois glove with two
buttons, her little hand which he would have liked to cover with
kisses leaned on his sleeve. Owing to the slipperiness of the
pavement, they teetered a little; it seemed to him as if they were
both rocked by the wind in the midst of a cloud.

The glitter of the lamps on the boulevard brought him back to
reality. The opportunity was a good one, there was no time to
lose. He gave himself as far as the Rue de Richelieu to declare his
love. But almost at that very moment, in front of a china shop, she
stopped abruptly and said to him:

'We're there. Thank you! On Thursday, I hope, as usual?'

The dinners were now renewed; and the more time he spent
with Madame Arnoux, the more his languor increased.

The contemplation of this woman had an enervating effect upon
him, like the use of a perfume that is too strong. It penetrated into
the very depths of his nature, and became almost a general way of
feeling, a new mode of existence.

The prostitutes whom he brushed past under the gaslight, the
female ballad-singers trilling their flourishes, the ladies rising on
horseback at full gallop, housewives on foot, working-girls at
their windows, all women reminded him of her, either by comparison or by violent contrast. As he walked along by the shops,
he gazed at the shawls, the laces, and the jewelled eardrops,
imagining how they would look draped around her hips, sewn in
her corsage, or glistening like fire in her black hair. In the flower-
girls' baskets the bouquets blossomed for her to choose one as she
passed; in the shoemakers' show-windows the little satin slippers
with swansdown edges seemed to be waiting for her foot; every
street led towards her house: the cabs stood on the squares only to
get there more quickly; Paris existed in relation to her, and the
great city, with all its voices, resounded around her like an
immense orchestra.

When he went to the Jardin des Plantes the sight of a palm tree
carried him off into distant countries. They were travelling together
on the backs of dromedaries, under the awnings of elephants, in the
cabin of a yacht amongst blue archipelagoes, or side by side on
two mules with little bells attached to them who went stumbling

through the grass against broken columns. Sometimes he stopped in the Louvre before old pictures; and, his love embracing her even back in vanished centuries, he substituted her for the personages in the paintings. Wearing a hennin on her head, she was praying on her knees behind a stained-glass window. As a Lady of Castile or Flanders, she sat with a stiff collar and boned bodice with big puffed sleeves. Then he saw her descending some wide porphyry staircase in the midst of senators under a daïs of ostriches' feathers in a robe of brocade. At other times he dreamed of her in yellow silk trousers on the cushions of a harem – and all that was beautiful, the sparkle of the stars, certain musical airs, the turn of a phrase, a contour, brought her to his thoughts in an abrupt, unconscious fashion.

As for trying to make her his mistress, he was sure that any such attempt would be futile.

One evening, Dittmer, on his arrival, kissed her on the forehead; Lovarias did the same, observing:

'You give me leave, don't you, as a friend's privilege?'

Frédéric stammered out:

'It seems to me that we are all friends?'

'Not all old friends!' she returned.

This was repelling him beforehand, indirectly.

What was he to do, anyway? Tell her that he loved her? She would certainly repulse him; or else she would become indignant and turn him out of her house! And he preferred every suffering imaginable rather than run the horrible risk of seeing her no more.

He envied pianists for their talents and soldiers for their scars. He longed for a dangerous illness, hoping in this way to make her take an interest in him.

One thing amazed him, that he felt in no way jealous of Arnoux; and he could not picture her in his imagination as anything other than dressed – so natural did her modesty appear, making her sex recede into a mysterious shadow.

Nevertheless, he dreamed of the happiness of living with her, of calling her 'tu', of passing his hand lingeringly over her hair, or being on the floor, on his knees with both arms clasped round her waist, drinking in her soul through his eyes! To accomplish this he would have had to counter Fate; and incapable of action, cursing God, and accusing himself of being a coward, he turned restlessly within the confines of his desire, like a prisoner in his dungeon. He was choked by a perpetual anxiety. For hours he would remain quite motionless, or else he would burst into tears; and one day when he had not had the strength to restrain his emotion, Deslauriers said to him:

'But goodness gracious! What's the matter with you?'

Frédéric's nerves were unstrung. Deslauriers did not believe a word of it. At the sight of such suffering, he had felt all his old affection reawakening, and he tried to comfort him. A man like him letting himself be depressed, how silly! It was all very well while one was young but, later on, it's just a waste of time.

'You're spoiling my Frédéric for me! I want the old one back. Waiter, same again! I liked him! Come on, smoke a pipe, old chap! Shake yourself up a little! You're breaking my heart!'

'It's true,' said Frédéric, 'I'm a fool!'

The Clerk went on:

'Ah! My old troubadour, I know what's wrong with you! A little affair of the heart? Confess it! Bah! One lost, four found! We console ourselves for virtuous women with the other sort. Would you like me to introduce you to some? You have only to come to the Alhambra. (This was a place for public dancing recently opened at the top of the Champs-Elysées, which went bankrupt in its second season owing to a display of luxury somewhat premature in establishments of the kind.) People have a good time there, by all accounts. Let's go! You can take your friends, if you like. I'll even allow you Regimbart!'

Frédéric did not invite the Citizen. Deslauriers sacrificed Sénécal. They took only Hussonnet and Cisy along with Dussardier; and the same cab set the group of five down at the entrance to the Alhambra.

Two Moorish galleries extended to right and left, parallel to one another. The wall of a house opposite occupied the entire background, and the fourth side (that in which the restaurant was) represented a Gothic cloister with stained-glass windows. A sort of Chinese roof covered the platform reserved for the musicians; the ground around was covered with asphalt, and Venetian lanterns fastened to posts, seen from a distance, formed a crown of many-coloured lights above the heads of the dancers. A pedestal here and there supported a stone basin, from which rose a thin streamlet of water. In the midst of the foliage could be seen plaster statues, Hebes or Cupids, painted in oil, and presenting a very sticky appearance; and the numerous walks, garnished with very yellow sand, carefully raked, made the garden look much larger than it was in reality.

Students were walking their mistresses up and down; drapers' clerks strutted about with canes in their hands; lads fresh from school were smoking their regalias; old bachelors smoothed their dyed beards with a comb; there were English, Russians, men from South America, and three Orientals in tarbooshes. Lorettes, grisettes, and girls of the town had come there in the hope of finding a protector, a lover, a gold coin, or simply for the pleasure of dancing; and their dresses, with tunics of water-green, blue, cherry-red, or violet, swept along, fluttered between the ebony trees and the lilacs. Nearly all the men wore clothes with checks, some of them had white trousers, in spite of the coolness of the evening. The gas was lighted.

Hussonnet knew a lot of the women through his connection with the fashion journals and the smaller theatres; he sent them kisses with the tips of his fingers, and from time to time he quitted his friends to go and chat with them.

Deslauriers felt jealous of these playful familiarities. He accosted in a cynical manner a tall, fair-haired girl, in a nankeen costume. After looking at him in a surly way, she said: 'No! I wouldn't trust you, my lad!' and turned on her heel.

His next attack was on a stout brunette, who apparently was a little mad, for she gave a bounce at the very first word he spoke to her, threatening, if he went any further, to call the police. Deslauriers made an effort to laugh; then, coming across a little woman sitting by herself under a gas-lamp, he asked her to be his partner in a quadrille.

The musicians, perched on the platform in the attitude of apes, kept scraping and blowing away with desperate energy. The conductor, standing up, beat time automatically. The dancers were much crowded and thoroughly enjoying themselves; bonnet-strings fell loose and brushed against cravats, boots sank under petticoats; and all this bouncing went on to the accompaniment of the music; Deslauriers hugged the little woman to him, and, seized with the delirium of the cancan, whirled about, like a great puppet, in the midst of the dancers. Cisy and Dussardier were still promenading up and down; the young aristocrat ogled the girls, and, in spite of Dussardier's exhortations, did not dare to talk to them, having an idea in his head that where these women lived there was always 'a man hidden in the cupboard with a pistol who would come out of it and force you to sign a bill of exchange.'

They came back and joined Frédéric. Deslauriers had stopped dancing; and they were all asking themselves how they were to finish up the evening, when Hussonnet exclaimed:

'Look! There's the Marquise d'Amaëgui!'

The person referred to was a pale woman with a turned-up nose, mittens up to her elbows, and big black curls hanging along her cheeks, like two dog's ears. Hussonnet said to her:

'We ought to organise a little party at your house, a sort of Oriental fling. Try to collect some of your friends for these French cavaliers! Come on, what's stopping you? Are you waiting for your hidalgo?'

The Andalusian hung down her head: being well aware of the by no means lavish habits of her friend, she was afraid of having to pay for the refreshments. When, at length, she let the word 'money' slip from her, Cisy offered five napoleons – all he had in his purse – and so it was settled that the thing should come off. But Frédéric was no longer there.

He had fancied that he had recognised the voice of Arnoux, had got a glimpse of a woman's hat, and had plunged into the nearby arbour.

Mademoiselle Vatnaz was alone there with Arnoux.

'Excuse me! Am I disturbing you?'

'Not in the least!' returned the picture-merchant.

Frédéric, from the closing words of their conversation, understood that Arnoux had come to the Alhambra to talk over a pressing matter of business with Mademoiselle Vatnaz; and it seemed that he was not completely reassured, for he said to her, with some uneasiness in his manner:

'You are quite sure?'

'Perfectly certain! You are loved! Ah! What a man you are!'

And she pouted at him, putting out her big lips, so red that they seemed tinged with blood. But she had wonderful eyes, of a tawny hue, with specks of gold in the pupils, full of vivacity, amorousness, and sensuality. They illuminated, like lamps, the rather yellow tint of her thin face. Arnoux seemed to enjoy her scoldings. He leaned towards her, saying:

'You are nice – give me a kiss!'

She caught hold of his two ears, and pressed her lips against his forehead.

At that moment the dancing stopped; and in the conductor's place appeared a handsome young man, too plump, with a waxen complexion. He had long lack hair, which he wore in the same fashion as Christ, and a blue velvet waistcoat embroidered with large gold palm branches. He looked as proud as a peacock, and as stupid as a turkey-cock; and having bowed to the audience, he broke into a ditty. A villager was supposed to be giving an account of his journey to the capital. The singer used the dialect of Lower Normandy, and pretended to be drunk. The refrain:

> 'Ah! How I laughed, how I laughed,
> In wicked old Paris!'

was greeted with enthusiastic stampings of feet. Delmas, 'a singer with soul', was too shrewd to let the excitement of his listeners cool. A guitar was quickly handed to him and he moaned forth a ballad entitled 'The Albanian Girl's Brother.'

The words recalled to Frédéric those which had been sung by the man in rags between the paddleboxes of the steamboat. His eyes involuntarily attached themselves to the hem of the dress spread out before him. After each couplet there was a long pause – and the blowing of the wind through the trees seemed like the sound of waves.

With one hand, Mademoiselle Vatnaz pushed aside the branches of a privet which was obstructing her view of the platform, and gazed fixedly at the singer, nostrils flared, her eyes narrowed, as if absorbed in a grave kind of joy.

'Aha!' said Arnoux. 'Now I know why you're at the Alhambra this evening! You're keen on Delmas, my dear'.

She would admit nothing.

'Ah! How coy you are!'

And, pointing to Frédéric, he said:

'Is it because of him? You needn't worry. That young man is the soul of discretion!'

The others came into the arbour looking for their friend. Hussonnet introduced them. Arnoux offered cigars all round and treated everyone to a sorbet.

Mademoiselle Vatnaz had blushed the moment she saw Dussardier. She soon rose, and stretching out her hand towards him:

'You don't remember me, Monsieur Auguste?'

'How do you know her?' asked Frédéric.

'We worked for the same business!' he replied.

Cisy pulled him by the sleeve; they went out; and, scarcely had he disappeared, when Mademoiselle Vatnaz began to sing his praises. She even went so far as to add that he possessed *the genius of the heart*.

Then they chatted about Delmas, who as a mimic might be a success on the stage; and a discussion followed in which Shakespeare, Censorship, Style, the People, the receipts of the Porte-Saint-Martin, Alexandre Dumas, Victor Hugo, and Dumersan were all mixed up together. Arnoux had known many celebrated actresses; the young men bent forward to hear what he had to say. But his words were drowned in the noise of the music; and, as soon as the quadrille or the polka was over, everybody rushed for the tables, called the waiter, and laughed; bottles of beer and fizzy lemonade popped amid the foliage, women squawked like hens; now and then, two gentlemen tried to fight; and a thief was arrested.

The dancers, in the rush of a gallop, spilled over onto the paths. Panting, with flushed, smiling faces, they filed off in a whirlwind which lifted up dresses as well as coat-tails; the trombones brayed more loudly; the rhythm grew faster; behind the medieval cloister could be heard crackling sounds, squibs went off; artificial suns began turning round; the gleam of the Bengal fires, like emeralds in colour, lighted up for the space of a minute the entire garden – and with the last rocket, a great sigh escaped from the assembled throng.

The crowd slowly melted away. A cloud of gunpowder hung in the air. Frédéric and Deslauriers were walking step by step through the midst of the crowd, when they happened to see something that made them suddenly stop: Martinon was getting some change back at the place where umbrellas were left; and he was accompanying a woman of about fifty, plain-looking, magnificently dressed, and of problematic social rank.

'That sly dog,' said Deslauriers, 'is not so simple as we imagine. But where in the world is Cisy?'

Dussardier pointed out the bar, where they perceived the knightly youth, with a bowl of punch before him, and a pink hat by his side, to keep him company.

Hussonnet, who had been away for five minutes, reappeared at the same moment.

A young girl was leaning on his arm, and addressing him in a loud voice as 'ducky'.

'Oh no!' said he to her. 'No! Not in public! I'd rather you called me "Vicomte". That has something of the gay cavalier about it, Louis XIII, soft boots – I like it! Yes, my friends, an old flame! Nice, isn't she?' – and he took her by the chin.

'Give greetings to these gentlemen! They are all the sons of peers of France! I keep company with them so that they'll appoint me ambassador!'

'How crazy you are!' sighed Mademoiselle Vatnaz.

She asked Dussardier to see her as far as her door.

Arnoux watched them go; then, turning towards Frédéric:

'Do you happen to like la Vatnaz? At any rate, you're not open about these affairs. I believe you keep your amours hidden?'

Frédéric, turning pale, swore that he kept nothing hidden.

'It's just that no one's heard of you having a mistress,' continued Arnoux.

Frédéric longed to mention a woman's name at random. But the story might be repeated to *her*. So he replied that indeed he had no mistress.

The picture-dealer reproached him for this.

'This evening you had a good opportunity! Why didn't you do like the others, who are all going off with a woman?'

'Well, and what about you?' said Frédéric, provoked by his persistence.

'Oh! Me! That's different, my son! I'm going back to my own!'

He called a cab, and disappeared.

The two friends went off on foot. An east wind was blowing. Neither spoke. Deslauriers was regretting that he had not succeeded in making a *shine* before the owner of a journal, and Frédéric sank deeper into his melancholy broodings. At length, he said that the dance hall had struck him as stupid.

'Whose fault is that? If you hadn't left us for that Arnoux of yours!'

'Bah! Anything I could have done would have been utterly useless.'

But the Clerk had theories. All that was necessary in order to get a thing was to desire it strongly.

'And yet you yourself, a little while ago . . . '

'I didn't care!' returned Deslauriers, cutting short Frédéric's allusion. 'Am I going to get entangled with women?'

And he declaimed against their affectations, their silly ways; in short, he disliked them.

'Don't pose!' said Frédéric.

Deslauriers became silent. Then, all at once:

'Will you bet me a hundred francs that I won't *get* the first woman that passes?'

'Yes – it's a bet!'

The first who passed was a hideous-looking beggar-woman; and they were giving up all hope of a chance presenting itself when, in the middle of the Rue de Rivoli, they saw a tall girl with a little bandbox in her hand.

Deslauriers accosted her under the arcades. She turned up abruptly by the Tuileries, and soon diverged into the Place du Carrousel; she kept looking to right and left. She ran after a cab; Deslauriers overtook her. He walked by her side, talking to her with expressive gestures. At length, she accepted his arm, and they went on together along the quays. Then, when they were up as far as Châtelet, they kept tramping up and down the pavement for at least twenty minutes, like two sailors keeping watch. But, all of a sudden, they passed over the Pont-au-Change, through the Flower Market, and along the Quai Napoléon. Frédéric entered the building behind them. Deslauriers gave him to understand that he would be in their way, and had only to follow his example.

'How much have you got still?'

'Two hundred sous pieces!'

'That's enough! Good night!'

Frédéric was seized with the astonishment one feels at seeing a piece of foolery succeed: 'He's having me on,' was his reflection.

'Suppose I went back up?' Perhaps Deslauriers would think that he was envious of this paltry love? 'As if I had not one a hundred times more rare, more noble, more powerful.' He felt a sort of anger impelling him onward. He arrived in front of Madame Arnoux's door.

None of the outer windows belonged to her apartment. Nevertheless, he remained with his eyes pasted on the front of the house – as if he fancied he could, by sheer looking, break open the walls. Now, no doubt, she was sunk in repose, tranquil as a sleeping flower, with her beautiful black hair resting on the lace of the pillow, her lips slightly parted, and one arm under her head.

Arnoux's head rose before him, and he rushed away to escape from this vision.

The advice which Deslauriers had given to him came back to his memory; it filled him with horror. Then he walked aimlessly about the streets.

When a pedestrian approached, he tried to distinguish his face. From time to time a ray of light passed between his legs, tracing a great quarter of a circle on the pavement; and in the shadow a man rose up with his basket and his lantern. The wind, at certain points, made an iron chimneypot shake; distant sounds reached his ears, mingling with the buzzing in his brain, and it seemed to him that he was listening to the indistinct flourish of quadrille music. His movements as he walked on kept up this illusion; he found himself on the Pont de la Concorde.

Then he recalled that evening in the previous winter – when, as he left her house for the first time, he had had to stand still, so rapidly did his heart beat with the hopes that held it in their grip. And now they had all withered!

Dark clouds were drifting across the face of the moon. He gazed at it, musing on the vastness of space, the wretchedness of life, the nothingness of everything. The day dawned; his teeth were chattering; and, half-asleep, wet with the morning mist, and bathed in tears, he asked himself why he should not make an end of it. All that was necessary was a single movement! The weight of his forehead dragged him down, he beheld his own dead body floating in the water; Frédéric leaned over. The parapet was rather wide, and it was through pure weariness that he did not make the attempt to climb over it.

Then a feeling of horror swept over him. He reached the boulevards once more, and sank down upon a seat. He was aroused by some police officers, who were convinced that he had been 'out on the town'.

He began to walk once more. But, as he was exceedingly hungry, and as all the restaurants were closed, he went to have something to eat in a tavern in the Halles. After which, thinking it too soon to go in yet, he wandered about the Hôtel de Ville till a quarter past eight.

Deslauriers had long since got rid of his wench; and he was writing at the table in the middle of the room. About four o'clock, M. de Cisy came in.

Thanks to Dussardier, he had enjoyed the society of a lady the previous evening; and he had even accompanied her home in the carriage with her husband to the very threshold of her house, where she had given him an assignation from which he had just come. And she wasn't a familiar name!

'What's that got to do with me?' said Frédéric.

Thereupon the young gentleman began to beat about the bush; he mentioned Mademoiselle Vatnaz, the Andalusian, and all the others. At length, with much circumlocution, he stated the object of his visit: relying on the discretion of his friend, he came to ask him to help him in taking an important step, after which he might definitely regard himself as a man; and Frédéric did not refuse him. He told the story to Deslauriers without relating the facts with reference to himself personally.

The Clerk was of the opinion that he was now 'going on very well'. This respect for his advice increased his good humour.

He owed to that quality his success, on the very first night he met her, with Mademoiselle Clémence Daviou, embroideress in gold for military outfits, the sweetest creature that ever lived, as slender as a reed, with large blue eyes, perpetually staring with wonder. The Clerk took advantage of her credulity to such an extent as to make her believe that he had been decorated; in their private encounters he had his frock-coat adorned with a red ribbon, but divested himself of it in public in order, as he put it, not to humiliate his employer. Besides, he kept her at a distance, allowed himself to be fawned upon, like a pasha, and, in a laughing sort of way, called her 'daughter of the people'. Every time they met, she brought him little bunches of violets. Frédéric would not have cared for a love affair of this sort.

Yet, whenever they set forth arm-in-arm to eat in a private room at Pinson's or Barillot's, he felt a strange sadness. Frédéric did not realise how much he had made Deslauriers suffer for the past year, every Thursday, while brushing his nails before going out to dine in the Rue de Choiseul!

One evening, when from up on his balcony he had just been watching them as they went out together, he saw Hussonnet, some distance off, on the Pont d'Arcole. The Bohemian began calling him by making signals, and, when Frédéric had descended his five flights of stairs:

'Here's the thing: it's next Saturday, the 24th, Madame Arnoux's feast-day.'

'How is that, when her name is Marie?'

'And Angèle also, no matter! They will entertain their guests at their country house in Saint-Cloud; I am instructed to give you due notice of it. You'll find a vehicle at the magazine office at three o'clock! So that's agreed! Excuse me for having disturbed you. But I have such a number of calls to make!'

Frédéric had scarcely turned round when his doorkeeper placed a letter in his hand:

'Monsieur and Madame Dambreuse beg of Monsieur F. Moreau to do them the honour to come and dine with them on Saturday the 24th inst. – R.S.V.P.'

'Too late,' he thought.

Nevertheless, he showed the letter to Deslauriers, who exclaimed:

'Ha! At last! But you don't look very pleased. Why?'

After some little hesitation, Frédéric said that he had another invitation for the same day.

'Do me the favour of sending the Rue de Choiseul packing. Don't be silly! I'll answer this for you if you're worried.'

And the clerk wrote an acceptance of the invitation in the third person.

Having seen nothing of the world save through the fever of his desires, he pictured it to himself as an artificial creation discharging its functions by virtue of mathematical laws. A dinner out, an accidental meeting with an important man, a smile from a pretty woman, might, by a series of consequential reactions, have gigantic results. Certain Parisian drawing-rooms were like those machines which take a material in its raw state and render it up a hundred times more valuable. He believed in courtesans advising diplomats, in wealthy marriages brought about by intrigues, in the cleverness of convicts, in the capacity of strong men for getting the better of fortune. In short, he considered it so useful to visit the Dambreuses, and talked about it so plausibly, that Frédéric was at a loss to know what was the best course to take.

All the same, as it was Madame Arnoux's feast-day, he ought nonetheless to make her a present; he naturally thought of a parasol, in order to make reparation for his awkwardness. Now he came across a shot-silk parasol with a little carved ivory handle, which had just come from China. But the price of it was a hundred and seventy-five francs, and he had not a sou, having in fact to live on the credit of his next quarter's allowance. However, he wished to get it, he was determined to have it, and, in spite of his repugnance to do so, he had recourse to Deslauriers.

Deslauriers answered by saying that he had no money.

'I need some,' said Frédéric – 'I need some very badly!'

As the other made the same excuse over again, he flew into a passion.

'You might just some time . . . '

'What?'

'Oh! Nothing.'

The Clerk had understood. He took the sum required out of his reserve fund, and when he had counted it out, coin by coin:

'I'm not asking you for a receipt, since I'm living off you!'

Frédéric threw himself on his friend's neck with a thousand affectionate protestations. Deslauriers received this display of emotion coldly. Then, next morning, noticing the parasol on the top of the piano:

'Ah! It was for that!'

'I will send it, perhaps,' said Frédéric, lamely.

Good fortune was on his side, for that evening he got a note with a black border from Madame Dambreuse announcing to him that she had lost an uncle, and excusing herself for having to defer till a later period the pleasure of making his acquaintance.

At two o'clock, he reached the office of the art journal. Instead of waiting for him in order to drive him in his carriage, Arnoux had left the city the night before, unable any longer to resist his desire to get some fresh air.

Every year it was his custom, for several days in succession, as soon as the leaves were budding forth, to start early in the morning and make long journeys across the fields, drinking milk at the farmhouses, romping with the village girls, asking about the harvest, and carrying back home with him stalks of salad in his handkerchief. At length, realising a long-cherished dream, he had bought a country house.

While Frédéric was talking to the picture-dealer's clerk, Mademoiselle Vatnaz suddenly made her appearance, and was disappointed at not seeing Arnoux. He would, perhaps, be remaining away another two days. The clerk advised her 'to go there' – she could not go; 'to write a letter' – she was afraid that the letter might get lost. Frédéric offered to be the bearer of it himself. She rapidly scribbled a note, and implored of him to let nobody see him delivering it.

Forty minutes later, he alighted at Saint-Cloud.

The house, which was about a hundred paces farther away than the bridge, stood halfway up the hill. The garden walls were hidden by two rows of linden trees, and a wide lawn descended to the bank of the river. The gate in the railings was open. Frédéric went in.

Arnoux, stretched on the grass, was playing with a litter of kittens. This amusement appeared to absorb him completely. Mademoiselle Vatnaz's letter drew him out of his torpor.

'The deuce! The deuce! This is a bore! She's right, though; I must go.'

Then, having stuck the missive into his pocket, he showed the young man through the grounds with manifest delight. He showed him everything, the stable, the cart-house, the kitchen. The drawing-room was on the right, and, on the side facing Paris, looked out on a trellised veranda, covered with clematis. But presently a few harmonious notes burst forth above their heads; Madame Arnoux, fancying that she was alone, was singing to amuse herself. She executed scales, trills, arpeggios. There were long notes which seemed to hang in the air; others fell in a rushing shower like the droplets of a waterfall; and her voice, passing out through the Venetian blind, cut its way through the deep silence and rose towards the blue sky.

It ceased all at once, when M. and Madame Oudry, two neighbours, presented themselves.

Then she appeared herself at the top of the steps; and, as she descended, he caught a glimpse of her foot. She wore little open shoes of bronzed leather, with three cross-straps which traced on her stockings a wirework of gold.

The guests arrived. With the exception of Maître Lefaucheux, lawyer, they were the same guests who came to the Thursday dinners. Each of them had brought some present: Dittmer a Syrian scarf, Rosenwald an album of ballads, Burrieu a watercolour, Sombaz his own caricature, and Pellerin a charcoal drawing, representing a kind of dance of death, a hideous fantasy, poorly executed. Hussonnet had dispensed with the formality of a present.

Frédéric waited to offer his, after the others.

She thanked him very much. Thereupon, he said:

'Why . . . it's almost a debt! I was so annoyed . . . '

'At what?' she returned. 'I don't understand.'

'Come! Dinner is waiting!' said Arnoux, catching hold of his arm; then in a whisper: 'You're not very bright, are you!'

Nothing could well be prettier than the dining-room, painted in water-green. At one end, a nymph of stone was dipping her toe into a basin formed like a shell. Through the open windows the entire garden could be seen with the long lawn flanked by an old Scotch pine, three-quarters stripped bare; beds of flowers swelled it out in unequal plots; and on the other side of the river there extended in a wide semicircle the Bois de Boulogne, Neuilly, Sèvres, and Meudon. Before the railed fence in front a canoe with sail outspread was tacking about.

They chatted first about the view in front of them, then about landscape in general; and they were beginning to plunge into discussions when Arnoux ordered his servant to prepare the carriage for about half past nine. He was summoned back to Paris by a letter from his cashier.

'Would you like me to go back with you?' said Madame Arnoux.

'Why, certainly!' And, making her a graceful bow: 'You know, madame, that it is impossible to live without you!'

Everyone congratulated her on having so good a husband.

'Ah! You see I'm not alone!' she replied quietly, pointing towards her little daughter.

Then, the conversation having turned once more on painting, there was some talk about a Ruysdaël, for which Arnoux expected a large sum, and Pellerin asked him if it were true that the celebrated Saul Mathias from London had come over during the past month to make him an offer of twenty-three thousand francs for it.

'Absolutely true!' And turning towards Frédéric: 'That was the very same gentleman I brought with me the other day to the Alhambra, much against my will, I assure you, for these English are by no means amusing companions!'

Frédéric, who suspected that Mademoiselle Vatnaz's letter was connected with a matter concerning some woman, had admired the facility with which my lord Arnoux found a way of passing it off as a perfectly honourable transaction; but his new lie, which was quite needless, made the young man open his eyes in speechless astonishment.

The picture-dealer added, with an air of simplicity:

'What's the name, by the by, of that young fellow, your friend?'

'Deslauriers,' said Frédéric quickly.

And, in order to repair the injustice which he felt he had done to his comrade, he praised him as one who possessed remarkable ability.

'Ah! Indeed? But he doesn't look such a fine fellow as the other – the clerk in the wagon office.'

Frédéric cursed Dussardier. She would think he associated with the common herd.

Then they began to talk about the improvements in the capital, the new districts of the city, and the worthy Oudry happened to refer to M. Dambreuse as one of the big speculators.

Frédéric, taking advantage of the opportunity to make a good figure, said that he knew him. But Pellerin launched into a harangue against shopkeepers; he saw no difference between them, whether they were sellers of candles or of money. Then Rosenwald and Burrieu talked about old china; Arnoux chatted with Madame Oudry about gardening; Sombaz, a humorist of the old school, amused himself by chaffing her husband, calling him

'Odry', as if he were the actor, and remarking that he must be descended from Oudry, the dog-painter, seeing that the bump for animals was visible on his forehead. He even wanted to feel M. Oudry's skull, but the latter excused himself on account of his wig; and dessert ended with gusts of laughter.

When they had taken their coffee, while they smoked, under the linden trees, and strolled about the garden for some time, they went for a walk along the river.

The party stopped in front of a fishmonger's shop, where a man was cleaning eels. Mademoiselle Marthe wanted to look at them. He emptied the box in which he had them out on the grass; and the little girl threw herself on her knees in order to catch them, laughed with delight, and screamed with terror. They all got lost. Arnoux paid for them.

He next took it into his head to go out for a sail.

One side of the horizon was beginning to pale, while on the other side a wide strip of orange colour spread across the sky, deepening to purple at the summits of the hills, which were steeped in shadow. Madame Arnoux was sitting on a big stone with this fiery splendour at her back. The other persons sauntered about here and there; Hussonnet, at the lower end of the river bank, went making ducks and drakes over the water.

Arnoux presently returned, followed by a weatherbeaten long boat, into which, in spite of the most prudent remonstrances, he packed his guests. The boat started to sink; they had to go ashore again.

Already candles were burning in the drawing-room, all hung with chintz, and with branched candlesticks of crystal fixed to the walls. Mère Oudry was nodding gently off in an armchair, and the others were listening to M. Lefaucheux expatiating on the glories of the Bar. Madame Arnoux was alone by the window; Frédéric came over to her.

They chatted about the remarks which were being made around them. She admired orators; he preferred the renown gained by writers. But, she ventured to suggest, it must give a man greater pleasure to move crowds directly by addressing them in person, to see that he is infusing into their souls all the sentiments that animate his own. Such triumphs as these did not tempt Frédéric much, as he had no ambition.

'Oh, why?' she said. 'One must have a little!'

They were standing close together, side by side in the window recess. Before them the night stretched out like a great dark veil, spangled with silver. It was the first time they had not talked about trivial matters. He even learned what she liked and disliked: certain perfumes upset her, she found history books interesting, and she believed in dreams.

Then he broached the subject of sentimental adventures. She spoke pityingly of the havoc wrought by passion, but was revolted by hypocritical deceivers; and this rectitude of spirit harmonised so well with the regular beauty of her face that it seemed part of it.

She smiled, every now and then, letting her eyes rest on him for a minute. Then he felt her gaze penetrating his soul like those great rays of sunlight which descend into the depths of the water. He loved her without reservation, without any hope of return, absolutely; and in those silent transports, which were like outbursts of gratitude, he longed to cover her forehead with a rain of kisses. At the same time, an inspiration from within carried him beyond himself; he felt moved by a longing for self-sacrifice, an imperative impulse towards immediate self-devotion, and all the stronger from the fact that he could not gratify it.

He did not leave along with the rest. Neither did Hussonnet. They were to go back in the carriage; and the vehicle was waiting just in front of the steps when Arnoux went down into the garden to gather some roses. Then the bouquet having been tied round with a thread, as the stems protruded unevenly, he searched in his pocket, which was full of papers, took out one at random, wrapped them up, completed his handiwork with the aid of a strong pin, and then offered it to his wife with a certain amount of emotion.

'Here, my darling. Forgive me for having forgotten you!'

But she uttered a little cry: the pin, having been awkwardly fixed, had pricked her, and she went back up to her room. They waited nearly a quarter of an hour for her. At last, she reappeared, carried off Marthe, and threw herself into the carriage.

'What about your bouquet?' said Arnoux.

'No, no! Don't bother!'

Frédéric was running off to fetch it for her; she called out to him: 'I don't want it!'

But he speedily brought it to her, saying that he had just put it back into the envelope, as he had found the flowers lying on the floor. She thrust them into the leather apron behind the seat, and off they started.

Frédéric, seated by her side, noticed that she was trembling frightfully. Then, when they had passed the bridge, as Arnoux was turning to the left:

'Why, no! That's wrong! That way, to the right!'

She seemed irritated; everything annoyed her. At length, Marthe having closed her eyes, Madame Arnoux drew forth the bouquet, and flung it out through the carriage door, then caught Frédéric's arm, making a sign to him with the other hand never to mention it.

After this, she pressed her handkerchief against her lips, and sat quite motionless.

The other two, on the box, were talking about printing and about subscribers. Arnoux, who was driving carelessly, lost his way in the middle of the Bois de Boulogne. Then they plunged down narrow paths. The horse proceeded along at a walking pace; the branches of the trees grazed the hood. Frédéric could see nothing of Madame Arnoux save her two eyes in the shadow; Marthe lay stretched across her lap while he supported the child's head.

'She is tiring you!' said her mother.

He replied:

'No! Oh, no!'

Slow whirlwinds of dust rose up; they were passing through Auteuil; all the houses were closed up; a gas-lamp here and there lighted up the angle of a wall, then once more they were surrounded by darkness; at one time he noticed that she was crying.

Was this remorse? Passion? What in the world was it? This grief, of whose exact nature he was ignorant, interested him as if it were a personal matter; there was now a new bond between them, as if, in a sense, they were accomplices; and he said to her in the most caressing voice he could assume:

'Are you unwell?'

'Yes, a little,' she returned.

The carriage rolled on, and the honeysuckles and the syringas hung out over garden fences, sending puffs of enervating perfumes into the night air. Her gown fell around her feet in numerous folds. It seemed to him as if he were in communication with her entire person through the medium of this child's body which lay stretched between them. He stooped over the little girl, and spreading out her pretty brown tresses, kissed her softly on the forehead.

'You are good!' said Madame Arnoux.

'Why?'

'Because you are fond of children.'

'Not all!'

He said no more, but he stretched out his left hand towards her and left it wide open – fancying that she would follow his example perhaps, and that he would find her palm touching his. Then he felt ashamed and withdrew it.

They soon reached the paved street. The carriage went on more quickly, the number of gaslights vastly increased, it was Paris. Hussonnet, at the Garde-Meuble, jumped down from his seat. Frédéric waited till they were in the courtyard before alighting; then he lay in wait at the corner of the Rue de Choiseul, and saw Arnoux slowly making his way back towards the boulevards.

Next morning he began working as hard as ever he could.

He saw himself in an Assize Court, on a winter's evening, at the close of the advocates' speeches, when the jurymen are looking pale, and when the breathless audience makes the partitions of the prætorium creak, having being four hours speaking, recapitulating all his proofs, creating new ones, feeling with every phrase, with every word, with every gesture, the blade of the guillotine, suspended behind him, rising up; then in the tribune of the Chamber, he saw himself as an orator bearing on his lips the safety of an entire people, drowning his opponents under his figures of rhetoric, crushing them with a repartee, with thunderings and musical intonations in his voice, ironical, pathetic, fiery, sublime: she would be there somewhere in the midst of the others, hiding beneath her veil her enthusiastic tears; after that they would meet – and he would be unaffected by discouragements, calumnies, and insults, if she would only say, 'Ah, that is beautiful!' while drawing her light hand across his brow.

These images flashed, like beacon-lights, on the horizon of his life. His intellect, thereby excited, became more active and more vigorous. He buried himself in study till the month of August, and was successful at his final examination.

Deslauriers, who had found it so troublesome to coach him once more for the second examination at the close of December, and for the third in February, was astonished at his ardour. Then the great expectations of former days returned. In ten years Frédéric must become a deputy; in fifteen a minister; why not? With his patrimony, which would soon come into his hands, he might begin by starting a newspaper; this would be the opening step in his career; after that they would see what the future would bring. As for himself, he was still ambitious of obtaining a chair in the Law School; and he defended his thesis for the degree of Doctor in such a remarkable fashion that it won for him the compliments of the professors.

Three days afterwards, Frédéric took his own degree. Before leaving for his holidays, he conceived the idea of getting up a picnic to bring to a close their Saturday reunions.

He displayed the utmost gaiety on the occasion. Madame Arnoux was now with her mother in Chartres. But he would soon be reunited with her, and would end by being her lover.

Deslauriers, admitted that very day to the Orsay debating society, had made a speech which had been greatly applauded. Although he was sober, he became a little tipsy, and said to Dussardier at dessert:

'You're honest, you are! And when I'm rich, I'll make you my agent.'

All were in a state of delight; Cisy was not going to finish his law course; Martinon intended to remain during the period before his admission to the Bar in the provinces, where he would be nominated a deputy-magistrate; Pellerin was preparing himself for a great picture representing 'The Genius of the Revolution'; Hussonnet, in the following week, was to read for the Director of the Délassements the scenario of a play, and had no doubt as to its success:

'Because everybody knows I can knock out the structure of a play! As for passions, I've been around long enough to understand them inside out; and witticisms are entirely in my line!'

He gave a spring, fell on his two hands, and walked in this fashion for some time around the table with his legs in the air.

This childish performance did not make Sénécal smile. He had just been dismissed from the boarding-school, in which he had been a teacher, for having given a whipping to an aristocrat's son. His straitened circumstances having worsened in consequence, he laid the blame for this on the social order, and cursed the wealthy; and he poured out his grievances into the sympathetic ears of Regimbart, who had become every day more and more disillusioned, saddened, and disgusted. The Citizen had now turned his attention towards questions arising out of the Budget, and accused the Camarilla of squandering millions in Algeria.

As he could not sleep without having paid a visit to the Alexandre tavern, he disappeared at eleven o'clock. The rest went away some time afterwards; and Frédéric, as he was parting from Hussonnet, learned that Madame Arnoux must have come back the night before.

He accordingly went to the coach office to change his ticket for the next day, and, at about six o'clock in the evening, presented himself at her house. Her return, the door keeper said, had been put off for a week. Frédéric dined alone, and then strolled about on the boulevards.

Rosy clouds, scarf-like in form, stretched beyond the roofs; shop awnings were beginning to be raised; water-carts were letting a shower of spray fall over the dusty pavement, and an unexpected coolness mingled with emanations from cafés, which afforded glimpses through their open doors, between silver ware and gilt ware, of flowers in sheaves, reflected in the tall mirrors. The crowd moved on at a leisurely pace. Groups of men were chatting in the middle of the pavement; and women passed by with an indolent expression in their eyes and that camellia tint in their complexions which the weariness of the hot season imparts to feminine flesh. Something immeasurable in its vastness seemed to pour itself out and envelope the houses. Never had Paris looked so beautiful to him. He saw nothing before him in the future but an interminable series of years all full of love.

He stopped in front of the theatre of the Porte-Saint-Martin to look at the bill; and, for want of something to occupy him, paid for a seat and went in.

An old fairytale was the piece on stage. There was a very small audience; and through the skylights of the top gallery the light was cut up into little blue squares, whilst the footlights formed a single line of yellow illuminations. The scene represented a slave-market at Peking, with handbells, tomtoms, sultanas, sharp-pointed caps, and lots of puns. Then, as soon as the curtain fell, he wandered about in the foyer all alone and gazed out with admiration at a large green landau which stood on the boulevard outside, before the front steps, yoked to two white horses, while a coachman with short breeches held the reins.

He was returning to his seat when, in the balcony, a lady and a gentleman entered the first box in front of the stage. The husband had a pale face with a narrow strip of grey beard round it, the rosette of the Legion of Honour, and that frigid look which is supposed to characterise diplomats.

His wife, who was at least twenty years younger, and who was neither tall nor undersized, neither ugly nor pretty, wore her fair hair in corkscrew curls in the English fashion, and displayed a flat-bodiced dress and a large black lace fan. To make people so fashionable as these come to the theatre in such a season one would imagine either that there was some accidental cause, or boredom at the prospect of spending the evening in one another's society. The lady nibbled at her fan, and the gentleman yawned. Frédéric could not remember where he had seen that face.

In the next interval between the acts, while passing through one of the lobbies, he came face to face with both of them; at his vague gesture of greeting, M. Dambreuse, recognising him, came up and apologised at once for having treated him with unpardonable neglect. This was an allusion to the numerous visiting cards he had sent on Deslauriers' advice. However, he confused the dates, supposing that Frédéric was in the second year of his law course. Then he said he envied the young man for the opportunity of going into the country. He sadly needed a little rest himself, but business kept him in Paris.

Madame Dambreuse, leaning on his arm, nodded her head slightly; and the agreeable sprightliness of her face contrasted with its gloomy expression of a short time before.

'But there are wonderful things to do here!' she said, after her husband's last remark. 'What a stupid play this is! Isn't it, Monsieur?'

And all three of them stood chatting about theatres and new plays.

Frédéric, accustomed to the grimaces of provincial ladies, had not seen in any woman such ease of manner combined with that simplicity which is the essence of refinement, and in which ingenuous souls see the expression of an immediate sympathy.

They would expect to see him as soon as he returned; M. Dambreuse told him to give his kind remembrances to Père Roque.

Frédéric, when he got home, did not fail to inform Deslauriers of this hospitable invitation.

'Grand!' was the Clerk's reply; 'and don't let your mamma get round you! Come back straight away!'

On the day after his arrival, as soon as they had finished lunch, Madame Moreau took her son out into the garden.

She said she was happy to see him in a profession, for they were not as rich as people imagined; the land brought in little; the people who farmed it paid badly; she had even been compelled to sell her carriage. Finally, she placed their situation in its true colours before him.

During the first embarrassments which followed the death of her late husband, M. Roque, a man of great cunning, had made her loans of money which had been renewed, and left long unpaid, in spite of her desire to clear them off. He had suddenly made a demand for immediate payment; and she had accepted his terms by giving up to him, at a contemptible figure, the farm of Presles. Ten years later, her capital disappeared with the failure of a banker at Melun. Through a horror which she had of mortgages, and to keep up appearances, which might be necessary in view of her son's future, she had, when Père Roque presented himself again, listened to him once more. But now she was free from debt. In short, there was left them an income of about ten thousand francs, of which two thousand three hundred belonged to him – his entire patrimony!

'It can't be true!' exclaimed Frédéric.

She nodded her head, as if to declare that it was indeed true.

But his uncle would leave him something?

Nothing could be more uncertain!

And they took a turn around the garden without speaking. At last she drew him to her heart, and in a voice choked with rising tears:

'Ah! My poor boy! I have had to give up so many dreams!'

He seated himself on the bench in the shadow of the great acacia.

Her advice was that he should become a clerk to M. Prouharam, solicitor, who would assign over his office to him; if he increased its value, he might sell it again and make a good marriage.

Frédéric was no longer listening. He was gazing automatically across the hedge into the other garden opposite.

A little girl of about twelve with red hair was there all alone. She had made earrings for herself with rowan berries; her bodice, made of grey linen-cloth, showed her bare shoulders, slightly gilded by the sun; her short white petticoat was spotted with jam stains – and there was something of the grace of a young wild animal about her entire person, both tense and slight. Apparently, the presence of a stranger astonished her, for she had stopped abruptly with her watering-can in her hand, darting glances at him with eyes of a limpid greenish-blue.

'That is M. Roque's daughter,' said Madame Moreau. 'He has just married his servant and legitimised his child.'

CHAPTER SIX

Ruined, stripped of everything, lost without hope!

He had remained seated on the bench, as if stunned by a shock. He cursed Fate, he would have liked to beat somebody; and, to intensify his despair, he felt a kind of outrage, a sense of disgrace, weighing down upon him — for Frédéric had been under the impression that the fortune coming to him through his father would mount up one day to an income of fifteen thousand livres, and he had so informed the Arnoux in an indirect sort of way. So then he would be looked upon as a braggart, a rogue, an obscure blackguard, who had introduced himself to them in the expectation of making some profit out of it! And as for her, Madame Arnoux, how could he ever see her again now?

That was in any case completely impossible with an income of only three thousand francs! He could not always lodge on the fourth floor, have the door keeper as a servant, and make his appearance with wretched black gloves turning blue at the ends, a greasy hat, and the same frock-coat for a whole year! No! No! Never! And yet without her life was intolerable. Many people were able to live well without any fortune, Deslauriers for one — and he thought himself a coward to attach so much importance to matters of trifling consequence. Need would perhaps multiply his faculties a hundredfold. He grew excited by thinking of great men who work in garrets. A soul like that of Madame Arnoux ought to be touched at such a spectacle, and she would be moved by it to sympathetic tenderness. So, after all, this catastrophe was a piece of good fortune; like those earthquakes which unveil treasures, it had revealed to him the hidden wealth of his nature. But there was only one place in the world where this could be turned to account: Paris! for to his mind art, science, and love (those three faces of God, as Pellerin would have said) were associated exclusively with the capital.

That evening, he informed his mother of his intention to go back there. Madame Moreau was surprised and indignant. She regarded it as a foolish and absurd course. He would do better to follow her advice, namely to remain near her in an office. Frédéric shrugged his shoulders: 'Come now!' – looking on this proposal as an insult to himself.

Thereupon, the good lady adopted another method. In a tender voice broken by sobs she began to speak of her solitude, her old age, and the sacrifices she had made. Now that she was more unhappy than ever, he was abandoning her. Then, alluding to the anticipated close of her life:

'Have a little patience, good heavens! You will soon be free!'

These lamentations were renewed twenty times a day for three months; and at the same time the luxuries of home weakened his resolve; he found it enjoyable to have a softer bed and napkins that were not torn; so that weary, enervated, overcome finally by the terrible force of gentle persuasion, Frédéric allowed himself to be taken to the office of the lawyer Mr Prouharam.

There, he displayed neither knowledge nor aptitude. Up to this time, he had been regarded as a young man of great means who would be the shining light of the province. There was general disappointment.

At first, he had said to himself: 'I must inform Madame Arnoux', and for a whole week he had kept formulating in his own mind dithyrambic letters and short notes in an eloquent and lapidary style. The fear of avowing his actual position restrained him. Then he thought that it was far better to write to the husband. Arnoux knew about life and would be able to understand him. At length, after a fortnight's hesitation:

'Bah! I ought not to see them any more; let them forget me! At least, I shall not have sunk in her memory of me! She'll believe that I'm dead, and will regret me . . . perhaps.'

As extravagant resolutions cost him little, he had sworn to himself that he would never return to Paris, and that he would not even make any enquiries about Madame Arnoux.

Yet he regretted the very smell of the gas and the din of the omnibuses. He mused on all the things which had been said to him, on the tone of her voice, on the light of her eyes – and, regarding himself as a dead man, he no longer did anything at all.

He rose very late, and looked through his window at the passing teams of wagoners. The first six months especially were dreadful.

On certain days, however, he was possessed by a feeling of indignation at himself. Then he would go out. He would wander through the meadows, half covered in winter time by the inundations of the Seine. They are divided by rows of poplar trees. Here and there arises a little bridge. He tramped about till evening, rolling the yellow leaves under his feet, inhaling the mist, and jumping over the ditches; as his arteries began to throb more vigorously, he felt himself carried away by desires to do something wild; he longed to become a trapper in America, to attend on a pasha in the East, to take ship as a sailor; and he gave vent to his melancholy in long letters to Deslauriers.

The latter was struggling to get on. The spineless behaviour of his friend and his eternal jeremiads appeared to him simply stupid. Their correspondence soon became a mere form. Frédéric had given up all his furniture to Deslauriers, who stayed on in the same lodgings. From time to time his mother spoke to him about it; at length one day he told her about the present he had made, and she was scolding him for it, when a letter was placed in his hands.

'What is the matter now?' she said. 'You're trembling?'

'There's nothing the matter with me!' replied Frédéric.

Deslauriers informed him that he had taken Sénécal under his roof, and that for the past fortnight they had been living together. So now Sénécal was taking his ease in the midst of things that had come from the Arnoux's shop! He might sell them, criticise, make jokes about them. Frédéric felt wounded in the depths of his soul. He went up to his room. He wanted to die.

His mother called him to consult him about some planting in the garden.

This garden was, after the fashion of an English park, cut in the middle by a stick fence, and half of it belonged to Père Roque, who had another for vegetables on the bank of the river. The two neighbours, having fallen out, abstained from making their appearance there at the same hour. But since Frédéric's return the old gentleman used to walk out there more frequently, and was not stinted in his courtesies towards Madame Moreau's son. He pitied the young man for having to live in a country town. One day he told him that Monsieur Dambreuse had asked for news of him. On another occasion he expatiated on the custom of Champagne, where nobility was conferred through the female line.

'At that time you would have been a noble, since your mother's name was De Fouvens. And, say what you will, there's something in name! After all,' he added, with a sly glance at Frédéric, 'that depends on the Keeper of the Seals.'

This pretension to aristocracy contrasted strangely with his personal appearance. As he was small, his big chestnut-coloured frock-coat exaggerated the length of his torso. When he took off his cap, a face almost like that of a woman with an extremely sharp nose could be seen; his hair, which was of a yellow colour, resembled a wig; he saluted people with a very low bow, passing close to the wall.

Up to his fiftieth year, he had been content with the services of Catherine, a native of Lorraine, of the same age as himself, who was strongly marked with smallpox. But in about 1834, he brought back with him from Paris a handsome blonde with a sheeplike countenance and a 'queenly carriage'. She was observed before long strutting about with large earrings, and everything was explained by the birth of a daughter who was introduced to the world under the name of Elisabeth-Olympe-Louise Roque.

Catherine, being jealous, expected that she would loathe this child. On the contrary, she loved her, She treated her with the utmost care, attention, and tenderness, in order to supplant her mother and render her odious – an easy task, inasmuch as Madame Éléonore entirely neglected the little one, preferring to gossip in the shops. On the day after her marriage, she went to pay a visit at the Subprefecture, no longer called the servants 'tu', and took it into her head that, as a matter of good form, she ought to be strict with the child. She was present at her lessons; the teacher, an old clerk who had been employed at the town hall, had no idea how to proceed. The pupil rebelled, got her ears boxed, and rushed away to shed tears on the lap of Catherine, who always took her part. So then the two women quarrelled, and M. Roque ordered them to hold their tongues. He had married out of tender regard for his daughter, and did not wish her to be tormented.

She often wore a tattered white dress, with drawers trimmed with lace; and on great festival days she would leave the house attired like a princess, in order to mortify a little the local worthies, who forbade their brats to associate with her on account of her illegitimate birth.

She passed her time always alone in her garden, went see-sawing on the swing, chased butterflies, then suddenly stopped to watch the floral beetles swooping down onto the rose trees. It was, no doubt, these habits which imparted to her face an expression at the same time of audacity and dreaminess. She was, moreover, the same size as Marthe, so that Frédéric said to her, at their second interview:

'Will you permit me to kiss you, mademoiselle?'

The little girl lifted up her head and replied:

'I will!'

But the stick hedge separated them from one another.

'You must climb up onto it,' said Frédéric.

'No, lift me up!'

He leaned over the hedge, and raising her off the ground with his hands, kissed her on both cheeks; then he put her back on her own side by a similar process, and this performance was repeated on the next occasions when they found themselves together.

Without more reserve than a child of four, as soon as she heard her friend coming, she sprang forward to meet him, or else, hiding behind a tree, she began yelping like a dog to frighten him.

One day, when Madame Moreau had gone out, he took her up to his room. She opened all the scent bottles, and pomaded her hair plentifully; then, without the slightest embarrassment, she lay down on the bed, where she remained stretched out full length, wide awake.

'I'm imagining that I'm your wife,' she said.

Next day he found her all in tears. She confessed that she was 'weeping for her sins', and, when he wished to know what they were, she looked down, and answered:

'Ask me no more!'

The time for first communion was at hand; she had been brought to confession that morning.

The sacrament scarcely made her any better behaved. Occasionally, she got into a real passion; and Frédéric was sent for to appease her.

He often took her with him on his walks. While he indulged in daydreams as he walked along, she would gather wild poppies at the edges of the cornfields, and, when she saw him more melancholy than usual, she tried to console him with kind words. His heart, bereft of love, fell back on the friendship of this child; he drew funny faces for her, told her stories, and began to read books to her.

He began with the *Annales Romantiques*, a collection of prose and verse celebrated at the period. Then, forgetting her age, so much was he charmed by her intelligence, he read for her in succession *Atala*, *Cinq-Mars*, and *Les Feuilles d'Automne*. But one night (she had that very evening heard *Macbeth* in Letourneur's simple trans-lation) she woke up, exclaiming: 'The spot! The spot!' Her teeth were chattering, she was trembling, and, fixing terrified glances on her right hand, she kept rubbing it, saying: 'Still a spot!' At last a doctor was brought, who directed that she should be kept free from violent emotions.

The townsfolk saw in this only an unfavourable prognostic for her morals. It was said that 'young Moreau' wished to make an actress of her later.

Soon another event became the subject of discussion, namely, the arrival of uncle Barthélemy. Madame Moreau gave up her bedroom to him, and was so gracious as to serve up meat to him on fast-days.

The old man was not very agreeable. He was perpetually making comparisons between Le Havre and Nogent, the air of which he considered heavy, the bread bad, the streets ill-paved, the food indifferent, and the inhabitants idle. 'What a poor state trade is in here!' He blamed his deceased brother for his extravagance, point-ing out by way of contrast that he had himself accumulated an income of twenty-seven thousand livres a year! At last, he left at the end of the week, and on the footboard of the carriage gave utterance to these by no means reassuring words:

'I am always very glad to know that you are comfortably off.'

'You will get nothing!' said Madame Moreau as they re-entered the dining-room.

He had come only at her urgent request; and for a week she had been seeking some statement of his intentions, too openly perhaps. She repented now of having done so, and remained seated in her armchair with her head bent down and her lips tightly pressed together. Frédéric sat opposite, watching her; and they were both silent, as they had been five years before on his return home from Montereau. This coincidence, which presented itself even to his mind, recalled Madame Arnoux to his recollection.

At that moment the crack of a whip outside the window reached their ears, while a voice was heard calling out to him.

It was Père Roque, who was alone in his tilted cart. He was going to spend the whole day at La Fortelle with M. Dambreuse, and cordially offered to drive Frédéric there.

'You have no need of an invitation as long as you're with me; don't worry!'

Frédéric felt inclined to accept. But how would he explain his permanent residence at Nogent? He had not a proper summer suit; and what would his mother say? He declined.

From that time, their neighbour exhibited less friendliness. Louise was growing up; Madame Eléonore fell dangerously ill; and the intimacy broke off, to the great delight of Madame Moreau, who feared lest her son's prospects of being settled in life might be affected by association with such people. .

Her dream was to purchase for him a clerkship to the court; Frédéric raised no particular objection to this idea. He now accompanied her to mass, in the evening he took a hand in a game of cards, he became accustomed to provincial life, let himself sink into it – and even his love had assumed a character of funereal sweetness, a kind of soporific charm. By dint of having poured out his grief in his letters, mixed it up with everything he read, walked it about with him in the country and infused it into everything, he had almost exhausted it, so that Madame Arnoux was for him, as it were, a dead woman whose tomb he wondered that he did not know, so tranquil and resigned had his affection for her now become.

One day, the 12th of December 1845, about nine o'clock in the morning, the cook brought up a letter to his room. The address, which was in big characters, was written in an unknown hand; and Frédéric, feeling sleepy, was in no great hurry to break the seal. At length, he read:

'Justice of the Peace at Le Havre, 3rd Arrondissement.
Monsieur,
Monsieur Moreau, your uncle, having died intestate . . . '

He was the heir!

As if a conflagration had broken out behind the wall, he jumped out of bed in his shirt, with his feet bare; he passed his hand over his face, doubting the evidence of his own eyes, believing that he was still dreaming, and in order to get a firmer grip on reality, he flung the window wide open.

There had been a fall of snow; the roofs were white – and he even recognised in the yard outside a washtub which had caused him to stumble the evening before.

He read the letter over three times in succession; it was absolutely true! His uncle's entire fortune! A yearly income of twenty-seven thousand livres! – and a wild joy possessed him at the idea of seeing Madame Arnoux once more. With the vividness of a hallucination he saw himself beside her, at her house, bringing her some present in silk paper, while at the door stood his tilbury – no, a brougham rather! A black brougham, with a servant in brown livery; he could hear his horse pawing the ground and the noise of the curb-chain mingling with the rippling sound of their kisses. And every day it would be the same, indefinitely. He would receive them at home in his own house; the dining-room would be furnished in red leather, the boudoir in yellow silk, sofas everywhere! And such a variety of whatnots, Chinese vases, and carpets! These images came in so tumultuous a fashion into his mind that he felt his head turning round. Then he remembered his mother; and he descended the stairs with the letter still in his hand.

Madame Moreau made an effort to control her emotion, but could not keep herself from swooning. Frédéric caught her in his arms and kissed her on the forehead.

'Dear mother, you can now buy back your carriage; come on, laugh, no more tears, be happy!'

Ten minutes later the news had travelled as far as the edges of town. Then Maître Benoist, M. Gamblin, M. Chambion, all their friends hurried to the house. Frédéric got away for a minute in order to write to Deslauriers. Then other visitors turned up. The afternoon passed in congratulations. They had forgotten all about Roque's wife, who, however, was declared to be 'very low'.

When they were alone, the same evening, Madame Moreau said to her son that she would advise him to set up as an advocate at Troyes. As he was better known in his own part of the country than in any other, he might more easily find a good match there.

'Ah, that's too much!' exclaimed Frédéric.

He had scarcely grasped his good fortune in his hands when

people tried to take it from him. He announced his express
determination to live in Paris.

'To do what?'

'Nothing!'

Madame Moreau, astonished at his manner, asked what he
intended to become of him.

'A minister!' was Frédéric's reply.

And he declared that he was not at all joking, that he meant to
plunge at once into diplomacy, and that his studies and his instincts
impelled him in that direction. He would first enter the Council of
State under M. Dambreuse's patronage.

'So you know him?'

'Oh, yes! Through M. Roque!'

'That is odd,' said Madame Moreau.

He had awakened in her heart her old dreams of ambition. She
gave herself up to them, privately, and spoke no more about the
others.

If he had heeded his impatience, Frédéric would have started
that very instant. Next morning every seat in the coaches had been
engaged; and so he ate his heart out till the following day, at seven
o'clock in the evening.

They were sitting down to dinner when three pronged tolls of
the church bell fell on their ears; and the housemaid, coming in,
informed them that Madame Éléonore had just died.

This death, after all, was not a misfortune for anyone, not even
for her child. The young girl would be all the better for it later.

As the two houses were close to one another, a great coming and
going and a clatter of voices could be heard; and the idea of this
corpse being so near them threw a certain funereal gloom over
their parting. Madame Moreau wiped her eyes two or three times.
Frédéric felt his heart oppressed.

When the meal was over, Catherine stopped him in the passage.
Mademoiselle must, absolutely must, see him. She was waiting for
him in the garden. He went out, strode over the hedge, and
bumping into the trees from time to time, directed his steps
towards M. Roque's house. Lights were glittering through a
window on the second floor; then a form appeared in the
darkness, and a voice whispered:

'It's me.'

She seemed to him taller than usual, owing to her black dress, no doubt. Not knowing what to say to her, he contented himself with taking her hands, and sighing:

'Ah! Poor Louise!'

She did not reply. She gazed at him for a long time with a look of deep earnestness. Frédéric was afraid of missing the coach; he fancied that he could hear the rolling of wheels some distance away, and, in order to put an end to things:

'Catherine told me that you had something . . . '

'Yes, that's right! I wanted to tell you . . . '

He was astonished to find that she addressed him as '*vous*'; and, as she had again relapsed into silence:

'Well, what?'

'I don't know. I've forgotten! Is it true you're going away?'

'Yes, I'm starting just now.'

She repeated:

'Ah! Just now? . . . For good? . . . We'll never see one another again?'

She was choking with sobs.

'Goodbye! Goodbye! Embrace me then!'

And she clasped him passionately in her arms.

SENTIMENTAL
EDUCATION

PART TWO

CHAPTER ONE

When he had taken his place in the back of the coupé, and the vehicle lurched into motion as the five horses started into a brisk trot all at the same time, he felt swept away on a wave of elation. Like an architect drawing up the plan of a palace, he mapped out his life in advance. He filled it with things dainty and splendid; it rose up to the sky; a huge array of objects appeared in it; and so deeply was he buried in the contemplation of these things that external reality disappeared.

At the foot of the hill of Sourdun, he noticed where they were. They had travelled only about five kilometres at the most! He was indignant. He pulled down the coach window in order to get a view of the road. He asked the driver several times at what hour, exactly, they would reach their destination. However, he eventually regained his composure, and remained seated in his corner, with eyes wide open.

The lantern, which hung from the postilion's seat, threw its light on the rumps of the shaft-horses. Beyond, he saw only the manes of the other horses undulating like white billows; their breaths caused a kind of fog to gather at each side of the team; the little metal chains of the harness rang, the windows shook in their frames; and the heavy coach went rolling at an even pace over the pavement. Here and there could be distinguished the wall of a barn, or else an inn standing by itself. Sometimes, as they passed through a village, a baker's oven threw out a fiery light, and the monstrous silhouettes of the horses ran along the walls of the house opposite. At every posting station, when the horses had been unhitched, there was a great silence for a minute. Overhead, under the awning, someone would be tramping about, while a woman standing in a doorway screened her candle with her hand. Then the conductor would jump on the footboard, and the vehicle would start on its way again.

At Mormans, the striking of the clocks announced that it was a quarter past one.

'So,' he thought, 'it's today, this very day, soon!'

But gradually his hopes and his recollections, Nogent, the Rue de Choiseul, Madame Arnoux, his mother, all became confused.

He was awakened by the dull sound of wheels passing over wooden boards: they were crossing the Pont de Charenton, it was Paris. Then his two travelling companions, the first taking off his cap, and the second his silk scarf, put on their hats, and began to chat. The first, a big, red-faced man in a velvet frock-coat, was a merchant; the second was coming to the capital to consult a physician – and, fearing that be had disturbed this gentleman during the night, Frédéric spontaneously apologised to him, so much had the young man's heart been softened by the feelings of happiness that possessed it.

The quayside terminus being flooded, no doubt, they went on, straight ahead, and once more they could see green fields. In the distance, tall factory chimneys were smoking. Then they turned into Ivry. They drove up a street; all at once, he saw the dome of the Panthéon.

The plain, quite broken up, seemed a waste of ruins. The enclosing wall of the fortifications made a horizontal swelling in it; and, on the unpaved paths at the side of the road, little branchless trees were protected by battens bristling with nails. Establishments for chemical products and timber-merchants' yards made their appearance alternately. High gates, like those seen in farmhouses, afforded glimpses, through their half-open leaves, of wretched yards within, full of filth, with puddles of dirty water in the middle of them. Long wine-shops, painted dark blood red, displayed on their first floor, between the windows, two billiard cues crossing one another in a wreath of painted flowers; here and there a half-built plaster hut had been abandoned. Then the double row of houses continued uninterrupted; and over their naked façades enormous tin cigars stood out at intervals, indicating tobacconists' shops. Midwives' signboards showed a matron in a cap, rocking a baby in a lace-trimmed quilt. The corners of the walls were covered with placards, which, three-quarters torn, were quivering in the wind like rags. Workmen in overalls passed by, brewers' drays, laundresses' vans and butchers' carts; a thin rain was falling, it was cold, the sky was pale, but two eyes, which to him were as precious as the sun, were shining behind the haze.

They had to wait a long time at the barrier, which was obstructed by egg-vendors, wagoners, and a flock of sheep. The sentry, with his greatcoat thrown back, walked to and fro in front of his box, to keep himself warm. The clerk who collected the city-dues clambered up to the roof of the coach, and there was a loud blast on a cornet. They went down the boulevard at a quick trot, the whipple trees clapping and the traces flying. The lash of the long whip went cracking through the moist air. The driver uttered his sonorous cry: 'Look alive! Look alive! Oho!' and the crossing-sweepers stood aside, the pedestrians sprang back, the mud spurted up against the coach windows, they passed tip-carts, cabs, and omnibuses. At length, the iron gate of the Jardin des Plantes came into view.

The Seine, which was yellowish, almost reached the deck of the bridges. A cool breath of air issued from it. Frédéric inhaled it with all his might, savouring this fine Paris air, which seems to contain exhalations of love and emanations of the intellect; he was touched with emotion at the sight of the first hackney cab. His heart went out even to the thresholds of the wine merchants' shops garnished with straw, to the shoe-blacks with their boxes, to the grocers' lads as they shook their coffee-roasters. Women trotted along with umbrellas over their heads; he bent forward to try to distinguish their faces; chance might have led Madame Arnoux to come out.

The shops sped by, the crowd grew denser, the noise grew louder. After the Quai Saint-Bernard, the Quai de la Tournelle, and the Quai Montebello, they drove along the Quai Napoléon; he tried to see his windows, but they were too far away. Then they once more crossed the Seine over the Pont-Neuf, and descended as far as the Louvre; and, having traversed the Rues Saint-Honoré, Croix-des-Petits-Champs, and du Bouloi, they reached the Rue Coq-Héron, and entered the courtyard of the hotel.

In order to prolong his pleasure, Frédéric dressed himself as slowly as possible, and even went on foot to the Boulevard Montmartre; he smiled at the thought of presently beholding once more the cherished name on the marble plate – he raised his eyes. No more shop windows, no more pictures, nothing!

He hastened to the Rue de Choiseul. M. and Madame Arnoux no longer lived there, and a woman next door was keeping an eye on the porter's lodge; Frédéric waited to see the porter himself; at last he made his appearance, it was no longer the same man. He did not know their address.

Frédéric went into a café, and, over lunch, consulted the Commercial Almanack. There were three hundred Arnoux in it, but no Jacques Arnoux! Where, then, were they living? Pellerin ought to know.

He made his way to the very top of the Faubourg Poissonnière, to the artist's studio. As the door had neither a bell nor a knocker, he rapped loudly on it with his fist, and then called out, shouted. But silence was the sole response.

After this he thought of Hussonnet. But where could such a man be found? On one occasion he had accompanied Hussonnet to his mistress's house in the Rue de Fleurus. Frédéric had just reached the Rue de Fleurus when he realised that he did not know the lady's name.

He had recourse to the Prefecture of Police. He wandered from staircase to staircase, from office to office. The information desk was closing. He was told to come back again the next day.

Then he called at all the picture-dealers' shops that he could discover, to see if anyone knew Arnoux. M. Arnoux was no longer in business.

At last, discouraged, weary, sickened, he returned to his hotel, and went to bed. Just as he was stretching himself between the sheets, an idea made him leap up with delight:

'Regimbart! What an idiot I was not to think of him!'

Next morning, at seven o'clock, he arrived in the Rue Notre-Dame-des-Victoires, in front of a dram-shop, where Regimbart was in the habit of drinking white wine. It was not yet open; he walked about the neighbourhood, and at the end of about half an hour, presented himself at the place once more. Regimbart had just left. Frédéric rushed out into the street. He fancied that he could even see Regimbart's hat some distance away; a hearse and some mourning coaches intercepted his progress. When they had got out of the way, the vision had disappeared.

Fortunately, he recalled to mind that the Citizen breakfasted every day at eleven o'clock sharp, at a little restaurant in the Place Gaillon. All he had to was to wait patiently till then; and, after sauntering about interminably from the Bourse to the Madeleine, and from the Madeleine to the Gymnase, Frédéric, just as the clocks were striking eleven, entered the restaurant in the Place Gaillon, certain of finding his quarry there.

'Don't know him!' said the restaurant-keeper, in an uncere-monious tone.

Frédéric persisted; the man replied:

'I have no longer any acquaintance with him, Monsieur!' And, as he spoke, he raised his eyebrows majestically and shook his head in a way which suggested some mystery.

But, in their last encounter, the Citizen had referred to the Alexandre tavern. Frédéric swallowed a brioche, jumped into a cab, and asked the driver whether there happened to be anywhere on the heights of Sainte-Geneviève a certain Café Alexandre. The cabman drove him to the Rue des Francs-Bourgeois-Saint-Michel, where there was an establishment of that name, and in answer to his question: 'M. Regimbart, if you please?' the keeper of the café said with an unusually gracious smile:

'We have not seen him as yet, Monsieur,' while he directed towards his wife, who sat behind the counter, a meaningful look.

And the next moment, turning towards the clock:

'But he'll be here, I hope, in ten minutes, or at most a quarter of an hour. Célestin, hurry with the newspapers! What would Monsieur like to take?'

Though he did not want to take anything, Frédéric swallowed a glass of rum, then a glass of kirsch, then a glass of curaçao, then different kinds of grog, both cold and hot. He read through the whole of that day's *Siècle*, and then read it again; he examined the caricature in the *Charivari* down to the very tissue of the paper; when he had finished, he knew the advertisements by heart. From time to time, the tramp of boots on the footpath outside reached his ears, it was he! And someone's form would trace its outlines on the windowpanes; but it invariably passed on!

To relieve his boredom, Frédéric shifted his seat; he moved to the back of the room, then to the right, after that to the left; and he remained in the middle of the bench with both arms outstretched. But a cat, stepping daintily along the velvet at the back of the seat, startled him by giving a sudden spring, in order to lick up the spots of syrup on the tray; and the child of the house, an insufferable brat of four, was playing noisily with a rattle on the bar steps. His mother, a wan-faced little woman, with decayed teeth, was smiling in a stupid sort of way. What in the world could Regimbart be doing? Frédéric waited for him in an agony of distress.

The rain clattered like hail on the covering of the cab. Through the opening in the muslin curtains he could see the poor horse in the street, more motionless than a horse made of wood. The gutter, swollen to enormous size, ran between two spokes of the wheels, and the coachman was nodding drowsily, sheltering under the apron; but fearing lest his fare might give him the slip, he opened the door every now and then, streaming with water, like a river – and, if things could get worn out by looking at them, the clock ought by now to have dissolved, so frequently did Frédéric set his eyes on it. However, it kept going. 'Mine host' Alexandre walked up and down repeating, 'He'll come! Cheer up! He'll come!' And, in order to divert his thoughts, chatted to him, talked politics. He even carried civility so far as to propose a game of dominoes.

At length, when it was half-past four, Frédéric, who had been there since midday, sprang to his feet, and declared that he would not wait any longer.

'I can't understand it at all myself,' replied the cafe-keeper, with an air of sincerity. 'This is the first time that M. Ledoux has failed to come!'

'What! Monsieur Ledoux?'

'Why, yes, Monsieur!'

'I said Regimbart!' cried Frédéric, exasperated.

'Ah! A thousand pardons! You're mistaken! Madame Alexandre, did not Monsieur say M. Ledoux?'

And, addressing the waiter:

'You heard him yourself, just as I did?'

No doubt to pay his master off for old scores, the waiter simply smiled.

Frédéric drove back to the boulevards, indignant at having wasted his time, raging against the Citizen, but craving his presence as if he were a god, and firmly resolved to extract him from the depths of the most remote cellars. His cab irritated him, and he got rid of it; his ideas were in a state of confusion; then all the names of cafés which he had heard pronounced by that idiot shot at once from his memory like the thousand pieces of a firework display: the Café Gascard, the Café Grimbert, the Café Halbout, the Bordelais tavern, the Havanais, the Havrais, the Bœuf-à-la-Mode, the Brasserie Allemande, and the Mère Morel; and he made his way to all of them in succession. But in one, Regimbart had just left; in another, he might perhaps call in later; in a third, they had not seen him for six months; elsewhere, he had the day before ordered a leg of mutton for Saturday. Finally, at Vautier's wine shop, Frédéric, opening the door, bumped into the waiter.

'Do you know M. Regimbart?'

'What, monsieur! Do I know him? I'm the one who has the honour of serving him. He's upstairs; he's just finishing his dinner!'

And, with a napkin under his arm, the master of the establishment himself accosted him:

'You're asking for M. Regimbart, Monsieur? He was here a moment ago.'

Frédéric gave vent to an oath, but the proprietor affirmed that he would find the gentleman for sure at Bouttevilain's.

'I assure you, on my honour, he left a little earlier than usual, for he has a business appointment with some gentlemen. But you'll find him, I tell you again, at Bouttevilain's, in the Rue Saint-Martin, No. 92, second row of steps on the left, at the far end of the courtyard, first floor, door on the right!'

At last, he saw Regimbart, in a cloud of tobacco smoke, by himself, at the lower end of the back room, after the billiard-table, with a glass of beer in front of him, and his chin lowered in a thoughtful attitude.

'Ah! I've been looking for you a long time!'

Quite unmoved, Regimbart extended towards him only two fingers, and, as if he had seen Frédéric the day before, he uttered a number of trivial remarks about the opening of the session.

Frédéric interrupted him, saying in the most natural tone he could assume:

'Is Arnoux well?'

The reply was a long time coming, as Regimbart was gargling with the liquor in his throat:

'Yes, not bad!'

'Where is he living now?'

'Why . . . in the Rue Paradis-Poissonnière,' the Citizen returned with astonishment.

'What number?'

'Thirty-seven – confound it! What a funny fellow you are!'
Frédéric rose.

'What! Are you going?'

'Yes, yes! I have to make a call – a business matter I'd forgotten! Goodbye!'

Frédéric went from the tavern to the Arnoux's residence, as if carried along by a warm wind and with a sensation of extreme ease such as people experience in dreams.

He found himself soon on the second floor of a building in front of a door, with the bell ringing; a servant appeared; a second door was opened; Madame Arnoux was seated near the fire. Arnoux jumped up and embraced him. She had on her lap a little boy of about three; her daughter, now as tall as herself, was standing up at the opposite side of the mantelpiece.

'Allow me to present this gentleman to you,' said Arnoux, taking hold of his son under the armpits.

And he amused himself for some minutes in making the child fly up into the air very high, and then catching him with both hands as he came down.

'You'll kill him! Ah, good heavens, do stop!' exclaimed Madame Arnoux.

But Arnoux, declaring that there was not the slightest danger, continued, and even addressed him in words of endearment such as nurses use in the Marseillaise dialect, his native tongue: 'Ah, my little old boy, what a good bubba!' Then, he asked Frédéric why he had been so long without writing to them, what he had found to do in the country, and what brought him back.

'Me, my friend, I at the moment am a dealer in porcelain. But let's talk about you!'

Frédéric gave as reasons for his absence a protracted lawsuit and the state of his mother's health; he laid special emphasis on the latter in order to make himself interesting. He ended by saying that this time he was going to settle in Paris for good; he said nothing about the inheritance – lest it might be prejudicial to his past.

The curtains, like the upholstering of the furniture, were of brown damask wool; two pillows were close beside one another on the bolster; on the coal fire a kettle was heating; and the shade of the lamp, which stood near the edge of the chest of drawers, darkened the apartment. Madame Arnoux wore a dark blue merino dressing-gown. With her face turned towards the ashes in the hearth and one hand on the shoulder of the little boy, she unfastened with the other the laces of the child's bodice; the youngster in his shirt was crying and scratching his head, like the son of M. Alexandre.

Frédéric had expected spasms of joy – but the passions grow pale when we change their settings, and, as he no longer saw Madame Arnoux in the environment in which he had known her, she seemed to him to have lost something, to have degenerated in some way that he could not comprehend, in fact, not to be the same. He was astonished at the serenity of his heart. He made enquiries about their old friends, about Pellerin, amongst others.

'I don't see him often,' said Arnoux.

She added:

'We no longer entertain as we used to!'

Was this to let him know that he would get no invitation from them? But Arnoux, continuing to exhibit the same cordiality, reproached him for not having come to dine with them uninvited; and he explained why he had changed his business.

'What are you to do in an age of decadence like ours? Great painting has gone out of fashion! Besides, you can put art into anything. You know me, I love Beauty! I must take you to my factory one of these days.'

And he insisted on showing Frédéric immediately some of his productions in his store on the first floor

Dishes, soup-tureens, plates, and wash handbasins encumbered the floor. Against the walls were laid out large squares of tiles for bathrooms and dressing-rooms, with mythological subjects in the Renaissance style, whilst in the centre, a double display-case, rising up to the ceiling, supported ice-urns, flowerpots, candelabra, little flower-stands, and large polychrome statuettes, representing a negro or a Pompadour shepherdess. Frédéric, who was cold and hungry, was bored with Arnoux's displays of his wares.

He hurried off to the Café Anglais, ordered a sumptuous supper, and while eating, said to himself:

'What a fool I was, back at home, feeling wretched! She hardly recognised me! How middle class she is, how dull!'

And in a sudden expansion of healthfulness, he resolved to lead a life of egoism. He felt his heart as hard as the table on which his elbows rested. So now he could plunge fearlessly into the vortex of society. The thought of the Dambreuses came to him; he would make use of them; then he recalled Deslauriers. 'Ah well, too bad!' Nevertheless, he sent him a note by a messenger, making an appointment with him for the following day in the Palais-Royal, to have lunch together.

Fortune had not been so kind to Deslauriers.

He had presented himself for his postgraduate examination with a thesis *on the law of wills*, in which he maintained that the powers of testators ought to be restricted as much as possible – and, as his adversary provoked him in such a way as to make him say foolish things, he had said a great deal of them without the examiners turning a hair. Then chance had so willed it that he should choose by lot, as a subject for a lecture, Prescription. Thereupon, Deslauriers had emitted some deplorable theories; old claims should be treated as new; why should the proprietor be deprived of his estate because he could furnish his title deeds only after the lapse of thirty-one years? This was giving the security of the honest man to the inheritor of the enriched thief. Every injustice was consecrated by the extension of this law, which was a form of tyranny, the abuse of force! He had even exclaimed:

'Abolish it; and the Franks will no longer oppress the Gauls, the English oppress the Irish, the Yankee oppress the Redskins, the Turks oppress the Arabs, the whites oppress the blacks, Poland . . . '

The President had interrupted him:

'Well, that's enough, Monsieur! We are not concerned with your political opinions – you will submit yourself for re-examination at a later date!'

Deslauriers had chosen not to submit himself for re-examination. But this wretched Article XX of the Third Book of the Civil Code had become a monstrous stumbling-block for him. He was elaborating a great work on 'Prescription considered as the Basis of the Civil Law and of the Law of Nature amongst Peoples'; and he was lost in Dunod, Rogerius, Balbus, Merlin, Vazeille, Savigny, Troplong, and other weighty authorities on the subject. In order to have more leisure for this task, he had resigned his post of head clerk. He lived by giving private tuitions and preparing other peoples's theses; and at the meetings of newly-fledged barristers to rehearse legal arguments he frightened the conservatives by his virulence, all the young doctrinaires who acknowledged M. Guizot as their master – so that in a certain set he had gained a sort of celebrity, mingled, to some degree, with a lack of confidence in him as an individual.

He came to keep the appointment in a great overcoat lined with red flannel, like the one Sénécal used to wear in former days.

Out of deference to the passers-by they refrained from a long embrace, and they made their way to Véfour's arm-in-arm, laughing with delight, though with teardrops lingering in the depths of their eyes. Then, as soon as they were alone, Deslauriers exclaimed:

'Ah! Damn it! We'll have a jolly good time of it now!'

Frédéric was not pleased to find Deslauriers all at once associating himself in this way with his good fortune. His friend exhibited too much pleasure on account of them both, and not enough on his account alone.

After this, Deslauriers gave details about the reverse he had met with, and gradually told Frédéric all about his occupations and his daily existence, speaking of himself in a stoical fashion, and of others in tones of intense bitterness. He found fault with everything. There was not a man in office who was not an idiot or a rascal. He flew into a passion against the waiter for having a glass badly rinsed and, when Frédéric uttered a mild reproach:

'As if I were going to worry about fellows like that who go and earn as much as six and even eight thousand francs a year, who are electors, perhaps eligible as candidates! Ah, no! No!'

Then, with a playful air:

'But I'm forgetting that I'm talking to a capitalist, to a Mondor, for you are a Mondor now!'

And, coming back to the question of inheritance, he gave expression to this view: that collateral successorship (a thing unjust in itself, though in the present case he was glad it was possible) would be abolished one of these days, at the next revolution.

'You think so?' said Frédéric.

'Be sure of it!' he replied. 'This sort of thing can't go on! There's too much suffering! When I see people like Sénécal living in poverty . . .'

'Always Sénécal!' thought Frédéric.

'Anyway, what's the news? Are you still in love with Madame Arnoux? That's over – eh?'

Frédéric, not knowing what answer to give, closed his eyes and lowered his head.

With regard to Arnoux, Deslauriers told him that his journal was now the property of Hussonnet, who had transformed it. It was called '*L'Art*, a literary institute, a company with shares of one hundred francs each; capital of the firm: forty thousand francs', each shareholder having the right to put into it his own contributions; for 'the company has for its object to publish the works of beginners, to spare talent, perchance genius, the painful crises which overwhelm, etc . . . , You see the line!' There was, however, something to be done, and that was to raise the tone of the said journal then, suddenly, while retaining the same writers, and promising a continuation of the feuilleton, to supply the subscribers with a political journal; the amount to be advanced would not be very great.

'What do you think, hey? Would you like to have a hand in it?'

Frédéric did not reject the proposal. But he had to wait for his affairs to be settled.

'So, if you require anything . . . '

'No thanks, my boy!' said Deslauriers.

Then, they smoked puros, leaning with their elbows on the plush-covered sill, by the window. The sun was shining, the air was balmy, flocks of birds, fluttering about, swooped down into the garden; the statues of bronze and marble, washed by the rain, were glistening; maids wearing aprons were seated on chairs, chatting together; and the laughter of children could be heard mingling with the continuous plash that came from the playing fountain.

Frédéric had been troubled by Deslauriers' bitterness; but under the influence of the wine which circulated through his veins, half-asleep, in a state of torpor, with the light full on his face, he was no longer conscious of anything save an immense wellbeing, sensual and stupid, like a plant saturated with heat and humidity. Deslauriers, with half-closed eyes, was staring vacantly into the distance. His breast swelled, and he began to speak:

'Ah! Those were the days, when Camille Desmoulins, standing over there on a table, drove the people on to the Bastille! Men really lived in those times, they could assert themselves, and prove their strength! Simple advocates commanded generals, kings were beaten by beggars, while now . . . '

He stopped, then added all of a sudden:

'Pooh! There are great things ahead!'

And, drumming a battle march on the windowpanes, he declaimed these lines by Barthélemy:

> 'That dread Assembly shall again appear,
> Which, after forty years, fills you with fear,
> Marching with giant stride and dauntless soul' –

I don't know how it goes on! But it's late, shall we go?'

And he went on expounding his theories in the street.

Frédéric, without listening to him, was looking at certain materials and articles of furniture in the shop-windows which would be suitable for his new residence; and it was, perhaps, the thought of Madame Arnoux that made him stop before a secondhand dealer's window, where three china plates were exposed to view. They were decorated with yellow arabesques with metallic reflections, and were worth a hundred crowns apiece. He got them put by.

'If I were in your shoes,' said Deslauriers, 'I would rather buy silver plate,' revealing by this love of display the man of humble origins.

As soon as he was alone, Frédéric took himself off to the establishment of the celebrated Pomadère, where he ordered three pairs of trousers, two coats, a fur cloak, and five waistcoats; then he called at a bootmaker's, a shirtmaker's, and a hatter's, giving them directions in each shop to make the greatest possible haste.

Three days later, on the evening of his return from Le Havre, he found his complete wardrobe awaiting him at home; and impatient to make use of it, he resolved to pay an immediate visit to the Dambreuses. But it was too early yet, scarcely eight o'clock.

'Suppose I went to see the others?' he said to himself.

Arnoux, all alone, was shaving in front of his glass. The latter proposed to take him to a place where he could enjoy himself, and when M. Dambreuse was referred to:

'Ah, that's just lucky! You'll see some of his friends there; come on, then! It'll be good fun!'

Frédéric asked to be excused. Madame Arnoux recognised his voice, and wished him good day, through the partition, for her daughter was indisposed, and she was also rather unwell herself; and the noise of a spoon against a glass could be heard, and all those gentle rustling sounds made by things being lightly moved about, which are usual in a sickroom. Then Arnoux disappeared to say goodbye to his wife. He brought forward a heap of reasons for going out:

'You know very well that it's important! I must go, I've got business, they'll be expecting me.'

'Go, go, my dear! Enjoy yourself!'

Arnoux hailed a hackney cab:

'Palais-Royal, No. 7, Galerie Montpensier.'

And, as he let himself sink back in the cushions:

'Ah! How tired I am, my dear fellow! It will be the death of me! However, I can tell it to you – to you.'

He bent towards Frédéric's ear in a mysterious fashion:

'I'm trying to rediscover the copper-red of the Chinese!'

And he explained the nature of the glaze and the slow fire.

On their arrival at Chevet's, a large hamper was brought to him, which he stowed away in the cab. Then he chose for his 'poor wife' grapes, pineapples and various dainties, and directed that they should be sent early next morning.

After this, they called at a costumier's establishment; it was to a ball they were going. Arnoux selected blue velvet breeches, a vest of the same material, and a red wig; Frédéric a mask; and they went down the Rue de Laval towards a house the second floor of which was illuminated by coloured lanterns.

At the foot of the stairs they heard violins playing above.

'Where the devil are you taking me?' said Frédéric.

'To see a nice girl! Don't worry!'

The door was opened for them by a groom, and they entered the anteroom, where overcoats, cloaks and shawls were thrown together in a heap on some chairs. A young woman in a costume of a dragoon of Louis XV's reign was on her way through it at that moment. It was Mademoiselle Rose-Annette Bron, the mistress of the place.

'Well?' said Arnoux.

'It's done!' she replied.

'Ah! Thanks, my angel!'

And he wanted to kiss her.

'Take care, now, silly! You'll spoil the paint on my face!'

Arnoux introduced Frédéric.

'Put it there, Monsieur, and welcome!'

She drew aside a door-curtain behind her, and cried out with a certain emphasis:

'Here's my lord Arnoux, scullion, and a princely friend of his!'

Frédéric was at first dazzled by the lights; he could see nothing save silk and velvet, naked shoulders, a mass of colours swaying to and fro to the sounds of an orchestra hidden behind green foliage, between walls hung with yellow silk, with pastel portraits here and there and crystal torch-lights in the style of Louis XVI. Tall lamps, whose globes of roughened glass looked like snowballs, stood above baskets of flowers placed on tables in the corners – and opposite, after a second room, smaller in size, one could distinguish, in a third, a bed with twisted columns, and at its head a Venetian mirror.

The dancing stopped, and there were bursts of applause, a hubbub of delight, as Arnoux was seen advancing with his hamper on his head; the eatables contained in it made a lump in the centre.

'Mind the chandelier!' Frédéric raised his eyes: it was the old Dresden china chandelier that had adorned the shop of *L'Art Industriel*; the memory of former days passed into his mind; but a footsoldier of the line in undress, with that silly expression ascribed by tradition to conscripts, planted himself right in front of him, spreading out his two arms in order to signify astonishment; and, in spite of the hideous ultra-pointed black moustaches which disfigured his face, Frédéric recognised his old friend Hussonnet. In a half-Alsatian, half-negro kind of gibberish, the Bohemian loaded him with congratulations, calling him his colonel. Frédéric, put out of countenance by all these people, was at a loss for an answer. At a tap on the music-stand from a fiddlestick, the partners in the dance fell into their places.

They were about sixty in number, the women being for the most part dressed either as village-girls or as marchionesses, and the men, who were nearly all of mature age, being got up as wagoners, longshoremen, or sailors.

Frédéric, having taken up his position close to the wall, stared at the quadrille being performed in front of him.

An old beau, dressed like a Venetian Doge in a long gown of purple silk, was dancing with Mme Rosanette, who wore a green coat, knitted breeches, and boots of soft leather with gold spurs. The pair in front of them consisted of an Albanian laden with yataghans and a Swiss girl with blue eyes and skin white as milk, who looked as plump as a quail in shirtsleeves and red bodice. In order to turn to account her hair, which fell down to her knees, a tall blonde, who played walk-on parts at the Opéra, had dressed up as a female savage; and on top of her brown body-garment she wore nothing save a leather loincloth, glass bead bracelets, and a tinsel diadem, from which rose a tall sheaf of peacocks' feathers. In front of her, a gentleman representing Pritchard, muffled up in a grotesquely big black coat, was beating time with his elbow on his snuffbox. A little Watteau shepherd in blue and silver, like moon-light, dashed his crook against the thyrsus of a Bacchante crowned with grapes, who wore a leopard's skin over her left side, and buskins with gold ribbons. On the other side, a Polish lady, in a spencer of nacarat-coloured velvet, made her gauze petticoat flutter over her pearl-grey stockings, caught in pink boots bordered with white fur. She was smiling on a big-paunched man of about forty, disguised as a choirboy, who was skipping very high, lifting up his surplice with one hand, and with the other holding on his red clerical cap. But the queen, the star, was Mademoiselle Loulou, a celebrated dancer at public balls. As she had now become wealthy, she wore a wide lace collar over her jacket of smooth black velvet; and her wide trousers of puce-coloured silk, clinging closely to her buttocks, and drawn tight round her waist by a cashmere scarf, had all along their seams little natural white camellias. Her pale face, a little puffy, and with the nose turned up, looked all the more pert from the disordered appearance of her wig, over which was a man's grey felt hat, knocked in with a touch of her fist and clapped over her right ear; and, with every bound she made, her pumps, adorned with diamond buckles, nearly reached the nose of her neighbour, a great mediaeval Baron, weighed down by a suit of armour. There was also an Angel, with a gold sword in its hand, and two swan's wings over its back, who kept rushing up and down, continually losing her partner Louis XIV, who was completely at sea in the figures and confused the quadrille.

Frédéric, as he gazed at these people, experienced a sense of forlornness, a feeling of unease. He was still thinking of Madame Arnoux and it seemed to him as if he were taking part in some plot that was being hatched against her.

When the quadrille was over, Mme Rosanette accosted him. She was slightly out of breath, and her gorget, as shiny as a mirror, swelled up softly under her chin.

'And you, Monsieur,' said she, 'you're not dancing?'

Frédéric excused himself; he did not know how to dance.

'Really! But with me? Are you quite sure?'

And, poising herself on one hip, with her other knee a little drawn back, while she stroked with her left hand the mother-of-pearl pommel of her sword, she stared at him for a minute with a half-beseeching, half-mocking air. At last she said 'Good night!' made a pirouette, and disappeared.

Frédéric, dissatisfied with himself, and not well knowing what to do, began to wander about observing the ball.

He entered the boudoir padded with pale blue silk, with bouquets of wild flowers, whilst on the ceiling, in a circle of gilt wood, Cupids, emerging out of an azure sky, played about on clouds which looked like eiderdowns. This display of elegance, which would today seem paltry to the Rosanettes of this world, dazzled him; and he admired everything: the artificial convolvuli which adorned the surround of the mirror, the curtains on the mantelpiece, the Turkish divan, and a sort of tent in a recess in the wall, with pink silk hangings and a covering of white muslin. Furniture made of black wood with brass inlay filled the bedroom, where, on a platform covered with swansdown, stood the great canopied bedstead trimmed with ostrich feathers. Pins, with heads made of precious stones, stuck into pincushions, rings trailing over trays, lockets in gold frames and little silver chests could be distinguished in the shadow in the light shed by a Bohemian urn suspended from three slim chains. Through a little door, which was slightly ajar, could be seen a hothouse occupying the entire breadth of a terrace, with an aviary at the other end.

Here indeed were surroundings specially calculated to charm. In a sudden revolt of his youthful blood he swore that he would enjoy such things, and grew bold; then, coming back to the entrance to the drawing-room, where there was now a larger gathering (everything moved about in a kind of luminous shimmer), he stood to watch the quadrilles, blinking his eyes to see better – and inhaling the soft perfumes of the women, which floated through the atmosphere like one huge kiss.

But, close to him, on the other side of the door, was Pellerin –

Pellerin in full dress, his left arm over his breast and with his hat and a torn white glove in his right.

'Well, it's a long time since we saw you! Where the deuce have you been? Travelling in Italy? Boring, Italy, wouldn't you say? Not so wonderful as people say it is? Never mind! Bring me your sketches one of these days.'

And, without giving him time to answer, the artist began talking about himself.

He had made considerable progress, having definitely satisfied himself as to the stupidity of Line. One should not look for Beauty and Unity in a work of art so much as for character and diversity of subject.

'For everything exists in nature, so everything is legitimate, everything is plastic. All you have to do is catch the note, that's all. I've discovered the secret!' And giving him a nudge, he repeated several times: 'I've discovered the secret, you see! Just look at that little woman with the sphinx's headdress dancing with a Russian postilion; that's neat, crisp, fixed, all in planes and in crude tones: indigo under the eyes, a patch of vermilion on the cheek, sepia on the temples; pif! paf!' And with his thumb he dabbed imaginary brush strokes in the air. 'Whereas the big one over there,' he went on, pointing towards a Fishwife 'in the cherry gown with a gold cross hanging from her neck and a lawn kerchief tied behind her back – nothing but curves; the nostrils are spread out just like the wings of her bonnet, the corners of the mouth turn up, the chin hangs down, it's all fleshy, smooth, abundant, tranquil, and sunshiny, a true Rubens! Yet they're both perfect! Where, then, is the type?' He grew warm with the subject. 'What is a beautiful woman? What is beauty? Ah, beauty, you'll tell me . . . ' Frédéric interrupted him to enquire who was the pierrot with the profile of a he-goat, who was in the act of blessing all the dancers in the middle of a pastourelle.

'Oh, nothing, no one! A widower, father of three boys. He leaves them without breeches, spends his time at the club, and sleeps with the maid.'

'And who is that dressed as a bailiff, talking in the window-bay to the pompadour Marquise?'

'The Marquise is Mme Vandaël, formerly an actress at the Gymnase, the mistress of the Doge, the Comte de Palazot.

They've been together now for twenty years; no one knows why. What wonderful eyes she used to have, that woman! As for the citizen by her side, they call him Captain d'Herbigny, one of the old guard, with nothing in the world except his Cross of the Legion of Honour and his pension. He acts as uncle to the grisettes at festival times, arranges duels, and dines out.'

'A rascal?' said Frédéric.

'No, an honest man!'

'Ah!'

The artist pointed out others to him as well, when, perceiving a gentleman who, like Molière's physicians, wore a big black serge gown, but opening very wide as it descended in order to display all his trinkets:

'That character is Dr des Rogis, furious at not having made a name for himself; has written a book of medical pornography, is happy to clean people's boots in society, is very discreet; the ladies adore him. He and his wife (that lean châtelaine in the grey dress) trip about together in every public gathering, and others. In spite of their domestic embarrassments, they have a *day* – artistic teas, at which poems are recited – Look out!'

Indeed, the doctor came up to them at that moment; and soon they formed all three, at the entrance to the drawing-room, a group of talkers, which was presently augmented by Hussonnet, then by the lover of the Female Savage, a young poet who displayed, under a short Francis I cloak, the most pitiful of anatomies, and finally a sprightly youth disguised as a sideshow Turk. But his yellow-braided jacket had taken so many voyages on the backs of itinerant dentists, his wide pleated trousers were of so faded a red, his turban, rolled about like an eel in the Tartar fashion, was so poor in appearance, in short, his entire costume was so wretched and successful, that the women did not conceal their disgust. The doctor consoled him by pronouncing eulogies on his mistress, the Longshorewoman. This Turk was a banker's son.

Between two quadrilles, Rosanette advanced towards the mantel-piece, where an obese little old man, in a brown coat with gold buttons, had seated himself in an armchair. In spite of his withered cheeks, which fell over his high white cravat, his hair, still fair, and curling naturally like that of a poodle, gave him a certain frivolity of aspect.

She listened to him with her face bent close to his. Presently, she mixed him a glass of syrup; and nothing could be more dainty than her hands under their laced sleeves, which showed beyond the cuffs of the green coat. When the old man had swallowed it, he kissed them.

'Why, that's M. Oudry, a neighbour of Arnoux's!'

'Former neighbour!' said Pellerin, laughing.

'What!'

A Longjumeau postilion caught her by the waist; a waltz was beginning. Then all the women, seated round the drawing-room on benches, quickly rose to their feet, one by one; and their skirts, their scarves and their head-dresses began to turn.

They turned so close to him that Frédéric could see the beads of perspiration on their foreheads – and this spinning movement, more and more fast and regular, dizzying, communicated to his mind a sort of intoxication, which made other images surge up within it, while all these women passed in the one dazzling impression, and each of them aroused him differently, according to her style of beauty. The Polish lady, surrendering herself in a languorous fashion, inspired him with a longing to clasp her to his heart while they sped forward together in a sleigh along a snow-covered plain. Horizons of a tranquil sensuality, in a chalet beside a lake, opened out under the footsteps of the Swiss girl, who was waltzing with her torso straight and her eyes lowered. Then, suddenly, the Bacchante, bending back her head with its dark locks, made him dream of devouring caresses in woods of oleanders, in the midst of a storm, to the confused sound of the tambourines. The Fishwife, who was panting from the rapidity of the music, which was far too great for her, was shrieking with laughter; and he would have liked to drink with her in some tavern in the 'Porcherons', and rumple her kerchief with both hands, as in the good old times. But the Longshorewoman, whose light toes barely skimmed the floor, seemed to conceal in the suppleness of her limbs and the seriousness of her face all the refinements of modern love, which possesses the exactitude of a science and the mobility of a bird. Rosanette was whirling with one hand on her hip; her wig, with its tail bobbing over her collar, flung iris-powder around her; and, at every turn, she was near catching Frédéric with the tips of her gold spurs.

With the closing bar of the waltz, Mademoiselle Vatnaz made her appearance. She had an Algerian kerchief on her head, a quantity of piastres on her forehead, kohl lining her eyes, with a kind of coat of black cashmere falling over a light-coloured petticoat of silver lamé, and in her hand she held a basque drum.

Behind her walked a tall fellow in the classical costume of Dante, who happened to be – she no longer hid the fact – the ex-singer of the Alhambra – who, being Auguste Delamare by name, had first called himself Anténor Dellamarre, then Delmas, then Belmar and last Delmar, thus modifying and perfecting his name as his celebrity increased; for he had forsaken the public house concert for the theatre, and had even just made a resounding *début* at the Ambigu in *Gaspardo le Pêcheur*.

Hussonnet, on seeing him, scowled. Since his play had been rejected, he hated actors. It was impossible to conceive the vanity of these gentlemen, and this one in particular! 'What a poser! Just look at him!'

After a light bow towards Rosanette, Delmar had leaned back against the mantelpiece; and he remained motionless, with one hand over his heart, his left foot thrust forward, his eyes raised towards heaven, with his wreath of gilt laurels above his cowl, while he strove to put into the expression of his face a great deal of poetry, in order to fascinate the ladies. People came over to form a large circle around him.

But Vatnaz, having given Rosanette a prolonged embrace, came to beg of Hussonnet to revise, with a view to the improvement of the style, an educational work which she intended to publish, under the title of 'The Young Ladies' Garland', a collection of literary pieces and moral aphorisms. The man of letters promised to assist her. Then she asked him whether he could not in one of the journals to which he had access give her friend a slight puff, and even assign to him, later, some part in a play. Hussonnet forgot, as a result, to take a glass of punch.

It was Arnoux who had brewed the beverage; and, followed by the Comte's groom carrying an empty tray, he offered it round with a satisfied air.

When he came to pass in front of M. Oudry, Rosanette stopped him.

'Well, what about that matter?'

He coloured slightly; finally, addressing the old man:

'Our fair friend tells me that you would have the kindness . . . '

'But of course, neighbour! At your service!'

And M. Dambreuse's name was pronounced; as they were talking to one another in low tones, Frédéric could hear them only indistinctly; and he made his way to the other side of the mantel-piece, where Rosanette and Delmar were chatting together.

This performer had a vulgar countenance, made, like the scenery of the stage, to be viewed from a distance: coarse hands, big feet, and a heavy jaw; and he disparaged the most distinguished actors, spoke of poets with patronising contempt, talked of 'my organ', 'my physique', 'my powers', embellishing his conversation with words that were scarcely intelligible even to himself, and of which he was fond, such as '*morbidezza*', 'analogue', and 'homogeneity'.

Rosanette listened to him with little nods of approbation. One could see her admiration blossoming under the paint on her cheeks, and a touch of moisture passed like a veil over her bright eyes, of an indefinable colour. How could such a man as this fascinate her? Frédéric internally urged himself on to yet greater contempt for him, in order to banish, perhaps, the kind of envy he felt of him.

Mademoiselle Vatnaz was now with Arnoux; and while laughing from time to time very loudly, she cast glances towards Rosanette, of whom M. Oudry did not lose sight.

Then Arnoux and Vatnaz disappeared; the old man came and talked in a subdued voice to Rosanette.

'All right, yes, it's settled! Leave me alone.'

And she asked Frédéric to go and give a look into the kitchen to see whether Monsieur Arnoux happened to be there.

A battalion of glasses half-full covered the floor; and the sauce-pans, the pots, the turbot-kettle, and the frying pan were all in a state of commotion. Arnoux was giving directions to the servants, whom he addressed as 'tu', beating up the *rémoulade*, tasting the sauces, and larking with the housemaid.

'Right,' he said; 'tell her! I'm ready to serve.'

The dancing had ceased, the women had just sat down, the men were walking about. In the centre of the drawing-room, one of the curtains stretched over a window was swelling in the wind; and the Sphinx, in spite of the observations of everyone, exposed her sweating arms to the draught. Where could Rosanette be? Frédéric went on further to find her, even into her boudoir and her bedroom. Some, in order to be alone, or to be in pairs, had found refuge there. Whispers mingled with the shadows. There were little laughs stifled under handkerchiefs, and at the edge of women's bodices could be seen glimpses of fans quivering with movements slow and gentle, like the beating of a wounded bird's wings.

As he entered the hothouse, he saw under the large leaves of a caladium near the fountain, Delmar lying on his stomach on the canvas sofa; Rosanette, seated beside him, had her fingers entwined in his hair; and they were gazing into each other's faces. At the same moment, Arnoux came in at the opposite side, that which was near the aviary. Delmar sprang to his feet, then he sauntered out, without turning round; and even paused close to the door to gather a hibiscus flower, with which he adorned his buttonhole. Rosanette hung down her head; Frédéric, who saw her profile, noticed that she was in tears.

'I say! Whatever's the matter with you?' exclaimed Arnoux.

She shrugged her shoulders without replying.

'Is it because of him?' he went on.

She threw her arms round his neck, and kissing him on the forehead, slowly:

'You know very well that I'll always love you, my pet. Let's forget it! Let's go to supper!'

A brass chandelier with forty wax tapers lit up the dining-room, the walls of which were covered entirely with fine old earthen-ware that was hung up there; and this crude light, falling perpendicularly, rendered still whiter, amid the side-dishes and the fruits, a huge turbot which occupied the centre of the tablecloth, with plates all round filled with *bisque*. With a rustle of garments, the women, having arranged their skirts, their sleeves, and their stoles, took their seats beside one another; the men, standing up, posted themselves at the corners. Pellerin and M. Oudry were placed near Rosanette; Arnoux was facing her. Palazot and his female companion had just left.

'Enjoy your trip!' she said. 'To work!'

And the Choirboy, a facetious man, made a big sign of the cross, and said grace.

The ladies were scandalised, and especially the Fishwife, the mother of a young girl of whom she wished to make an honest woman. Neither did Arnoux like 'that sort of thing', as he considered that religion ought to be respected.

A German clock with a cockerel attached to it happening to chime out the hour of two, gave rise to a number of jokes about the cuckoo. All kinds of talk followed: puns, anecdotes, boasts, bets, lies taken for truth, improbable assertions, a tumult of words, which soon became dispersed in the form of conversations between particular individuals. The wines went round, the dishes succeeded each other, the doctor carved. An orange or a cork would every now and then be flung from a distance; people would quit their seats to go and talk to someone at another end of the table. Rosanette often turned round towards Delmar, who stood motionless behind her; Pellerin gossiped, M. Oudry smiled. Mademoiselle Vatnaz ate, almost alone, the dish of crayfish, and the shells crackled under her long teeth. The Angel, poised on the piano stool (the only place on which its wings allowed it to sit down) was placidly masticating without stopping.

'What an appetite!' the Choirboy kept repeating in amazement. 'What an appetite!'

And the Sphinx drank brandy, shouted at the top of her voice, and threw herself around like a demon. Suddenly her cheeks swelled, and no longer being able to keep down the blood which choked her, she pressed her napkin against her lips, then threw it under the table.

Frédéric had seen her.

'It's nothing!'

And to his entreaties that she should go home and look after herself, she replied slowly:

'Pooh! What's the good? May as well go this way as any other! Life's not that much fun!'

At that he shivered, a feeling of icy sadness taking possession of him, as if he had caught a glimpse of whole worlds of wretchedness and despair, a charcoal brazier beside a folding bed, and the corpses of the Morgue in leathern aprons, with the tap of cold water running over their hair.

Meanwhile, Hussonnet, squatted at the feet of the Female Savage, was braying in a hoarse voice in imitation of the actor Grassot:

'Be not cruel, O Celuta! This little family celebration is charming! Intoxicate me with delight, my loves! Let us be gay! Let us be gay!'

And he began kissing the women on the shoulders. They quivered under the tickling of his moustaches; then he conceived the idea of breaking a plate against his head by giving it a gentle tap. Others followed his example; bits of china flew about like slates in a high wind, and the Longshorewoman exclaimed:

'Break all you like! It costs nothing! Compliments of the house, from the fellow who makes them!'

Every eye was riveted on Arnoux. He replied:

'Ah! But invoiced, please!' Desiring, no doubt, to pass for not being, or for no longer being, Rosanette's lover.

But two angry voices made themselves heard:

'Idiot!'

'Rascal!'

'At your orders!'

'At yours!'

It was the medieval Knight and the Russian Postilion who were disputing; the latter having maintained that armour dispensed with the need for courage, while the other regarded this view as an insult. He desired to fight, all interposed to prevent him, and in the midst of the uproar the Captain tried to make himself heard.

'Listen to me, messieurs! One word! I have some experience, messieurs!'

Rosanette, tapping with her knife on a glass, succeeded eventually in restoring silence; and, addressing the Knight, who had kept his helmet on, and then the Postilion, whose head was covered with a hairy cap:

'You can start by taking off that saucepan of yours! It's making me hot! And you there, your wolf's head – Are you going to obey me, damn you? Pray show respect to my epaulets! I am your Maréchale!'

They complied, and everyone present applauded, exclaiming:

'Long live the Maréchale! Long live the Maréchale!'

Then she took a bottle of champagne off the stove, and poured out its contents from a great height into the outstretched glasses. As the table was too wide, the guests, especially the women, leaned over to her side, and stood erect on tiptoe on the slats of the chairs, so as to form, for the space of a minute, a pyramidal group of headdresses, naked shoulders, extended arms, and stooping bodies; and long jets of wine played over all that, for the Pierrot and Arnoux, at opposite corners of the room, each let fly the cork of a bottle, splashing everybody's faces. The little birds of the aviary, the door of which been left open, burst into the room, terrified, fluttering round the chandelier, knocking against the windowpanes and against the furniture; and some of them, alighting on the heads of the guests, looked like large flowers set in their hair.

The musicians had gone. The piano was pulled out of the antechamber into the drawing-room. Vatnaz seated herself before it, and, accompanied by the Choirboy, who thumped the Basque drum, she tore furiously into a quadrille, striking the keys like a horse pawing the ground, and swaying from the waist, the better to mark time. The Maréchale dragged out Frédéric, Hussonnet did cartwheels, the Longshorewoman dislocated her joints like a circus clown, the Pierrot pretended to be an orang-utan, the Female Savage, with outspread arms, imitated the swaying motion of a boat. At last, unable to go on, everybody stopped; and a window was flung open.

The broad daylight entered, with the cool breath of morning. There was an exclamation of astonishment, and then silence. The yellow flames flickered, making the sockets of the candlesticks crack from time to time; the floor was strewn with ribbons, flowers, and pearls; the side-tables were sticky with stains of punch and syrup; the hangings were soiled, clothes rumpled and dusty; the plaits of the women's hair hung loose over their shoulders; and make-up, trickling down with the sweat, revealed pallid faces and red, blinking eyelids.

The Maréchale, fresh as if she had come out of a bath, had rosy cheeks and sparkling eyes. She flung her wig far away; and her hair fell around her like a fleece, allowing none of her uniform to be seen except her breeches, which produced an effect both comical and pretty.

The Sphinx, whose teeth were chattering with fever, wanted a shawl.

Rosanette rushed up to her room to look for one, and, as the other came after her, she quickly shut the door in her face.

The Turk remarked, in a loud tone, that M. Oudry had not been seen leaving. Nobody took up this malicious observation, so worn out were they all.

Then, while waiting for their vehicles, they muffled themselves up in capes and cloaks. It struck seven. The Angel was still in the dining-room, seated at the table eating sardine and butter paste; and close beside her was the Fishwife, smoking cigarettes, and giving her advice about life.

At last, the cabs having arrived, the guests took their departure. Hussonnet, who had an engagement as correspondent for the provinces, had to read through fifty-three newspapers before lunch; the Female Savage had a rehearsal at the theatre, Pellerin had to see a model, and the Choirboy had three appointments. But the Angel, attacked by the preliminary symptoms of indigestion, was unable to rise. The mediaeval Baron carried her to the cab.

'Mind her wings!' cried the Longshorewoman through the window.

At the top of the stairs, Mademoiselle Vatnaz said to Rosanette:

'Goodbye, darling! That was a very nice evening party of yours.'

Then, bending close to her ear:

'Keep him!'

'Till better times come,' returned the Maréchale, slowly turning her back.

Arnoux and Frédéric returned together, just as they had come. The dealer in china looked so gloomy that his companion thought he was ill.

'I? Not at all!'

He was biting at his moustache, knitting his brows, and Frédéric asked him whether he was worried about his business affairs.

'By no means!'

Then all of a sudden:

'You know him, don't you, Père Oudry?'

And, with a spiteful look on his face:

'He's rich, the old scoundrel!'

After this, Arnoux spoke about an important piece of firing, which was to be finished that day at his works. He wanted to see it. The train left in an hour.

'Meantime, I must go and embrace my wife.'

'Ah! His wife!' thought Frédéric.

Then he went to bed, with his head aching terribly; and, to appease his thirst, he swallowed a whole carafe of water.

Another thirst had come to him, the thirst for women, for luxury, and all that life in Paris implies. He felt somewhat stunned, like a man leaving a ship; and in the visions that haunted his first sleep, he saw the shoulders of the Fishwife, the hips of the Longshorewoman, the calves of the Polish lady, and the headdress of the Female Savage flying past him and coming back again continually. Then, two large black eyes, which had not been at the ball, appeared before him; and, light as butterflies, burning as torches, they came and went, vibrated, ascended to the cornice and descended to his very mouth. Frédéric made desperate efforts to recognise those eyes, without success. But already the dream had taken hold of him; it seemed to him that he was yoked beside Arnoux to the pole of a hackney cab, and that the Maréchale, astride of him, was disembowelling him with her gold spurs.

Frédéric found a little town house at the corner of the Rue Rumfort, and he bought it along with the brougham, the horse, the furniture, and two flower-stands acquired from Arnoux, to be placed on each side of his drawing-room door. In the rear of this apartment were a bedroom and a closet. The idea occurred to his mind to put up Deslauriers there. But how could he receive her, *her*, his future mistress? The presence of a friend would be an obstacle. He knocked down the partition wall in order to enlarge the drawing-room, and converted the closet into a smoking-room.

He bought the works of the poets whom he loved, books of travel, atlases, and dictionaries, for he had innumerable plans of study; he hurried on the workmen, rushed about to the different shops, and in his impatience to enjoy, carried off everything without holding out for bargains.

From the tradesmen's bills, Frédéric ascertained that he would have to expend very soon some forty thousand francs, not including the succession duties, which would exceed thirty-seven thousand; as his fortune was in landed property, he wrote to the notary at Le Havre to sell a portion of it in order to pay off his debts, and to have some money at his disposal. Then, anxious to become acquainted at last with that vague entity, glittering and undefinable, which is known as 'society', he sent a note to the Dambreuses to know whether he might be at liberty to call upon them. Madame, in reply, said she would expect a visit from him the following day.

This happened to be their reception day. Carriages were standing in the courtyard. Two footmen rushed forward under the awning, and a third at the head of the stairs began walking in front of him.

He was conducted through an anteroom, a second room, and then a great drawing-room with high windows and a monumental fireplace which supported a timepiece in the form of a sphere, and two enormous porcelain vases, in each of which bristled, like two golden bushes, two clusters of sconces. Pictures in the manner of Ribera hung on the walls; the heavy tapestry door-curtains fell majestically; and the armchairs, the side-tables, the tables, the entire furniture, which was in the Empire style, had a certain imposing and diplomatic air. Frédéric smiled with pleasure in spite of himself.

At last he reached an oval apartment panelled in rosewood, stuffed with dainty furniture, and letting in the light through a single sheet of plate-glass, which looked out onto a garden. Madame Dambreuse was seated at the fireside, with a dozen persons gathered round her in a circle. With a polite greeting, she made a sign to him to take a seat, without, however, exhibiting any surprise at not having seen him for so long a time.

Just at the moment when he was entering the room, they had been praising the eloquence of the Abbé Cœur. Then they deplored the immorality of servants, a topic suggested by a theft which a footman had committed; and the gossip began. Old Madame de Sommery had a cold, Mademoiselle de Turvisot was to marry, the Montcharrons would not return before the end of January, neither would the Bretancourts, people now remained in the country very late; and the triviality of the conversation was, so to speak, intensified by the luxuriousness of the surroundings; but what they said was less stupid than their way of talking, which was aimless, disconnected, and utterly devoid of animation. And yet there were present men versed in life, an ex-minister, the curé of a great parish, two or three Government officials of high rank; they adhered to the most hackneyed commonplaces. Some of them resembled weary dowagers, others looked like horsedealers; and old men accompanied their wives, of whom they were old enough to be the grandfathers.

Madame Dambreuse received them all graciously. When it was mentioned that anyone was ill, she knitted her brows with a sorrowful expression on her face, and when balls or evening parties were discussed, assumed a joyous air. She would soon be compelled to deprive herself of these pleasures, for she was going to take out from her boarding-school a niece of her husband, an orphan. The guests extolled her devotedness; this was behaving like a true mother of a family.

Frédéric watched her attentively. The dull skin of her face looked as if it had been stretched, and had a bloom in which there was no brilliancy, like that of a preserved fruit. But her hair, which was in corkscrew curls, after the English fashion, was finer than silk, her eyes of a sparkling blue, and all her movements were dainty. Seated at the back of the room, on the small sofa, she stroked the red flock of a Japanese screen, no doubt in order to let her hands be seen to greater advantage, long narrow hands, a little thin, with fingers tilting up at the points. She wore a grey silk gown with a high-necked bodice, like a Puritan lady.

Frédéric asked her whether she intended to go to La Fortelle this year. Madame Dambreuse was unable to say. He quite understood: Nogent must bore her. More and more visitors arrived. There was an incessant rustling of robes on the carpet; ladies, seated on the edges of their chairs, gave vent to little snickering laughs, articulated two or three words, and at the end of five minutes left, along with their young daughters. It soon became impossible to follow the conversation, and Frédéric was leaving when Madame Dambreuse said to him:

'Every Wednesday, I hope, Monsieur Moreau?' making up for her previous display of indifference by these simple words.

He was satisfied. Nevertheless, he took a deep breath of fresh air when he got out into the street; and, feeling the need of a less artificial environment, Frédéric recalled to mind that he owed the Maréchale a visit.

The door of the anteroom was open. Two Havana lapdogs rushed forward. A voice exclaimed:

'Delphine! Delphine! Is that you, Felix?'

He stood here without advancing a step; the two little dogs kept yelping. At length Rosanette appeared, wrapped up in a sort of dressing-gown of white muslin trimmed with lace, and with her stockingless feet in Turkish slippers.

'Ah! Excuse me, Monsieur! I took you for the hairdresser. One minute! I'll be back!'

And he was left alone in the dining-room.

The Venetian blinds were closed. Frédéric was looking round, recalling the hubbub of the other night, when he noticed on the table, in the middle of the room, a man's hat, an old felt hat, bruised, greasy, disgusting. To whom then did this hat belong?

Impudently displaying its torn lining, it seemed to say: 'Why should I care, after all! I am the master!'

The Maréchale suddenly reappeared. She took up the hat, opened the conservatory, flung it in there, shut the door again (other doors flew open and closed again at the same moment), and, having brought Frédéric through the kitchen, she introduced him into her dressing-room.

It could at once be seen that this was the most frequented room in the house, and, so to speak, its true moral centre. The walls, the armchairs, and a huge springy divan were covered in chintz patterned with a great deal of foliage; on a white marble table stood two large wash handbasins, some distance apart, of fine blue earthenware; crystal shelves, forming a whatnot overhead, were laden with phials, brushes, combs, sticks of cosmetic, and powder-boxes; the fire was reflected in a tall cheval-glass; a cloth was hanging outside a bath, and the air was thick with the odours of almond-paste and of benzoin.

'You'll excuse the disorder! I'm dining out tonight.'

And as she turned on her heel, she was near crushing one of the little dogs. Frédéric declared that they were charming. She lifted up the pair of them, and raising their black snouts up to his face:

'Come! Give the nice gentleman a smile and a kiss.'

A man dressed in a dirty frock-coat with a fur collar entered abruptly.

'Felix, my dear man,' said she, 'that little business of yours will be settled next Sunday without fail.'

The man proceeded to dress her hair. He gave her news of her friends, Madame de Rochegune, Madame de Saint-Florentin, and Madame Lombard, every woman being noble, as if it were at the mansion of the Dambreuses. Then he talked theatres; an extra-ordinary performance was to be given that evening at the Ambigu.

'Shall you go?

'My word, no! I'm staying at home.'

Delphine appeared. Her mistress gave her a scolding for having gone out without permission. The other vowed that she was 'just returning from market'.

'Well, bring me your book! You don't mind, do you?'

And, reading the notebook in a low tone, Rosanette made remarks on every item. The sum was not correct.

'Hand me over four sous!'

Delphine handed them over, and, when she had sent the maid away:

'Ah! Holy Virgin! What a blight these creatures are!'

Frédéric was shocked at this complaint about servants. It recalled the others too vividly to his mind, and established between the two houses a kind of vexatious equality.

When Delphine came back again, she drew close to the Maréchale's side in order to whisper something in her ear.

'Ah, no! I don't want to!'

Delphine presented herself once more.

'Madame, she insists.'

'Ah, what a plague! Throw her out!'

At the same moment, an old lady, dressed in black, pushed forward the door. Frédéric heard nothing, saw nothing; Rosanette had rushed into the bedroom to meet her.

When she reappeared her cheeks were flushed, and she sat down in one of the armchairs without speaking. A tear fell down her face; then, turning towards the young man, gently:

'What is your Christian name?'

'Frédéric.'

'Ha! Federico! You don't mind if I call you that?'

And she gazed at him in a coaxing sort of way which was almost amoroûs. All of a sudden she uttered an exclamation of delight at the sight of Mademoiselle Vatnaz.

The lady artist had no time to lose before presiding at her *table d'hôte* at six o'clock sharp; and she was panting for breath, completely exhausted. She first took out of her shopping-bag a watch chain with a piece of paper, then various objects that she had bought.

'You should know that there are in the Rue Joubert splendid suede gloves at thirty-six sous! Your dyer wants another week. As for the lace, I told them we'd come back. Bugneaux has got the instalment you paid. That's all, I think. You owe me a hundred and eighty-five francs!'

Rosanette went to a drawer to get ten napoléons. Neither of the pair had any change; Frédéric offered some.

'I'll pay you back,' said Vatnaz, as she stuffed the fifteen francs into her handbag. 'But you are a naughty boy. I don't love you any

more, you didn't get me to dance with you even once the other
evening! Ah! My dear, I came across a case of stuffed humming-
birds which are perfect loves at a shop on the Quai Voltaire. If I
were in your place, I would make myself a present of them. Look
here! What do you think of this?'

And she exhibited an old remnant of pink silk which she had
purchased at the Temple to make a medieval doublet for Delmar.

'He came today, didn't he?'

'No!'

'That's strange!'

And, after a minute's silence:

'Where are you going this evening?'

'To Alphonsine's,' said Rosanette.

This was the third version given by her as to the way in which
she was going to pass the evening.

Mademoiselle Vatnaz went on:

'And what news about the old man of the mountain?'

But, with a sharp look, the Maréchale bade her hold her tongue;
and she accompanied Frédéric out as far as the anteroom to
ascertain from him whether he would soon see Arnoux.

'Do please ask him to come; not in front of his wife, of course!'

At the top of the stairs an umbrella was placed against the wall
near a pair of clogs.

'Vatnaz's galoshes,' said Rosanette. 'What a foot, eh? My little
friend is rather strongly built.'

And, in a melodramatic tone, making the final letter of the word
roll:

'Don't trust herrrr!'

Frédéric, emboldened by this confidential-seeming remark,
tried to kiss her on the neck. She said, coldly:

'Oh, do it! It costs nothing!'

He felt rather light-hearted as he left her, having no doubt that
the Maréchale would be his mistress before long. This desire
awakened another in him; and, in spite of the kind of grudge that
he bore her, he had a desire to see Madame Arnoux.

Besides, he would have to call at her house in order to execute
the commission with which he had been entrusted by Rosanette.

'But now,' thought he (it was just striking six), 'Arnoux is
probably at home.'

He put off his visit till the following day.

She was seated in the same attitude as on the first day, and was sewing a child's shirt. The little boy, at her feet, was playing with a wooden menagerie; Marthe, a short distance away, was writing.

He began by complimenting her on her children. She replied without any exaggeration of maternal silliness.

The room had a tranquil aspect. A glow of sunshine stole in through the windowpanes, lighting up the angles of the different articles of furniture, and, as Madame Arnoux sat close beside the window, a large ray, falling on the curls over the nape of her neck, penetrated with liquid gold her skin, which assumed the colour of amber. Then he said:

'This young lady here has grown very tall during the past three years! Do you remember, Mademoiselle, when you slept on my lap in the carriage?' Marthe did not remember. 'One evening, returning from Saint-Cloud?'

There was a look of peculiar sadness on Madame Arnoux's face. Was it in order to prevent any allusion on his part to the memories they possessed in common?

Her beautiful black eyes, with their shining sclerotic coat, moved gently under their somewhat drooping lids, and her pupils revealed in their depths an immense kindness of heart. He was seized with a love stronger than ever, a passion that knew no bounds; it enervated him to contemplate her; however, he shook off this feeling. How was he to make the most of himself? By what means? And, having turned the matter over thoroughly in his mind, Frédéric could think of none that seemed more effectual than money. He began talking about the weather, which was less cold than it had been at Le Havre.

'You have been there?'

'Yes, about a matter . . . to do with the family . . . an inheritance.'

'Ah! I'm very glad,' she said, with an air of such genuine pleasure that he felt as touched as if she had rendered him a great service.

Then she asked him what he intended to do, as it was necessary for a man to occupy himself with something. He remembered his lie, and said that he hoped to reach the Council of State with the help of M. Dambreuse, the deputy.

'You are acquainted with him, perhaps?'

'Merely by name.'

Then, in a low tone:

'*He* took you to the ball the other night, did he not?'

Frédéric remained silent.

'That was what I wanted to know; thank you.'

After that she put two or three discreet questions to him about his family and the part of the country in which he lived. It was very kind of him not to have forgotten them after having lived so long away from Paris.

'But . . . could I?' he rejoined. 'Had you any doubt about it?'

Madame Arnoux arose.

'I believe that you entertain towards us a true and solid affection. Goodbye . . . au revoir!'

And she extended her hand towards him in a sincere and virile fashion. Was this not an engagement, a promise? Frédéric felt a sense of delight at merely living; he had to restrain himself to keep from singing, he wanted to burst out, to do generous deeds, and to give alms. He looked around him to see if there were anyone near who needed help. No poverty-stricken wretch happened to be passing by; and his desire for self-devotion evaporated, for he was not a man to go out of his way to find opportunities for benevolence.

Then he remembered his friends. The first of whom he thought was Hussonnet, the second, Pellerin. The lowly position of Dussardier naturally called for consideration; as for Cisy, he was glad to let that young aristocrat get a slight glimpse as to the extent of his fortune. He wrote accordingly to all four to come to a housewarming the following Sunday at eleven o'clock sharp, and he told Deslauriers to bring Sénécal.

The tutor had been dismissed from his third boarding-school for not having given his consent to the distribution of prizes, a custom which he looked upon as dangerous to equality. He was now with an engine-builder, and for the past six months had been no longer living with Deslauriers.

There had been nothing painful about their parting. Latterly, Sénécal had received visits from men in overalls, all patriots, all workmen, all honest fellows, but at the same time men whose society seemed distasteful to the advocate. Besides, he disliked certain ideas of his friend, excellent though they might be as weapons of warfare. He held his tongue on the subject through motives of ambition, deeming it prudent to pay deference to him in order to exercise control over him, for he looked forward impatiently to a great revolution, in which he calculated on making an opening for himself and occupying a prominent position.

Sénécal's convictions were more disinterested. Every evening, when his work was finished, he returned to his garret and sought in books for something that might justify his dreams. He had annotated the *Contrat Social*. He crammed himself with the *Revue Indépendante*. He was acquainted with Mably, Morelly, Fourier, Saint-Simon, Comte, Cabet, Louis Blanc, the heavy cartload of Socialistic writers, those who demand for humanity the equality of the military barracks, those who would like to amuse it in a brothel or bend it over a counter; and from a medley of all these things he had constructed an ideal of virtuous democracy, with the dual aspect of a farm in which the landlord was to receive a share of the produce, and a spinning-mill, a sort of American Sparta, in which the individual would only exist for the benefit of society, which was to be more omnipotent, absolute, infallible, and divine than the Grand Lamas and the Nebuchadnezzars. He had no doubt as to the approaching realisation of this ideal; and Sénécal raged against everything that he considered hostile to it with the reasoning of a geometrician and the zeal of an Inquisitor. Titles of nobility, crosses, crests, liveries above all, and even reputations that were too loud-sounding scandalised him — his studies as well as his sufferings intensifying every day his essential hatred of every kind of distinction and every form of superiority.

'What do I owe to this gentleman that I should be polite to him? If he wanted me, he could come to me!'

Deslauriers dragged him along.

They found their friend in his bedroom. Blinds and double curtains, a Venetian mirror, nothing was lacking; Frédéric, in a velvet jacket, was lying back in an easy-chair, smoking cigarettes of Turkish tobacco.

Sénécal scowled, like a bigot arriving in the midst of a pleasure-party. Deslauriers took everything in with a single glance; then, with a very low bow:

'Monseigneur! Allow me to present my respects!'

Dussardier leaped on his neck.

'So you're a rich man now? Ah! So much the better, upon my soul, so much the better!'

Cisy made his appearance with a mourning band on his hat. Since the death of his grandmother, he was in the enjoyment of a considerable fortune, and was less bent on amusing himself than on being distinguished from others, on not being the same as every-one else, in short, on 'having *cachet*'. This was his phrase.

However, it was now midday, and they were all yawning; Frédéric was waiting for someone. At the mention of Arnoux's name, Pellerin pulled a face. He looked on him as a renegade since he had abandoned the fine arts.

'Suppose we forget about him? What do you say?'

They all approved of this suggestion.

The door was opened by a manservant in long gaiters, and the dining-room could be seen with its lofty oak plinth relieved with gold, and its two sideboards laden with plate. The bottles of wine were warming on the stove; the blades of the new knives were glittering beside oysters; in the milky tint of the muslin glasses there was a kind of alluring sweetness, and the table disappeared from view under its load of game, fruit and meats of the rarest quality. These attentions were lost on Sénécal.

He began by asking for home-made bread (the hardest that could be got), and in connection with this subject, spoke of the murders of Buzançais and the crisis arising from lack of the means of subsistence.

Nothing of this sort would have happened if agriculture had been better protected, if everything had not been given up to competition, to anarchy, and to the deplorable maxim of 'Let things alone! Let things go their own way!' It was in this way that the feudalism of money was established, the worst form of feudal-ism! But let them take care! The people in the end will get tired of it, and may make the capitalists pay for their sufferings either by bloody proscriptions or by the plunder of their houses.

Frédéric saw, as if by a lightning-flash, a flood of men with bare arms invading Madame Dambreuse's drawing-room, and smashing the mirrors with blows of pikes.

Sénécal went on to say that the workman, owing to the insuffi-ciency of wages, was more unfortunate than the helot, the negro, and the pariah, especially if he has children.

'Ought he to get rid of them by asphyxia, as some English doctor, whose name I don't remember, a disciple of Malthus, advises him?'

And, turning towards Cisy:

'Are we to be reduced to following the advice of the infamous Malthus?'

Cisy, who was ignorant of the infamy and even of the existence of Malthus, said by way of reply, that after all, much human misery was being relieved, and that the higher classes . . .

'Ha! The higher classes!' said the Socialist, with a sneer. 'In the first place, there are no higher classes; it's the heart alone that makes anyone higher than another! We want no alms, understand! But equality, the fair distribution of products.'

What he demanded was that the workman might become a capitalist, just as the soldier might become a colonel. The guilds, at least, in limiting the number of apprentices, prevented workmen from growing inconveniently numerous, and the sentiment of fraternity was kept alive by means of festivals and banners.

Hussonnet, as a poet, regretted the banners; so did Pellerin – a predilection which had taken possession of him at the Café Dagneaux, while listening to Phalansterians talking. He expressed the opinion that Fourier was a great man.

'Come now!' said Deslauriers. 'An old fool, who sees in the overthrow of empires effects of Divine vengeance! He's just like my lord Saint-Simon and his church, with his hatred of the French Revolution: a set of buffoons who would like to re-establish Catholicism!'

M. de Cisy, no doubt seeking enlightenment, or wanting to make a good impression, broke in with this remark, which he uttered in a mild tone:

'These two men of science are not, then, of the same way of thinking as Voltaire?'

'Him! I make you a present of him!' answered Sénécal.

'How is that? Why, I thought . . . '

'Oh no! He didn't love the people!'

Then the conversation came down to contemporary events: the Spanish marriages, the dilapidations of Rochefort, the new chapter house of Saint-Denis, which would lead to the taxes being doubled. Yet, according to Sénécal, they were quite high enough!

'And why, my God? To erect palaces for the apes at the Museum, to make showy staff officers parade along our squares, or to maintain a Gothic style of etiquette amongst the flunkeys of the Château!'

'I read in *La Mode*,' said Cisy, 'that at the Tuileries ball on the feast of Saint-Ferdinand, everyone was disguised as for a public ball.'

'Pathetic!' said the socialist, with a shrug of disgust.

'And the Museum of Versailles!' exclaimed Pellerin. 'Let's talk about that! These idiots have shortened a Delacroix and lengthened a Gros! At the Louvre they've restored, scratched, and fiddled about with the canvases so much that in ten years probably not one will be left. As for the errors in the catalogue, a German has written a whole book on the subject. Upon my word, the foreigners are laughing at us!'

'Yes, we're the laughing-stock of Europe,' said Sénécal.

'It's because Art is in thrall to the Crown.'

'As long as you haven't got universal suffrage . . . '

'Allow me!' For the artist, having been rejected at every *Salon* for the last twenty years, was filled with rage against Authority. 'Ah! Let them leave us alone. I, personally, ask for nothing! Only the Chambers ought to pass statutes in the interests of Art. A chair of aesthetics should be established with a professor who, being a practical man as well as a philosopher, would succeed, I hope, in grouping the multitude. You'd do well, Hussonnet, to say a word or two about this in your newspaper?'

'Are the newspapers free? Are we ourselves free?' said Deslauriers in an angry tone. 'When you think that there might be as many as twenty-eight different formalities to set up a boat on the river, it makes me want to go and live with the cannibals! The Government is eating us up! Everything belongs to it: philosophy, law, the arts, the very air of heaven; and France, bereft of all energy, lies under the boot of the gendarme and the cassock of the devil-dodger, with the death-rattle in her throat!'

The future Mirabeau thus poured out his bile, in abundance. Finally he took his glass, rose, and with his hand on his hip, and his eyes flashing:

'I drink to the utter destruction of the existing order of things, that is to say, of everything included in the words Privilege,

Monopoly, Regulation, Hierarchy, Authority, State!' And in a louder voice: 'which I would like to smash as I do this!' dashing on the table the beautiful wineglass, which broke into a thousand pieces.

They all applauded, and especially Dussardier.

The spectacle of injustice made his heart leap with indignation. He was anxious about Barbès; he was one of those persons who fling themselves under vehicles to help horses who have fallen. His erudition was limited to two works, one entitled *Crimes of the Kings*, and the other *Mysteries of the Vatican*. He had listened to the advocate with open-mouthed delight. At length, unable to restrain himself any longer:

'For my part, the thing I blame Louis-Philippe for is abandoning the Poles!'

'One moment!' said Hussonnet. 'In the first place, Poland doesn't exist; it's an invention of Lafayette! The Poles, as a general rule, all belong to the Faubourg Saint-Marceau, the real ones having been drowned with Poniatowski.' In short, 'he no longer believed all that stuff', he had 'got over all that sort of thing!' It was just like the sea-serpent, the revocation of the Edict of Nantes, and 'that old humbug about the Saint Bartholomew massacre!'

Sénécal, while he did not defend the Poles, picked up the final remarks made by the man of letters. The Popes had been slandered, inasmuch as they, at any rate, defended the people, and he called the League 'the dawn of Democracy, a great egalitarian movement against the individualism of the Protestants.'

Frédéric was a little surprised at these views. They probably bored Cisy, for he changed the conversation to the *tableaux vivants* at the Gymnase, which at that time were attracting a great number of people.

Sénécal deplored them. Such exhibitions corrupted the daughters of the proletariat; then they went in for such displays of shameless luxury. Therefore he approved of the conduct of the Bavarian students who had insulted Lola Montez. In imitation of Rousseau, he showed more esteem for the wife of a charcoal-burner than for the mistress of a king.

'You don't appreciate dainties!' retorted Hussonnet in a majestic tone.

And he took up the championship of ladies of this class in order to defend Rosanette. Then, as he was talking about her ball and Arnoux's costume:

'People maintain that he's getting a bit shaky,' remarked Pellerin.

The picture-dealer had just been engaged in a lawsuit with reference to his land at Belleville, and he was presently in a kaolin company in Lower Brittany with other rogues of the same sort.

Dussardier knew more about it; for his own master, M. Moussinot, having made enquiries about Arnoux from the banker, Oscar Lefebvre, the latter had said in reply that he considered him a risk, as he knew about bills of his that had been renewed.

The dessert was over; they passed into the drawing-room, which was hung, like that of the Maréchale, in yellow damask in the style of Louis XVI.

Pellerin found fault with Frédéric for not having chosen in preference the Neo-Greek style; Sénécal struck matches against the hangings; Deslauriers did not make any remark. He did in the library, which he called 'a little girl's library'. The principal contemporary writers were to be found there. It was impossible to speak about their works, for Hussonnet immediately began relating anecdotes with reference to their personal characteristics, criticising their faces, their morals, their dress, glorifying fifth-rate intellects and disparaging those of the first, and all the while making it clear that he deplored modern decadence. Any village ditty contained in itself alone more poetry than all the lyric poets of the nineteenth century; Balzac was overrated, Byron discredited, Hugo knew nothing about the stage, etc.

'Why,' said Sénécal, 'have you not got the volumes of our working-men poets?'

And M. de Cisy, who dabbled in literature, was astonished at not seeing on Frédéric's table 'some of those new physiological studies, the physiology of the smoker, of the angler, of the toll-keeper'.

They finished by irritating him to such an extent that he wanted to take them by the shoulders and throw them out. 'Come, I'm being stupid!' And he drew Dussardier aside, and asked him whether he could do him any service.

The honest fellow was moved. His post of cashier entirely sufficed for his wants.

After that, Frédéric led Deslauriers into his bedroom, and, taking out of his desk two thousand francs:

'Look here, old boy, put this money in your pocket! It's the balance of my old debts to you.'

'But . . . what about the journal?' said the advocate. 'You are, of course, aware that I spoke about it to Hussonnet.'

And, when Frédéric replied that he was 'a little short of cash just now', the other gave a sour smile.

After the liqueurs they drank beer; after the beer, grog; and they smoked some more pipes. At last they all left, at five o'clock in the evening; and they were walking along at each others' side without speaking, when Dussardier broke the silence by saying that Frédéric had entertained them in excellent style. They all agreed.

Hussonnet declared that his luncheon was a little too heavy. Sénécal found fault with the trivial character of his household arrangements. Cisy took the same view. It was absolutely devoid of 'cachet'.

'For my part, I think,' said Pellerin, 'he might have had the grace to give me an order for a picture.'

Deslauriers fingered the banknotes in his trouser pocket and said nothing.

Frédéric was left by himself. He was thinking about his friends, and it seemed to him as if a huge, dark gulf separated him from them. He had nevertheless held out his hand to them, and they had not responded to the sincerity of his heart.

He recalled to mind what Pellerin and Dussardier had said about Arnoux. It must be an invention, a slander? But why? And he had a vision of Madame Arnoux, ruined, weeping, selling her furniture. This idea tormented him all night long; next day he presented himself at her house.

At a loss to find any way of communicating to her what he had heard, he asked her, as if in casual conversation, whether Arnoux still held possession of his land at Belleville.

'Yes, he has it still.'

'He is now, I believe, a shareholder in a kaolin company in Brittany.'

'That's true.'

'His workshop is going on very well, isn't it?

'Well . . . I suppose so.'

And, as he hesitated:

'What's the matter with you? You frighten me!'

He told her the story about the renewals. She hung down her head, and said:

'I thought so!'

Indeed, Arnoux, in order to maximise his speculation, had refused to sell his land, had borrowed money extensively on it, and finding no purchasers, had thought of rehabilitating himself by establishing the earthenware factory. The expense of this had exceeded his calculations. She knew nothing more about it; he evaded all her questions, and declared repeatedly that 'everything was fine'.

Frédéric tried to reassure her. These in all probability were mere temporary embarrassments. However, if he got any information, he would impart it to her.

'Oh, yes, please do,' said she, clasping her two hands with an air of charming supplication.

So then, he had it in his power to be useful to her. He was now entering into her life, finding a place in her heart!

Arnoux appeared.

'Ah! How nice of you to come to take me out to dinner.'

Frédéric was speechless.

Arnoux spoke about general topics, then informed his wife that he would be returning home very late, as he had an appointment with M. Oudry.

'At his house?'

'Why, certainly, at his house.'

'As they went down the stairs, he confessed that, as the Maréchale was free, they were going on a secret pleasure-party to the Moulin Rouge; and, as he always needed somebody to be the recipient of his confidences, he got Frédéric to take him to the door.

Instead of entering, he walked about on the footpath, looking up at the windows on the second floor. Suddenly the curtains parted.

'Ah! Bravo! Père Oudry has left. Good evening!'

So it was Père Oudry who was keeping her? Frédéric did not know what to think now.

From this day forth, Arnoux was still more cordial than before; he invited the young man to dine with his mistress, and soon Frédéric frequented both houses at the same time.

Rosanette's was amusing, People called there of an evening on the way back from the club or the play; they took a cup of tea, or played a game of lotto; on Sundays they played charades; Rosanette, more noisy than the rest, excelled in droll inventions, such as running on all fours or muffling her head in a cotton cap. In order to watch the passers-by through the window, she had a hat of waxed leather; she smoked chibouks, she sang Tyrolean airs. In the afternoon, to pass the time, she cut out flowers in a piece of chintz and pasted them onto the windowpanes, smeared her two little dogs with make-up, burned pastilles, or had her fortune told. Incapable of resisting a desire, she became infatuated about some trinket which she had happened to see, and could not sleep till she had gone and bought it, then bartered it for another; she ruined material, lost her jewellery, squandered money, would have sold her chemise for a stage box at the theatre. Often she asked Frédéric to explain to her some word she had read, but did not pay any attention to his answer, for she jumped quickly to another idea, while heaping questions on top of each other. After spasms of gaiety came childish outbursts of rage; or else she sat on the ground dreaming before the fire with her head down and her hands clasping her knees, more inert than a torpid adder. Without minding it, she dressed in his presence, slowly drew on her silk stockings, then washed her face with great splashes of water, throwing back her body as if she were a shivering naïad; and her laughing white teeth, her sparkling eyes, her beauty, her gaiety, dazzled Frédéric, and lashed his nerves till they tingled.

Nearly always he found Madame Arnoux teaching her little boy how to read, or standing behind Marthe's chair while she played her scales on the piano; when she was doing a piece of sewing, it was a great source of delight to him to pick up her scissors now and then. In all her movements there was a tranquil majesty; her little hands seemed made to scatter alms and to wipe away tears; and her voice, naturally rather muffled, had caressing intonations and a sort of lightness like a breeze.

She had no deep feeling for literature, but her intelligence exercised a charm by the use of a few simple and penetrating words. She loved travelling, the sound of the wind in the woods, and to walk bareheaded in the rain. Frédéric listened to these confidences with rapture, fancying that he saw in them the beginning of a certain self-abandonment on her part.

His association with these two women made, as it were, two different strains of music in his life: the one playful, passionate, diverting, the other grave and almost religious; and vibrating both at the same time, they continually increased in volume and gradually blended with one another — for if Madame Arnoux happened merely to touch him with her finger, the image of the other immediately presented itself to his desire, because his chances in that direction were less remote — and when his heart happened to be touched while in Rosanette's company, he was immediately reminded of his consuming passion.

This confusion was due to a similarity which existed between the interiors of the two houses. One of the chests which was formerly to be seen in the Boulevard Montmartre now adorned Rosanette's dining-room, the other was in Mme Arnoux's drawing-room. The dinner-services in the two houses were the same, and even the same velvet cap was to be found lying about on the easychairs; then, a heap of little presents, screens, boxes, fans, went from the mistress's house to the wife's and returned again, for Arnoux, without the slightest embarrassment, often took back from the one what he had given to her in order to make a present of it to the other.

The Maréchale laughed with Frédéric at Armoux's bad behaviour. One Sunday, after dinner, she led him behind the door, and showed him in the pocket of his overcoat a bag of cakes which he had just pilfered from the table, in order, no doubt, to regale his little family with it. Some of M. Arnoux's little tricks bordered on the criminal. It seemed to him a duty to practise fraud with regard to the city dues; he never paid when he went to the theatre, or if he took a ticket for the second seats always tried to make his way into the first, and he used to relate as an excellent joke that it was a custom of his at the cold baths to put into the attendant's collection-box a trouser button instead of a ten sous piece; and this did not prevent the Maréchale from loving him.

One day, however, she said, while talking about him:

'Ah! I'm fed up with him! I've had enough! Well, too bad for him, I'll find someone else!'

Frédéric believed that the 'someone else' had already been found, and that his name was M. Oudry.

'Well,' said Rosanette, 'what does that signify?'

Then, in a voice choked with rising tears:

'Yet I ask very little from him, and he won't give me that, the mean creature! He won't! As for promising things, oh, that's different.'

He had even promised her a fourth of his profits in the famous kaolin mines; no profit made its appearance, any more than the cashmere with which he had been luring her on for the last six months.

Frédéric immediately thought of making her a present of one. Arnoux might regard it as a lesson for himself, and be annoyed.

For all that, he was a goodnatured soul, his wife herself said so. But so crazy! Instead of bringing people to dine every day at his house, he now entertained his acquaintances at a restaurant. He bought things that were utterly useless, such as gold chains, time-pieces, and household articles. Madame Arnoux even pointed out to Frédéric in the corridor an enormous supply of kettles, footwarmers, and samovars. Finally, she one day confessed her anxieties: Arnoux had made her sign a promissory note payable to M. Dambreuse.

Meanwhile Frédéric still cherished his literary projects as if it were a point of honour with himself to do so. He wished to write a history of aesthetics, a result of his conversations with Pellerin, then, to write dramas dealing with different epochs of the French Revolution, and to compose a great comedy, an idea traceable to the indirect influence of Deslauriers and Hussonnet. In the midst of his work, often the face of one or other of the women passed before his mental vision; he struggled against the longing to see her, but soon yielded; and he felt sadder as he came back from Madame Arnoux.

One morning, while he was brooding over his melancholy thoughts by the fireside, Deslauriers came in. The incendiary speeches of Sénécal had made his master uneasy, and once more he found himself without resources.

'What do you expect me to do?' said Frédéric.

'Nothing! I know you have no money. But it wouldn't be much trouble for you to get him a post either through M. Dambreuse or else through Arnoux, would it?'

The latter ought to have need of engineers in his establishment. Frédéric had an inspiration: Sénécal would be able to let him know when the husband was away, carry letters for him and assist

him on a thousand occasions when opportunities presented themselves. Services of this sort are always rendered between one man
and another. Besides, he would find means of employing him
without arousing any suspicion on his part. Chance offered him an
auxiliary, it was a circumstance that augured well for the future, he
had to seize it; and, with an affectation of indifference, he replied
that the thing was feasible perhaps, and that he would devote some
attention to it.

He did so at once. Arnoux was taking a great deal of trouble in
his factory. He was endeavouring to discover the copper-red of
the Chinese; but his colours evaporated in the firing. In order to
avoid cracks in his ware, he mixed lime with his potter's clay; but
the articles broke, for the most part, the enamel of his paintings on
the raw material boiled away, his large plates became warped; and,
attributing these mischances to the inferior plant of his factory, he
was anxious to start other grinding-mills and other drying-rooms.
Frédéric recalled some of these things to mind; and he approached
Arnoux, saying that he had discovered a very able man who would
be capable of finding his famous red. Arnoux gave a jump, then,
having listened to what the young man had to tell him, replied that
he did not need anyone.

Frédéric spoke in a very laudatory style about Sénécal's prodigious
attainments, pointing out that he was at the same time an engineer,
a chemist, and an accountant, being a mathematician of the first
rank.

Our dealer in china consented to see him.

They squabbled over the emoluments. Frédéric interposed, and,
at the end of a week, succeeded in getting them to come to an
agreement.

But as the works were situated at Creil, Sénécal could not assist
him in any way. This thought alone was enough to make his
courage flag, as if he had met with some misfortune.

His notion was that the more detached Arnoux was from his
wife, the better would be his own chance with her. So he
proceeded to make repeated apologies for Rosanette; he referred
to all the wrongs she had sustained at the other's hands, referred to
the vague threats which she had uttered the other day, and even
spoke about the cashmere, without concealing the fact that she had
accused Arnoux of avarice.

Arnoux, nettled at the word (and, furthermore, feeling some unease), brought Rosanette the cashmere, but scolded her for having made any complaint to Frédéric; when she told him that she had reminded him a hundred times of his promise, he pretended that, owing to pressure of business, he had forgotten all about it.

The next day Frédéric presented himself at her abode. He found the Maréchale still in bed, though it was two o'clock, with Delmar at her bedside, finishing a slice of *foie gras* at a little round table. He had scarcely entered, when she cried out: 'I've got it! I've got it!' Then she seized him by the ears, kissed him on the forehead, thanked him effusively, called him 'tu', and even wanted to make him sit down on the bed. Her fine eyes, full of tender emotion, were sparkling, there was a smile on her moist mouth, her two round arms emerged through the sleeveless opening of her night-dress; and from time to time, he could feel through the cambric the firm outlines of her body. All this time Delmar kept rolling his eyeballs about.

'But really, my dear, my own pet!'

It was the same on his next visits. As soon as Frédéric entered, she would stand up on a cushion so that he could embrace her more easily, called him a darling, a sweetie, put a flower in his buttonhole, and settled his cravat; these delicate attentions were always redoubled when Delmar happened to be there.

Were they advances on her part? So it seemed to Frédéric. As for deceiving a friend, Arnoux, in his place, would not have any scruples! And he had every right not to be virtuous with his mistress, having always been so with his wife; for so he thought, or rather he would have liked to convince himself of this, as a justification for his prodigious cowardice. Nevertheless he decided he was stupid, and resolved to lay siege boldly to the Maréchale.

So, one afternoon, just as she was stooping down in front of her chest of drawers, he came across to her, and made a gesture so eloquent and unambiguous that she straightened up, blushing scarlet. He did it again; thereupon, she burst into tears, saying that she was very unfortunate, and that that was no reason for people to treat her with disrespect.

He repeated his attempts. She now adopted a different method, which was always to laugh. He thought it a clever thing to answer her in the same strain, and even to exaggerate. But he made too great a display of gaiety to convince her that he was in earnest; and their friendship was an impediment to any outpouring of serious feeling. At last, one day, she replied that she would not take another woman's leavings.

'What other woman?'

'Ah, yes, go back to Madame Arnoux!'

For Frédéric used to talk about her often; Arnoux, too, had the same mania; at last she lost patience at always hearing this woman's praises sung; and her insinuation was a kind of revenge.

Frédéric did not forgive her for that.

Anyway, Rosanette was beginning to irritate him enormously. Sometimes, assuming the attitude of a woman of experience, she spoke ill of love with a sceptical laugh that made him feel inclined to box her ears. A quarter of an hour afterwards, it was the only thing of any consequence in the world, and, with her arms crossed over her breast, as if she were clasping someone close to her, she would murmur: 'Oh, yes, it's good! It's so good!' her eyes half-closed in a kind of rapturous swoon. It was impossible to understand her, to know, for instance, whether she loved Arnoux, for she made fun of him, and yet seemed jealous of him. So likewise with Vatnaz, whom she would sometimes call a wretch, and at other times her best friend. In short, there was about her entire person, even to the very arrangement of her chignon, an inexpressible something, which seemed like a challenge – and he desired her for the satisfaction, above all, of conquering her and being her master.

How was he to accomplish this? For she often sent him away unceremoniously, appearing only for a moment between two doors in order to whisper: 'I'm engaged; come back this evening!' Or else he found her surrounded by a dozen persons, and when they were alone, so many impediments presented themselves one after the other, that one would have sworn there was a bet to keep matters from going any further. He invited her to dinner and she always refused; once, she accepted, but did not come.

A Machiavellian idea arose in his brain.

Having heard from Dussardier about Pellerin's complaints against himself, he thought of giving the artist a commission to paint the Maréchale's portrait, a life-sized portrait, which would necessitate a good number of sittings; he would not miss one of them; the habitual unpunctuality of the painter would facilitate their private conversations. So he urged Rosanette to get her picture painted in order to make a present of her face to her dear Arnoux. She consented, for she saw herself in the midst of the Grand Salon in the most prominent position with a crowd of people staring at her, and the newspapers would all talk about it, which at once would 'launch her'.

As for Pellerin, he eagerly snatched at the offer. This portrait was to make a great man of him, it was to be a masterpiece.

He passed in review in his memory all the portraits by great masters with which he was acquainted, and decided finally in favour of a Titian, which would be set off with ornaments in the style of Veronese. Therefore, he would carry out his design without artificial shadows, in a bold light, which would illuminate the flesh-tints with a single tone, and which would make the accessories glitter.

'Suppose I were to put on her,' he thought, 'a pink silk dress with an Oriental burnous? Oh, no, the burnous is vulgar! Or suppose, rather, I were to make her wear blue velvet with a grey background, richly coloured? We might likewise give her a white lace collar with a black fan and a scarlet curtain behind.'

And thus, seeking for ideas, he broadened his conception from day to day, and marvelled at it.

He felt his heart beating when Rosanette, accompanied by Frédéric, called at his house for the first sitting. He placed her standing up on a sort of platform in the midst of the apartment; and, finding fault with the light and expressing regret at the loss of his former studio, he first made her lean on her elbow against a pedestal, then sit down in an armchair, and drawing away from her and coming near her again by turns in order to adjust with a flick of his fingers the folds of her dress, he looked at her with eyelids half-closed, and appealed to Frédéric's taste with a passing word.

'Well, no!' he exclaimed. 'I return to my original idea! I'm going to do you as a Venetian.'

She would have a puce velvet gown with a jewelled girdle, and her wide sleeve lined with ermine would afford a glimpse of her bare arm, which was to touch the balustrade of a staircase rising behind her. On her left, a great column would mount as far as the top of the canvas to meet certain structures forming an arch. Underneath would be seen, vaguely, groups of orange trees almost black, against which the blue sky, with its streaks of white cloud, would stand out. On the baluster, covered with a rug, there would be, on a silver dish, a bouquet of flowers, a chaplet of amber, a dagger, and a little chest of antique ivory rather yellow with age, which would appear to be disgorging gold sequins; some of them, falling on the ground here and there, would form a series of brilliant splashes, in such a way as to direct the eye towards the tip of her foot, for she would be standing on the last step but one in a natural position as if in the act of moving, in full light.

He went to look for a picture-case, which he laid on the platform to represent the step; then he arranged as accessories, on a stool by way of balustrade, his jacket, a buckler, a tin of sardines, a bundle of pens, and a knife, and when he had flung in front of Rosanette a dozen big sous, he made her assume the attitude he required.

'Just try to imagine that these things are riches, magnificent presents. The head a little to the right! Perfect! And don't move! This majestic posture exactly suits your style of beauty.'

She wore a tartan dress and carried a big muff, and was trying hard not to laugh.

'As for your hair, we will mingle with it a circle of pearls: that always produces a good effect with red hair.'

The Maréchale protested that her hair was not red.

'Relax! The red of painters is not that of ordinary people!'

He began to sketch the position of the masses; and he was so much preoccupied with the great artists of the Renaissance that he spoke about them. For a whole hour he mused aloud on those splendid existences full of genius, glory, and luxury, with triumphal entries into towns, and galas by torchlight among half-naked women, beautiful as goddesses.

'You were made to live in those days. A creature of your calibre would have deserved a monseigneur!'

Rosanette thought these compliments very pretty. The day was fixed for the next sitting; Frédéric took it on himself to bring the accessories.

As the heat of the stove had stupefied her a little, they went home on foot through the Rue du Bac, and reached the Pont Royal.

It was fine weather, piercingly bright and splendid. The sun was setting; some windows of houses in the Cité shone in the distance, like plates of gold, whilst behind, on the right, the towers of Notre-Dame showed their outlines in black against the blue sky, softly bathed on the horizon in grey vapours. The wind began to blow; and Rosanette having declared that she felt hungry, they entered the 'Pâtisserie Anglaise'.

Young women with their children stood eating in front of the marble buffet, where plates of little cakes were stacked under glass covers. Rosanette swallowed two cream tarts. The powdered sugar formed moustaches at the corners of her mouth. From time to time, in order to wipe it, she drew out her handkerchief from her muff; and her face, under her green silk hood, looked like a rose blossoming in the midst of its leaves.

They resumed their walk; in the Rue de la Paix she stopped before a goldsmith's shop to look at a bracelet; Frédéric wished to make her a present of it.

'No,' she said; 'keep your money.'

He was hurt by these words.

'What's the matter now with the ducky? Are we sad?'

And, the conversation having been renewed, he began making protestations of love to her as usual.

'You know perfectly well it's impossible!'

'Why?'

'Ah! Because . . . '

They went on side by side, she leaning on his arm, and the flounces of her gown flapping against his legs. Then he recalled to mind one winter twilight when on the same footpath Madame Arnoux walked thus by his side; and he became so absorbed in this recollection that he no longer saw Rosanette, and did not give her a thought.

She kept looking straight before her in a careless fashion, lagging a little, like a lazy child. It was the hour when people came home from their outings, and carriages were making their way at a quick trot over the hard pavement. Pellerin's flatteries having probably recurred to her mind, she heaved a sigh.

'Ah! There are some lucky women in the world! I was certainly made for a rich man.'

He replied, with a certain roughness in his tone:

'You have one though!' For M. Oudry was looked upon as a millionaire three times over.

She asked for nothing better than to get free from him.

'What's stopping you?'

And he gave utterance to some bitter jokes about this old bewigged bourgeois, pointing out to her that such a liaison was unworthy of her, and that she ought to break it off!

'Yes,' replied the Maréchale, as if talking to herself. 'That's what I shall end by doing, no doubt!'

Frédéric was charmed by this disinterestedness. She slackened her pace, and he fancied that she was tired. She obstinately refused to let him take a cab, and she parted with him at her door, sending him a kiss with her fingertips.

'Ah! What a pity! And to think that some fools think I'm rich!'

He reached home in a gloomy frame of mind.

Hussonnet and Deslauriers were waiting for him.

The Bohemian, seated before the table, was drawing Turks' heads, and the lawyer, in muddy boots, lay asleep on the sofa.

'Ha! At last!' he exclaimed. 'But how sullen you look! Will you listen to me?'

His vogue as a tutor had fallen off, for he crammed his pupils with theories unfavourable for their examinations. He had appeared in two or three cases which he had lost, and each new disappointment flung him back with greater force on the dream of his earlier days: a journal in which he could spread himself, avenge himself, and spit forth his bile and his opinions. Fortune and reputation, moreover, would follow as a necessary consequence. It was in this hope that he had won round the Bohemian, Hussonnet happening to be the possessor of a periodical.

At present, he printed it on pink paper; he invented hoaxes, composed puzzles, tried to start up debates, and even intended (in spite of the situation of the premises) to get up concerts! A year's subscription was to 'give a right to a place in the orchestra in one of the principal theatres of Paris; in addition, the board of management took on itself to furnish persons from abroad with all necessary information, artistic and otherwise'. But the printer was threatening him, there were three quarters' rent due to the landlord, all sorts of embarrassments were arising; and Hussonnet would have allowed *L'Art* to perish, were it not for the exhortations of the lawyer, who raised his spirits daily. He had brought the other with him, in order to give more weight to the application he was now making.

'We've come about the journal,' he said.

'What! Are you still thinking about that?' said Frédéric, in an absent tone.

'Of course I'm thinking about it!'

And he explained his plan anew. By reporting on the Stock Exchange, they would get into communication with financiers, and would thus obtain the hundred thousand francs indispensable as security. But, in order that the periodical might be transformed into a political journal, it was necessary beforehand to have a large *clientèle*, and for that purpose to make up their minds to go to some expense for the cost of paper and printing, and for outlay at the office, in short, a sum of fifteen thousand francs.

'I have no capital,' said Frédéric.

'Do you think we have?' said Deslauriers, with folded arms.

Frédéric, hurt by the attitude which Deslauriers was assuming, replied:

'Is that my fault?'

'Ah! Very fine! A man has wood for his fire, truffles on his table, a good bed, a library, a carriage, every kind of comfort! But let another man shiver under the slates, dine at twenty sous, work like a convict, and sprawl through want in the mire! Is it the rich man's fault?'

And he repeated, 'Is it the rich man's fault?' with a Ciceronian irony which smacked of the law courts. Frédéric tried to speak.

'However, I understand, one has certain wants . . . aristocratic wants; for, no doubt . . . some woman . . . '

'Well, and what if that were so? Am I not free?'

'Oh, quite free!'

And, after a minute's silence:

'Promises are so convenient!'

'Good God! I'm not taking them back!' said Frédéric.

The lawyer went on:

'At school we swear oaths, we'll form a phalanx, we'll be like Balzac's *Thirteen*! Then, when we meet again, it's: "Cheerio, old fellow! Go about your business!" For the one who might help the other carefully keeps everything for his precious self.'

'What?'

'Yes, you haven't even introduced me to the Dambreuses!'

Frédéric looked at him; with his shabby frock-coat, his dirty spectacles and his sallow face, the lawyer seemed to him such a poor creature that he could not help his lips curling with a disdainful smile. Deslauriers saw it, and reddened.

He had already taken his hat to leave. Hussonnet, filled with unease, tried to mollify him with pleading looks, and, as Frédéric was turning his back on him:

'Come on, old man! Be my Mæcenas! Protect the arts!'

Frédéric, with an abrupt movement of resignation, took a sheet of paper, and, having scrawled some lines on it, handed it to him. The Bohemian's face lighted up. Then, passing across the sheet of paper to Deslauriers:

'Apologise, my fine fellow!'

Their friend begged his notary to send him fifteen thousand francs as quickly as possible.

'Ah! Now I recognise you!' said Deslauriers.

'On the faith of a gentleman,' added the Bohemian, 'you are a noble fellow, you'll be placed in the gallery of useful men!'

The lawyer continued:

'You'll lose nothing by it, it's an excellent speculation.'

'My word!' exclaimed Hussonnet, 'I'd stake my head at the scaffold on its success!'

And he said so many foolish things, and promised so many marvels (in which perhaps he believed) that Frédéric did not know whether he did this in order to laugh at others or at himself.

The same evening he received a letter from his mother.

She expressed astonishment at not seeing him yet a minister, while indulging in a little banter at his expense. Then she spoke of her health, and informed him that M. Roque had now become one of her visitors. 'Since he has become a widower, I thought there would be no objection to inviting him to the house. Louise is greatly changed for the better.' And in a postscript: 'You have told me nothing about your fine acquaintance, M. Dambreuse; if I were you, I would make use of him.'

Why not? His intellectual ambitions had left him, and his fortune (he noticed) was insufficient; for when his debts had been paid, and the sum agreed on remitted to the others, his income would be diminished by four thousand at least! Anyway, he felt the need of giving up this sort of life, and attaching himself to something. So, next day, when dining at Madame Arnoux's, he said that his mother was tormenting him in order to make him take up a profession.

'But I was under the impression,' she said, 'that M. Dambreuse was going to get you into the Council of State? That would suit you very well.'

So, then, she wished it. He obeyed.

The banker, as on the first occasion, was seated at his desk, and, with a gesture, asked him to wait a few minutes, for a gentleman who was standing at the door with his back turned was discussing some serious topic with him. The subject of their conversation was coal and the proposed amalgamation of different companies.

On each side of the glass hung portraits of General Foy and Louis-Philippe; filing shelves rose along the panelling up to the ceiling, and there were six straw chairs, M. Dambreuse not requiring a more fashionably furnished apartment for the transaction of his business; it was like those gloomy kitchens in which great banquets are prepared. Frédéric noticed particularly two chests of prodigious size which stood in the corners. He wondered how many millions they might contain. The banker unlocked one of them, and as the iron plate revolved, it disclosed to view nothing inside but blue paper books full of entries.

At last, the person who had been talking to M. Dambreuse passed in front of Frédéric. It was Père Oudry. The two greeted one another, their faces colouring, a circumstance which seemed to surprise M. Dambreuse. However, he exhibited the utmost affability. Nothing would be easier than to recommend his young friend to the Keeper of the Seals. They would be too happy to have him; and he concluded his polite attentions by inviting him to an evening party which he would be giving in a few days.

Frédéric was stepping into a brougham on his way to this party when a note from the Maréchale arrived. By the light of the carriage-lamps he read:

'Darling, I have followed your advice. I have just expelled my Red Indian. After tomorrow evening, freedom! Now say I am not a fine creature.'

Nothing more! But it was clearly an invitation to him to take the vacant place. He uttered an exclamation, squeezed the note into his pocket, and set forth.

Two municipal guards on horseback were stationed in the street. A row of lamps burned over the two front gates; and servants were calling out in the courtyard to have the carriages brought up to the bottom of the steps under the awning. Then suddenly in the vestibule the noise ceased.

Great trees filled up the stairwell; the porcelain globes shed a light which shimmered like white moiré satin on the walls. Frédéric tripped lightly up the stairs. An usher announced his name; M. Dambreuse extended his hand; almost at the very same moment, Madame Dambreuse appeared.

She wore a mauve dress trimmed with lace, the ringlets of her hair more abundant than usual, and not a single jewel.

She complained of his coming to visit them so rarely, and managed to say a word or two. The guests began to arrive; their manner of saluting was to jerk their bodies to one side or bend double, or merely lower their heads a little; then a married pair, a family, passed in, and all scattered themselves about the drawing-room, which was already full.

Under the chandelier in the centre, an enormous ottoman seat supported a stand, the flowers of which, bending forward like plumes of feathers, hung over the heads of the ladies seated all around in a ring, while others occupied the easy chairs, which formed two straight lines symmetrically interrupted by the large red velvet curtains of the windows and the lofty bays of the doors with their gilded lintels.

The crowd of men who remained standing on the floor with their hats in their hands seemed, from a distance, like one black mass, into which the ribbons in the buttonholes introduced red points here and there, and which was further darkened by the monotonous whiteness of their cravats. With the exception of some very young men with down on their faces, all appeared to be bored; a few dandies, looking sullen, were rocking on their heels. There were numbers of men with grey hair or wigs; here and there glistened a bald pate; and the faces, either flushed or exceedingly pale, showed in their worn aspect the traces of immense fatigue – for the men who were there devoted themselves to political or commercial pursuits. M. Dambreuse had also invited a number of scholars and magistrates, two or three celebrated doctors, and he deprecated with an air of humility the praise he received for his entertainment and the allusions to his wealth.

An immense number of menservants, with heavily gold-braided livery, were moving about on every side. The large candelabra, like bouquets of flame, spread their branches against the hangings; they were reflected in the mirrors; and at the end of the dining-room, the walls of which were covered with a trellis of jasmine, the sideboard looked like the high altar of a cathedral or an exhibition of jewellery – there were so many dishes, dish-covers, knives, forks and spoons, in silver and silver-gilt, surrounded by all sorts of crystal, whose facets shot their iridescence back and forth over the food. The three other reception-rooms overflowed with artistic objects: landscapes by the masters on the walls, ivory and porcelain on the tables, and Chinese ornaments on the side-tables; lacquered screens were opened out in front of the windows, clusters of camellias filled the fireplaces; and a light music vibrated in the distance, like the humming of bees.

The quadrilles were not numerous, and the dancers, judging by the indifferent fashion in which they dragged their slippers along, seemed to be going through the performance of a duty. Frédéric heard phrases such as the following:

'Were you at the last charity fête at the Hôtel Lambert, Mademoiselle?'

'No, Monsieur!'

'It will soon be intolerably warm!'

'Oh, yes indeed, quite suffocating!'

'Whose polka, pray, is this?'

'Good heavens, Madame, I don't know!'

And, behind him, three greybeards, who had posted themselves in the recess of a window, were whispering obscene remarks; others talked about the railways and free trade; a sportsman told a hunting story; a Legitimist carried on a discussion with an Orleanist.

And, wandering from group to group, he reached the card-room, where, in the midst of grave-looking men gathered in a circle, he recognised Martinon, now 'attached to the Bar of the capital'.

His big face, with its waxen complexion, filled up the space encircled by his collar-like beard, which was a marvel, so evenly matched were its rows of black hairs; and, observing the golden mean between the elegance which his age required and the dignity which his profession exacted from him, he kept his thumbs stuck under his armpits, according to the custom of beaux, and then slipped his arms into his waistcoat after the manner of learned persons. Though his boots were polished to excess, he kept his temples shaved, to give himself the forehead of a thinker.

After he had addressed a few chilling words to Frédéric, he turned once more towards those who were chatting around him. A landowner was saying:

'This is a class of men who dream of overturning society!'

'They're calling for the organisation of labour!' said another. 'Can this be conceived?'

'What could you expect!' said a third, 'when we see M. de Genoude giving his assistance to the *Siècle*?'

'And even Conservatives style themselves Progressives! To lead us to what? To the Republic! As if such a thing were possible in France!'

All declared that the Republic was impossible in France.

'No matter!' remarked one gentleman in a loud tone. 'There's too much interest in the Revolution; they're publishing masses of histories, of different kinds of books about it . . . '

'Without taking into account,' said Martinon, 'that there are perhaps subjects of more importance to be studied!'

A gentleman occupying a ministerial office launched an attack on the scandals associated with the stage:

'So, for instance, this new drama of *La Reine Margot* really goes too far! Where was the need for telling us about the Valois? All this shows royalty in an unfavourable light! It's the same with your press! There's no use talking, the September laws are altogether far too mild! For my part, I would like to have court-martials, to gag the journalists! At the slightest display of insolence, drag them before a council of war, and then let them have it!'

'Oh, take care, Monsieur! Take care!' said a professor. 'Don't attack the precious boons we gained in 1830! Let us respect our liberties!' It would be better to adopt a policy of decentralisation, and to distribute the surplus populations of the towns through the country districts.

'But they're rotten to the core!' exclaimed a Catholic. 'Let religion be more firmly established!'

Martinon hastened to observe:

'Indeed, it is a restraining force!'

All the evil lay in this modern longing to rise above one's class and to possess luxuries.

'But,' urged a manufacturer, 'luxury aids commerce. Therefore, I approve of the Duc de Nemours' action in insisting on having short breeches at his evening parties.'

'M. Thiers came in a pair of trousers. You know his joke on the subject?'

'Yes, charming! But he's turning into a demagogue, and his speech on the question of incompatibilities was not without its influence in bringing about the insurrection of the twelfth of May.'

'Oh, pooh!'

'Ay, ay!'

The circle had to make a little opening to make way for a manservant carrying a tray, who was trying to make his way into the card-room.

Under the green shades covering the candles the table was covered with rows of cards and gold coins. Frédéric stopped by one of them, lost the fifteen napoleons which he had in his pocket, whirled lightly about, and found himself in the doorway of the boudoir in which Madame Dambreuse happened to be at that moment.

It was filled with women sitting close to one another on seats without backs. Their long skirts, swelling round them, seemed like waves from which their torsos emerged, and their breasts offered themselves to view in the point of their bodices. Nearly every one of them had a bouquet of violets in her hand. The dull shade of their gloves showed off the human whiteness of their arms; over their shoulders hung fringes or foliage, and, every now and then, as they quivered with emotion, it seemed as if their dress was about to fall off. But the decorum of their countenances tempered the provocative nature of their costumes; several of them had an almost bestial placidity, and this assembly of half-naked women made him think of the interior of a harem; a grosser comparison suggested itself to the young man's mind. Indeed every variety of beauty was to be found there: English ladies, with the profile familiar in 'keepsakes'; an Italian, whose black eyes flashed like a Vesuvius; three sisters dressed in blue; three from Normandy, fresh as April apple trees; a tall red-haired girl, with a set of amethysts – and the white glitter of the diamonds which trembled in the aigrettes worn in their hair, the luminous patches of the precious stones spread over their breasts, and the gentle radiance of the pearls which adorned their foreheads mingled with the glitter of gold rings, with the lace, the powder, the feathers, the vermilion of dainty mouths, and the mother-of-pearl of teeth. The ceiling, rounded into a dome, gave the boudoir the form of a basket; and a draught of perfumed air circulated with the beating of their fans.

Frédéric, planted behind them with his eyeglass to his eye, did not consider all the shoulders irreproachable; he thought of the Maréchale, and this dispelled the temptations that beset him or consoled him for them.

He gazed, however, at Madame Dambreuse, and he considered her charming, in spite of her mouth being rather wide and her nostrils too dilated. But she had a particular grace. There was a kind of passionate languor in the curls of her hair, and her forehead, which was the colour of agate, seemed to contain a great many things, and indicated a masterful intelligence.

She had placed beside her her husband's niece, a rather plain-looking young person. From time to time she left her seat to receive those who had just come in; and the murmur of feminine voices, made, as it grew, a kind of twittering, as of birds.

They were talking about the Tunisian ambassadors and their costumes. One lady had been present at the last reception of the Academy; another referred to the *Don Juan* of Molière, which had recently been performed at the Théâtre Français. But with a significant glance towards her niece, Madame Dambreuse laid a finger on her lips, while the smile which escaped from her contradicted this display of austerity.

Suddenly, Martinon appeared at the other door directly in front of her. She arose. He offered her his arm. Frédéric, in order to watch the progress of these gallantries on Martinon's part, walked past the card-tables and came up with them in the large drawing-room; Madame Dambreuse immediately quitted her cavalier, and began chatting with Frédéric himself in a familiar tone.

She understood that he did not play cards or dance.

'Young people have a tendency to be melancholy!'

Then, with a single comprehensive glance at the scene:

'Besides, this sort of thing is not amusing! At least for certain natures!'

And she drew up in front of the row of armchairs, uttering a few polite remarks here and there, while some old men with double eyeglasses came to pay court to her. She introduced Frédéric to some of them. M. Dambreuse touched him lightly on the elbow, and led him out on the terrace.

He had seen the Minister. The thing was not easy to manage. Before qualifying for the post of auditor to the Council of State, one had to take an examination; Frédéric, seized with an unaccountable self-confidence, replied that he had a knowledge of the subjects prescribed for it.

The financier was not surprised at this, after all the eulogies M Roque had pronounced on his abilities.

At the mention of this name, a vision of little Louise, her house and her room, passed through his mind; and he remembered how he had on nights like this stood at his window listening to the wagoners driving past. This recollection of his sadness brought back the thought of Madame Arnoux; and he relapsed into silence as he continued to pace up and down the terrace. The windows shone amid the darkness like long slabs of flame; the buzz of the ball was growing fainter; the carriages were beginning to leave.

'Why in the world,' M. Dambreuse went on, 'are you so anxious to be attached to the Council of State?'

And he declared, in the tone of a man of broad views, that the public functions led to nothing, he could speak with some authority on that point; business was much better. Frédéric urged as an objection the difficulty of learning the ropes.

'Pooh! I could post you up well in them in a very short time.'

Was he thinking of asking him to be an associate in any of his own undertakings?

The young man saw, as by a lightning-flash, an enormous fortune coming into his hands.

'Let's go in again,' said the banker. 'You're staying for supper with us, aren't you?'

It was three o'clock, people were leaving. In the dining-room, a table at which supper was served awaited the private guests.

M. Dambreuse perceived Martinon, and, drawing near his wife, in a low tone:

'Was it you who invited him?'

She answered dryly:

'Yes, of course!'

The niece was not present. The guests drank a great deal of wine, and laughed very loudly; and broad jokes did not give any offence, all present experiencing that sense of relief which follows a somewhat prolonged period of constraint. Martinon alone displayed anything like gravity; he refused to drink champagne, as he thought this good form, and, moreover, was the soul of tact and very polite, for when M. Dambreuse, who was narrow-chested, complained of an oppression, he made repeated enquiries about his health; and then he let his pale blue eyes wander in the direction of Madame Dambreuse.

She questioned Frédéric in order to find out which of the young ladies he liked best. He had noticed none of them in particular, and besides, he preferred women of thirty.

'There, perhaps, you show your good sense!' she returned.

Then, as they were putting on their cloaks and overcoats, M. Dambreuse said to him:

'Come and see me one of these mornings and we'll have a chat!'

Martinon, at the foot of the stairs, lit a cigar; and, as he puffed it, he presented such a heavy profile that his companion allowed this remark to escape from him:

'My word, you've a fine head!'

'It's turned a few!' replied the young magistrate, with an air of mingled complacency and annoyance.

As Frédéric got into bed, he reviewed the evening. In the first place, his own toilet (he had looked at himself several times in the mirrors), from the cut of his coat to the knot of his pumps, was irreproachable; he had spoken to influential men, and seen wealthy ladies at close quarters. M. Dambreuse had treated him admirably, and Madame Dambreuse had been almost encouraging. He weighed one by one her slightest words, her looks, a thousand things incapable of being analysed and yet significant. It would be absolutely splendid to have a mistress like that! And, after all, why should he not? He was as good as the next man! Perhaps she was not so hard to win? Then Martinon came back to his recollection; and, as he fell asleep, he smiled with pity for this worthy fellow.

He woke up with the thought of the Maréchale in his mind; those words of her note: 'After tomorrow evening', were certainly an appointment for this very day. He waited until nine o'clock, and then hurried to her house.

Someone who had been going up the stairs before him shut the door. He rang the bell; Delphine came out and told him that Madame was not there.

Frédéric persisted, begging of her to admit him. He had something of a very serious nature to communicate to her – just a quick word. At length, the argument of the hundred-sous-piece proved successful, and the maid left him alone in the anteroom.

Rosanette appeared. She was in her chemise, with her hair loose; and, shaking her head, she waved her arms from afar to indicate that she could not receive him.

Frédéric descended the stairs slowly. This caprice was worse than any of the others. He could not understand it at all.

In front of the porter's lodge, Mademoiselle Vatnaz stopped him.

'Did she receive you?'

'No!'

'You've been sent away?'

'How do you know that?'

'It's quite obvious! But come on! Let's go! I can't breathe!'

She took him into the street. She was gasping for breath. He could feel her thin arm trembling on his own. Suddenly, she broke out:

'Ah! The wretch!'

'Who?'

'Why, it's he! He! Delmar!'

This revelation humiliated Frédéric; he next asked:

'Are you quite sure?'

'Why, I tell you I followed him!' exclaimed Vatnaz. 'I saw him go in! Now do you understand? I ought to have expected it anyway; I was the one, in my stupidity, who introduced him to her. And if you only knew all, my God! I picked him up, fed him, clothed him; and then all the paragraphs I got into the newspapers for him! I loved him like a mother!' Then, with a sneer: 'Ha! Monsieur wants velvet dresses! You may be sure it's a speculation on his part! And as for her! To think that I knew her when she earned her living sewing underwear! If it weren't for me, she would have fallen into the mire twenty times over. But I'll plunge her into it yet! Oh yes! I'll see her dying in a public hospital! And everything about her will be out in the open!'

And, like a torrent of dirty washing water with its cargo of filth, her rage poured out in a tumultuous fashion into Frédéric's ear the recital of her rival's disgraceful acts.

'She's slept with Jumillac, with Flacourt, with little Allard, with Bertinaux, with Saint-Valéry, the pockmarked one. No, the other one! They're two brothers — it makes no difference! And when she had problems, I arranged everything. And what good did it do me? She's so mean! And then, you'll agree with me, it was really generous of me to associate with her, because, after all, we're not in the same class! I'm not a tart, am I! Do I sell myself! Not to mention that she's as thick as they come! She spells category with a th. Anyway, they're well matched; they're a good pair, for all he calls himself an artist and thinks he's a genius! But, my God! If he only had any intelligence, he wouldn't have done such an infamous thing! You don't abandon a superior woman for a hussy! Oh, I don't care. He's losing his looks! I hate him! If I met him, see, I'd spit in his face.' She spat. 'Yes, that's all I care about him now! And what about Arnoux, hey? Isn't it dreadful? He's forgiven her so many times! You can't imagine all he's sacrificed for her! She ought to kiss his feet! He's so generous and kind!'

Frédéric was delighted to hear Delmar disparaged. He had accepted Arnoux. This perfidy on Rosanette's part seemed to him an abnormal and inexcusable thing; and, catching the old maid's emotion, he began to feel a sort of tenderness for him. Suddenly, he found himself in front of Arnoux's door; Mlle Vatnaz, without his noticing, had led him down the Faubourg Poissonnière.

'Here we are,' she said. 'I can't go up. But you, surely there's nothing to prevent you.'

'Go up to do what?'

'To tell him everything, of course!'

Frédéric, as if waking up with a start, saw the baseness towards which she was urging him.

'Well?' she said.

He raised his eyes towards the second floor. Madame Arnoux's lamp was burning. Indeed there was nothing to stop him going up.

'I'll wait for you here. Go on then!'

This command cooled his spirit still further, and he said:

'I'll be up there a long time. You'd do better to go home. I'll call on you tomorrow.'

'No, no!' replied Vatnaz, stamping her foot. 'Fetch him! Take him there! Let him catch them together!'

'But Delmar will have left!'

She hung down her head.

'Yes, that's true, perhaps.'

And she remained without speaking in the middle of the street, with vehicles all around her; then, fixing on him her wild cat's eyes:

'I can count on you, can't I? There's a sacred bond between us now! Go on then. Till tomorrow!'

Frédéric, in passing through the lobby, heard two voices arguing. Madame Arnoux's voice was saying:

'Don't lie! Just don't lie!'

He went in. The voices suddenly ceased.

Arnoux was walking up and down, and Madame was seated on the little chair near the fire, extremely pale and staring straight before her. Frédéric made as if to retire. Arnoux grasped his hand, glad that someone had come to his rescue.

'But I'm afraid . . . ' said Frédéric.

'Stay here, I beg of you!' Arnoux whispered in his ear.

Madame continued:

'You must make some allowance, Monsieur Moreau. Such things do sometimes unfortunately occur in households.'

'They do when we put them there,' said Arnoux jovially. 'Women get such weird ideas! This one, for instance, is not a bad one. No, quite the contrary! Well, she's been amusing herself for the last hour plaguing me with a heap of silly stories.'

'They're true!' retorted Madame Arnoux, losing patience. 'Because in fact, you did buy it.'

'I?'

'Yes, you! At the Persian House!'

'The cashmere!' thought Frédéric.

He felt guilty and afraid.

She quickly added:

'It was last month, a Saturday, the fourteenth.'

'Ah! That day, precisely, I was at Creil! So you see.'

'Not at all! Because we had dinner with the Bertins on the fourteenth.'

'The fourteenth . . . ' said Arnoux, looking up, as if he were searching for a date.

'And, furthermore, the assistant who sold it to you was a fair-haired young man!'

'How could I remember the assistant!'

'And yet it was at your dictation that he wrote the address: 18 Rue de Laval.'

'How do you know?' said Arnoux in amazement.

She shrugged her shoulders.

'Oh, it's perfectly simple: I went to get my cashmere repaired, and the head of the department told me that they had just sent another of the same sort to Madame Arnoux.'

'Is it my fault if there is a Madame Arnoux in the same street?'

'Yes! But not Jacques Arnoux,' she returned.

Thereupon, he began to talk in an incoherent fashion, protesting his innocence. It was a misunderstanding, an accident, one of those unaccountable things that happen sometimes. People should not be condemned on mere suspicion, vague probabilities; and he cited the example of the unfortunate Lesurques.

'In short, I say you are mistaken! Do you want me to take my oath on it?'

'It isn't worth it!'

'Why?'

She looked him straight in the face without speaking; then stretched out her hand, took down the little silver chest from the mantelpiece, and handed him a bill which was spread open.

Arnoux coloured up to his ears, and his face lost its composure and began to look puffy.

'Well?'

'But . . . ' he said slowly, 'What does that prove?'

'Ah!' she said, with a peculiar ring in her voice, in which sorrow and irony were blended. 'Ah!'

Arnoux held the bill in his hands, and turned it round without removing his eyes from it, as if he were going to find in it the solution of a great problem.

'Ah! Yes, yes, I remember,' said he at length. 'It was a commission. You ought to know about it, Frédéric?' Frédéric remained silent – 'A commission entrusted to me . . . by . . . by Père Oudry.'

'And for whom?'

'For his mistress!'

'For yours!' exclaimed Madame Arnoux, springing to her feet and standing erect before him.

'I swear to you . . . '

'Don't start again! I know everything!'

'Ha! Very nice! So I'm being spied on!'

She returned coldly:

'Perhaps that wounds your delicacy?'

'Once people lose their tempers,' said Arnoux, looking for his hat, 'and can't be reasoned with . . . '

Then, with a deep sigh:

'Don't marry, my poor friend, don't, believe me!'

And he took himself off, feeling the need for some air.

Then there was a deep silence; and it seemed as if everything in the room had become stiller than before. A luminous circle above the lamp whitened the ceiling, while in the corners the shadows gathered like pieces of black gauze placed on top of one another; the ticking of the clock could be heard and the crackling of the fire.

Madame Arnoux had just sat down again in the armchair at the opposite side of the fireplace; she bit her lip and shivered; she drew her hands up to her face, a sob broke from her, and she began to weep.

He sat down on the little chair; and in the soothing tone in which one addresses an invalid:

'You don't doubt that I share . . . ?'

She made no reply. But, continuing her reflections aloud:

'I leave him perfectly free! He had no need to lie!'

'That's quite true,' said Frédéric.

It was the result of Arnoux's habits. No doubt he had acted thoughtlessly, but perhaps in matters of a graver character . . .

'Whatever do you see that can be graver?'

'Oh, nothing!'

Frédéric bowed, with a smile of acquiescence. Nevertheless, Arnoux possessed certain good qualities; he was fond of his children.

'Ah! And he does all he can to ruin them!'

That was due to an excessively easy-going disposition; for, after all, he was a good fellow.

She exclaimed:

'But what does that mean, a good fellow?'

He defended him thus, in the vaguest kind of language he could think of, and, while expressing his sympathy with her, he rejoiced, he was delighted, in the depths of his soul. Through vengeance or need for affection she would fly to him for refuge. His love was intensified by the hope which had now grown immeasurably stronger.

Never had she appeared to him so captivating, so profoundly beautiful. From time to time a deep breath lifted her bosom; her two eyes, gazing fixedly into space, seemed dilated by a vision in the depths of her consciousness, and her lips were slightly parted, as if to breathe out her soul. Sometimes she pressed her hand-kerchief over them tightly; he would have liked to be this little piece of cambric all moistened with her tears. In spite of himself, he cast a look at the couch deep in the alcove, imagining her head lying on the pillow; and he saw this so vividly that he had to restrain himself from clasping her in his arms. She closed her eyelids, and now she appeared quiescent and languid. Then he drew closer to her, and, bending over her, he eagerly scanned her face. The noise of boots sounded in the passage, it was the other. They heard him shutting the door of his room. Frédéric made a sign to ask Madame Arnoux whether he should go and see him.

She replied 'Yes,' in the same way; and this mute exchange of thoughts between them was, as it were, an assent, the beginnings of adultery.

Arnoux was just taking off his coat to go to bed.

'Well, how is she going on?'

'Oh! Better!' said Frédéric. 'It will pass!'

But Arnoux was injured.

'You don't know her! She has such nerves now! . . . That fool of an assistant! This is what comes of being too kind! If I hadn't given that blasted shawl to Rosanette!'

'Don't regret a thing! She's tremendously grateful to you!'

'Do you really think so?'

Frédéric had not a doubt of it. The best proof of it was that she had just dismissed Père Oudry.

'Ah! Poor little thing!'

And in the excess of his emotion, Arnoux wanted to rush off to her forthwith.

'Don't bother! I've just been there. She's ill!'

'All the more reason for my going!'

He quickly put on his coat again, and took up his candlestick. Frédéric cursed his own stupidity, and pointed out to him that for decency's sake he ought to remain this night with his wife. He could not leave her, it would be very bad of him.

'I tell you candidly you would be wrong! There's no hurry about Rosanette! You can go tomorrow! Come! Do this for my sake.'

Arnoux put down his candlestick, and, embracing him, said:

'You're a good fellow, you are!'

Then began for Frédéric a wretched existence. He became the parasite of the house.

If anyone were indisposed, he called three times a day to know how the patient was, went to the piano-tuner's, contrived to do a thousand acts of kindness; and he endured with an air of contentment Mademoiselle Marthe's poutings and the caresses of little Eugène, who was always drawing his dirty hands over the young man's face. He was present at dinners at which Monsieur and Madame, facing each other, did not exchange a word; unless it happened that Arnoux provoked his wife with jocular remarks. When the meal was over, he would play about the room with his son, conceal himself behind the furniture, or carry him on his back, walking about on all fours, like the Béarnais. At last, he would go out; and she would at once plunge into the eternal subject of complaint: Arnoux.

It was not his misconduct that excited her indignation. But her pride appeared to be wounded, and she did not hide her repugnance towards this man, who had no delicacy, dignity, or sense of honour.

'Or rather, he's mad!' she said.

Frédéric artfully drew her out. Before long he knew all the details of her life.

Her parents were humble people from Chartres. One day, Arnoux, while sketching on the bank of the river (at this period he believed himself to be a painter), had seen her leaving the church, and made her an offer of marriage; on account of his wealth, he was unhesitatingly accepted. Besides, he was desperately in love with her. She added:

'Good heavens, he loves me still! After his fashion!'

They had spent the few months immediately after their marriage travelling in Italy.

Arnoux, in spite of his enthusiasm for the scenery and the masterpieces, had done nothing but complain about the wine, and, to find some kind of amusement, had organised picnics with

English people. The profit which he had made by reselling some pictures had encouraged him to take up fine art as a commercial speculation. Then he had become keen on a china factory. Just now other commercial ventures attracted him: and, as he sank further and further, he was falling into coarse and extravagant ways. It was not so much for his vices she had to reproach him as for everything he did. No change could be expected, and her unhappiness was irreparable.

Frédéric declared that his own life, in the same way, was a failure.

He was still very young, however. Why should he despair? And she gave him good advice: 'Work! And marry!' He answered her with bitter smiles; for instead of telling her the real cause of his unhappiness, he pretended that it was something else, something sublime, and he played the Antony to some extent, the man accursed by fate, an attitude which was not, in fact, completely at odds with the complexion of his thoughts.

For certain men action becomes all the more difficult as desire becomes stronger. They are paralysed by self-distrust, and terrified by the fear of giving offence; besides, deep attachments are like virtuous women; they are afraid of being discovered, and pass through life with downcast eyes.

Though he was now better acquainted with Madame Arnoux (for that very reason perhaps), he was even more fainthearted than before. Each morning he swore to himself to be bold. He was prevented from doing so by an unconquerable feeling of self-restraint; and he had no example to guide him, inasmuch as this one was different from other women. From the force of his dreams, he had placed her outside the ordinary pale of humanity. At her side he felt himself of less importance in the world than the sprigs of silk that escaped from her scissors.

Then he thought of some monstrous and absurd devices, such as surprises at night, with narcotics and false keys – anything appearing easier to him than to face her disdain.

Besides, the children, the two maids, and the relative position of the rooms caused insurmountable obstacles. So then he made up his mind to possess her for himself alone, and to take her to live with him far away in the depths of some lonely place; he even asked himself what lake would be blue enough, what seashore would be delightful enough for her, whether it would be in Spain, Switzerland, or the East; and expressly fixing on days when she seemed more irritated than usual, he told her that she must break away, think of something, and that he saw no way out but a separation. But, for the sake of the children whom she loved, she would never resort to such an extreme course. So much virtue served to increase his respect for her.

He spent each afternoon in recalling the visit he had paid the night before, and in longing for the evening visit to come. When he was not dining with them, he posted himself about nine o'clock at the corner of the street; and as soon as Arnoux had slammed the main door behind him, Frédéric quickly ascended the two flights of stairs, and asked the maid in an ingenuous fashion:

'Is Monsieur in?'

Then he would exhibit surprise at finding that Arnoux was out.

The latter frequently came back unexpectedly. Then Frédéric had to accompany him to a little café in the Rue Sainte-Anne, which Regimbart now frequented.

The Citizen began by giving vent to some fresh grievance against the Crown. Then they would chat, exchanging friendly insults; for the factory-owner took Regimbart for a thinker of a high order, and, vexed at seeing him neglecting so many gifts, teased him for his laziness. It seemed to Regimbart that Arnoux was a man full of heart and imagination, but decidedly of lax morals; and therefore he was quite unceremonious towards him, refusing even to dine at his house on the grounds that 'formality was a bore'.

Sometimes, at the moment of parting, Arnoux would feel peckish. He 'needed' an omelette or some cooked potatoes; and, as there was never anything to eat in the establishment, he sent out for something. They waited. Regimbart did not leave, and ended, grumbling, by agreeing to eat something.

He was nevertheless gloomy, for he remained for hours seated before the same half-filled glass. As Providence did not regulate things in harmony with his ideas, he was becoming a hypo-chondriac, no longer cared even to read the newspapers, and at the mere mention of England's name began to bellow with rage. On one occasion, referring to a waiter who attended on him carelessly, he exclaimed:

'Have we not enough insults from the Foreigner!'

Except at these critical periods he remained taciturn, contemplating 'one foolproof act to blow the whole business sky-high'.

Whilst he was lost in his reflections, Arnoux, in a monotonous voice, and with a slightly drunken look, related incredible anecdotes in which he had always shone, thanks to his cool head; and Frédéric (this was, no doubt, due to some deep-rooted resemblances) felt a certain attraction to him. He reproached himself for this weakness, believing that on the contrary he ought to have hated him.

Arnoux complained to him of his wife's ill-temper, her obstinacy, her unfair prejudices. She had not been like that in former days.

'If I were you,' said Frédéric, 'I would make her an allowance and live alone.'

Arnoux made no reply; and the next moment he began to sound her praises. She was kind, devoted, intelligent, and virtuous; and, passing to her physical attributes, he was prodigal in his revelations, with the thoughtlessness of people who display their treasures in inns.

His equilibrium was disturbed by a catastrophe.

He had been appointed one of the Board of Superintendence in a kaolin company. But trusting everything he was told, he had signed inaccurate reports and approved, without verification, the annual inventories fraudulently prepared by the manager. The company had now failed, and Arnoux being legally responsible, had, along with the others, just been condemned to pay damages, which meant a loss to him of about thirty thousand francs, not to speak of the costs of the judgment.

Frédéric learned this from a newspaper, and hurried off to the Rue de Paradis.

He was ushered into Madame's apartment. It was breakfast-time. A round table close to the fire was cluttered with bowls of *café au lait*. Slippers trailed over the carpet, and clothes over the armchairs. Arnoux, wearing underpants and a knitted vest, had bloodshot eyes and his hair in disorder; little Eugène was crying because of his mumps, while nibbling at a slice of bread and butter; his sister was eating calmly; Madame Arnoux, a little paler than usual, was waiting on all three of them.

'Well,' said Arnoux, heaving a deep sigh, 'you know all about it!' And, as Frédéric made a gesture of compassion – 'There, you see, I have been the victim of my own trustfulness!'

Then he relapsed into silence; and so great was his prostration, that he pushed his breakfast away. Madame Arnoux raised her eyes with a shrug of the shoulders. He passed his hand across his forehead.

'After all, I'm not guilty. I've nothing to reproach myself with. It's just bad luck! We'll get over it! Ah well, too bad!'

He took a bite of brioche, however, in obedience to his wife's entreaties.

That evening, he wanted to dine alone with her in a private room at the Maison d'Or. Madame Arnoux did not at all understand this emotional impulse, taking offence, in fact, at being treated as if she were a light woman – which, from Arnoux, on the contrary, was a proof of affection. Then, as he was beginning to get bored, he went to find some distraction from the Maréchale.

Up to the present, he had been pardoned for many things owing to his good nature. His lawsuit classed him amongst men of shady reputation. People ceased to visit.

Frédéric considered that he was bound in honour to frequent them more than ever. He hired a box at the Italian Opera, and took them there every week. But the pair had reached that period in ill-matched unions when an invincible lassitude springs from the concessions which each has made and renders life intolerable. Madame Arnoux struggled to contain herself, Arnoux became more and more gloomy; and Frédéric grew sad at witnessing the spectacle of these two unhappy beings.

She had asked him, since he was in Arnoux's confidence, to make enquiries as to the state of her husband's affairs. But shame prevented him from doing so; it was painful to him to eat his dinners while coveting his wife. Nevertheless, he continued to do so, excusing himself on the ground that he was bound to protect her, and that an occasion might present itself for being of service to her.

A week after the ball, he had paid a visit to M. Dambreuse. The financier had offered him twenty or so shares in a coalmining speculation; Frédéric had not returned. Deslauriers wrote letters to him; he left them unanswered. Pellerin had invited him to go and see the portrait; he always put him off. He gave way, however, to Cisy's persistent appeals to be introduced to Rosanette.

She received him very nicely, but without springing on his neck as she used to do. His comrade was delighted at being received by a woman of easy virtue, and above all at having a chat with an actor; Delmar was there.

A drama in which he had appeared as a peasant lecturing Louis XIV and prophesying '89 had brought him so much into the public eye that the same part was continually being created for him; and now his function consisted in attacking the monarchs of all nations. As an English brewer, he inveighed against Charles I, as a student at Salamanca, he cursed Philip II; or, as a sensitive father, he expressed indignation against the Pompadour, this was the best! The brats of the street used to wait at the stage-door to see him; and his biography, sold in the intervals, described him as taking care of his aged mother, reading the Bible, assisting the poor, in short, as a Saint Vincent de Paul mixed with a dash of Brutus and of Mirabeau. People spoke of him as 'Our Delmar'. He had a mission, he was becoming another Christ.

All this had fascinated Rosanette; and she had got rid of Père Oudry, without caring one jot for the consequences, for she was not covetous.

Arnoux, who knew her, had taken advantage of the state of affairs for some time past in order to keep her as his mistress at little cost; the old chap had appeared on the scene, and all three of them had carefully avoided anything like a candid explanation. Then, fancying that she had got rid of the other solely on his account, Arnoux had increased her allowance. But she renewed her demands with a frequency hard to explain, for she was living at a less expensive rate; she had even sold the cashmere in her anxiety to pay off her old debts, she said; and he gave and gave again, she bewitched him, she abused him, pitilessly. Therefore, bills and stamped paper rained into the house. Frédéric felt that a crisis was approaching.

One day he called to see Madame Arnoux. She had gone out. Monsieur was at work below stairs in the shop.

Indeed, Arnoux, surrounded by his vases, was trying to 'persuade' a newly-married pair, well-to-do people from the provinces. He talked about wheel-moulding and fine-moulding, about spotted porcelain and glazed porcelain ; the others, not wishing to appear utterly ignorant, listened with nods of approbation, and bought.

When the customers had gone out, he told Frédéric that he had that very morning had a little altercation with his wife. In order to obviate any remarks about expense, he had declared that the Maréchale was no longer his mistress.

'I even told her that she was yours.'

Frédéric was indignant; but to utter reproaches might betray him; he stammered:

'Ah! You were wrong, very wrong!'

'What does that matter?' said Arnoux. 'Where's the disgrace in passing for her lover? I am, aren't I? Wouldn't you be flattered at being in that position?'

Had she spoken? Was this an allusion? Frédéric hastened to reply:

'No, not at all! On the contrary!'

'Well then?'

'Yes, all right! It makes no difference.'

Arnoux went on:

'Why don't you come there any more?'

Frédéric promised that he would make it his business to go there again.

'Ah! I was forgetting! You ought . . ., when talking about Rosanette . . . to let out something to my wife . . . I don't know what, but you'll think of something . . . something to persuade her that you are her lover. I ask this of you as a special favour – eh?'

The young man's only answer was an equivocal grimace. This calumny would destroy him. He called on her that very evening, and swore that Arnoux's allegation was false.

'Is that really so?'

He seemed sincere; and, when she had taken a long breath of relief, she said to him: 'I believe you', with a beautiful smile; then she hung down her head, and, without looking at him:

'Besides, nobody has any claim on you!'

So then she guessed nothing, and she despised him, since she did not think he could love her enough to be faithful to her! Frédéric, forgetting his overtures to the other, found this indulgence insulting.

After this she asked him to pay a visit from time to time 'to that woman', to get some idea of the position.

Arnoux presently made his appearance, and, five minutes later, wished to carry him off to see Rosanette.

The situation was becoming intolerable.

His attention was diverted by a letter from the notary, who was to send him fifteen thousand francs the following day; and, in order to make up for his neglect of Deslauriers, he went forthwith to tell him this good news.

The lawyer was living in the Rue des Trois-Maries, on the fifth floor over a courtyard. His study, a little tiled apartment, chilly, and with a greyish paper on the walls, had as its principal decoration a gold medal, the prize for hs doctorate, which was fixed in an ebony frame near the mirror. A mahogany bookcase enclosed under its glass front a hundred volumes, more or less. The leather-covered writing-desk occupied the centre of the apartment. Four old arm-chairs upholstered in green velvet were placed in the corners; and a heap of shavings made a blaze in the fireplace, where there was always a bundle of sticks ready to be lighted as soon as someone rang the bell. It was his consultation hour; the lawyer had on a white cravat.

The announcement as to the fifteen thousand francs (he had, no doubt, given up all hope of it) made him chuckle with delight.

'That's good, old fellow, that's good, that's very good!'

He threw some wood on to the fire, sat down again, and immediately began talking about the journal. The first thing to do was to get rid of Hussonnet.

'I'm tired of that idiot! As for officially professing opinions, my own notion is that the most equitable and powerful position is to have no opinions at all.'

Frédéric appeared astonished.

'Why, it's perfectly plain! It's time for politics to be dealt with scientifically. The old chaps of the eighteenth century were beginning to when Rousseau and the men of letters introduced philanthropy, poetry, and other nonsense into it, which pleased the Catholics no end; a natural alliance, however, since the modern reformers (I can prove it) all believe in the Revelation. But, if you sing high masses for Poland, if, in place of the God of the Dominicans, who was an executioner, you take the God of the Romantics, who is an upholsterer; if, in fact, you haven't got a broader conception of the Absolute than your ancestors, Mon-archy will penetrate through your Republican forms, and your red cap will never be more than the headpiece of a priest! The only difference will be that the cell system will have taken the place of torture, the insulting of Religion that of sacrilege, and the

European Concert that of the Holy Alliance; and in this beautiful order which we admire, composed of bits and pieces left over from Louis XIV, ruins from the age of Voltaire, with some Imperial whitewash on top, and some fragments of the British Constitution, you will see the municipal councils trying to annoy the Mayor, the general councils their Prefect, the Chambers the King, the Press those in Power, and the Administration trying to annoy everybody! But naive souls get enraptured about the Civil Code, which is a work fabricated – let them say what they like – in a mean and tyrannical spirit; for the legislator, instead of fulfilling his role, which is to regularise custom, has aspired to model society like another Lycurgus! Why does the law impede fathers of families with regard to the making of wills? Why does it place shackles on the compulsory sale of real estate? Why does it punish vagrancy as a crime, when it shouldn't even be regarded as a technical contravention? And there is so much else! I know all about them! And so I am going to write a little novel, entitled *The History of the Idea of Justice*, which will be amusing! But I'm infernally thirsty! What about you?'

He leaned out through the window, and called to the porter to go and fetch them some grog from the public house.

'To sum up, I see three parties . . . No! Three groups – in none of which do I take the slightest interest: those who have, those who have no longer, and those who are trying to have. But all agree in their idiotic worship of Authority! For example: Mably recommends that philosophers should be prevented from publishing their doctrines; M. Wronsky, the geometrician, describes censorship as the "critical repression of speculative spontaneity"; Père Enfantin gives his blessing to the Hapsburgs for "having passed a heavy hand across the Alps in order to keep Italy down"; Pierre Leroux wishes people to be compelled to listen to an orator, and Louis Blanc inclines towards a State religion; so much rage for government have these vassals whom we call the "people"! Nevertheless, there is not a single legitimate government, in spite of their sempiternal principles. But "principle" signifies "origin". It is always necessary to go back to a revolution, to an act of violence, to a transitory fact. Thus, the principle of ours is national sovereignty, embodied in Parliamentary institutions, though the Parliament does not assent to this! But in what way could the sovereignty of the people be more sacred than Divine Right? They're both fictions! Enough of metaphysics, no more phantoms! There's no need of dogmas to get the streets swept! It will be said that I'm turning society upside down! Well, what if I am? Where would be the harm in that? Because it's a nice thing, this society of yours.'

Frédéric could have said a great deal in reply. But, seeing that his theories were far removed from those of Sénécal, he was full of indulgence towards Deslauriers. He contented himself with objecting that such a system would make them generally hated.

'On the contrary, as we should have given to each party a pledge of hatred against his neighbour, all of them will count on us. You'll take a hand in this, too, and furnish us with some transcendent criticism!'

It was necessary to attack accepted ideas, the Academy, the École Normale, the Conservatoire, the Comédie-Francaise, everything that resembled an institution. That was how they would give theoretical uniformity to their review. Then, as soon as their doctrine had been thoroughly well-established, the journal would suddenly be converted into a daily publication; thereupon they would start attacking individuals.

'And people will respect us, you may be sure!'

Deslauriers was about to fulfil his old dream: the position of editor-in-chief, so that he might have the unutterable happiness of directing others, of carving up their articles, of ordering or declining them. His eyes sparkled behind his glasses, he grew excited and drank glasses of spirits, one after the other, in an automatic fashion.

'You'll have to give a dinner once a week. That's indispensable, even if half your income had to go on it! People will want to come, it will be a centre for the others, a lever for yourself; and by manipulating public opinion at its two ends, literature and politics, you'll see, before six months have passed, we'll dominate Paris.'

Frédéric, as he listened, experienced a sensation of rejuvenescence, like a man who, after having been confined in a room for a long time, is suddenly transported into the open air. He caught the enthusiasm of his friend.

'Yes, I've been an idler, an idiot, you're right!'

'Excellent!' cried Deslauriers; 'I've found my Frédéric again!'

And, placing his fist under Frédéric's chin:

'Ah! You've made me suffer. Never mind! I love you all the same.'

They stood there gazing into each other's faces, both deeply affected, and were on the point of embracing each other.

A woman's bonnet appeared on the threshold of the anteroom.

'What brings you here?' said Deslauriers.

It was Mademoiselle Clémence, his mistress.

She replied that, as she happened to be passing, she had not been able to resist the desire to go in to see him; and in order that they might have a little meal together, she had brought him some cakes, which she laid on the table.

'Mind my papers!' said the advocate, sharply. 'Besides, this is the third time that I have forbidden you to come at my consultation hours.'

She tried to embrace him.

'All right! Go away! Buzz off!'

He pushed her away, she let out a great sob.

'Ah, you make me tired!'

'It's because I love you!'

'I don't want people to love me, but to oblige me!'

This remark, so harsh, stopped Clémence's tears. She took up her station before the window, and remained there motionless, with her forehead against the pane.

Her attitude and her silence had an irritating effect on Deslauriers.

'When you've finished, you'll order your carriage, won't you?'

She turned round with a start.

'Are you sending me away?'

'Exactly!'

She fixed on him her large blue eyes, no doubt as a last appeal, then drew the two ends of her tartan across each other, lingered for another minute or two, and went away.

'You ought to call her back,' said Frédéric.

'Don't be silly!'

And, as he needed to go out, Deslauriers went into the kitchen, which also served as his dressing-room. On the stone floor, beside a pair of boots, were to be seen the remains of a meagre breakfast, and a mattress with a coverlet was rolled up on the floor in a corner.

'This will show you,' said he, 'that I receive few marchionesses! It's easy to do without them, you know! And the others, too. Those who cost nothing take up your time; that's money under another form; now, I'm not rich! And then they're all so silly, so silly! Can *you* talk to a woman?'

They parted at the corner of the Pont-Neuf.

'It's agreed, then! You'll bring the stuff to me tomorrow as soon as you have it.'

'Agreed!' said Frédéric.

When he awoke next morning, he received through the post a cheque on the bank for fifteen thousand francs.

This scrap of paper represented to him fifteen big bags of money; and he said to himself that with such a sum he could: first of all, keep his carriage for three years instead of selling it, as he would soon be forced to do; or buy for himself two beautiful damascene pieces of armour, which he had seen on the Quai Voltaire, then a quantity of other things, paintings, books and however many bouquets of flowers, presents for Madame Arnoux! Anything, in short, would have been preferable to risking, to losing so much money in that journal! Deslauriers seemed to him presumptuous, his insensitivity the day before having chilled Frédéric's affection for him; and the young man was indulging in these feelings of regret, when he was quite surprised by the appearance of Arnoux – who sat down heavily on the side of the bed, like a man overwhelmed.

'What ever is the matter?'

'I'm ruined!'

He had to deposit that very day at the office of Maître Beaumont, notary, in the Rue Saint-Anne, eighteen thousand francs lent him by one Vanneroy.

'It's an unaccountable disaster! I've given him a mortgage, which ought to have kept him quiet! But he threatens me with a writ if he isn't paid this afternoon promptly!'

'So?'

'So, it's very simple! He will take possession of my real estate. Once the thing is publicly announced, it means ruin to me, that's all! Ah, if I could find someone to advance me this cursed sum, he might take Vanneroy's place, and I should be saved! You don't happen to have it?'

The cheque had remained on the night-table near a book. Frédéric took up the volume, and placed it on the cheque, while he replied:

'Good heavens, my dear friend, no!'

But it was painful to him to refuse Arnoux.

'What, don't you know anyone who would . . . ?'

'Nobody! And to think that in a week I shall be getting in money! I'm owed maybe . . . fifty thousand francs at the end of the month!'

'Couldn't you ask the persons that owe you money to make you an advance . . . ?'

'No chance!'

'But haven't you any securities or promissory notes?'

'Not one!'

'What's to be done?' said Frédéric.

'That's what I'm wondering,' replied Arnoux.

He fell silent, and paced up and down the room.

'It isn't for myself, my God, but for my children and my poor wife!'

Then, pronouncing each word separately:

'Well . . . I'll be strong . . . I'll sell everything up . . . and I'll go and seek my fortune . . . somewhere or other!'

'You can't do that!' exclaimed Frédéric.

Arnoux replied with an air of calmness:

'How do you think I could live in Paris now?'

There was a long silence.

Frédéric began to speak:

'When could you pay back this money?'

Not that he had it; quite the contrary! But there was nothing to prevent him from seeing some friends, and making an application to them. And he rang for his servant to get himself dressed. Arnoux thanked him.

'The amount you want is eighteen thousand francs, isn't it?'

'Oh! I could easily manage with sixteen thousand! For I could make two thousand five hundred, or three thousand with my silver plate, if, of course, Vanneroy will give me till tomorrow; and, I repeat to you, you may inform the lender, give him a solemn undertaking, that in a week, maybe even in five or six days, the money will be reimbursed. Besides, the mortgage will be security for it. So there is no risk, you understand?'

Frédéric assured him that he understood and that he would go out immediately.

He stayed where he was, cursing Deslauriers, for he wished to keep his word and at the same time oblige Arnoux.

'Suppose I applied to M. Dambreuse? But on what pretext could I ask for money? It's I, on the contrary, who should give him some for his coalmining shares! Ah, let him go hang himself with his shares! I don't owe for them!'

And Frédéric applauded himself for his independence, as if he had refused some service for M. Dambreuse.

'Well,' he then said to himself, 'since I'm making a loss there – for with fifteen thousand francs I could gain a hundred thousand! Such things do sometimes happen on the Stock Exchange . . . So, since I'm breaking my promise to one of them, am I not free? . . . Besides, what would it matter if Deslauriers has to wait? No, no, that's wrong, let's go!'

He looked at his clock.

'Ah, there's no hurry! The bank doesn't close till five o'clock.'

And, at half-past four, when he had cashed the cheque:

'There's no point now! I shouldn't find him in; I'll go this evening!' Thus giving himself the opportunity of changing his mind, for there always remains in the conscience something of those sophistries which we have poured into it; it retains an aftertaste, as of some unwholesome liquor.

He walked along the boulevards, and dined alone at the restaurant. Then he listened to one act of a play at the Vaudeville, in order to divert his thoughts. But his banknotes caused him as much embarrassment as if he had stolen them. He would not have been very sorry if he had lost them.

When he reached home again he found a letter containing these words:

What news?
    My wife joins me, dear friend, in the hope, etc.
    Yours,

With a flourish.

'His wife! She appeals to me!'

At the same moment Arnoux appeared, wanting to know whether he had obtained the sum so sorely needed.

'Here it is, take it!' said Frédéric.

And, twenty-four hours later, he gave this reply to Deslauriers:

'Nothing has come.'

The lawyer came back every day for three days. He urged Frédéric to write to the notary. He even offered to make the trip to Le Havre.

'No! Don't trouble yourself! I'll go!'

At the end of the week, Frédéric timidly asked the honourable Arnoux for his fifteen thousand francs.

Arnoux put him off till the following day, and then till the day after. Frédéric ventured out after dark, fearing lest Deslauriers might come on him by surprise.

One evening, somebody bumped into him at the corner of the Madeleine. It was he.

'I'll go and get it,' he said.

And Deslauriers accompanied Frédéric as far as the door of a house in the Faubourg Poissonnière.

'Wait for me!'

He waited. At last, after forty-three minutes, Frédéric came out, accompanied by Arnoux, and made signs to him to have patience a little longer. The dealer in china and his companion went up the Rue Hauteville arm-in-arm, and then turned into the Rue de Chabrol.

The night was dark, with gusts of warm wind. Arnoux was strolling along, talking about the Galeries du Commerce: a succession of covered passages which would have led from the Boulevard Saint-Denis to the Châtelet, a marvellous speculation, into which he was very tempted to enter; and he stopped from time to time to look at the faces of the young shop-girls in the shop windows, and then resumed the thread of his conversation.

Frédéric heard Deslauriers' steps behind him like reproaches, like blows falling on his conscience. But he did not dare to make his demand, through a sneaking sense of shame, and also through the fear that it would be useless. The other was drawing nearer. He made up his mind.

Arnoux, in a very detached tone, said that, as he had not got in his outstanding debts, he was unable to pay back the fifteen thousand francs just now.

'You don't need it, I assume?'

At that moment Deslauriers came up to Frédéric, and, taking him aside:

'Be honest, have you got it, yes or no?'

'Well, then, no,' said Frédéric, 'I've lost it!'

'Ah! And in what way?'

'Gambling!'

Deslauriers said nothing in reply, made a very low bow, and went away. Arnoux had taken advantage of the opportunity to light a cigar in a tobacconist's shop. When he came back, he asked who that young man was.'

'Nobody! A friend!'

Then, three minutes later, in front of Rosanette's door:

'Come on up,' said Arnoux, 'she'll be glad to see you. What a hermit you are these days!'

A street-lamp, opposite, threw its light on him; and, with his cigar between his white teeth and his air of contentment, there was something intolerable about him.

'Ha! Now that I think of it, my notary went to yours this morning about that mortgage registry business. It was my wife who reminded me.'

'An efficient woman!' returned Frédéric mechanically.

'I should say so!'

And once more Arnoux began to sing his wife's praises. She had no equal for intelligence, good-heartedness, and thrift; he added in a low voice, rolling his eyes:

'And what a body!'

'Goodbye!' said Frédéric.

Arnoux started.

'Hey! Why?'

And, with his hand half-stretched out towards Frédéric, he stared at him, quite disconcerted by the look of anger in his face.

Frédéric repeated in a dry tone:

'Goodbye!'

He went off down the Rue de Bréda like a stone rolling headlong, furious at Arnoux, swearing that he would never see him again, nor her either, so brokenhearted and desolate did he feel. In place of the rupture which he had anticipated, here now was the other, on the contrary, starting to cherish her, all over, from the ends of her hair to the inmost depths of her soul. Frédéric was exasperated by the vulgarity of this man. Everything, then, belonged to him! Up he turned once again at Rosanette's door; and the mortification of a rupture fed his rage at his own powerlessness. Besides, he felt humiliated by the other's display of integrity in offering him guarantees for his money; he would have liked to strangle him; and over and above the pangs of disappointment floated in his conscience, like a fog, the sense of his baseness towards his friend. Tears choked him.

Deslauriers descended the Rue des Martyrs, swearing aloud with indignation; for his project, like an obelisk that has fallen, now assumed extraordinary proportions. He considered himself robbed, as if he had suffered a great loss. His friendship for Frédéric was dead, and he experienced a feeling of joy at it; it was a sort of compensation! A hatred of all rich people took possession of him. He felt sympathetic towards Sénécal's opinions, and resolved to make every effort to propagate them.

Meanwhile, Arnoux was comfortably seated in an easy-chair near the fire, sipping his cup of tea, with the Maréchale on his knees.

Frédéric did not go back so see the Arnoux; and, in order to distract his attention from his disastrous passion, seizing the first topic which presented itself, he determined to write a *History of the Renaissance*. He heaped his desk pell-mell with the humanists, the philosophers, and the poets; he went to the Print Room to inspect the engravings of Marcantonio; he tried to understand Machiavelli. Gradually, the serenity of intellectual activity soothed him. Immersing himself in other people's personalities, he forgot his own, which is the only way, perhaps, not to suffer from it.

One day, while he was quietly taking notes, the door opened, and the manservant announced Madame Arnoux.

It was she, indeed! And alone? Why, no! For she was holding little Eugène by the hand, followed by her maid in a white apron. She sat down; and after a preliminary cough:

'It's a long time since you came to the house.'

As Frédéric could think of no excuse, she added:

'It was delicacy on your part!'

He asked in return:

'Delicacy about what?'

'About what you have done for Arnoux!' said she.

Frédéric made a gesture signifying: 'What do I care about him! It was for you!'

She sent off the child to play with the maid in the drawing-room. Two or three words passed between them as to their state of health, then the conversation ceased.

She was wearing a brown silk gown, the colour of Spanish wine, with a black velvet coat bordered with sable; this fur made him yearn to pass his hands over it, and her long headbands, so exquisitely smooth, seemed to draw his lips towards them. But she was troubled by some emotion and, turning her eyes towards the door:

'It's rather warm in here!'

Frédéric understood what her discreet glance meant.

'Excuse me! The two leaves of the door are simply touching.'

'Ah, yes!'

And she smiled, as much as to say: 'I'm not afraid!'

He asked her presently what was the object of her visit.

'My husband,' she replied with an effort, 'has urged me to call on you, not daring to take this step himself.'

'Why?'

'You know M. Dambreuse, don't you?'

'Yes, slightly!'

'Ah, slightly.'

She fell silent.

'No matter! Finish what you were going to say.'

Thereupon she told him that, two days before, Arnoux had found himself unable to meet four bills of a thousand francs, made payable at the banker's order and on which he had made her put her signature. She regretted having compromised her children's fortune. But anything was preferable to dishonour; and, if M. Dambreuse stopped the proceedings, they would certainly pay him soon; for she was going to sell a little house which she had in Chartres.

'Poor woman!' murmured Frédéric. 'I'll go. Rely on me.'

'Thank you!'

And she arose to go.

'Oh, there's no hurry yet!'

She remained standing, examining the trophy of Mongolian arrows suspended from the ceiling, the bookcase, the bindings, all the utensils for writing; she lifted up the bronze bowl which held his pens; her feet rested on different portions of the carpet. She had visited Frédéric several times before, but always accompanied by Arnoux. They were now alone together – alone in his own house – it was an extraordinary event, almost an amorous adventure.

She asked to see his little garden; he offered her his arm to show her his property, thirty feet of ground enclosed by houses, adorned with shrubs at the corners and flower-borders in the middle.

The early days of April had arrived. The leaves of the lilacs were already showing green, a breath of pure air was diffused around, and little birds chirped, their song alternating with the distant sound that came from a coachmaker's forge.

Frédéric went to look for a fire-shovel; and, while they walked on side by side, the child made sand-pies on the path.

Madame Arnoux did not believe that he would have a great imagination when he grew up, but he had an affectionate nature. His sister, on the other hand, possessed an innate coldness that sometimes wounded her.

'It will change,' said Frédéric. 'We must never despair.'

She returned:

'We must never despair!'

This automatic repetition of his phrase appeared to him a sort of encouragement; he plucked a rose, the only one in the garden.

'Do you remember . . . a certain bouquet of roses one evening, in a carriage?'

She coloured a little; and, with an air of bantering compassion:

'Ah, how young I was!'

'And this one,' went on Frédéric in a low tone, 'will it go the same way?'

She replied, turning the stem between her fingers, like the thread of a spindle:

'No! I'll keep it!'

She beckoned to the maid, who took the child in her arms; then, on the threshold of the door, in the street, Madame Arnoux breathed in the perfume of the flower, leaning her head on her shoulder with a look as sweet as a kiss.

When he had gone back up to his study, he gazed at the armchair in which she had sat, and every object which she had touched. Something of her circulated in the air around him. The caress of her presence lingered there still.

'So she came here!' he said to himself.

And he was submerged in waves of an infinite tenderness.

Next morning, at eleven o'clock, he presented himself at M. Dambreuse's house. He was received in the dining-room. The banker was seated opposite his wife, eating breakfast. Beside her sat his niece, and at the other side of the table the governess, an English woman, strongly pitted with smallpox.

M. Dambreuse invited his young friend to take his place among them, and when he declined:

'What can I do for you? I'm listening.'

Frédéric confessed, while affecting indifference, that he had come to make a request on behalf of one Arnoux.

'Ha! Ha, the ex-picture-dealer,' said the banker, with a noiseless laugh which exposed his gums. 'Oudry used to stand security for him; they fell out.'

And he proceeded to read the letters and newspapers which lay beside his plate.

Two servants attended without making the least noise on the floor; and the loftiness of the room, which had three tapestry door-curtains and two white marble fountains, the gleaming dishwarmers, the arrangement of the side-dishes, and even the rigid folds of the napkins, all this sumptuous comfort impressed Frédéric's mind with the contrast between it and another breakfast at the Arnoux's house. He did not dare to interrupt M. Dambreuse.

Madame noticed his embarrassment.

'Do you occasionally see our friend Martinon?'

'He'll be here this evening,' said the young girl swiftly.

'Ah, you know that, do you?' said her aunt, fixing on her a cold look.

Then, one of the menservants having leaned over to whisper in her ear:

'Your dressmaker, my dear! . . . Miss Johnson!'

And the governess, in obedience to this summons, left the room with her pupil.

M. Dambreuse, annoyed at the disarrangement of the chairs by this movement, asked what was the matter.

'It's Madame Regimbart.'

'Oh! Regimbart! I know that name. I've come across his signature.'

Frédéric at length broached the question; Arnoux deserved some consideration; he was even going, for the sole purpose of fulfilling his engagements, to sell a house belonging to his wife.

'They say she's very pretty,' said Madame Dambreuse.

The banker added with a jovial air:

'Are you . . . intimate with them?'

Frédéric, without giving an explicit reply, said that he would be very much obliged to him if he would take into consideration . . .

'Well, since it pleases you, so be it! We'll wait! I have some time in hand yet. Suppose we go down to my office, would you care to?'

They had finished breakfast; Madame Dambreuse bowed slightly towards Frédéric, smiling in a singular fashion, with a mixture of politeness and irony. Frédéric had no time to think about it, for M. Dambreuse, as soon as they were alone:

'You didn't come to get your shares.'

And, without permitting him to make any excuses:

'Well! Well! It's right that you should know a little more about the business.'

He offered Frédéric a cigarette, and began.

The General Union of French Coal Mines had been constituted; all that they were waiting for was the order for its incorporation. The mere fact of the amalgamation diminished the cost of super-intendence, and of manual labour, and increased the profits. Besides, the company had conceived a new idea, which was to involve the workmen in its undertaking. It would build houses for them, healthy dwellings; finally, it would constitute itself the purveyor of its employees and would supply everything to them at net prices.

'And they will be the gainers by it, Monsieur: there's true progress; that's the way to reply effectively to certain Republican bleatings! We have on our Board (he showed the prospectus) a peer of France, a scholar who is a member of the Institut, a retired senior officer of the Engineers, well-known names! Details such as these reassure timid capitalists, and appeal to intelligent capitalists!' The Company would have in its favour the orders of the State, then the railways, the steamship lines, the metallurgical establishments, the gas companies, and ordinary households. 'Thus we heat, we light, we penetrate to the very hearth of the humblest homes. But how, you will say to me, can we be sure of selling? By the aid of protective laws, dear Monsieur, and we shall get them; that will be our concern! For my part, anyhow, I am a downright prohibitionist! The Country before anything!' He had been appointed a director; but he had no time to occupy himself with certain details, amongst other things with the writing of their reports. 'I'm a bit out of touch with my authors, I've forgotten my Greek! I need someone . . . who could translate my ideas.' And suddenly: 'Would you like to be that man, with the title of general secretary?'

Frédéric did not know what reply to make.

'Well, what is there to prevent you?'

His functions would be confined to writing a report every year for the shareholders. He would find himself in daily communication with the most important men in Paris. Representing the Company with the workmen, he would be worshipped by them, naturally, which would enable him, later, to get into the General Council, and into the position of a deputy.

Frédéric's ears tingled. Whence came this goodwill? He thanked the banker profusely.

But he must not, said the banker, be dependent on anyone. The best course was to take out some shares, 'a splendid investment besides, for your capital guarantees your position, as your position does your capital.'

'About how much should it amount to?' said Frédéric.

'Oh, well, whatever you please; from forty to sixty thousand francs, I suppose.'

This sum was so trifling for M. Dambreuse and his authority so great, that the young man immediately resolved to sell a farm. He accepted. M. Dambreuse would arrange a meeting one of these days to finish their arrangements.

'So I can tell Jacques Arnoux . . . ?'

'Anything you like! The poor chap! Anything you like!'

Frédéric wrote to Arnoux that he could set his mind at rest, and he despatched the letter by his manservant, who brought back the reply:

'Good!'

His action deserved better recognition, however. He expected a visit, or, at the very least, a letter. He did not receive a visit. No letter was forthcoming.

Was it forgetfulness on their part, or was it deliberate? Since Madame Arnoux had come once, what was to prevent her from coming again? The kind of hint, of avowal, which she had given him was then nothing but a stratagem prompted by self-interest? 'Were they making a fool of me? Is she his accomplice?' A sort of delicacy, in spite of his desire, prevented him from returning to their house.

One morning (three weeks after their interview), M. Dambreuse wrote to him, saying that he expected him the same day in an hour's time.

On the way, the thought of the Arnoux assailed him once more; and, unable to discover any reason for their conduct, he was seized with a feeling of anxiety, a dark sense of foreboding. In order to shake it off, he hailed a cab, and drove to the Rue Paradis.

Arnoux was away travelling.

'And Madame?'

'In the country, at the factory!'

'When is Monsieur coming back?'

'Tomorrow, without fail!'

He would find her alone; this was the moment. Something imperious seemed to cry out in the depths of his consciousness: 'Go, then!'

But M. Dambreuse? 'Ah well, too bad! I'll say I was ill.' He rushed to the railway station; then, as soon as he was in the carriage: 'I've done the wrong thing, perhaps? Bah, what does it matter!'

Green plains stretched out to the right and to the left; the train rolled on; the little station-houses slid past like stage scenery, and the smoke of the locomotive spilled out, always on the same side, its big fleecy masses, which danced for a little while on the grass, and then were dispersed.

Frédéric, who sat alone on his bench, gazed at these objects through sheer weariness, lost in that languor which is produced by the very excess of impatience. Cranes and warehouses appeared. It was Creil.

The town, built on the slopes of two low-lying hills (the first of which is bare, and the second crowned by a wood), with its church tower, its houses of unequal size and its stone bridge, seemed to him to present an aspect of mingled gaiety, reserve, and propriety. A long flat barge descended with the current, and the water splashed

up, whipped by the wind; chickens pecked about in the straw at the
foot of the calvary; a woman passed with wet linen on her head.

After crossing the bridge, he found himself on an island, where
can be seen on the right the ruins of an abbey. A mill with its
wheels revolving barred up the entire width of the second arm of
the Oise, over which the factory projected. Frédéric was greatly
surprised by the imposing character of this structure. He felt more
respect for Arnoux on account of it. Three paces further on, he
turned up an alley, which had a grating at its lower end.

He went in. The doorkeeper called him back, exclaiming:

'Have you a permit?'

'For what?'

'For visiting the establishment!'

Frédéric said in a curt tone that he had come to see M. Arnoux.

'Who is this M. Arnoux?'

'Why, the head, the master, the proprietor, of course!'

'No, monsieur, this factory belongs to M. Lebœuf and M.
Milliet!'

The good woman must be joking. Some workmen arrived; he
spoke to two or three of them; they gave the same response.

Frédéric left the yard, staggering like a drunken man; he looked
so stunned that on the Pont de la Boucherie an inhabitant of the
town, who was smoking his pipe, asked him whether he was
looking for something. This man knew Arnoux's factory. It was
situated at Montataire.

Frédéric asked about a vehicle. The only place there were any
was at the station. He went back there. A shaky-looking trap, to
which was yoked an old horse, with torn harness hanging over the
shafts, stood all alone in front of the luggage office.

An urchin offered to go and find 'Père Pilon'. In ten minutes'
time he came back; Père Pilon was having his lunch. Frédéric,
unable to stand this any longer, walked away. The gates of the
crossing were closed. He had to wait till two trains had passed. At
last, he made a dash into the open country.

The monotonous greenery made it look like an immense billiard-
table. Heaps of iron slag were ranged on both sides of the road, like
mile-markers of stones. A little further on, some factory chimneys
were smoking close beside each other. In front of him, on a round
hillock, stood a little turreted château, with the quadrangular

belfry of a church. At a lower level, long walls formed irregular lines among the trees; and, further down again, the houses of the village spread out.

They have only a single storey, with staircases consisting of three steps made of uncemented blocks. Every now and then the bell of a grocery-shop could be heard. Heavy steps sank into the black mire, and a fine rain was falling, which cut the pale sky with a thousand hatchings.

Frédéric pursued his way along the middle of the street; then he saw on his left, at the opening of a side-street, a large wooden arch, whereon was traced, in letters of gold, the word 'CERAMICS'.

It was not without an object that Jacques Arnoux had selected the vicinity of Creil; by placing his works as close as possible to the other (which had long enjoyed a high reputation), he created a certain confusion in the public mind which was favourable to his interests.

The main body of the building was built on the very bank of a river which flowed through the meadow. The master's house, surrounded by a garden, could be distinguished by the steps in front of it, adorned with four vases containing spiky cacti. Heaps of white clay were drying under sheds; there were others in the open air; and in the middle of the yard stood Sénécal with his everlasting blue overcoat lined with red.

The ex-tutor extended towards Frédéric his cold hand.

'You've come to see the boss? He's not here.'

Frédéric, nonplussed, replied stupidly:

'I know.' But the next moment, correcting himself: 'It's about a matter that concerns Madame Arnoux. Can she receive me?'

'Ah! I haven't seen her for three days,' said Sénécal.

And he broke into a long string of complaints. When he accepted Arnoux's terms, he had understood that he would be living in Paris, and not be forced to bury himself in this country district, far from his friends, deprived of newspapers. No matter! He had got over all that! But Arnoux appeared to pay no heed to his merits. He was, moreover, shallow and retrograde – no one could be more ignorant. Instead of seeking for artistic improvements, it would have been better to introduce coal and gas heating. The fellow was *going under*; Sénécal laid stress on the last words. In short, he disliked his present occupation; and he all but ordered Frédéric to say a word on his behalf so that he might get an increase of salary.

'Don't worry!' said the other.

He met nobody on the staircase. On the first floor, he put his head into an empty room; it was the drawing-room. He called out at the top of his voice. There was no reply; no doubt, the cook had gone out, and so had the maid; at length, having reached the second floor, he pushed open a door. Madame Arnoux was alone, in front of a wardrobe mirror. The belt of her half-open dressing-gown hung down along her hips. One entire half of her hair fell in a dark wave over her right shoulder; and she had raised both arms in order to hold up her chignon with one hand and to put a pin through it with the other. She gave a cry, and disappeared.

Then, she came back again properly dressed. Her figure, her eyes, the sound of her dress, her entire appearance, charmed him. Frédéric could barely restrain himself from covering her with kisses.

'I beg your pardon,' she said, 'but I couldn't . . . '

He had the boldness to interrupt her:

'Nevertheless . . . you looked very nice . . . just now.'

She probably thought this compliment a little coarse, for her cheeks reddened. He was afraid that he might have offended her. She went on:

'What lucky chance has brought you here?'

He did not know what reply to make; and, after a little nervous laugh, which gave him time for reflection:

'If I told you, would you believe me?'

'Why not?'

Frédéric informed her that he had had a frightful dream the other night:

'I dreamt that you were seriously ill, near dying.'

'Oh! My husband and I are never ill!'

'I dreamt only of you,' said he.

She gazed at him calmly.

'Dreams don't always come true.'

Frédéric stammered, sought to find appropriate words, and plunged into a flowing period about the affinity of souls. There existed a force which could, through the intervening bounds of space, bring two persons into communication with each other, make known to each the other's feelings, and enable them to reunite.

She listened to him with her head down, while she smiled with that beautiful smile of hers. He watched her out of the corner of his eye with delight, and poured out his love all the more freely through the easy channel of a commonplace remark. She offered to show him the factory; and, as she insisted, he accepted.

In order to divert his attention at first with something amusing, she showed him the species of museum that decorated the staircase. The specimens hung up against the wall or laid on shelves bore witness to the efforts and the successive fads of Arnoux. After seeking vainly for the copper-red of the Chinese, he had wished to manufacture majolicas, faïence, Etruscan and Oriental ware, and had attempted some of the improvements which were realised at a later period. So it was that one could observe in the series big vases covered with figures of mandarins, bowls of iridescent bronze, pots adorned with Arabian inscriptions, ewers in the style of the Renaissance, and large plates on which two personages were to be seen as if drawn in red chalk, in a delicate, aerial fashion. He now made letters for signboards and wine labels; but his intelligence was not high enough to attain to Art, nor commonplace enough to look merely to profit, so that, without satisfying anyone, he was ruining himself. They were both considering these objects when Mademoiselle Marthe passed by.

'Don't you recognise him?' said her mother to her.

'Oh yes I do!' she replied, bowing to him, while her clear and sceptical glance, the glance of a virgin, seemed to whisper: 'What are *you* doing here?' and she climbed the stairs with her head turned slightly backwards over her shoulder.

Madame Arnoux led Frédéric into the yard, then explained to him in a grave tone how different clays were ground, cleaned, and sifted.

'The most important thing is the preparation of the pastes.'

And she introduced him into a hall filled with vats, in which a vertical axis with horizontal arms was turning. Frédéric felt some regret that he had not flatly declined her offer a little while before.

'Those are the puggers,' said she.

He thought the word grotesque, and as if unseemly in her mouth.

Wide straps ran from one end of the ceiling to the other, so as to roll themselves round drums, and everything moved continuously with a provoking mathematical regularity.

They left the spot, and passed close to a ruined hut, which had formerly been used as a repository for gardening implements.

'It's no longer in use,' said Madame Arnoux.

He replied in a tremulous voice:

'You could be happy in it!'

The din of the fire-pump drowned his words, and they entered the workshop where the roughing-in was done.

Some men, seated at a narrow table, placed each in front of himself on a revolving disc a piece of paste; their left hand scooped out the insides, their right stroked the outer surface, and vases could be seen rising into shape like flowers bursting into bloom.

Madame Arnoux had the moulds for more difficult works shown to him.

In another portion of the building, people were working on the fillets, the necks, and the projecting lines. On the floor above, they were removing the joins, and stopping up with plaster the little holes that had been left by the preceding operations.

Pots were lined up everywhere, on gratings, in corners, in the middle of the corridors.

Frédéric began to feel bored.

'Perhaps this is tiring you?' she said.

Fearing that he would have to terminate his visit there and then, he affected, on the contrary, a tone of great enthusiasm. He even expressed regret at not having devoted himself to this branch of industry.

She appeared surprised.

'Certainly! I would have been able to live near you!'

And as he tried to catch her eye, Madame Arnoux, in order to avoid this, took from a table some little balls of paste, left over from abortive readjustments, flattened them out into a thin cake, and imprinted her hand on them.

'May I take that away with me?' said Frédéric.

'How childish you are, good heavens!'

He was about to reply when in came Sénécal.

As soon as he came in, the sub-manager noticed a breach of the rules. The workshops should be swept every week; this was

Saturday, and, as the workmen had not done what was required, Sénécal announced that they would have to remain an hour longer. 'You've only yourselves to blame!'

They stooped over the work assigned to them unmurmuringly; but their rage could be divined by their hoarse breathing. They were, anyway, very hard to control, having all been dismissed from the big factory. The Republican ruled them harshly. A man of theory, he regarded the people only in the mass, and exhibited an utter absence of pity for individuals.

Frédéric, hampered by his presence, asked Madame Arnoux in a low tone whether they could have an opportunity of seeing the kilns. They descended to the ground floor; and she was just explaining the use of caskets, when Sénécal, who had followed them, placed himself between them.

He continued the explanation himself, expatiated on the various kinds of combustibles, the process of placing in the kiln, the pyroscopes, the kiln hearths, the slips, the lustres, and the metals, making a prodigious display of chemical terms, such as chloride, sulphur, borax, and carbonate. Frédéric could not understand a word, and kept turning every minute towards Madame Arnoux.

'You're not listening,' she said. 'M. Sénécal, however, is very clear. He knows all these things much better than I.'

The mathematician, flattered by this eulogy, proposed a visit to the colouring-shop. Frédéric gave Madame Arnoux an anxious, questioning look. She remained impassive, not caring to be alone with him, very probably, and yet unwilling to leave him. He offered her his arm.

'No, thank you very much! The staircase is too narrow!'

And, when they had reached the top, Sénécal opened the door to an apartment full of women.

They were handling brushes, phials, shells, and plates of glass. Along the cornice, close to the wall, were rows of engraved plates; scraps of thin paper floated about; and a cast-iron stove pumped out a nauseating heat, mingled with the odour of turpentine.

The workwomen were nearly all wearing filthy clothes. One of them, however, stood out; she wore a Madras cotton kerchief, and long earrings. Both slight and, at the same time, plump, she had great black eyes and the fleshy lips of a negress. Her ample bosom swelled up under her blouse, which was fastened round her waist by the string of her skirt; and, with one elbow on the bench and the other arm hanging down, she gazed vaguely into the distance, at the open country. Beside her were a bottle of wine and some sausage.

The regulations prohibited eating in the workshops, a rule intended to secure cleanliness for the work and hygiene for the workers.

Sénécal, through a sense of duty or a need to exercise despotic authority, shouted out to her across the room, pointing towards a framed placard:

'Hey! You there, the Bordelaise! Read out for me Article 9!'

'So what?'

'So, mademoiselle? So it's a three-franc fine you have to pay!'

She looked him straight in the face in an impudent fashion.

'What do I care? The master will take off your fine when he comes back! I don't care about you, laddy!'

Sénécal, who was walking up and down with his hands behind his back, like an usher in the study-room, contented himself with smiling;

'Article 13, insubordination, ten francs!'

The Bordelaise resumed her work. Madame Arnoux, through a sense of propriety, said nothing, but her brows contracted. Frédéric murmured:

'Ah! For a democrat, you're very hard!'

The other replied in a magisterial tone:

'Democracy is not the unbounded licence of individualism. It's the equality of all before the law, the distribution of work, order!'

'You're forgetting humanity!' said Frédéric.

Madame Arnoux took his arm; Sénécal, offended, perhaps, by this silent approbation, went away.

Frédéric experienced an immense relief. Since the morning he had been looking out for the opportunity to declare himself; now it had arrived. Madame Arnoux's spontaneous gesture seemed to him to contain promises; and he asked her, as if to warm his feet, if he might go up to her room. When he was seated beside her, he began once more to feel awkward; he was at a loss for a starting-point. Sénécal, luckily, came to his mind.

'Nothing could be more stupid,' said he, 'than this punishment!'

Madame Arnoux replied:

'Some severe measures are indispensable.'

'What! You who are so kind! Oh, I am mistaken! For you sometimes take pleasure in making other people suffer!'

'I don't understand riddles, my friend.'

And her austere look, still more than the words she used, checked him. Frédéric was determined to go on. A volume of Musset chanced to be on the chest of drawers. He turned over a few pages, then began to talk about love, about its despairs and its transports.

All that, according to Madame Arnoux, was criminal or factitious.

The young man felt wounded by this negative attitude; and, in order to combat it, he cited, by way of proof, the suicides which are read about every day in the newspapers, extolled the great literary types, Phèdre, Dido, Romeo, Desgrieux. He became stuck on his own eloquence.

The fire was no longer burning in the hearth, the rain lashed against the windowpanes. Madame Arnoux, without stirring, remained with both her hands resting on the arms of her chair; the flaps of her bonnet fell like the fillets of a sphinx; her pure profile traced out its pale outlines in the midst of the shadow.

He wanted to cast himself at her feet. There was a creaking in the corridor; he did not dare.

He was, moreover, restrained by a kind of religious awe. That dress, mingling with the surrounding shadows, appeared to him boundless, infinite, incapable of being lifted; and for this very reason his desire redoubled. But the fear of doing too much, and of not doing enough, deprived him of all judgment.

'If she dislikes me,' he thought, 'let her drive me away! If she cares for me, let her encourage me!'

He said, with a sigh:

'So, then, you don't admit that a man may love . . . a woman?'

Madame Arnoux replied:

'When she can be married, he marries her; when she belongs to another, he goes away.'

'So happiness is impossible?'

'No! But it is never to be found in falsehood, anxiety, and remorse.'

'What does it matter, if one is compensated by supreme bliss?'

'The experience is too costly!'

He sought to assail her with irony.

'Would not virtue in that case be merely cowardice?'

'Say rather, clear-sightedness. Even for those women who might forget duty or religion, simple good sense is sufficient. Egoism is a firm base for good behaviour.'

'Ah, what bourgeois maxims you have!'

'But I don't pretend to be a fine lady!'

At that moment the little boy rushed in.

'Mamma, are you coming to dinner?'

'Yes, in a moment.'

Frédéric arose; at the same instant, Marthe appeared.

He could not make up his mind to go; and, with a look full of entreaty:

'These women you speak of are very unfeeling, then?'

'No! But deaf when they have to be.'

And she remained standing on the threshold of her room with her two children at her sides. He bowed without saying a word. She mutely returned his salutation.

What he first experienced was an immense astonishment. This way of letting him understand the futility of his hopes crushed him. He felt lost like a man who has fallen to the bottom of an abyss and knows that no one will come to help him and he must die.

He walked on, however, but at random, seeing nothing; he tripped over stones; he mistook his way. A clatter of wooden shoes sounded close to his ear; the working-girls were leaving the foundry. Then he realised where he was.

The railway lamps traced on the horizon a line of fire. He arrived just as a train was leaving, let himself be pushed into a carriage, and fell asleep.

An hour later on the boulevards, the gaiety of Paris by night made his journey all at once recede into an already far-distant past. He resolved to be strong, and relieved his heart by vilifying Madame Arnoux with insulting epithets:

'She's an idiot, a goose, a soulless brute, let's not give her another thought!'

When he got home, he found in his study a letter of eight pages on blue glazed paper, and signed with the initials 'R. A.'

It began with friendly reproaches:

'What has become of you, my dear? I'm bored.'

The handwriting was so abominable, that Frédéric was about to fling away the entire bundle of sheets, when he noticed in the postscript:

'I count on you to come tomorrow and drive me to the races.'

What was the meaning of this invitation? Was it another trick of the Maréchale's? But a woman does not make a fool of the same man twice without some object; and, seized with curiosity, he read the letter over again attentively.

Frédéric was able to distinguish: 'Misunderstanding . . . having taken the wrong path . . . disillusions . . . Poor children that we are! . . . Like two rivers that join each other! etc.'

This style was quite unlike Rosanette's usual way of speaking. What change had occurred?

He kept the sheets for a long time between his fingers. They smelt of iris; and there was in the form of the characters and the irregular spaces between the lines something suggestive of disarranged clothing, that fired his blood.

'Why shouldn't I go?' he said to himself at length. 'But if Madame Arnoux were to know about it? Ah, let her know! So much the better! And let her feel jealous over it! Then I'll be avenged!'

CHAPTER FOUR

The Maréchale was ready, and was waiting for him.

'This is so nice of you!' she said, fixing a glance of her fine eyes on his face, with an expression at the same time tender and gay.

When she had fastened her bonnet-strings, she sat down on the divan, and remained silent.

'Shall we go?' said Frédéric.

She looked at the clock.

'Oh, no! Not before half-past one' – as if she had imposed on herself this limit to her indecision.

At last, when the hour had struck:

'Ah well, *andiamo, caro mio!*'

And she gave a final touch to her hair, and left directions for Delphine.

'Is Madame coming home to dinner?'

'Why should we, indeed? We'll dine together somewhere, at the Café Anglais, wherever you wish!'

'All right!'

Her little dogs were yelping around her.

'We can take them with us, can't we?'

Frédéric carried them himself to the vehicle. It was a hired berlin with two post-horses and a postilion; he had put his manservant on the seat behind. The Maréchale appeared satisfied with his arrangements; then, as soon as she had seated herself, she asked him whether he had been round to see the Arnoux lately.

'Not for the past month,' said Frédéric.

'I met him the day before yesterday; he was even thinking of coming today. But he has all sorts of troubles, another lawsuit, something. What a funny man!'

'Yes! Very funny!'

Frédéric added with an air of indifference:

'Now that I think of it, do you still see . . . what's his name, that ex-singer . . . Delmar?'

She replied tersely:

'No! That's all over!'

So their break-up was definite. Frédéric derived some hope from this circumstance.

They descended the Quartier Bréda at an easy pace; as it was Sunday, the streets were deserted, and householders' faces appeared at the windows. The carriage went on more rapidly; the noise of the wheels made the passers-by turn round, the leather of the hood, which was lowered, glittered, the manservant stuck out his chest, and the two Havana dogs, side by side, seemed like two ermine muffs laid on the cushions. Frédéric let himself sway with the rocking of the carriage-straps. The Maréchale turned her head to the right and to the left with a smile on her face.

Her hat of pearly straw was trimmed with black lace. The hood of her burnous floated in the wind; and she sheltered herself from the sun under a parasol of lilac satin, pointed at the top like a pagoda.

'What lovely little fingers!' said Frédéric, gently taking her other hand, the left one, which was adorned with a gold bracelet in the form of a curb-chain. 'I say, that's pretty; where did it come from?'

'Oh, I've had it a long time,' said the Maréchale.

The young man did not challenge this hypocritical answer. He preferred to 'profit by the circumstance'. And, still keeping hold of the wrist, he pressed his lips to it between the glove and the cuff.

'Stop! People will see us!'

'Pooh! What does that matter!'

After the Place de la Concorde, they drove along the Quai de la Conférence and the Quai de Billy, where there is a cedar in a garden. Rosanette believed that the Lebanon was in China; she laughed herself at her ignorance and asked Frédéric to give her lessons in geography. Then, leaving the Trocadéro on the right, they crossed the Pont d'Iéna, and drew up at length in the middle of the Champ de Mars, near some other vehicles already drawn up in the Hippodrome.

The grass hillocks were covered with the common people. Some spectators could be seen on the balcony of the École Militaire; and the two pavilions outside the weighing-room, the two galleries contained within its enclosure, and a third in front of that of the king, were filled with a fashionably dressed crowd whose deportment showed their regard for this as yet novel form of amusement. The race-going public, more select at this period, looked more refined; it was the era of trouser-straps, velvet collars, and white gloves. The ladies, attired in bright colours, wore dresses with long waists, and, seated on the tiers of the stands, they looked like huge beds of flowers, spotted here and there with black by the dark costumes of the men. But every glance was directed towards the celebrated Algerian Bou-Maza, who sat, impassive, between two staff officers in one of the private galleries. That of the Jockey Club contained none but grave-looking gentlemen.

The more enthusiastic portion of the throng was seated lower down, close to the track, protected by two lines of sticks linked by ropes; in the immense oval described by this pathway, coconut-sellers were shaking their rattles, others were selling programmes of the races, others were hawking cigars, in a vast buzz of noise; the municipal guards passed to and fro; a bell, hung from a post covered with numbers, began ringing. Five horses appeared, and the spectators in the galleries resumed their seats.

Meanwhile, big clouds touched with their spirals the tops of the elms opposite. Rosanette was afraid that it was going to rain.

'I have umbrellas,' said Frédéric, 'and everything we need to amuse ourselves,' he added, opening the boot, in which there was a stock of provisions in a basket.

'Bravo! We understand each other!'

'And we'll understand each other still better, won't we?'

'That may be!' she said, blushing.

The jockeys, in silk jackets, were trying to draw up their horses in order, and were holding them back with both hands. Somebody lowered a red flag. Then all five bent over the bristling manes, and off they went. At first they remained pressed close to each other in a single mass; this presently stretched out and broke up; the jockey in the yellow jacket was near falling in the middle of the first circuit; for a long time it was uncertain whether Filly or Tibi should be ahead; then Tom Thumb appeared in the lead; but Clubstick, who had been in the rear since the start, came up with the others and came in first, beating Sir Charles by two lengths; it was a surprise; the crowd shouted; the wooden stands shook with the stamping of feet.

'We are having fun!' said the Marechale. 'I love you, darling!'

Frédéric no longer doubted that his happiness was secure; Rosanette's last words were confirmation.

A hundred paces away from him, in a four-wheeled cabriolet, a lady appeared. She was leaning out of the carriage door, and then quickly drawing back; this movement was repeated several times; Frédéric could not distinguish her face. He was seized by a strong suspicion, however, that it was Madame Arnoux. And yet this seemed impossible! Why should she have come here?

He stepped out of the carriage, pretending that he wished to stroll around the weighing-room.

'You're not very gallant!' said Rosanette.

He paid no heed and went on. The four-wheeled cabriolet, turning round, broke into a trot.

Frédéric at the same moment found himself buttonholed by Cisy.

'Hello, my dear boy! How are you? Hussonnet is over there! Listen to me!'

Frédéric tried to shake him off in order to get up with the cabriolet. The Maréchale was beckoning to him to come back to her. Cisy saw her, and insisted on bidding her good day.

Since the period of mourning for his grandmother was over, he was successfully putting his ideal into practice and succeeding in *having some cachet*. A tartan waistcoat, a short coat, large bows on his pumps, and an entrance card stuck in the ribbon of his hat, nothing, in fact, was wanting to produce what he described himself as his *chic*, a *chic* redolent of England and the musketeer. He began by finding fault with the Champ de Mars, with its execrable turf, then spoke of the Chantilly races, and the droll things people did there, swore that he could drink a dozen glasses of champagne while the clock was striking the twelve strokes of midnight, suggested that the Marechale should lay a bet, gently stroked her two lapdogs; and, leaning against the carriage door with the other elbow, he kept on talking nonsense, with the knob of his walking-stick in his mouth, his legs wide apart, and hip stuck out. Frédéric, standing beside him, was smoking, while endeavouring to make out what had become of the cabriolet.

The bell having rung, Cisy took himself off, to the great delight of Rosanette, who said he had been boring her to death.

The second race had nothing special about it, neither had the third, except for a man who was carried off on a stretcher. The fourth, in which eight horses contested the City Stakes, was more interesting.

The spectators in the gallery had clambered on to their seats. The others, standing up in the carriages, followed with opera-glasses in their hands the movements of the jockeys; they could be seen speeding like red, yellow, white or blue patches across the entire space occupied by the crowd that had gathered around the ring of the hippodrome. At a distance, their speed did not appear to be very great; at the opposite side of the Champ de Mars, they seemed even to be slowing down, and to be merely sliding along, so that the horses' bellies touched the ground without their outstretched legs bending at all. But, coming back fast, they grew larger; they cut the air as they passed, the ground trembled, pebbles went flying; the wind, blowing out the jockeys' jackets, made them flutter like veils; each of them lashed the animal he rode with great blows of his whip in order to reach the finishing post. The numbers were removed, another was hoisted in their place and, to the sounds of applause, the victorious horse dragged himself along to the weighing-room, all covered with sweat, his knees stiff, his neck bowed, while his rider, looking as if he were expiring in his saddle, held his sides.

The final race was delayed by a dispute. The crowd, bored, began to scatter. Groups of men were chatting at the lower end of the stands. The talk had a free and easy tone; some fashionable ladies left, scandalised by seeing fast women in their immediate vicinity.

There were also some specimens of the ladies who appeared at public balls, boulevard actresses – and it was not the best-looking who received the most appreciation. The elderly Georgine Aubert, she whom a writer of vaudevilles called the Louis XI of prostitution, horribly painted, and giving vent every now and then to a kind of laugh resembling a grunt, remained reclining at full length in her long trap, covered with a sable tippet as if it were midwinter. Madame de Remoussot, who had become fashionable because of her lawsuit, sat enthroned on the seat of a brake in company with some Americans; and Thérèse Bachelu, with her look of a Gothic virgin, filled with her dozen furbelows the interior of a tiny snail-carriage which had, in place of an apron, a flower-stand filled with roses. The Maréchale was jealous of these magnificences; in order to attract attention, she began to make large gestures and to speak in a very loud voice.

Gentlemen recognised her, and bowed to her. She returned their salutations while telling Frédéric their names. They were all counts, viscounts, dukes, and marquises; and he swelled with pride, for in all eyes he could read a certain respect for his good fortune.

Cisy had a no less happy air in the midst of the circle of mature men that surrounded him. They were smiling from above their cravats, as if they were mocking him; at length he gave a tap in the hand of the oldest of them, and made his way towards the Maréchale.

She was eating, with an affectation of gluttony, a slice of *foie gras*; Frédéric, in order to make himself agreeable to her, followed her example, with a bottle of wine on his knees.

The four-wheeled cabriolet reappeared; it was Madame Arnoux. Her face turned extraordinarily pale.

'Give me some champagne!' said Rosanette.

And, lifting up her glass, full to the brim, as high as possible, she exclaimed:

'Hey, you over there! Here's to respectable women, the wife of my protector, hey!'

There was a great burst of laughter all round her and the cabriolet disappeared. Frédéric tugged at her by the dress, and was on the point of flying into a passion. But Cisy was there, in the same attitude as before; and, more confident than ever, he invited Rosanette to dine with him that very evening.

'Impossible!' she replied. 'We're going together to the Café Anglais.'

Frédéric, as if he had heard nothing, remained silent; and Cisy quitted the Maréchale with a look of disappointment on his face.

While he had been standing talking to her by the right-hand door of the carriage, Hussonnet had appeared on the left, and, catching the words 'Café Anglais':

'It's a nice place! Suppose we had a bite there, eh?'

'Just as you like,' said Frédéric, who, sunk down in the corner of the berlin, was gazing at the horizon as the four-wheeled cabriolet vanished from his sight, feeling that an irreparable thing had just happened, and that there was an end of his great love. And the other was there beside him, the gay and easy love! But, worn out, full of conflicting desires, and no longer even knowing what he wanted, he was possessed by a feeling of infinite sadness, a longing to die.

A great noise of footsteps and voices made him raise his head; the little ragamuffins, climbing over the ropes of the track were coming to stare at the stands; people were leaving. A few drops of rain began to fall. The crush of vehicles increased. Hussonnet got lost.

'Well! All the better!' said Frédéric.

'Do we prefer to be alone?' said the Maréchale, as she placed her hand on his.

Then there swept past them with a glitter of brass and steel a magnificent landau drawn by four horses driven in the Daumont style by two jockeys in velvet jackets with gold fringes. Madame Dambreuse was by her husband's side, and Martinon was on the other seat facing them; all three gazed at Frédéric in astonishment.

'They recognised me!' he said to himself.

Rosanette wished to stop in order to get a better view of the people driving away from the course. Madame Arnoux might again make her appearance. He called out to the postilion:

'Go on! Go on! Forward!'

And the berlin dashed towards the Champs-Élysées in the midst of the other carriages, the traps, britzkas, wurts, tandems, tilburies, dog-carts, tilted carts with leather curtains, in which workmen on the spree were singing, or one-horse chaises driven with prudence by fathers of families. In victorias crammed with people, some young fellow seated on the others' feet let both his legs hang down outside. Large broughams, with cloth seats, carried dozing dowagers; or else a splendid stepper went by drawing a gig as simple and coquettish as the black coat of a dandy. Meanwhile, the shower grew heavier. Umbrellas, parasols and mackintoshes were taken out; people called to each other from afar: 'Good day!' 'Are you quite well?' 'Yes!' 'No!' 'Bye-bye!' – and the faces succeeded each other with the rapidity of Chinese shadows. Frédéric and Rosanette did not speak to each other, feeling a sort of numbness at seeing all these wheels continually turning by their side.

At times, the rows of carriages, too closely pressed together, stopped all at the same time in several lines. Then people remained side by side and examined each other. Over panels adorned with coats-of-arms, indifferent glances were cast on the crowd; eyes full of envy gleamed from the interiors of hackney coaches; supercilious smiles responded to the haughty manner in which some people carried their heads; mouths gaping wide expressed idiotic admiration; and, here and there, some lounger, in the middle of the road, fell back with a bound, in order to avoid a rider who was galloping through the midst of the vehicles, and had succeeded in getting away from them. Then, everything set itself in motion once more; the coachmen let go the reins, and lowered their whips; the horses, excited, shook their curb-chains, and flung foam around them; and the damp rumps and harness steamed in the watery mist, through which struggled the rays of the sinking sun. Passing under the Arc de Triomphe, there stretched out at the height of a man, a reddish light, which shed a glittering lustre on the hubs of the wheels, the handles of the carriage doors, the ends of the shafts, and the rings of the saddles, and on the two sides of the great avenue – like a river in which manes, garments, and human heads were undulating – the trees, all glittering with rain, rose up like two green walls. The blue of the sky overhead, reappearing in certain places, had the softness of satin.

Then, Frédéric recalled the days, already distant, when he used to yearn for the inexpressible happiness of finding himself in one of these carriages by the side of one of these women. He had attained this happiness, and was none the more joyous.

The rain had ceased falling. The pedestrians, who had sought shelter between the columns of the Garde-Meuble, took their departure. People walking along the Rue Royale, went back up towards the boulevard. In front of the residence of the Minister of Foreign Affairs, a group of sightseers had taken up their posts on the steps.

When it had got up as high as the Chinese Baths, as there were holes in the pavement, the berlin slackened its pace. A man in a light brown overcoat was walking on the edge of the footpath. A splash, spurting out from under the springs, spread over his back. The man turned round, furious. Frédéric grew pale; he had recognised Deslauriers.

At the door of the Café Anglais he sent away the carriage.

Rosanette had gone up before him while he was paying the postilion.

He found her on the stairs chatting with a gentleman. Frédéric took her arm. But in the middle of the corridor a second gentleman stopped her.

'Go ahead!' said she; 'I won't be a minute!'

And he entered the private room alone. Through the two open windows people could be seen at the casements of the other houses opposite. Large silky streaks were shimmering on the asphalt as it began to dry, and a magnolia, placed on the edge of the balcony, sent its perfume through the room. This fragrance and freshness had a relaxing effect on his nerves; and he sank down on the red divan underneath the glass.

The Maréchale came back; and, kissing him on the forehead:

'Is my poor pet upset?'

'Perhaps!' was his reply.

'You're not the only one, you know!'

Which was as much as to say: 'Let's each forget our own troubles in a bliss which we shall share!'

Then she placed the petal of a flower between her lips and held it out for him to nibble. This movement, full of a voluptuous grace and almost benediction, had a softening influence on Frédéric.

'Why do you hurt me?' he said, thinking of Madame Arnoux.

'I, hurt you?'

And, standing before him, she looked at him with her eyes half closed and her two hands resting on his shoulders.

All his virtue, all his rancour gave way before an infinite weakness of will.

He continued:

'Because you won't love me!' And he took her on his knees.

She did not resist; he put both arms round her waist; the crackling sound of her silk dress inflamed him.

'Where are they?' said Hussonnet's voice in the corridor.

The Maréchale arose abruptly, and went across to the other side of the room, turning her back to the door.

She ordered oysters, and they sat down.

Hussonnet was not amusing. By dint of writing every day on all sorts of subjects, reading many newspapers, listening to a great number of discussions, and uttering paradoxes in order to dazzle, he had in the end lost the exact idea of things, blinding himself with his own feeble fireworks. The embarrassments of a life which had formerly been frivolous, but was now a hard one, kept him in a state of perpetual agitation; and his impotence, which he would not admit to himself, rendered him snappish and sarcastic. Referring to a new ballet entitled *Ozaï*, he uttered a diatribe against dancing and from there to the Opéra; and thence to the Italian Opera, now replaced by a company of Spanish actors, 'as if people had not had enough of the Castiles!' Frédéric was shocked at this, owing to his romantic attachment to Spain; and with a view to diverting the conversation into a new channel, he enquired about the Collège de France, from which Edgar Quinet and Mickiewicz had just been excluded. But Hussonnet, an admirer of M. de Maistre, declared himself on the side of Authority and Spiritualism. But he cast doubt on the most well-established facts, denied history, and queried the most undisputed certainties, even exclaiming at the word 'geometry': 'What nonsense geometry is!' All this intermingled with imitations of actors. Sainville specially was his model.

These absurdities were driving Frédéric to distraction. In a gesture of impatience he accidentally kicked one of the little dogs under the table.

Both animals began barking in a horrible fashion.

'You ought to get them taken home!' he said abruptly.

Rosanette did not know anyone to whom she could entrust them.

So he turned to the Bohemian:

'Look here, Hussonnet, make yourself useful!'

'Oh yes, my sweet! That would be so kind!'

Hussonnet left without further urging.

What was his reward for being so obliging? Frédéric did not want to think about it. He was even beginning to enjoy being alone with her, when a waiter entered.

'Madame, somebody is asking for you!'

'What! Again?'

'But I must see who it is!' said Rosanette.

He was thirsting for her; he needed her. This disappearance seemed to him an act of felony, almost an obscenity. Whatever did she want? Was it not enough to have insulted Madame Arnoux?

As for the latter, it served her right! Now he hated all women; and he felt the tears choking him, for his love had been misunderstood and his desire eluded.

The Maréchale returned, and presented Cisy to him:

'I've invited Monsieur to join us. I've done right, haven't I?'

'What! Oh, but of course!'

Frédéric, with the smile of a soul in torment, beckoned to the gentleman to take a seat.

The Maréchale began to run her eye through the menu, stopping at every fantastic name.

'Suppose we ate a turban of rabbits *à la Richelieu* and a pudding *à la d'Orléans*?'

'Oh! No Orléans, pray!' exclaimed Cisy, who was a Legitimist, and imagined he was being witty.

'Would you prefer a turbot *à la Chambord*?' she next asked.

Frédéric was disgusted with this display of politeness.

The Maréchale made up her mind to order a simple tournedos, some crayfish, truffles, a pineapple salad, and vanilla sorbets.

'Then we'll see. Go on for the present. Ah, I was forgetting! Bring me a sausage! Not with garlic!'

And she called the waiter 'young man', struck her glass with her knife, and flung up the crumb of her bread to the ceiling. She wished to drink some Burgundy immediately.

'It is not taken at the beginning of a meal,' said Frédéric.

It was sometimes done, according to the Vicomte.

'Oh no! Never!'

'Yes, indeed, I assure you!'

'Ha! You see!'

The look with which she accompanied these words meant: 'This is a rich man, pay attention to what he says!'

Meantime, the door was opening every moment, the waiters were bawling, and on an infernal piano in the adjoining room someone was strumming a waltz. Then the races led to a discussion about horsemanship and the two rival systems. Cisy was upholding Baucher, and Frédéric the Comte d'Aure, when Rosanette shrugged her shoulders:

'Enough, please! He's a better judge of these things than you are. Come now!'

She was biting into a pomegranate, with her elbow resting on the table; the wax candles of the candelabrum in front of her were flickering in the wind; this white light penetrated her skin with mother-of-pearl tones, gave a pink hue to her lids, and made her eyeballs glitter; the red colour of the fruit blended with the scarlet of her lips, her thin nostrils quivered; and there was about her entire person an air of insolence, intoxication and abandonment that exasperated Frédéric, and yet filled his heart with wild desires.

Then she asked, in a calm voice, who owned that big landau with chestnut-coloured livery.

'The Comtesse Dambreuse,' replied Cisy.

'They're very rich, aren't they?'

'Oh, very rich! Although Madame Dambreuse, who was merely a Mademoiselle Boutron and the daughter of a prefect, had a very modest fortune.'

Her husband, on the other hand, must have inherited several estates. Cisy enumerated them: as he visited the Dambreuses, he knew their family history.

Frédéric, in order to make himself disagreeable to him, persisted in contradicting him. He maintained that Madame Dambreuse's maiden name was de Boutron, which proved that she was of a noble family.

'No matter! I'd really like to have her equipage!' said the Maréchale, throwing herself back in the armchair.

And the sleeve of her dress, slipping up a little, showed on her left wrist a bracelet adorned with three opals.

Frédéric noticed it.

'Oh, but . . .'

All three looked into one another's faces, and reddened.

The door was cautiously half-opened, the brim of a hat appeared, and then Hussonnet's profile.

'Pray excuse me if I disturb the lovers!'

But he stopped, astonished at seeing Cisy, and that Cisy had taken his place.

Another cover was brought; and, as he was very hungry, he snatched up at random from what remained of the dinner some meat from a dish, fruit out of a basket, and drank with one hand while he helped himself with the other, all the time telling them the result of his mission. The two bow-wows had been taken home. Nothing to report at the house. He had found the cook in the company of a soldier, a fictitious story which he had invented simply for the sake of effect.

The Maréchale took down her cloak from the hook. Frédéric made a rush towards the bell, calling out to the waiter, who was some distance away:

'A carriage!'

'I have mine,' said the Vicomte.

'But, Monsieur!'

'Nevertheless, Monsieur!'

And they stared into each other's eyes, both pale and their hands trembling.

At last, the Maréchale took Cisy's arm, and pointing towards the Bohemian seated at the table:

'You'd better look after him! He's choking himself. I wouldn't care to let his devotion to my pugs be the cause of his death!'

The door closed behind them.

'Well?' said Hussonnet.

'Well, what?'

'I thought . . . '

'What did you think?'

'Weren't you . . . ?'

He completed the sentence with a gesture.

'Oh no! Absolutely not!'

Hussonnet did not press the matter further.

He had had an object in inviting himself to dinner. His journal, which was no longer called *L'Art*, but *Le Flambard*, with this epigraph: 'Gunners, to your cannons!' not being at all in a flourishing condition, he had a mind to change it into a weekly review, conducted by himself, without any assistance from Deslauriers. He again referred to the old project and explained his latest plan.

Frédéric, probably not understanding what he was talking about, replied with some vague words. Hussonnet snatched up several cigars from the table, said 'Goodbye, old chap,' and disappeared.

Frédéric called for the bill. It had a long list of items; and the waiter, with his napkin under his arm, was waiting for his money, when another, a sallow-faced individual who looked like Martinon, came and said to him:

'Beg pardon, they forgot at the bar to add in the charge for the cab.'

'What cab?'

'The cab the gentleman took a short time ago for the little dogs.'

And the waiter's face lengthened, as if he pitied the poor young man. Frédéric wanted to hit him. He gave the waiter the twenty francs' change as a tip.

'Thank you, my lord!' said the man with the napkin, bowing low.

Frédéric passed the whole of the next day brooding over his anger and humiliation. He reproached himself for not having given a slap in the face to Cisy. As for the Maréchale, he swore not to see her again; there were plenty of others just as good-looking; and, as money was required in order to possess these women, he would speculate on the Bourse with the purchase-money of his farm, he would get rich, he would crush the Maréchale and everyone else with his opulence. When the evening came, he was surprised at not having thought of Madame Arnoux.

'So much the better! What's the good of it?'

Two days after, at eight o'clock, Pellerin came to pay him a visit. He began by expressing his admiration of the furniture and flattering him. Then, abruptly:

'You were at the races on Sunday?'

'Yes, alas!'

Thereupon the painter decried the anatomy of English horses, and praised the horses of Géricault and the horses of the Parthenon.

'Was Rosanette with you?'

And he artfully proceeded to sing her praises.

Frédéric's freezing manner put him a little out of countenance. He did not know how to bring up the question of her portrait.

His first idea had been to do a Titian. But gradually the varied colouring of his model had bewitched him; and he had gone on boldly with the work, heaping up layer on layer and light on light. Rosanette, in the beginning, was enchanted; her appointments with Delmar had interrupted the sittings, and left Pellerin time enough to get bedazzled. Then, as his admiration began to subside, he had asked himself whether the painting might not be on a larger scale. He had gone to have another look at the Titians, recognized the gap between them and his, and seen wherein his own short-comings lay; and he had begun to go over the outlines again in the most simple fashion. After that, he had sought, by scraping them off, to lose and to mingle the tones of the head and those of the background; and the face had assumed consistency and the shadows vigour; the whole work had a look of greater firmness. At length the Maréchale had come back. She had even indulged in some hostile criticisms; the painter naturally had persevered. After getting into a violent passion at her silliness, he had said to himself that perhaps she was right. Then had begun the era of doubts, twinges of reflection which cause cramps in the stomach, insomnia, feverishness and disgust with oneself; he had had the courage to make some retouchings, but without much heart, and with a feeling that his work was bad.

He complained merely of having been refused a place in the Salon, then he reproached Frédéric for not having come to see the Maréchale's portrait.

'What do I care about the Maréchale?'

Such an expression of unconcern emboldened him.

'Would you believe that that stupid girl has no interest in the thing any longer?'

What he did not mention was that he had asked her for a thousand crowns. Now the Maréchale had not given herself much bother about ascertaining who was going to pay, and, preferring to get money out of Arnoux for things of a more urgent character, had not even spoken to him on the subject.

'Well, what about Arnoux?' said Frédéric.

She had referred him to Arnoux. The ex–picture–dealer wished to have nothing to do with the portrait.

'He maintains that it belongs to Rosanette.'

'Yes, it is hers.'

'What! She's the one who sent me to you!' was Pellerin's answer.

If he had believed in the excellence of his work, he would not have thought perhaps of making capital out of it. But a sum of money (and a big sum) would be an effective reply to the critics, and would strengthen his own position. To get rid of him, Frédéric courteously enquired his terms.

The extravagance of the figure named by Pellerin quite took away his breath, and he replied:

'No! Oh no!'

'But you're her lover, you're the one who commissioned it!'

'Excuse me, I was only the intermediary!'

'But I can't remain with this on my hands!'

The artist was losing his temper.

'Ah! I didn't imagine you were so greedy!'

'Nor you so stingy! I wish you good day!'

He had just gone out when Sénécal came in.

Frédéric, taken aback, stirred uneasily.

'What's the matter?'

Sénécal told his story.

'On Saturday, at about nine o'clock, Madame Arnoux got a letter summoning her to Paris; as there happened to be nobody in the place at the time to go to Creil for a vehicle, she asked me to go there myself. I refused, for is this not part of my duties. She left, and came back on Sunday evening. Yesterday morning, Arnoux turns up at the factory. The Bordelaise made a complaint to him. I don't know what is going on between them, but he cancelled her fine in front of everybody. Some sharp words passed between us. In short, he closed accounts with me, and here I am!"

Then, stressing each word:

'Anyway, I'm not sorry, I've done my duty. No matter – you were the cause of it.'

'What?' exclaimed Frédéric, alarmed lest Sénécal might have guessed his secret.

Sénécal had not, however, guessed anything, for he replied:

'I mean that, but for you I might have done better.'

Frédéric was seized with a kind of remorse.

'In what way can I be of service to you now?'

Sénécal wanted some employment, a situation.

'That is an easy thing for you to manage. You know so many people, Monsieur Dambreuse among others, so Deslauriers told me.'

This reminder of Deslauriers was by no means agreeable to his friend. He scarcely cared to call on the Dambreuses again after his meeting with them in the Champ de Mars.

'I am not on sufficiently intimate terms with them to recommend anyone.'

The democrat endured this refusal stoically, and after a minute's silence:

'All this, I'm sure, is due to the Bordelaise and also to your Madame Arnoux.'

This 'your' had the effect of wiping out of Frédéric's heart the slight modicum of good will he retained for Sénécal. Nevertheless, out of courtesy he took up the key of his desk.

Sénécal forestalled him.

'No thanks!'

Then, forgetting his troubles, he talked about the affairs of the nation, the lavish awarding of crosses of the Legion of Honour on the king's birthday, the question of a change of ministry, the Drouillard case and the Bénier case, scandals of the day, declaimed against the bourgeois, and predicted a revolution.

His eyes were attracted by a Japanese dagger hanging on the wall. He took hold of it, tried the handle, then flung it on the sofa with an air of disgust.

'Come, then! Goodbye! I must go to Notre-Dame-de-Lorette.'

'Goodness! Why?'

'Today is the anniversary service for Godefroy Cavaignac. He died in harness, that man! But all is not over! . . . Who knows?'

And Sénécal, with a show of fortitude, put out his hand:

'Perhaps we shall never see each other again! Goodbye!'

This 'goodbye,' repeated twice, his knitted brows as he gazed at the dagger, his resignation, and the solemnity of his manner, above all, plunged Frédéric into a thoughtful mood, but very soon he thought no more of it.

During the same week, his notary in Le Havre sent him the sum realised by the sale of his farm – one hundred and seventy-four thousand francs. He divided it into two portions, invested the first half in government bonds, and took the second half to a stock-broker to risk it on the Stock Exchange

He dined at fashionable taverns, went to the theatres, and was trying to amuse himself as best he could, when Hussonnet addressed a letter to him announcing in a gay fashion that the Maréchale had got rid of Cisy the very day after the races. Frédéric was delighted at this news, without taking the trouble to ascertain what the Bohemian's motive was in giving him the information.

It so happened that he met Cisy, three days later. That aristo-cratic young gentleman put a brave face on things, and even invited him to dine on the following Wednesday.

On the morning of that day, Frédéric received a notification from a process-server, in which M. Charles-Jean-Baptiste Oudry apprised him that by the terms of a legal judgment he had become the purchaser of a property situated at Belleville, belonging to M. Jacques Arnoux, and that he was ready to pay the two hundred and twenty-three thousand francs for which it had been sold. But, as it appeared by the same decree that the amount of the mortgages with which the estate was encumbered exceeded the purchase money, Frédéric's claim would in consequence be completely forfeited.

The entire mischief arose from not having renewed the registration of the mortgage within the proper time. Arnoux had undertaken to attend to this matter, and had then forgotten all about it. Frédéric got into a rage with him for this, and when his anger had passed off:

'Well, anyway . . . so what? If this can save him, so much the better! It won't kill me! Let's think no more about it!'

But, while moving his papers about on the table, he came across Hussonnet's letter, and noticed the postscript, which had not at first attracted his attention. The Bohemian was asking for just five thousand francs to give the journal a start.

'Ah! This fellow is getting on my nerves!'

And he sent a curt answer, unceremoniously refusing the application. After that, he dressed himself to go to the Maison d'Or.

Cisy introduced his guests, beginning with the most respectable of them, a big, white haired gentleman:

'The Marquis Gilbert des Aulnays, my godfather. Monsieur Anselme de Forchambeaux,' he said next (this was a slender, fair-haired young man, already bald); then, pointing towards a simple-mannered man of about forty: 'Joseph Boffreu, my cousin; and this is my old tutor Monsieur Vezou', a person who seemed a mixture of a ploughman and a seminarist, with large whiskers and a long frock-coat fastened at the bottom by a single button, so that it fell over his chest like a shawl.

Cisy was expecting someone else, the Baron de Comaing, 'who might perhaps come, but it was not certain.' He left the room every minute, and appeared to be worried about something; finally, at eight o'clock, they proceeded into a dining room splendidly illuminated and too spacious for the number of guests. Cisy had selected it on purpose, for show.

A vermilion epergne laden with flowers and fruit occupied the centre of the table, which was covered with silver dishes, after the old French fashion; glass dishes full of salted titbits and spices formed a border all around it; jugs of chilled rosé wine stood at regular distances from each other; five glasses of different sizes were ranged before each plate, with things of which the use could not be divined, countless dinner utensils of an ingenious description – and for the first course alone, there were: a sturgeon's cheeks moistened with champagne, a York ham with tokay, thrushes *au gratin*, roast quail, a béchamel vol-au-vent, a stew of red-legged partridges, and at the two ends of all this, finely sliced potatoes mixed with truffles. The apartment was illuminated by a chandelier and some candelabra, and was hung with red damask. Four menservants in black coats stood behind the Moroccan leather armchairs. At the sight of all this the guests cried out, especially the Tutor.

'My word, our host has offered us a veritable feast! It's too splendid!'

'This?' said the Vicomte de Cisy. 'Come now!'

And, as they were swallowing the first spoonful:

'Well, my dear old friend des Aulnays, have you been to the Palais-Royal to see *Père et Portier*?'

'You know that I haven't the time!' replied the Marquis.

His mornings were taken up with a course of arboriculture, his evenings were spent at the Agricultural Club, and all his afternoons were occupied by research in factories manufacturing ploughing equipment. As he lived in Saintonge for three fourths of the year, he took advantage of his visits to the capital to broaden his education; and his large-brimmed hat, which lay on a side-table, was crammed with pamphlets.

But Cisy, observing that M. de Forchambeaux refused to take wine:

'Go on, damn it, drink! You're not showing much spirit for your last meal as a bachelor!'

At this remark all bowed and congratulated him.

'And the young lady,' said the Tutor, 'is charming, I'm sure?'

'I should say so!' exclaimed Cisy. 'No matter, he's making a mistake; marriage is such a stupid thing!'

'You talk in a thoughtless fashion, my friend!' returned M. des

Aulnays, while tears began to gather in his eyes at the recollection of his own dead wife.

And Forchambeaux repeated several times in succession, sniggering:

'You'll come to it, you'll come to it!'

Cisy protested. He preferred to enjoy himself, to 'be Regency'. He wanted to learn foot-boxing, in order to visit the thieves' taverns in the Cité, like prince Rodolphe in the *Mysteries of Paris*, drew out of his pocket a rough clay pipe, abused the servants, and drank a great quantity; and, in order to create a good impression of himself, he denigrated all the dishes. He even sent away the truffles, and the Tutor, who was enjoying them exceedingly, said cravenly:

'They're not as good as your grandmother's snow eggs!'

Then he went on chatting with the person sitting next to him, the agriculturist, who found many advantages from his sojourn in the country, if it were only to be able to bring up his daughters with simple tastes. The Tutor approved of his ideas and toadied to him, supposing that this gentleman possessed influence over his former pupil, whose man of business he was secretly anxious to become.

Frédéric had come there filled with hostility to Cisy; his idiocy had disarmed him. But as his gestures, face, and entire person brought back to his recollection the dinner at the Café Anglais, he got more and more irritated; and he lent his ears to the uncomplimentary remarks made in a low tone by Joseph, the cousin, a fine young fellow without any money, who was a lover of hunting and speculated on the Stock Exchange. Cisy, for the sake of a laugh, called him a 'thief' several times; then suddenly:

'Ah! Here comes the Baron!'

There entered a jovial-looking chap of thirty, with something tough-looking in his features and athletic-looking about his limbs, wearing his hat over his ear and a flower in his buttonhole. He was the Vicomte's ideal. He was delighted at having him there; and stimulated by his presence, he even attempted a pun, for he said, as they passed round a woodcock:

'There's the best of La Bruyère's characters!'

After that, he put a heap of questions to M. de Comaing about persons unknown to the other guests; then, as if an idea had suddenly seized him:

'Tell me! Did you give some thought to me?'

The other shrugged his shoulders:

'You're not old enough, my little man! It's impossible!'

Cisy had begged of the Baron to get him admitted into his club. But the other, no doubt taking pity on his vanity:

'Ah! I was forgetting! A thousand congratulations on having won your bet, my dear fellow!'

'What bet?'

'The bet you made at the races to go back that evening to that lady's house.'

Frédéric felt as if he had been lashed with a whip. He was speedily appeased by the look of utter confusion in Cisy's face.

Indeed, the Maréchale, the very next morning, had already begun to regret her action, when Arnoux, her first lover, her man, had presented himself the same day. They had both given the Vicomte to understand that he was 'in the way', and kicked him out without much ceremony.

He pretended not to have heard. The Baron went on:

'How's she getting along, dear old Rose? . . . Are her legs as pretty as ever?' showing by these words that he knew her intimately.

Frédéric was chagrined by this discovery.

'There's nothing to blush at,' said the Baron; 'she's a very good thing!'

Cisy clicked his tongue.

'Pooh! Not as good as all that!'

'Really?'

'Oh dear, yes! In the first place, I found her nothing extraordinary, and then, you pick up the likes of her as often as you please, for, after all . . . she's for sale!'

'Not for everyone!' remarked Frédéric, with some bitterness.

'He thinks he's different from everyone else!' was Cisy's comment. 'That's a joke!'

And a laugh ran round the table.

Frédéric felt as if the palpitations of his heart would suffocate him. He swallowed two glasses of water one after the other.

But the Baron had preserved a warm memory of Rosanette.

'Is she still with a fellow named Arnoux?'

'I haven't the faintest idea,' said Cisy, 'I don't know that gentleman!'

Nevertheless, he suggested that he believed Arnoux was a sort of crook.

'One moment!' exclaimed Frédéric.

'Come on, there's no doubt about it! Legal proceedings have been taken against him.'

'That's not true!'

Frédéric began to defend Arnoux. He vouched for his honesty, ended by convincing himself of it, and concocted figures and proofs. The Vicomte, full of spite, and tipsy moreover, persisted in his assertions, so that Frédéric said to him gravely:

'Is the object of this to give offence to me, Monsieur?'

And he looked Cisy full in the face, with eyes which burned as hot as his cigar.

'Oh, not at all! I grant you that he possesses something very nice: his wife.'

'Do you know her?'

'I should say so! Sophie Arnoux; everyone knows old Sophie!'

'What did you say?'

Cisy, who had staggered to his feet, stammered out once more:

'Everyone knows old Sophie!'

'Hold your tongue! It's not with women of her sort you pass your time!'

'I'm very glad I don't!'

Frédéric flung his plate at his face.

It passed like a flash of lightning over the table, knocked down two bottles, demolished a fruit-dish, and breaking into three pieces, by knocking against the epergne, hit the Vicomte in the stomach.

All the other guests arose to hold him back. He struggled and shouted, possessed by a kind of frenzy; M. des Aulnays kept repeating:

'Come! Be calm! My dear boy!'

'Why, this is frightful!' bellowed the Tutor.

Forchambeaux, of the same livid hue as the plums, was trembling; Joseph was hooting with laughter; the attendants were wiping up the wine and gathering up the remains of the dinner from the floor; and the Baron went and shut the window, for in spite of the noise of carriage wheels the uproar might be heard on the boulevard.

As all present at the moment the plate had been flung had been talking at the same time, it was impossible to discover the cause of the attack, whether it was on account of Arnoux, Madame Arnoux, Rosanette, or somebody else. One thing only they were certain of, was that Frédéric had acted with indescribable brutality; he positively refused to express the slightest regret.

M. des Aulnays tried to calm him down. Cousin Joseph, the Tutor, and Forchambeaux himself joined in the effort. The Baron, all this time, was comforting Cisy, who, yielding to a nervous weakness, began to shed tears. Frédéric, on the contrary, was getting more and more angry; and they would have stayed there till daybreak if the Baron had not said, in order to bring matters to a close:

'The Vicomte, Monsieur, will send his seconds to call on you tomorrow.'

'Your hour?'

'Twelve, if it suits you.'

'Perfectly, Monsieur.'

Frédéric, as soon as he was in the open air, drew a deep breath. He had been keeping his feelings too long under restraint. He had satisfied them at last; he felt something like the pride of virility, a superabundance of energy within him which intoxicated him. He required two seconds. The first person he thought of was Regimbart; and he immediately directed his steps towards a tavern in the Rue Saint-Denis. The shop-front was closed. But some light shone through a pane of glass over the door. It opened and he went in, stooping very low as he passed under the porch.

A candle on the edge of the bar lighted up the deserted room. All the stools, with their feet in the air, were piled on the tables. The master and mistress, with their waiter, were at supper in a corner near the kitchen; and Regimbart, with his hat on his head, was sharing their meal, and even crowding the waiter, who was compelled at every mouthful to turn a little to one side. Frédéric, having briefly explained the matter to him, asked Regimbart to assist him. The Citizen at first made no reply; he rolled his eyes about, looked as if he were plunged in reflection, walked up and down the room a few times, and at last said:

'Yes, by all means!'

And his face lit up with a homicidal smile when he learned that the adversary was a nobleman.

'Never fear, we'll make him run! In the first place . . . with the sword . . . '

'But perhaps,' broke in Frédéric, 'I haven't the right . . . '

'I tell you you must use the sword!' the Citizen replied roughly. 'Do you know how to make passes?'

'A little.'

'Oh! A little! That's how they all are! And yet they're all mad to fight! What does the fencing-school teach? Listen to me: keep a good distance off, always confining yourself in circles, and keep back! Keep back! It's allowed. Tire him out! Then boldly make a lunge on him! And, above all, no tricks, no strokes of the La Fougère kind! No! Just simple one-two's, and some disengagements. Look, do you see? While you turn your wrist as if opening a lock – Père Vauthier, give me your cane! Ha! That will do.'

He grasped the rod which was used for lighting the gas, rounded his left arm, bent his right, and began to make thrusts against the partition. He stamped with his foot, got animated, and even pretended to be encountering difficulties, while he called: 'Are you there? Are you there?' and his enormous silhouette projected itself on the wall with his hat apparently touching the ceiling. From time to time the owner of the café said 'Bravo! Very good!' His wife, though a little unnerved, was likewise filled with admiration; and Théodore, who had been in the army, remained riveted to the spot with amazement, being, anyway, fanatically devoted to M. Regimbart.

Next morning, at an early hour, Frédéric hurried to Dussardier's shop. After having passed through a succession of rooms all full of material, either on shelves or lying across tables, while here and there shawls were fixed on wooden mushrooms, he saw him in a sort of cage with bars, surrounded by account books, and standing in front of a desk at which he was writing. The good fellow immediately left his work.

The seconds arrived at twelve o'clock. Frédéric, as a matter of good taste, thought he ought not to be present at the conference.

The Baron and M. Joseph declared that they would be satisfied with the simplest excuses. But Regimbart's principle being never to yield, and his contention being that Arnoux's honour should be vindicated (Frédéric had not spoken to him about anything else), he asked that the Vicomte should apologise. M. de Comaing was incensed at this presumption. The Citizen would not abate an inch. As all conciliation proved impracticable, there was nothing for it but to fight.

Other difficulties arose; for the choice of weapons, legally, lay with Cisy, as the person to whom the insult had been offered. But Regimbart maintained that by sending the challenge he had constituted himself the offending party. His seconds loudly protested that a slap, however, was the most cruel of offences. The Citizen quibbled over the words, pointing out that a blow was not a slap. Finally, they decided to refer the matter to a military man; and the four seconds went off to consult some officers in one of the barracks.

They drew up at the one on the Quai d'Orsay. M. de Comaing, having accosted two captains, explained to them the question in dispute.

The captains did not understand a word of what he was saying, owing to the confusion caused by the Citizen's incidental remarks. In short, they advised the gentlemen to draw up a minute of the proceedings; after which they would give their decision. Thereupon, they repaired to a café; and they even, in order to do things with more circumspection, referred to Cisy as H, and Frédéric as K.

Then they returned to the barracks. The officers had gone out. They reappeared, and declared that the choice of arms manifestly belonged to Monsieur H. They all returned to Cisy's abode. Regimbart and Dussardier remained on the pavement.

The Vicomte, when he was informed of the solution, was seized with such extreme agitation that they had to repeat it for him several times; and when M. de Comaing came to deal with Regimbart's contentions, he murmured 'Nevertheless', not being very reluctant himself to comply with them. Then he let himself sink into an armchair, and declared that he would not fight.

'Eh? What?' said the Baron.

Then Cisy indulged in a confused flood of gibberings. He wished to fight with a blunderbuss, to discharge one single pistol at point-blank range.

'Or else we'll put arsenic into a glass, and draw lots to see who drinks it. That's sometimes done; I've read about it!'

The Baron, naturally rather an impatient man, was rough with him.

'These gentlemen are waiting for your answer. This is getting indecent! What weapons are you going to take? Come! Is it the sword?'

The Vicomte nodded 'yes'; and it was arranged that the meeting should take place next morning at seven o'clock sharp at the Porte Maillot.

Dussardier being compelled to go back to work, Regimbart went to inform Frédéric.

He had been left all day without any news; and his impatience had become unbearable.

'So much the better!' he exclaimed.

The Citizen was satisfied with his attitude.

'Would you believe it? They wanted an apology from us. Nothing much, just one word! But I sent them off with a flea in their ear! The right thing to do, wasn't it?'

'Undoubtedly,' said Frédéric, thinking that he would have done better to choose a different second.

Then, when he was alone, he repeated several times aloud:

'I'm going to fight! Goodness, I'm going to fight! How odd!'

And, as he walked up and down his room, passing in front of the mirror, he noticed that he was pale.

'I wouldn't be afraid, would I?'

He was seized with a feeling of intolerable anxiety at the prospect of exhibiting fear on the ground.

'And yet, suppose I were killed? My father met his death the same way. Yes, I shall be killed!'

And, suddenly, he saw his mother, in a black dress; incoherent images floated through his mind. His own cowardice exasperated him. A paroxysm of courage, a thirst for human blood, took possession of him. A battalion could not have made him retreat. When this feverish excitement had cooled down, he was over-joyed to feel that his nerves were perfectly steady. In order to divert his thoughts, he went to the Opéra, where a ballet was being performed. He listened to the music, looked at the *danseuses* through his opera-glass, and drank a glass of punch during the interval. But when he got home again, the sight of his study, of his furniture, in the midst of which he found himself perhaps for the last time, made him feel ready to swoon.

He went down to the garden. The stars were shining; he gazed up at them. The idea of fighting for a woman gave him a greater stature in his own eyes, ennobling him. Then he went to bed in a tranquil frame of mind.

It was not so with Cisy. After the Baron's departure Joseph had tried to revive his drooping spirits, and, as the Vicomte remained impervious:

'Look, old boy, if you prefer to drop it, I'll go and say so.'

Cisy dared not answer 'of course I do', but he was cross with his cousin for not doing him this service without asking him.

He wished that Frédéric would die during the night of an attack of apoplexy, or that a riot would break out so that next morning there would be enough barricades to seal off all the approaches to the Bois de Boulogne, or that some emergency might prevent one of the seconds from being present; for in the absence of seconds the duel would fall through. He wanted to escape on an express train no matter where. He regretted that he did not understand medicine so as to be able to take something which, without endangering his life, would cause it to be believed that he was dead. He even went so far as to wish to be seriously ill.

In order to get advice and assistance from someone, he sent for M. des Aulnays. That worthy man had gone back to Saintonge on receiving a telegram informing him of the illness of one of his daughters. This appeared an ominous circumstance to Cisy. Luckily, M. Vezou, his Tutor, came to see him. Then he unbosomed himself.

'What am I to do? My God, what am I do?'

'If I were in your place, Monsieur le Comte, I should pay some strapping fellow to go and give him a drubbing.'

'He would still know who arranged it!' replied Cisy.

And from time to time he uttered a groan; then:

'But are people allowed to fight duels?'

'It's a relic of barbarism! What are you to do?'

Out of kindness the pedagogue invited himself to dinner. His pupil did not eat anything, and, after the meal, felt the need to take a short walk.

As they were passing a church, he said:

'Suppose we go in for a little while . . . just to see?'

M. Vezou asked nothing better, and even offered him holy water.

It was the month of May, the altar was covered with flowers, voices were chanting, the organ was resounding. But he found it impossible to pray, as the pomp of religion inspired him merely with thoughts of funerals; he fancied he could hear the murmurs of the *De Profundis*.

'Let's go! I don't feel well!'

They spent the whole night playing cards. The Vicomte made an effort to lose in order to exorcise ill-luck, a thing which M. Vezou turned to his own advantage. At last, at the first streak of dawn, Cisy, who could stand it no longer, sank down on the green cloth, and was soon plunged in a sleep full of unpleasant dreams.

If courage, however, consists in wishing to get the better of one's weakness, the Vicomte was courageous, for at the sight of his seconds, who were coming to fetch him, he stiffened his resolve with all the strength he could command, vanity making him realise that to draw back now would destroy him. M. de Comaing congratulated him on his good appearance.

But, on the way, the jolting of the cab and the heat of the morning sun weakened him. His energy had given way again. He could not even distinguish any longer where they were.

The Baron amused himself by increasing his terror, talking about the 'corpse', and of the way they meant to get it back clandestinely into town. Joseph gave the rejoinder; both, considering the affair ridiculous, were certain that it would be settled.

Cisy kept his head on his breast; he lifted it up slowly, and drew attention to the fact that they had not taken a doctor with them.

'We don't need one,' said the Baron.

'There's no danger, then?'

Joseph answered in a grave tone:

'Let us hope so!'

And nobody in the carriage made any further remark.

At ten minutes past seven they arrived at the Porte Maillot. Frédéric and his seconds were there, all three dressed in black. Regimbart, instead of a cravat, wore a stiff horsehair collar, like a trooper; and he was carrying a kind of long violin-case adapted for adventures of this kind. They exchanged a cold bow. Then they all plunged into the Bois de Boulogne, taking the route de Madrid, in order to find a suitable place.

Regimbart said to Frédéric, who was walking between him and Dussardier:

'Well, and what do we do about this funk you're in? If you want anything, don't worry about it, I know all about it! Fear is natural to man.'

Then, in a low tone:

'Don't smoke any more, it weakens you!'

Frédéric threw away his cigar, which had been bothering him, and went on with a firm step. The Vicomte advanced behind, leaning on the arms of his two seconds.

Occasional wayfarers crossed their path. The sky was blue, and from time to time they heard rabbits skipping about. At the turn of the path, a woman in a Madras cotton kerchief was chatting with a man in overalls, and in the main avenue under the chestnut trees grooms in linen jackets were walking horses up and down. Cisy recalled the happy days when, mounted on his own chestnut horse, and with his glass stuck in his eye, he rode along at carriage doors; these recollections intensified his wretchedness; an intolerable thirst parched his throat; the buzzing of the flies mingled with the throbbing of his arteries; his feet sank into the sand; it seemed to him as if he had been walking forever.

The seconds, without stopping, were examining with keen eyes each side of the path. They hesitated as to whether they would go to the Croix-Catalan or under the walls of the Bagatelle. At last they took a turn to the right; and they drew up in a clearing in the midst of the pine trees.

The spot was chosen so as to divide the level of the ground evenly. The two places at which the principals were to take their stand were marked out. Then Regimbart opened his case. It was lined with red leather, and contained four charming swords hollowed in the centre, with handles adorned with filigree. A ray of light passing through the leaves fell on them; and they appeared to Cisy to glitter like silver vipers on a sea of blood.

The Citizen showed that they were of equal length; he took the third for himself, in order to separate the combatants in case of necessity. M. de Comaing held a walking-stick. There was a silence. They looked at each other. All the faces looked either rather horrified or cruel.

Frédéric had taken off his coat and his waistcoat. Joseph helped

Cisy to do the same; when his cravat was removed a holy medal could be seen on his neck. This made Regimbart smile contemptuously.

Then M. de Comaing (in order to allow Frédéric another moment for reflection) tried to raise some quibbles. He demanded the right to put on a glove and to catch hold of the adversary's sword with the left hand; Regimbart, who was in a hurry, made no objection to this. At last the Baron, addressing Frédéric:

'Everything depends on you, Monsieur! There is never any dishonour in acknowledging one's faults.'

Dussardier made a gesture of approval. The Citizen was indignant:

'Do you think we came here to twiddle our fingers, damn it? On guard!'

The combatants were facing one another, with their seconds by their sides. He gave the signal:

'Go!'

Cisy became dreadfully pale. The end of his blade quivered like a whip. His head fell back, his arms opened, and he sank unconscious to the ground, on his back. Joseph raised him up, and, holding a scent-bottle to his nose, gave him a good shaking. The Vicomte reopened his eyes, then suddenly leaped for his sword like a madman. Frédéric had kept hold of his: and now awaited him with steady eye and uplifted hand.

'Stop! Stop!' cried a voice, which came from the road simultaneously with the sound of a horse at full gallop; and the hood of a cab broke the branches! A man leaning out of the carriage was waving a handkerchief, and calling continuously: 'Stop! Stop!'

M. de Comaing, believing that this meant the intervention of the police, lifted up his walking-stick.

'Make an end of it! The Vicomte is bleeding!'

'I?' said Cisy.

Indeed, he had in his fall taken off the skin of his left thumb.

'But that was when he fell over,' observed the Citizen.

The Baron pretended not to hear.

Arnoux had jumped out of the cab.

'I'm too late! No! Thanks be to God!'

He threw his arms around Frédéric, felt him, and covered his face with kisses.

'I know why you did it; you wanted to defend your old friend! That's good, that's good! Never shall I forget it! How kind you are! Ah, my own dear boy!'

He gazed at Frédéric and shed tears, at the same time as he chuckled with delight. The Baron turned towards Joseph:

'I think we are in the way at this little family party. It's over, messieurs, is it not? Vicomte, put your arm into a sling; here, take my silk scarf.' Then, with an imperious gesture: 'Come! No hard feelings! Do the right thing!'

The two adversaries shook hands in a very lukewarm fashion. The Vicomte, M. de Comaing, and Joseph disappeared in one direction, and Frédéric left with his friends in the opposite direction.

As the Madrid Restaurant was not far off, Arnoux proposed that they should go and drink a glass of beer there.

'We might even have breakfast,' said Regimbart.

But, as Dussardier had not the time, they confined themselves to taking some refreshment in the garden. They all experienced that sense of satisfaction which follows happy endings. The Citizen, nevertheless, was annoyed at the duel having been interrupted just at the most critical stage.

Arnoux had been apprised of it by a person named Compain, a friend of Regimbart; and in an impulse of his heart he had rushed to the spot to prevent it, under the impression, moreover, that he was the cause of it. He begged Frédéric to give him some details about it. Frédéric, touched by these proofs of his affection, felt some scruples at the idea of increasing his misapprehension:

'For mercy's sake, let's not say any more about it!'

Arnoux thought that this reserve showed great delicacy. Then, with his habitual levity, he passed on to a new subject:

'What news, Citizen?'

And they began talking about banking transactions, and dates due. In order to be more undisturbed, they even went to another table, where they exchanged whispered confidences.

Frédéric could make out the words: 'You'll underwrite it for me.' 'Yes, but you, mind . . . ' 'I finally negotiated it for three hundred!' 'A nice commission, my word!' In short, it was clear that Arnoux was mixed up in a great many shady transactions with the Citizen.

Frédéric thought of reminding him about his fifteen thousand francs. But his action that morning forbade the utterance of even the mildest of reproaches. Besides, he felt tired, and this was not a suitable place. He put it off till some future day.

Arnoux, seated in the shade of a privet, was smoking, with a look of huge enjoyment on his face. He raised his eyes towards the doors of the private rooms which all looked out on to the garden, and said he had often paid visits to the house in former days.

'Not alone, no doubt?' returned the Citizen.

'What do you think!'

'What a rascal you are! You, a married man!'

'Well, and what about you!' retorted Arnoux; and, with an indulgent smile: 'I'm even sure that this rogue has a room somewhere where he receives nice young girls.'

The Citizen confessed that this was true by simply raising his eyebrows. Then these two gentlemen declared their respective tastes: Arnoux now preferred youth, working girls; Regimbart hated 'stuck-up' women, and went in for the genuine article before anything else. The conclusion which the ceramics–dealer laid down at the close of this discussion was that women were not to be taken seriously.

'Yet he's fond of his own!' thought Frédéric, as he made his way home; and he decided that he was a dishonest man. He bore him a grudge on account of this duel, as if it had been for his sake that he had just risked his life.

But he felt grateful to Dussardier for his loyalty; before long the draper's clerk came at his invitation to pay him a visit every day.

Frédéric lent him books: Thiers, Dulaure, Barante, and Lamartine's *Girondins*. The honest fellow listened to everything the other said with a thoughtful air, and accepted his opinions as those of a master.

One evening he arrived in a great fright.

That morning, on the boulevard, a man who was running like the wind had jostled against him; and having recognised in him a friend of Sénécal, had said to him:

'He's just been taken, I'm making my escape!'

There was no doubt about it. Dussardier had spent the day making enquiries. Sénécal was in jail charged with an attempted crime of a political nature.

The son of an overseer, he was born in Lyons, and having had as his teacher a former disciple of Chalier, he had, on his arrival in

Paris, obtained admission into the 'Society of Families'; his habits were known; the police kept an eye on him. He had fought in the affair of May 1839; and since then he had remained in the shade, but becoming more and more fanatical, a passionate admirer of Alibaud, mixing up his own grievances against society with those of the people against the monarchy, and waking up every morning in the hope of a revolution which in a fortnight or a month would transform the world. At last, disgusted at the inactivity of his brethren, enraged at the delays which inhibited the realisation of his dreams, and despairing of the nation, he had entered in his capacity of chemist into the conspiracy for the use of incendiary bombs; and he had been caught carrying gunpowder, of which he was going to make a trial at Montmartre – a final attempt to establish the Republic.

Dussardier was no less attached to the Republican idea, for, from his point of view, it meant liberation and universal happiness. One day – at the age of fifteen – in the Rue Transnonain, in front of a grocer's shop, he had seen soldiers with bayonets reddened with blood and with human hairs stuck to the butt-ends of their guns; since that time, the Government had filled him with feelings of rage as the very incarnation of Injustice. He tended to confuse assassins with police; and in his eyes a police spy was just as bad as a parricide. All the evil scattered over the earth he ingenuously attributed to Power; and he hated it with a deep-rooted, undying hatred that held possession of his entire heart and sharpened his sensibilities. He had been dazzled by Sénécal's declamations. It was of little consequence whether he happened to be guilty or not, or whether the attempt with which he was charged could be characterised as odious! Once he had become the victim of Authority, it was only right to help him.

'The Peers will condemn him, certainly! Then he will be conveyed in a prison-van, like a convict, and will be shut up in the Mont Saint-Michel, where the Government lets them die! Austen went mad! Steuben killed himself! In order to transfer Barbès into a dungeon, they dragged him by the legs and by the hair! They trampled on his body, and his head rebounded along the staircase at every step they took. What an abomination! The wretches!'

He choked with sobs of anger, and he walked about the room in a very excited frame of mind.

'We have to do something, though! Come! I don't know! What if we tried to rescue him, eh? While they're taking him to the Luxembourg, we could throw ourselves on the escort in the passage! A dozen resolute men can do anything.'

There was so much fire in his eyes that Frédéric trembled.

Sénécal appeared of greater stature than he had thought. He recalled to mind his sufferings and his austere life; without feeling the same enthusiasm about him as Dussardier, he experienced nevertheless that admiration which is inspired by any man who sacrifices himself for an idea. He said to himself that, if he had helped him, Sénécal would not be in his present position; and the two friends laboriously sought to devise some plan for saving him.

It was impossible for them to get access to him.

Frédéric examined the newspapers to try to find out what had become of him, and for three weeks he was a constant visitor at the reading-rooms.

One day several numbers of the *Flambard* fell into his hands. The leading article was invariably devoted to cutting up some distinguished man. After that came society gossip and scandals. Then there were some chaffing observations about the Odéon, Carpentras, pisciculture, and prisoners under sentence of death, when there happened to be any. The disappearance of a steamer furnished material for a whole year's jokes. In the third column an art section, in the form of anecdotes or advice, gave advertisements for tailors, together with accounts of evening parties, notifications of auctions, and analysis of artistic productions, writing in the same strain about a volume of poetry and a pair of boots. The only serious portion of it was the criticism of the small theatres, in which fierce attacks were made on two or three managers; and the interests of Art were invoked in connection with the décors of the Funambules or a leading lady at the Délassements.

Frédéric was about to toss it all away when his eyes alighted on an article entitled 'A Pullet and three Cuckoos'. It was the story of his duel related in a lively Gallic style. He had no difficulty in recognising himself, for he was indicated by this little joke, which frequently recurred: 'A young man from the College of Sens who has no sense.' He was even represented as a poor devil from the provinces, an obscure booby trying to mix with persons of high rank. As for the Vicomte, he had the starring role, first in the supper-party, into which he forced his way, then in the episode of the bet for having carried off the lady, and, finally, in the duel, where he behaved like a gentleman. Frédéric's courage was not denied exactly, but it was intimated that an intermediary, the *protector* himself, had come on the scene just in time. The article concluded with this phrase, pregnant perhaps with sinister meaning:

'What is the origin of their affection? A problem! And, as Don Basilio says, "Who the deuce is being deceived here?" '

This was, beyond all doubt, Hussonnet's revenge against Frédéric for having refused the five thousand francs.

What was he to do? If he demanded an explanation from him, the Bohemian would protest that he was innocent, and nothing would be gained. The best course was to swallow the affront in silence. Nobody, after all, read the *Flambard*.

As he left the reading-room, he saw some people standing in front of a picture-dealer's shop. They were staring at the portrait of a woman, with this line traced underneath in black letters: 'Mademoiselle Rose-Annette Bron, belonging to M. Frédéric Moreau of Nogent.'

It was indeed she – almost – full face, her breasts uncovered, her hair hanging loose, and with a purse of red velvet in her hands, while behind her a peacock leaned his beak over her shoulder, covering the wall with his great feathers in the shape of a fan.

Pellerin had got up this exhibition in order to compel Frédéric to pay, persuaded that he was a celebrity, and that the whole of Paris, rising in his defence, would be interested in this wretched piece of work.

Was this a conspiracy? Had the painter and the journalist prepared their attack on him together?

His duel had not put a stop to anything. He was becoming an object of ridicule, everyone was laughing at him.

Three days afterwards, at the end of June, the Northern shares having had a rise of fifteen francs, as he had bought two thousand of them the month before, he found that he had made thirty thousand francs. This caress of fortune gave him renewed self-confidence. He said to himself that he needed nobody, and that all his embarrassments were the result of his timidity and indecision. He ought to have begun his intrigue with the Maréchale with brutal directness, refused Hussonnet the very first day, and should not have compromised himself with Pellerin; and, in order to show that he was not a bit embarrassed, he presented himself at one of Madame Dambreuse's ordinary evening parties.

In the middle of the anteroom, Martinon, who was arriving at the same time as he was, turned round.

'What! You here?' with a look of surprise, and as if displeased at seeing him.

'Why not?'

And, asking himself what could be the cause of such a reception, Frédéric made his way into the drawing-room.

The light was dim, in spite of the lamps placed in the corners; for the three windows, which were wide open, made three large squares of black shadow, parallel with each other. Beneath the pictures, flower-stands as tall as a man occupied the spaces on the walls; and a silver teapot with a samovar cast its reflection in a mirror at the end of the room. There arose a murmur of hushed voices and the sound of pumps creaking over the carpet.

He could see a number of black coats, then a round table lighted up by a large shaded lamp, seven or eight ladies in summer toilets, and at some little distance Madame Dambreuse in a rocking chair. Her dress of lilac taffeta had slashed sleeves, through which fell frothy puffs of muslin, the subdued tone of the material harmonising with the shade of her hair; and she sat slightly thrown back with the tip of her foot on a cushion – with the repose of an exquisitely delicate work of art, a flower of high culture.

M. Dambreuse and an old gentleman with white hair were walking from one end of the drawing-room to the other. Some of the guests chatted here and there, sitting on the edges of the little divans; the others, standing up, formed a circle in the centre.

They were talking about votes, amendments, counter-amendments, M. Grandin's speech, and M. Benoist's reply. The third party was decidedly going too far! The Centre Left ought to have had a better recollection of its origins! Serious attacks had been made on the ministry! It must be reassuring, however, that no successor could be seen. In short, the situation was analogous in all respects to that of 1834.

As these things bored Frédéric, he drew near the ladies. Martinon was beside them, standing up, with his hat under his arm, showing himself in three-quarter profile, and looking so perfectly posed that he resembled a piece of Sèvres porcelain. He took up a copy of the *Revue des Deux Mondes* which was lying on the table between an *Imitation* and an *Annuaire de Gotha*, and spoke of a distinguished poet in a contemptuous tone, said he was going to the Saint-Francis lectures, complained of his larynx, swallowed a lozenge from time to time; and in the meantime talked about music, and played the part of the elegant trifler. Mademoiselle Cécile, M. Dambreuse's niece, who was embroidering a pair of ruffles, gazed at him surreptitiously from time to time with her pale blue eyes; and he caused Miss Johnson, the governess, who had a flat nose, to lay aside her tapestry; both of them appeared to be exclaiming internally:

'How handsome he is!'

Madame Dambreuse turned round towards him.

'Please give me my fan which is on that side-table over there. You're taking the wrong one! The other one!'

She got up; and when he came back, they met in the middle of the drawing-room face to face; she addressed a few sharp words to him, reproaches no doubt, judging by the haughty expression of her face; Martinon tried to smile; then he went to join the circle in which grave men were holding discussions. Madame Dambreuse resumed her seat, and, bending over the arm of her chair, said to Frédéric:

'I saw somebody the day before yesterday who spoke to me about you – Monsieur de Cisy; you know him, don't you?'

'Yes . . . slightly.'

Suddenly Madame Dambreuse uttered an exclamation:

'Duchess! Oh, what a pleasure to see you!'

And she advanced towards the door to meet a little old lady in a light brown taffeta dress and a lace bonnet with long tabs. The daughter of a companion in exile of the Comte d'Artois, and the widow of a marshal of the Empire, who had been created a peer of France in 1830, she adhered to the court of a former generation as well as to the new court, and possessed sufficient influence to procure many things. Those who stood talking stepped aside, and then resumed their discussion.

It had now turned on to pauperism, of which, according to these gentlemen, all the descriptions that had been given were grossly exaggerated.

'And yet,' urged Martinon, 'let us confess that there is such a thing as want! But the remedy depends neither on Science nor on Power. It is purely an individual question. When the lower classes are willing to get rid of their vices, they will free themselves from their needs. Let the people be more moral, and they will be less poor!'

According to M. Dambreuse, no good could be attained without a superabundance of capital. Therefore, the only practicable method was to entrust, 'as the Saint-Simonians, by the way, proposed (good heavens, there was some merit in their views! Let us be just to everybody), to entrust, I say, the cause of Progress to those who can increase the public wealth.' Imperceptibly they began to touch on the subject of the great industrial enterprises, the railways, the coalmines. And M. Dambreuse, addressing Frédéric, said to him in a low voice:

'You didn't call about that business of ours.'

Frédéric pleaded illness; but, feeling that this excuse was too absurd:

'Besides, I needed my capital.'

'To buy a carriage?' asked Madame Dambreuse, who was brushing past him with a cup of tea in her hand, and for a minute she looked at him with her head turned slightly over her shoulder.

She believed that he was Rosanette's lover; the allusion was obvious. It seemed even to Frédéric that all the ladies were staring at him from a distance and whispering to one another. In order to get a better idea as to what they were thinking, he once more drew near to them.

On the other side of the table, Martinon, seated near Mademoiselle Cécile, was turning over the leaves of an album. It contained lithographs representing Spanish costumes. He read the descriptive titles aloud: 'A Lady of Seville', 'A Valencia Gardener', 'An Andalusian Picador'; and once, going down to the bottom of the page, he continued all in one breath:

'Jacques Arnoux, publisher . . . One of your friends, eh?'

'That's true,' said Frédéric, nettled by his manner.

Madame Dambreuse again interposed:

'Indeed, you came here one morning . . . about . . . a house, I believe? Yes, a house belonging to his wife.' (This meant: 'She is your mistress.')

He reddened up to his ears; and M. Dambreuse, who joined them at the same moment, added:

'You even seemed to be particularly interested in them.'

These last words completed Frédéric's discomfiture. His confusion, which he could not help feeling was obvious, was on the point of confirming their suspicions, when M. Dambreuse drew close to him, and, in a tone of great seriousness, said:

'I suppose you don't do business together?'

He protested by repeated shakes of the head, without understanding the capitalist's intention, which was to give him advice.

He felt a desire to leave. The fear of appearing a coward restrained him. A servant carried away the teacups; Madame Dambreuse was talking to a diplomat in a blue coat; two young girls, drawing their foreheads close together, were showing each other a ring; the others, seated in a semicircle on armchairs, kept gently moving their white faces crowned with black or fair hair; nobody, in fact, was paying him any attention. Frédéric turned on his heels; and, by a succession of long zigzags, he had almost reached the door, when, passing close to a side-table, he remarked, on the top of it, between a Chinese vase and the wainscoting, a journal folded in two. He drew it out a little, and read these words: *Le Flambard*.

Who had brought it? Cisy! Manifestly no one else. What did it matter, anyway! They would believe – already, perhaps, everyone did believe – in the article. Why this rancour? He was enveloped in an ironical silence. He felt like one lost in a desert. But suddenly he heard Martinon's voice:

'Talking of Arnoux, I saw in the newspapers, amongst the names of those accused of preparing incendiary bombs, that of one of his employees, Sénécal. Is that our Sénécal?'

'The very same,' said Frédéric.

Martinon repeated in a very loud voice:

'What, our Sénécal! Our Sénécal!'

Then he was questioned about the conspiracy; it was assumed that his connection with the prosecutor's office ought to furnish him with some information on the subject.

He declared that he had none. Anyway, he hardly knew this individual, having seen him only two or three times; he regarded him, to put it bluntly, as quite a shady character! Indignant, Frédéric exclaimed:

'Not at all! He's a very honest fellow!'

'But Monsieur,' said a landowner, 'no conspirator can be an honest man!'

Most of the men assembled there had served at least four governments; and they would have sold France or the human race in order to preserve their own incomes, to save themselves from any discomfort or embarrassment, or even through sheer baseness, through instinctive worship of force. They all maintained that political crimes were inexcusable. But crimes provoked by want should be forgiven! And they did not fail to put forward the eternal illustration of the father of a family stealing the eternal loaf of bread from the eternal baker.

A gentleman occupying an administrative office even went so far as to exclaim:

'For my part, Monsieur, if I were told that my brother were a conspirator I would denounce him!'

Frédéric invoked the right of resistance; and recalling to mind some phrases that Deslauriers had used in their conversations, he cited Desormes, Blackstone, the English Bill of Rights, and Article 2 of the Constitution of '91. It was even by virtue of that right that the fall of Napoleon had been proclaimed; it had been recognised in 1830, and inscribed at the head of the Charter.

'Besides, when the sovereign fails to fulfil the contract, justice requires that he should be overthrown.'

'Why, this is abominable!' exclaimed a prefect's wife.

All the other women remained silent, filled with a vague terror, as if they had heard the noise of bullets. Madame Dambreuse rocked herself in her chair, and smiled as she listened to him.

A manufacturer, who had formerly been a member of the Carbonari, tried to show him that the Orléans were a fine family; no doubt there were abuses . . .

'Well then?'

'But we mustn't say so, my dear Monsieur! If you knew what harm all these clamourings of the Opposition do to business!'

'I couldn't care less about business!' said Frédéric.

He was exasperated by the rottenness of these old men; and, carried away by the recklessness which sometimes takes possession of even the most timid, he attacked financiers, deputies, the government, the king, took up the defence of the Arabs, and said a great many silly things. Some of those present urged him on in a spirit of irony:

'Go on! Pray continue!' whilst others muttered: 'The deuce! What a hothead!' At last he thought it was time to retire; and, as he was leaving, M. Dambreuse said to him, alluding to the post of secretary:

'Nothing is settled, yet! But make haste!'

And Madame Dambreuse:

'Do come again soon, won't you?'

Frédéric considered their parting salutation a final mockery. He was resolved never to come back to this house, or to visit any of these people again. He imagined that he had offended them, not realising what vast funds of indifference society possesses! The women especially excited his indignation. Not one of them had backed him up even with a look of sympathy. He resented them for not having been moved by his words. As for Madame Dambreuse, he found in her something at the same time languid and cold, which prevented him from defining her character by a formula. Had she a lover? And, if so, who was it? Was it the diplomat or someone else? Perhaps it was Martinon? Impossible! Nevertheless, he experienced a sort of jealousy of Martinon, and an unaccountable ill-will towards her.

Dussardier, having called that evening as usual, was waiting for him. Frédéric's heart was full; he unburdened it, and his grievances, though vague and hard to understand, saddened the kindly draper's clerk; he even complained of his isolation. Dussardier, after a little hesitation, suggested that they should call on Deslauriers.

Frédéric, at the mention of the lawyer's name, was seized with a powerful longing to see him once more. His intellectual solitude was profound, and Dussardier's company inadequate. In reply, he told him to arrange matters any way he liked.

Deslauriers had likewise, since their quarrel, felt a void in his life. He responded promptly to the cordial advances which were made to him.

The pair embraced each other, then began chatting about matters of no consequence.

Frédéric's heart was touched by Deslauriers' display of reserve; and in order to make him a sort of reparation, he told him next day how he had lost the fifteen thousand francs, without mentioning that these fifteen thousand francs had been originally intended for him. The lawyer, nevertheless, had no doubt of it. This misadventure, which justified his prejudices against Arnoux, entirely disarmed his rancour, and he did not refer to the old promise.

Frédéric, misled by his silence, thought he had forgotten all about it. A few days afterwards, he asked him whether there was any way in which he could get back his money.

They might look into the previous mortgages, take Arnoux to court for misrepresentation, and might take proceedings against the wife personally.

'No! No! Not against her!' exclaimed Frédéric; and, yielding to the ex-law-clerk's questions, he confessed the truth. Deslauriers was convinced that Frédéric was not telling him the entire truth, no doubt through a feeling of delicacy. He was hurt by this want of confidence.

They were, however, on the same intimate terms as before, and they even found so much pleasure in each other's society that Dussardier's presence was a nuisance. Under the pretence that they had appointments, they managed gradually to get rid of him. There are men whose only mission amongst their fellow-men is to serve as go-betweens; people use them in the same way as if they were bridges, by stepping over them and going on their way.

Frédéric concealed nothing from his old friend. He told him about the coalmine speculation and M. Dambreuse's proposal. The lawyer grew thoughtful.

'That's odd! For a job like that you need a man with a good knowledge of the law!'

'But you could help me,' returned Frédéric.

'Yes . . . er . . . damn it! Of course.'

That same week Frédéric showed Deslauriers a letter from his mother.

Madame Moreau accused herself of having misjudged M. Roque, who had given a satisfactory explanation of his conduct. Then she spoke of his means, and of the possibility, later, of a marriage with Louise.

'That might not be so stupid!' said Deslauriers.

Frédéric said it was entirely out of the question; besides, Père Roque was an old trickster. That in no way affected the matter, in the lawyer's opinion.

At the end of July, an unaccountable diminution in value made the Northern shares fall. Frédéric had not sold his; he lost sixty thousand francs in one day. His income was considerably reduced. He would have either to curtail his expenditure, or take up some calling, or make a brilliant marriage.

Then Deslauriers spoke to him about Mademoiselle Roque. There was nothing to prevent him from going to get some idea of things by seeing for himself. Frédéric was rather tired; provincial existence and the maternal roof would refresh him. He left.

The appearance of the streets of Nogent, as he passed through them in the moonlight, brought back old memories; and he experienced a kind of pang, like people returning after a long period of travel.

At his mother's house, all the visitors were there as in former days: MM. Gamblin, Heudras, and Chambrion, the Lebrun family, 'those young ladies, the Augers'; and, in addition, Père Roque, and, sitting opposite to Madame Moreau at a card-table, Mademoiselle Louise. She was now a woman. She sprang to her feet with a cry. They were all in a flutter of excitement. She had remained standing motionless; and the four silver candelabra on the table intensified her pallor. When she resumed play, her hand was trembling. This emotion was exceedingly flattering to Frédéric, whose pride had been sorely wounded; he said to himself: 'You, at any rate, will love me!' and, taking his revenge for the humiliations he had endured in the capital, he began to affect the Parisian lion, retailed all the theatrical gossip, told anecdotes about society, which he had borrowed from the columns of the cheap newspapers, and, in short, dazzled his compatriots.

Next morning, Madame Moreau expatiated on Louise's fine qualities; then she enumerated the woods and farms of which she would be the owner. Père Roque's wealth was considerable.

He had acquired it while making investments for M. Dambreuse; for he lent money to persons who were able to give good security in the shape of mortgages, which enabled him to demand supplements or commissions. The capital, owing to his energetic vigilance, was in no danger. Besides, Père Roque never had any hesitation in foreclosing; then he bought up the mortgaged property at a low price, and M. Dambreuse, having got back his money, found his affairs in very good order.

But this manipulation in a way which was not strictly legal compromised him with his agent. He could refuse him nothing. It was owing to the latter's solicitations that M. Dambreuse had received Frédéric so cordially.

The truth was that in the depths of his soul Père Roque cherished an ambition. He wished his daughter to be a countess; and to achieve that aim, without imperilling the happiness of his child, he knew no other young man but Frédéric.

Through the influence of M. Dambreuse, he could obtain the title of his grandfather, Madame Moreau being the daughter of a Comte de Fouvens, besides being connected with the oldest families in Champagne, the Lavernades and the D'Etrignys. As for the Moreaus, a Gothic inscription near the mills of Villeneuve-l'Archevêque referred to one Jacob Moreau, who had rebuilt them in 1596; and the tomb of his son, Pierre Moreau, first esquire of the king under Louis XIV, was to be seen in the chapel of Saint-Nicholas.

So much family distinction fascinated M. Roque, the son of a former servant. If the coronet of a count did not come, he would console himself with something else; for Frédéric might get a deputyship when M. Dambreuse had been raised to the peerage, and might then be able to assist him in his commercial pursuits, and to obtain for him supplies and grants. He liked the young man personally. In short, he wanted him for a son-in-law, because for a long time past he had been keen on the idea, which only grew all the stronger day by day.

Now he went to church – and he had won Madame Moreau over to his views, mainly through the prospect of the title. She had, however, been careful not to give him a firm answer.

So it was that, a week later, without any formal engagement, Frédéric was regarded as Mademoiselle Roque's 'intended'; and Père Roque, who was not troubled with many scruples, sometimes left them alone together.

Deslauriers had carried away from Frédéric's house the copy of the deed of subrogation, with a power of attorney in proper form, giving him full authority to act; but, when he had climbed back up his own five flights and found himself alone in the midst of his dismal office, in his leather armchair, the sight of the stamped paper disgusted him.

He was tired of these things, and of restaurants at thirty-two sous a meal, of travelling in omnibuses, of his enduring want and his life of effort. He took up the papers again; there were others beside them; they were prospectuses of the coalmining company, with a list of the mines and the particulars as to their contents, Frédéric having left all these matters in his hands in order to have his opinion.

An idea occurred to him: to go and see M. Dambreuse and apply for the post of secretary. This post, it was perfectly certain, could not be obtained without purchasing a certain number of shares. He recognised the folly of his project, and said to himself:

'Oh, no! That would be wrong.'

Then he ransacked his brains to think of the best way in which he could recover the fifteen thousand francs. Such a sum was nothing to Frédéric! But, if *he* had had it, what a lever it would have been! And the ex-law-clerk was indignant at the other being so well off.

'He makes a pitiful use of his money. He's selfish. Ah! What do I care for his fifteen thousand francs!'

Why had he lent the money? For the sake of Madame Arnoux's bright eyes. She was his mistress! Deslauriers had no doubt about it. 'That's another way in which money is useful!' He was assailed by malignant thoughts.

Then he thought about Frédéric himself. Frédéric had always exercised over him an almost feminine charm; and he soon came to admire him for a success of which he realised that he was himself incapable.

'Nevertheless, was not the will the key element in every enterprise? And, since by its means we may triumph over everything . . . '

'Ha! That would be funny!'

But he felt ashamed of such treachery, and the next moment:

'Pooh! Am I afraid?'

Madame Arnoux (from having heard her spoken about so often) had come to be depicted in his imagination as something extraordinary. The persistency of this passion irritated him as if it were a problem. Its rather theatrical austerity now annoyed him. Besides, the woman of the world (or what he judged to be so) dazzled the lawyer as the symbol and the epitome of a thousand unfamiliar pleasures. Poor, he hankered after luxury in its most conspicuous form.

'After all, even if he should get angry, too bad! He's behaved too badly to me for me to bother on his account! I've no assurance that she's his mistress. He denied it to me. So I'm free to act as I please!'

Henceforth, the desire to take this step never left him. He wished to make a trial of his own strength – so that one day, all of a sudden, he polished his boots himself, bought some white gloves, and set forth on his way, substituting himself for Frédéric, and almost imagining that he was him, by a singular intellectual evolution, in which there was, at the same time, vengeance and sympathy, imitation and audacity.

He announced himself as 'Doctor Deslauriers'.

Madame Arnoux was surprised, as she had not sent for any physician.

'Ah! Do please forgive me! It's doctor of law. I've come in Monsieur Moreau's interest.'

This name appeared to disturb her.

'So much the better!' thought the ex-law-clerk. 'Since she has

a liking for him, she will like me, too!' buoying up his courage with the accepted idea that it is easier to supplant a lover than a husband.

He had had the pleasure of meeting her once at the law courts; he even mentioned the date. This remarkable power of memory astonished Madame Arnoux. He went on in an oily tone:

'You were already experiencing . . . some difficulties . . . in your affairs!'

She made no reply; so it must be true.

He began to chat about this and that, about her house, about the factory; then, noticing some medallions at the sides of the mirror:

'Ah! Family portraits, no doubt?'

He noticed that of an old lady, Madame Arnoux's mother.

'She has the appearance of being an excellent woman, a southern type.'

And, on being met with the objection that she was from Chartres:

'Chartres! Pretty town!'

He praised its cathedral and its pies; then, coming back to the portrait, traced resemblances between it and Madame Arnoux, and cast flatteries at her indirectly. She did not appear to be offended. He took confidence, and said that he had known Arnoux a long time.

'He is a fine fellow! But he does compromise himself! Take this mortgage, for example – one can't imagine such a reckless act . . . '

'Yes I know,' said she, shrugging her shoulders.

This involuntary evidence of contempt induced Deslauriers to continue.

'That kaolin business of his was near turning out very badly, you may not be aware of that, and even his reputation . . . '

A frown made him pause.

Then, falling back on generalities, he expressed his pity for the poor women whose husbands fritter away their means . . .

'But in this case, monsieur, the means belong to him; as for me, I have nothing!'

No matter! One never knew . . . A person with experience might be useful. He made offers of devotion, exalted his own merits; and he looked into her face through his shining spectacles.

She was seized with a vague torpor; but suddenly said:

'Let's look into the matter, I beg of you!'

He exhibited the bundle of papers.

'This is Frédéric's letter of attorney. With such a document in the hands of a process-server, who would make out an order, nothing could be easier: in twenty-four hours . . . ' (she remained impassive; he changed his tactic.) 'As for me, however, I don't understand what impels him to demand this sum; for, in fact, he doesn't need it!'

'What! Monsieur Moreau was good enough to . . . '

'Oh, granted!'

And Deslauriers sang his praises, then in a mild fashion began to denigrate him, calling him forgetful, self-centred, and mean.

'I thought he was your friend, Monsieur?'

'That doesn't stop me seeing his defects. For example, he shows very little recognition of . . . how shall I put it? Affection . . . '

Madame Arnoux was turning over the leaves of the big notebook. She interrupted him in order to get him to explain a certain word.

He bent over her shoulder, and his face came so close that he grazed her cheek. She blushed; this heightened colour inflamed Deslauriers; he hungrily kissed her hand.

'What are you doing, Monsieur!'

And, standing up against the wall, she held him motionless under the glance of her great, black, angry eyes.

'Listen to me! I love you!'

She broke into a laugh, a shrill, heart-breaking, dreadful laugh. Deslauriers felt himself suffocating with anger. He contained himself; and, with the look of a beaten man pleading for mercy:

'Ah, you're wrong! I wouldn't be like him. I'd never . . . '

'Of whom, pray, are you talking?'

'Of Frédéric!'

'Ah! Monsieur Moreau troubles me little. I told you that!'

'Oh! Excuse me! . . . Excuse me! . . . '

Then, drawling his words, in a cutting voice:

'I even imagined that you were sufficiently interested in his person to learn with pleasure . . . '

She became quite pale. The ex-law-clerk added:

'He's going to be married.'

'He!'

'In a month at the latest, to Mademoiselle Roque, the daughter of M. Dambreuse's agent. He has even gone down to Nogent for no other purpose but that.'

She placed her hand over her heart, as if at the shock of a great blow; but immediately she rang the bell. Deslauriers did not wait to be thrown out. When she turned round he had disappeared.

Madame Arnoux was gasping a little. She drew near the window to get her breath.

On the other side of the street, on the pavement, a packer in his shirtsleeves was nailing down a box. Hackney coaches passed. She closed the window and then came and sat down. As the high houses in the vicinity intercepted the sun's rays, the light of day stole coldly into the apartment. Her children had gone out; there was not a stir around her. It seemed as if she were utterly deserted.

'He is going to be married! Is it possible!'

And she was seized with a fit of nervous trembling.

'Why is this? Does it mean that I love him?'

Then all of a sudden:

'Why, yes, I love him . . . I love him!'

It seemed to her as if she were sinking into an abyss which continued without end. The clock struck three. She listened to the vibrations of the sounds as they died away. And she remained on the edge of her armchair, with her eyes fixed, and smiling continually.

The same afternoon, at the same moment, Frédéric and Mademoiselle Louise were walking in the garden belonging to M. Roque at the end of the island. Old Catherine was watching them, some distance away; they were walking side by side and Frédéric was saying:

'You remember when I took you out into the country?'

'How good you were to me!' she replied. 'You helped me to make sandcastles, to fill my watering-can, and to push me on the swing!'

'All your dolls, who had the names of queens or marchionesses – what has become of them?'

'Gracious, I don't know!'

'And your little dog Blacky?'

'He drowned, poor darling!'

'And the *Don Quixote* of which we coloured the engravings together?'

'I have it still!'

He recalled to her mind the day of her first communion, and how pretty she had been at vespers, with her white veil and her tall candle, whilst the girls were all taking their places in a row around the choir, and the bell was ringing.

These memories, no doubt, held little charm for Mademoiselle Roque; she had not a word to say in reply; and, a minute later:

'Naughty fellow! Never to have written a line to me, even once!'

Frédéric urged by way of excuse his numerous occupations.

'What do you do then?'

He was embarrassed by the question then told her that he was studying politics.

'Ah!'

And without questioning him further:

'That keeps you busy, whereas I . . . '

Then she spoke to him about the barrenness of her existence, as there was nobody to see, and nothing to amuse her or distract her! She wanted to go riding.

'The vicar maintains that this is improper for a young lady; how stupid these proprieties are! They used to let me do whatever I pleased; now, they won't let me do anything!'

'But your father is fond of you!'

'Yes; but . . . '

She heaved a sigh, which meant: 'That's not enough to make me happy.'

Then there was silence. They heard only the crunching sound of the sand beneath their feet, together with the murmur of the weir; for the Seine, above Nogent, is cut into two arms. The one which turns the mills discharges in this place the surplus of its water and unites further down with the natural course of the river; and a person coming from the bridge sees on the right, on the other bank, a grassy slope dominated by a white house. On the left, in the meadow, a row of poplar trees extends, and the horizon in front is bounded by a curve of the river; it was flat, like a mirror; large insects skated over the calm water. Tufts of reeds and rushes mark its edge, unevenly; all kinds of plants which happened to spring up there bloomed out as golden buds, trailed their yellow clusters, raised distaffs of purple flowers, and emerged as green rockets here and there. In a cove of the river was a carpet of water-lilies; and a row of ancient willows, in which wolf-traps were hidden, formed, on this side of the island, the sole protection of the garden.

In the interior, on this side, four walls with a slate coping enclosed the kitchen-garden, in which the square patches of earth, freshly dug, looked like brown plates. The bell-glasses of the melons shone in a row on their narrow bed; the artichokes, beans, spinach, carrots and tomatoes succeeded each other as far as a bed of asparagus, which looked like a little wood of feathers.

All this piece of land had been under the Directory what is called 'a folly'. The trees had, since then, grown enormously. Clematis choked the arbours, the walks were covered with moss, brambles abounded everywhere. Fragments of statues let their plaster crumble in the grass. As you walked, you tripped over odd bits of wire. All that was left of the pavilion were two rooms on the ground floor, with some blue paper hanging in shreds. Before the façade extended an Italian-style pergola, where a vine was supported on columns of brick by a trellis of sticks.

The two of them placed themselves beneath it, and, as the light fell through the irregular gaps in the foliage, Frédéric, turning to speak to Louise, watched the shadow of the leaves on her face.

She had in her red hair, stuck in her chignon, a needle, terminated by a glass ball in imitation of an emerald; and, in spite of her mourning, she wore (so artless was her bad taste) straw slippers trimmed with pink satin, a vulgar curiosity probably bought at some fair.

He noticed them, and ironically congratulated her.

'Don't laugh at me!' she replied.

Then surveying him from head to foot, from his grey felt hat to his silk socks:

'How exquisite you are!'

After this, she asked him to recommend some books for her to read. He gave her the names of several; and she said:

'Oh! How learned you are!'

While yet very small, she had been smitten with one of those childish passions which have, at the same time, the purity of a religion and the violence of a need. He had been her comrade, her brother, her master, had diverted her mind, made her heart beat more quickly, and, unconsciously, had poured into the very depths of her being a latent and continuous intoxication. Then he had left her at the moment of a tragic crisis in her existence, when her mother had only just died, and those two sorrows had fused. Absence had idealised him in her memory; he had come back with a sort of halo round his head and she gave herself up ingenuously to the pleasure of seeing him.

For the first time in his life Frédéric felt himself loved; and this new pleasure, which did not transcend the ordinary run of agreeable sensations, made him swell with an internal satisfaction; so that he spread out both his arms and flung back his head.

A large cloud passed across the sky.

'It's going towards Paris,' said Louise. 'You'd like to follow it – wouldn't you?'

'I! Why?'

'Who knows?'

And surveying him with a sharp look:

'Perhaps you have there . . . ' (she searched her mind for the appropriate phrase) 'something to engage your affections.'

'Oh! I have nothing to engage my affections!'

'Are you sure?'

'Why, yes, Mademoiselle, perfectly sure!'

In less than a year there had taken place in the young girl an extraordinary transformation, which astonished Frédéric. After a minute's silence he added:

'We ought to call each other 'tu', as we used to do – shall we?'

'No.'

'Why?'

'Because!'

He persisted. She answered, with downcast face:

'I dare not!'

They had reached the end of the garden, on the bank of the Livon. Frédéric, in a spirit of boyish fun, began to send pebbles skimming over the water. She bade him sit down. He obeyed; then, looking at the weir:

'It's like Niagara!'

He began to talk about distant countries and long voyages. The idea of travelling was very attractive to her. She would not have been afraid of anything, neither tempests nor lions.

Seated close beside each other, they collected in front of them handfuls of sand, then let it slip through their fingers as they talked; and the hot wind, which came from the plains, brought to them in waves odours of lavender, together with the smell of tar escaping from a boat behind the lock. The sun beat down onto the cascade; the greenish blocks of stone in the little wall over which the water slipped looked as if they were covered with a silver gauze that was perpetually unrolling. A long strip of foam spurted up with a regular rhythm at its foot. Then it formed bubblings and whirlpools, a thousand opposing currents, which ended by intermingling in a single limpid sheet of water.

Louise murmured that she envied the existence of fishes.

'It must be so delightful to tumble about in there at your ease, and to feel yourself caressed all over.'

And she shivered, quivering with a sensual affection for him.

But a voice called out:

'Where are you?'

'Your maid is calling you,' said Frédéric.

'All right! All right!'

Louise did not trouble to move.

'She'll be cross,' he went on.

'I don't care! And besides . . . ' Mademoiselle Roque gave him to understand by a gesture that her maid was entirely subject to her will.

She arose, however, and then complained of a headache. And, as they were passing in front of a large shed containing piles of faggots:

'Suppose we sat down there, *under shelter*?'

He pretended not to understand this dialect expression, and even teased her about her accent. Gradually the corners of her mouth drew in, she bit her lips; she moved away from him, sulking.

Frédéric came over to her, swore he had not meant to hurt her, and that he was very fond of her.

'Is that true?' she exclaimed, looking at him with a smile which lit up her entire face, with its light powdering of freckles.

He could not resist this frankness of feeling, the freshness of her youth, and he replied:

'Why should I lie to you? . . . Have you any doubt about it . . . Well?' And he passed his left arm round her waist.

A cry, soft as the cooing of a dove, burst from her throat; her head fell back, she was going to faint, he held her up. And he had no need of honourable scruples; at the sight of this virgin offering herself to him he had been seized with fear. Then he helped her to take a few steps, slowly. He had ceased his verbal caresses, and no longer caring to talk of anything save the most trifling subjects, he spoke to her about people in the society of Nogent.

Suddenly she pushed him away, and in a bitter tone:

'You wouldn't have the courage to take me away!'

He remained motionless, with a look of utter amazement. She burst into sobs, and hiding her face in his breast:

'Can I live without you?'

He tried to calm her. She laid her two hands on his shoulders in order to get a better view of his face, and fixing her green eyes on his with an almost fierce tearfulness:

'Will you be my husband?'

'But . . . ' Frédéric began, casting about for a reply. 'Of course . . . I ask for nothing better.'

At that moment M. Roque's cap appeared behind a lilac.

He took his 'young friend' on a two-day trip through the district, to view his properties; and when Frédéric returned, he found three letters awaiting him at his mother's house.

The first was a note from M. Dambreuse, containing an invitation to dinner for the previous Tuesday. What was the occasion of this politeness? Had they forgiven him his misdemeanour?

The second was from Rosanette. She thanked him for having risked his life on her behalf; Frédéric did not at first understand what she meant; finally, after a considerable amount of circumlocution, she implored him, while appealing to his friendship, relying on his delicacy, and down on her knees, as she put it, on account of the pressing necessity of the case, and as if begging for bread, for a small loan of five hundred francs. He at once made up his mind to supply her with them.

The third letter, which was from Deslauriers, spoke of the letter of attorney, and was long and obscure. The lawyer had not yet taken any definite action. He urged him not to disturb himself: 'There's no need for you to come back!' even laying singular stress on this point.

Frédéric got lost in conjectures of every sort, and he felt anxious to return to Paris; this assumption of a right to control his conduct excited in him a feeling of revolt.

Moreover, he began to miss the life of the boulevards; and then, his mother was pressing him so hard, M. Roque dogged him so constantly, and Mademoiselle Louise loved him so much, that it was no longer possible for him to stay on without declaring his intentions. He wanted to think, and he would be better able to form a right estimate of things at a distance.

In order to assign a motive for his journey, Frédéric invented a story; and he left home, telling everyone, and himself believing, that he would soon return.

His return to Paris gave him no pleasure; it was an evening at the end of August, the boulevards seemed empty, the passers-by succeeded each other with scowling faces, here and there a boiler of asphalt was smoking, many houses had their blinds entirely drawn. He arrived home; he found the hangings covered with dust; and, dining all alone, Frédéric was seized with a strange feeling of forlornness; then his thoughts reverted to Mademoiselle Roque.

The idea of getting married no longer appeared to him preposterous. They would travel, they would go to Italy, to the East! And he saw her standing on a hillock, gazing at a landscape, or else leaning on his arm in a Florentine gallery, pausing to look at the pictures. What a pleasure it would be to watch this good little creature expanding in response to the splendours of Art and Nature! Once away from her normal environment, she would soon become a charming companion. M. Roque's wealth, moreover, tempted him. Yet he shrank from taking such a step, regarding it as a weakness, a degradation.

But he was firmly resolved (whatever he might do) on changing his mode of life, that is to say, to lose his heart no more in fruitless passions, and he even hesitated about executing the commission with which he had been entrusted by Louise. This was to buy for her from Jacques Arnoux two large polychrome statues representing negroes, like those which were at the Prefecture at Troyes. She knew the manufacturer's number, and would not have any other. Frédéric was afraid that, if he went back to see 'them', he might once again fall victim to his old passion.

These reflections occupied his mind during the entire evening; and he was just about to go to bed when a woman presented herself.

'It's me,' said Mademoiselle Vatnaz, with a laugh. 'I have come on behalf of Rosanette.'

So, then, they were reconciled?

'Good heavens, yes! I'm not ill-natured, as you're well aware.

And besides, the poor girl . . . It would take too long to tell you all about it.'

In short, the Maréchale wanted to see him; she was waiting for an answer, her letter having travelled from Paris to Nogent; Mademoiselle Vatnaz did not know what was in it. So Frédéric asked her how the Maréchale was going on.

She was now *with* a very rich man, a Russian, Prince Tzernoukoff, who had seen her at the races at the Champ de Mars last summer.

'We have three carriages, a saddle-horse, livery servants, a groom got up in the English fashion, a country house, a box at the Italian opera, and a heap of other things. There you are, my dear.'

And, as if she had profited by this change of fortune, Vatnaz appeared gayer and even happy. She took off her gloves and examined the furniture and the ornaments in the room. She estimated them at their exact prices like a dealer. He ought to have consulted her in order to get them cheaper; and she congratulated him on his good taste:

'Ah! This is pretty, exceedingly nice! There's nobody like you for these ideas.'

Then, as her eyes fell on a door close to the head of the alcove:

'That's the way you let your little lady-friends out, eh?'

And, in a familiar fashion, she took him by the chin. He quivered at the touch of her long hands, which were at the same time thin and soft. Round her wrists she wore an edging of lace, and the bodice of her green dress was braided like a hussar's jacket. Her bonnet of black tulle, with its drooping brim, concealed her forehead a little; her eyes shone underneath; an odour of patchouli escaped from her hair; the lamp placed on a round table, shining on her from below like the footlights of a theatre, made her jaw protrude – and all at once, in the presence of this ugly woman whose body moved with the sinuosity of a panther, Frédéric felt an immense surge of lust, a desire for animalistic sexuality.

She said to him, in an unctuous tone, while she drew forth from her purse three square slips of paper:

'You must have these!'

They were three tickets for a benefit performance for Delmar.

'What! Him?'

'Certainly!'

Mademoiselle Vatnaz, without giving any further explanation, added that she adored him more than ever. If she were to be believed, the actor was now definitely classed amongst 'the leading celebrities of the age'. And it was not such or such a personage that he represented, but the very genius of France, the People! He had 'the humanitarian spirit; he understood the priesthood of Art'! Frédéric, in order to put an end to these eulogies, gave her the money for the three seats.

'You needn't say anything about this over the way! How late it is, good heavens! I must leave you. Ah, I was forgetting the address: it's Rue Grange-Batelière, number 14.'

And, at the door:

'Goodbye, beloved man!'

'Beloved by whom?' wondered Frédéric. 'What a strange creature!'

And he remembered that Dussardier had said to him one day, when talking about her: 'Oh, she's not much to write home about!' as if alluding to some rather shady history.

Next day he went to see the Maréchale. She lived in a new house, whose blinds projected into the street. On every landing there was a mirror against the wall, before each window there was a rustic flower-stand, and the stairs were covered with a canvas carpet; and when one got inside the door, the coolness of the staircase was refreshing.

It was a manservant who came to open the door, a footman in a red waistcoat. On a bench in the anteroom a woman and two men, tradespeople, no doubt, were waiting as if in a minister's vestibule. To the left, the door of the dining-room, slightly ajar, afforded a glimpse of empty bottles on the sideboards, and napkins on the backs of chairs; and parallel with it ran a gallery in which gold-coloured sticks supported an espalier of roses. In the court-yard below, two boys with bare arms were scrubbing a landau. Their voices rose to Frédéric's ears, mingled with the intermittent sounds made by a currycomb knocking against a stone.

The manservant returned. 'Madame would receive Monsieur'; and he led Frédéric through a second anteroom, and then into a large drawing-room hung with yellow brocatelle with twisted mouldings in the corners which were joined at the ceiling, and which seemed to be continued by the arabesques of the chandelier which looked like cables. No doubt there had been a party the night before. The tables were dusted with cigar-ash.

At last he made his way into a kind of boudoir with stained-glass windows which shed a dim light. Trefoils cut in wood adorned the upper part of the doors; behind a balustrade, three scarlet mattresses formed a divan, and the stem of a platinum hookah had been left on top of it. Instead of a mirror, there was on the mantelpiece a pyramid-shaped whatnot, displaying on its shelves an entire collection of curiosities: old silver watches, Bohemian horns, jewelled clasps, jade studs, enamels, grotesque figures in china, and a little Byzantine virgin with a vermilion cape; and all this was mingled in a golden twilight with the bluish shade of the carpet, the mother-of-pearl reflections of the footstools, and the tawny hue of the walls covered with brown leather. In the corners, on little pedestals, there were bronze vases containing clusters of flowers, which made the atmosphere heavy.

Rosanette appeared, attired in a pink satin jacket with white cashmere trousers, a necklace of piastres, and a red cap encircled with a branch of jasmine.

Frédéric started back in surprise; then said he had brought the 'thing in question', and handed her the banknote.

She gazed at him in utter astonishment; and, as he still kept the note in his hand, without knowing where to put it:

'Do take it!'

She seized it; then, as she flung it on the divan:

'You are very kind.'

She wanted it to help buy a piece of ground at Bellevue, which she was paying for like this, in annual instalments. Such lack of ceremony offended Frédéric. However, so much the better! This would avenge him for the past.

'Sit down!' said she. 'There, closer.' And in a grave tone: 'In the first place, I have to thank you, my dear friend, for having risked your life.'

'Oh, it was nothing!'

'What! But it was a very noble act!'

And the Maréchale exhibited an embarrassing sense of gratitude; for she must be thinking that he had fought entirely on account of Arnoux, as the latter, who believed it himself, must have yielded to the temptation to tell her so.

'She may be laughing at me,' thought Frédéric.

He had nothing further to detain him, and, pleading that he had an appointment, he rose.

'Oh no! Stay!'

He resumed his seat, and complimented her on her costume.

She replied, with an air of oppression:

'It's the prince who likes me to dress like that! And I have to smoke things like this!' Rosanette added, pointing towards the hookah. 'Shall we try it? Would you like to?'

A light was brought; and, finding it hard to set fire to the tombac, she began to stamp impatiently with her foot. Then she fell into a torpor; and she remained motionless on the divan, with a cushion under her armpit and her body twisted a little on one side, one knee bent and the other leg straight out. The long serpent of red leather, which formed rings on the floor, rolled itself round her arm. She pressed the amber mouthpiece to her lips, and gazed at Frédéric while she blinked her eyes in the midst of the spirals of smoke that enveloped her. A gurgling sound came from the water as she inhaled the fumes, and from time to time she murmured:

'The poor darling! The poor pet!'

He tried to find something of an agreeable nature to talk about; the thought of Vatnaz recurred to his memory.

He remarked that she had appeared very elegant to him.

'Yes, isn't she!' replied the Maréchale. 'She's very lucky to have me, she is!' – without adding another word, so much reserve was there in their conversation.

Each of them felt a sense of constraint, a barrier. In fact, Rosanette's vanity had been flattered by the duel, of which she believed herself to be the occasion. Then, she had been very much astonished that he did not hasten to take advantage of his achievement; and, in order to compel him to return to her, she had invented this story that she wanted five hundred francs. How was it that Frédéric did not ask for a little love from her in return! This was a piece of refinement that filled her with wonder, and, with a rush of emotion, she said to him:

'Would you like to come with us to the seaside?'

'What does "us" mean?'

'Myself and my friend; I'll pass you off as my cousin, as in the old comedies.'

'No thank you very much!'

'Well, then, you can take lodgings near ours.'

The idea of hiding himself from a rich man humiliated him.

'No, that's impossible!'

'Just as you please!'

Rosanette turned away with tears in her eyes. Frédéric noticed this; and in order to demonstrate the interest he took in her, he said that he was delighted to see her at last in a comfortable position.

She shrugged her shoulders. What ever was troubling her? Was it, perhaps, that she was not loved?

'Oh! I always have people to love me!'

She added:

'It remains to be seen in what way!'

Complaining that she was 'suffocating with the heat', the Maréchale unfastened her jacket; and, without any other garment round her body, save her silk chemise, she leaned her head on his shoulder with the air of a slave, full of provocation.

A man of a less introspective egoism would not have thought that the Vicomte, M. de Comaing, or anyone else might appear on the scene. But Frédéric had been too many times the dupe of these very glances to compromise himself by a fresh humiliation.

She wished to know all about his relationships and his amusements; she even went so far as to enquire about his financial affairs, and offered to lend him money if he wanted it. Frédéric, who had had enough, took up his hat.

'I'm off, my pet! Have a nice time at the seaside; goodbye!'

She opened her eyes wide; then, in a curt tone:

'Goodbye!'

He made his way out through the yellow drawing-room, and through the second anteroom. There was on the table, between a vase full of visiting cards and an inkstand, a chased silver chest. It was Madame Arnoux's! Then he experienced a feeling of tenderness, and, at the same time, a sense of scandal, of profanation. He longed to touch it, open it. He was afraid of being seen, and went away.

Frédéric was virtuous. He did not go back to the Arnoux's.

He sent his manservant to buy the two negroes, having given him all the necessary directions; and the case containing them set forth the same evening for Nogent. Next morning, as he was on his way to see Deslauriers, on the corner of the Rue Vivienne and the boulevard, Madame Arnoux presented herself before him face to face.

The first movement of each of them was to draw back; then the same smile came to the lips of both, and they advanced to meet each other. For a minute, neither of them spoke.

The sunlight fell round her; and her oval face, her long eye-lashes, her black lace shawl, which moulded the outline of her shoulders, her gown of shot silk, the bouquet of violets at the corner of her bonnet, all seemed to him to possess an extraordinary splendour. An infinite softness poured out of her beautiful eyes; and in a faltering voice, uttering at random the first words that came to his lips:

'How is Arnoux?' said Frédéric.

'Well, I thank you!'

'And your children?'

'They are very well!'

'Ah! . . . Ah! . . . What fine weather we're getting, are we not?'

'Wonderful, indeed!'

'You're shopping?'

'Yes.'

And, with a slow inclination of the head:

'Goodbye!'

She had not put out her hand, had not spoken one word of affection, and had not even invited him to her house. No matter! He would not have exchanged this meeting for the most delightful of adventures, and he pondered over its sweetness as he proceeded on his way.

Deslauriers, surprised at seeing him, concealed his annoyance – for he cherished still through obstinacy some hope with regard to Madame Arnoux; and he had written to Frédéric to prolong his stay in the country, in order to be more free in his manoeuvres.

He informed Frédéric, however, that he had presented himself at her house in order to ascertain if their contract stipulated for a community of property between husband and wife: in that case, proceedings might be taken against the wife; 'and she put on a queer face when I told her about your marriage.'

'Oh! What an invention!'

'It was necessary in order to show that you wanted your capital! A person who was indifferent wouldn't have nearly fainted, as she did.'

'Really?' exclaimed Frédéric.

'Ah! Old lad, you're giving yourself away! Come! Be honest!'

An immense weakness stole over Madame Arnoux's lover.

'Why, no! . . . I assure you! . . . On my word of honour!'

These feeble denials banished any further doubt in Deslauriers' mind. He congratulated his friend. He asked him for 'details'. Frédéric gave him none, and even resisted the desire to invent some.

As for the mortgage, he told him to do nothing about it, but to wait. Deslauriers thought he was wrong, and even remonstrated with him in rather a brutal fashion.

He was, anyway, more gloomy, malignant, and irascible than ever. In a year, if fortune did not change, he would embark for America or blow out his brains. Indeed, he appeared to be in such a rage against everything, and so uncompromising in his radicalism, that Frédéric could not keep from saying to him:

'Now you're like Sénécal.'

Deslauriers, at this remark, informed him that Sénécal had been discharged from Sainte-Pélagie, the magisterial investigation having failed to supply sufficient evidence, no doubt, to justify his being sent for trial.

Dussardier was so much overjoyed at the release of Sénécal, that he wanted to invite his friends to 'come and take punch' with him, and begged of Frédéric 'to be one of the party', giving him, at the same time, to understand that he would be in the company of Hussonnet, who had proved himself a very good friend to Sénécal.

Indeed, the *Flambard* had just become associated with a business establishment whose prospectus contained the following references: 'Vineyard Agency – Office of Publicity – Debt Recovery and Intelligence Office, etc.' But the Bohemian was afraid that his connection with trade might be prejudicial to his literary reputation, and he had taken the mathematician to keep the accounts. Although the situation was a poor one, Sénécal would have died of starvation without it. Not wishing to mortify the kindly clerk, Frédéric accepted his invitation.

Dussardier, three days beforehand, had himself waxed the red floor of his garret, beaten the armchair, and dusted the chimney-piece, on which might be seen under a globe an alabaster time-piece between a stalactite and a coconut. As his two chandeliers and his candlestick were not sufficient, he had borrowed two sconces from the doorkeeper; and these five lights shone on the top of the chest of drawers, which was covered with three napkins in order to display more fittingly some macaroons, biscuits, a brioche, and a dozen bottles of beer. Opposite, close to the wall, which was hung with yellow paper, there was a little mahogany bookcase containing the *Fables of Lachambeaudie*, the *Mysteries of Paris*, and Norvins' *Napoléon* – and, in the middle of the alcove, the face of Béranger was smiling in a rosewood frame!

The guests (in addition to Deslauriers and Sénécal) were an apothecary who had just been admitted, but who had not enough capital to start in business for himself; a young man of his own place of employment, a traveller in wines, an architect, and a gentleman employed in an insurance office. Regimbart had not been able to come. Regret was expressed at his absence.

They welcomed Frédéric with a great display of sympathy, as they all knew through Dussardier what he had said at M. Dambreuse's party. Sénécal contented himself with putting out his hand in a dignified manner.

He remained standing near the mantelpiece. The others, seated, with their pipes in their mouths, listened to him, as he held forth on universal suffrage, from which he predicted as a result the triumph of Democracy and the practical application of the principles of the Gospel. Moreover, the hour was at hand; the banquets of the party of reform were becoming more numerous in the provinces, Piedmont, Naples, Tuscany . . .

'It's true,' said Deslauriers, interrupting him abruptly. 'This can't go on!'

And he began to draw a picture of the situation.

We had sacrificed Holland to obtain from England the recognition of Louis-Philippe; and this precious English alliance was lost, owing to the Spanish marriages! In Switzerland, M. Guizot, in tow to the Austrian, maintained the treaties of 1815. Prussia, with her Zollverein, was preparing embarrassments for us. The Eastern question was still pending.

'The fact that the Grand Duke Constantine sends presents to M. d'Aumale is no reason to trust Russia. As for home affairs, never has there been such blindness, such stupidity! The Government no longer even keeps up its majority! Everywhere, indeed, according to the well-known expression, there's nothing! Nothing! Nothing! And in the teeth of such public scandals,' continued the lawyer, with his hands on his hips, 'they declare themselves satisfied.'

This allusion to a notorious vote called forth applause. Dussardier uncorked a bottle of beer; the froth splashed on the curtains. He did not mind; he filled the pipes, cut the brioche, offered it round, and had several times gone downstairs to see whether the punch was coming up; and soon everyone was in a state of excitement, as they all felt equally exasperated against Power. Their rage was violent for no other reason than that they hated injustice; and they mixed their legitimate grievances with the most idiotic complaints.

The apothecary groaned over the pitiable condition of our fleet. The insurance agent could not tolerate the two sentinels of Maréchal Soult. Deslauriers denounced the Jesuits, who had just installed themselves publicly in Lille. Sénécal execrated M. Cousin far more, for eclecticism, by teaching that certitude can be deduced from reason, developed selfishness and destroyed solidarity; the traveller in wines, knowing very little about these matters, remarked in a loud tone that he was forgetting many infamous things:

'The royal carriage on the Northern line is to cost eighty thousand francs! Who'll pay for it?'

'Yes, who'll pay for it?' echoed the clerk, as angry as if this amount had been drawn out of his own pocket.

Then followed recriminations against the sharks of the Stock Exchange and the corruption of officials. According to Sénécal they ought to go higher up, and lay the blame, first of all, on the princes who were reviving the morals of the Regency period.

'Didn't you see, recently, the Duc de Montpensier's friends coming back from Vincennes, drunk no doubt, and disturbing with their songs the workmen of the Faubourg Saint-Antoine?'

'They even called out "Down with thieves!" ' said the apothecary. 'I was there, and I joined in!'

'Good! The people are at last waking up since the Teste-Cubières case.'

'Well, I was troubled by that case,' said Dussardier, 'because it casts a slur on an old soldier!'

'Do you know,' Sénécal went on, 'that they have discovered at the Duchesse de Praslin's house . . . ?'

But here the door was sent flying open with a kick. Hussonnet entered.

'Hail, my lords,' said he, as he seated himself on the bed.

No allusion was made to his article, which he was sorry, moreover, for having written, the Maréchale having sharply scolded him for it.

He had just seen at Dumas's theatre the *Chevalier de Maison-Rouge*, and 'thought it was boring'.

Such a criticism astonished the democrats, as this drama, by its tendencies, or rather by its scenery, flattered their passions. They protested. Sénécal, in order to bring this discussion to a close, asked whether the play served the cause of Democracy.

'Yes . . . perhaps; but it is written in such a style . . . '

'Well, then, it's a good play. What is style? It's the idea!'

And, without allowing Frédéric to speak:

'Now, I was arguing that in the Praslin case . . . '

Hussonnet interrupted him.

'Ah! There's another worn-out old story! I'm sick of it!'

'And others as well as you,' returned Deslauriers. 'It's only got five papers suppressed! Listen while I read this note.'

And drawing his notebook out of his pocket, he read:

' "We have, since the establishment of the best of republics, been subjected to twelve hundred and twenty-nine press prosecutions, from which the results to the writers have been: imprisonment extending over a period of three thousand one hundred and forty-one years, and the light sum of seven million one hundred and ten thousand five hundred francs by way of fine." – That's charming, isn't it?'

They all sneered bitterly. Frédéric, as animated as the others, broke in:

'The *Démocratie Pacifique* has had proceedings taken against it on account of its serial, a novel entitled *The Woman's Share*.'

'Come! That's good,' said Hussonnet. 'If they're preventing us getting our share of women now!'

'But what is there that's not prohibited?' exclaimed Deslauriers. 'To smoke in the Luxembourg is prohibited, to sing the Hymn to Pius IX is prohibited!'

'And the typographers' banquet has been banned,' exclaimed a hollow voice.

It was that of the architect, who had sat concealed in the shadow of the alcove, and had remained silent up to that moment. He added that, the week before, a man named Mullet had been convicted of offering insults to the king.

'Mullet's in the soup,' said Hussonnet.

This joke appeared so improper to Sénécal, that he reproached Hussonnet for defending 'the Juggler of the Hôtel de Ville, the friend of the traitor Dumouriez'.

'I? Quite the contrary!'

He considered Louis-Philippe commonplace, one of the National Guard types of men, all grocer's shop and cotton nightcap! And laying his hand on his heart, the Bohemian proclaimed the consecrated phrases: 'It is always with a new pleasure . . . Polish nationality will not perish . . . Our great works will be continued . . . Give me money for my little family . . .' They all laughed hugely, declaring that he was a delightful fellow, full of wit; their joy was redoubled at the sight of the bowl of punch which was brought in by the keeper of a café.

The flames of the alcohol and those of the candles soon heated the apartment; and the light from the garret, passing across the courtyard, illuminated the edge of a roof opposite, with the flue of a chimney standing black against the darkness of the night. They talked in very loud tones all at the same time; they had taken off their coats; they knocked against the furniture, they clinked glasses.

Hussonnet exclaimed:

'Send up some great ladies, in order that this may be more Tour de Nesle, local colour, and Rembrandtesque, gadzooks!'

And the apothecary, who kept on and on stirring the punch, began to sing at the top of his lungs:

'I've two big oxen in my stable,
Two big white oxen . . . '

Sénécal laid his hand on the apothecary's mouth: he did not like disorderly conduct; and the other lodgers pressed their faces against the windowpanes, surprised at the unwonted uproar that was emanating from Dussardier's room.

The honest fellow was happy, and said that this recalled to his mind their little parties on the Quai Napoléon in days gone by;

however, they missed many who used to be present at these reunions, 'Pellerin, for instance . . .'

'We can do without him,' observed Frédéric.

And Deslauriers enquired about Martinon.

'What has become of that interesting gentleman?'

Frédéric, immediately giving vent to the ill-will which he bore Martinon, attacked his mental capacity, his character, his false elegance, his entire personality. He was a perfect specimen of an upstart peasant! The new aristocracy, the mercantile class, was not as good as the old, the nobility. He maintained this; and the democrats expressed their approval – as if he had been a member of the one, and they were in the habit of frequenting the other. They were delighted with him. The apothecary compared him to M. d'Alton Shée, who, though a peer of France, defended the cause of the People.

The time had come for taking their departure. They all separated with great handshakings; Dussardier, in a spirit of affectionate solicitude, saw Frédéric and Deslauriers home. As soon as they were in the street, the lawyer assumed a thoughtful air, and, after a moment's silence:

'You have a great grudge, then, against Pellerin?'

Frédéric did not hide his rancour.

The painter, however, had withdrawn the notorious picture from show. People should not quarrel over trifles! What was the good of making an enemy for oneself?

'He yielded to a burst of ill-temper, excusable in a man who hasn't a penny. You, of course, can't understand that!'

And, when Deslauriers had gone up to his own apartments, the clerk did not let Frédéric go; he even urged him to buy the portrait. In fact, Pellerin, abandoning the hope of being able to intimidate him, had got round them so that they might use their influence to make him buy the thing.

Deslauriers spoke about it again, and pressed him on the point. The artist's claims were reasonable.

'I'm sure that for a sum of, perhaps, five hundred francs . . . '

'Oh, give it to him! See, here it is,' said Frédéric.

The picture was brought the same evening. It appeared to him a still more atrocious daub than when he had seen it first. The half-tints and the shades had darkened under the excessive retouchings, and they seemed obscured in relation to the lights, which had remained very brilliant here and there, destroying the harmony of the whole.

Frédéric revenged himself for having had to pay for it by denigrating it bitterly. Deslauriers took him at his word, and expressed approval of his conduct, for he still nurtured the ambition of constituting a phalanx of which he would be the leader; certain men take delight in making their friends do things which are disagreeable to them.

Meanwhile, Frédéric had not renewed his visits to the Dambreuses. He lacked the capital. He would have to enter into endless explanations; he hesitated about making up his mind. Perhaps he was right? Nothing was certain now, the coalmining speculation no more than other things; he had to give up society of that sort; Deslauriers, finally, dissuaded him from having anything further to do with the undertaking. From sheer force of hatred he was growing virtuous; and then he preferred Frédéric in a position of mediocrity. In this way he remained his equal and in a more intimate relationship with him.

Mademoiselle Roque's commission had been very badly executed. Her father wrote and told him this, supplying him with the most precise directions, and concluded his letter with the witticism: 'At the risk of making you have niggers on the brain'.

Frédéric could not do otherwise than call upon the Arnoux once more. He went up into the warehouse, where he could see nobody. The firm being on the point of collapse, the employees were as careless as their master.

He passed along beside the long line of shelves laden with ceramics, which filled up the entire space in the centre of the apartment; then, when he had reached the end, facing the counter, he walked with a heavier tread in order to make himself heard.

The door-curtain lifted, and Madame Arnoux appeared.

'What! You here! You!'

'Yes,' she faltered, with some agitation. 'I was looking for . . . '

He saw her handkerchief near the desk, and guessed that she had come down to her husband's warehouse to see how things stood, to clear up some anxiety perhaps.

'But . . . perhaps there is something you want?' she said.

'A mere nothing, madame.'

'These shop-assistants are intolerable! They're never there.'

They ought not to be blamed. On the contrary, he was delighted to find her alone.

She looked at him ironically.

'Well, and this marriage?'

'What marriage?'

'Yours!'

'Mine? Never!'

She made a gesture as if to contradict his words.

'What if I did, anyway? We take refuge in the mediocre, in our despair of realising the beautiful ideal of which we dreamed!'

'All your dreams, however, were not so . . . pure!'

'What do you mean?'

'When you drive around at the races with . . . certain persons!'

He cursed the Maréchale. Then something recurred to his memory.

'But it was you yourself, a long time ago, who begged me to see her, in the interests of Arnoux!'

She replied with a shake of her head:

'And you took advantage of it to amuse yourself.'

'Good God! Let's forget all this nonsense!'

'That's right, since you're going to be married!'

And she stifled a sigh, biting her lips.

So then he exclaimed:

'But I tell you again I'm not! Can you believe that I, with my intellectual requirements, my habits, would go and bury myself in the provinces in order to play cards, supervise masons, and walk about in clogs? To what end, pray? You've been told she was rich, haven't you? Ah! What do I care about money! Could I, after yearning for all that's most lovely, most tender, most enchanting, a sort of Paradise in human form, and having found this sweet ideal at last, when this vision hides every other from my view . . . '

And taking her head between his two hands, he began to kiss her on the eyelids, repeating:

'No! No! No! Never will I marry! Never! Never!'

She accepted these caresses, transfixed by surprise and delight.

The warehouse door to the staircase slammed. She jumped; and remained with hand outstretched, as if to bid him keep silence. Steps drew near. Then someone said from outside:

'Is Madame there?'

'Come in!'

Madame Arnoux had her elbow on the counter, and was quietly twisting a pen between her fingers when the bookkeeper threw aside the door-curtain.

Frédéric rose.

'My respects, Madame. The set will be ready, will it not? I may count on this?'

She made no reply. But this silent complicity made her face flush with all the crimson of adultery.

On the following day he paid her another visit, she received him; and, in order to follow up the advantages he had gained, Frédéric immediately, without any preamble, attempted to offer some justification for the meeting in the Champ de Mars. It was by the merest chance that he had been in that woman's company. While admitting that she was pretty (which was not the case), how could she for even a moment absorb his thoughts, seeing that he loved another!

'You know perfectly well, I told you.'

Madame Arnoux lowered her head.

'I'm sorry you told me.'

'Why?'

'The most basic proprieties now demand that I should see you no more!'

He protested the innocence of his love. The past ought to be a guarantee as to the future; he had promised himself not to disturb her existence, not to deafen her with his complaints.

'But yesterday my heart overflowed.'

'We must forget that moment, my friend!'

And yet, where would be the harm in two wretched beings sharing their sadness?

'For you're not happy any more than I am! Oh! I know you, you have no one to respond to your craving for affection, for devotion; I will do anything you wish! I will not offend you! . . . I swear to you that I won't!'

And he sank to his knees, in spite of himself, giving way beneath a weight of the feelings that was too great.

'Get up!' she said, 'I insist!'

And she declared in an imperious tone that if he did not obey, he would never see her again.

'Ah! I defy you to do it!' returned Frédéric. 'What is there for me to do in the world? Other men strive for riches, celebrity, power! But I have no profession, you are my exclusive occupation, my whole wealth, the object, the centre of my existence and of my thoughts. I can no more live without you than without the air of heaven! Don't you feel the aspiration of my soul rising towards yours, and that they must intermingle, and that it's killing me?'

Madame Arnoux began to tremble in every limb.

'Oh! Leave me! I beg of you!'

The look of utter disarray on her face made him pause. Then he advanced a step. But she drew back, with her two hands clasped.

'Leave me! In the name of Heaven! For mercy's sake!'

And Frédéric loved her so much that he went away.

Soon afterwards, he was filled with rage against himself, declared himself an idiot, and, twenty-four hours later, returned.

Madame was not there. He remained on the landing, stupefied with rage and indignation. Arnoux appeared, and informed him that his wife had left that very morning to instal herself in a little country house which he they rented in Auteuil, as they no longer owned the house in Saint-Cloud.

'This is another of her whims! Never mind, if that's what she wants! It suits me, too, for that matter; so much the better! Shall we dine together this evening?'

Frédéric pleaded as an excuse some urgent business, then he rushed to Auteuil.

Madame Arnoux allowed an exclamation of joy to escape her lips. Then all his bitterness vanished.

He did not talk about his love. In order to inspire her with more confidence in him, he even exaggerated his reserve; and when he asked if he might call again, she replied: 'Why, of course', putting out her hand, which she withdrew almost immediately.

From that time forth, Frédéric called upon her often. He promised large tips to the cabman. But often, growing impatient at the slow pace of the horse, he would get down; then, out of breath, he would climb on to an omnibus; then with what disdain he would survey the faces of the people sitting around him, who were not going to see her!

He could recognise her house from a distance by an enormous honeysuckle covering, on one side, the planks of the roof; it was a kind of Swiss châlet, painted red, with a balcony outside. In the garden there were three old chestnut trees, and on a mound in the centre was a parasol made of thatch, held up by the trunk of a tree. Under the slatework of the walls, a great vine, badly attached, hung down here and there like a rotten cable. The gate-bell, which was rather hard to pull, rang for a long time, and a long time always elapsed before anyone came. On each occasion he experienced a pang of suspense, a vague fear.

Then his ears would be greeted with the flapping of the maid's slippers over the sand; or else Madame Arnoux herself would appear. One day he came up behind her just as she was stooping down looking for violets on the lawn.

Her daughter's capricious disposition had forced her to send her to a convent. Her little son was at school every afternoon. Arnoux now took long lunches at the Palais-Royal with Regimbart and their friend Compain. No unwelcome visitor could take them by surprise.

It was clearly understood that they should not belong to each other. By this convention they were preserved from danger, and they found it easier to pour out their hearts to each other.

She told him all about her early life at Chartres which she spent with her mother; her piety when she was about twelve; then her passion for music, when she used to sing till nightfall in her little room, from which you could see the ramparts. He told her how melancholy broodings had haunted him at school, and how a woman's face had cast its rays over the cloudland of his imagination, so that, when he first laid eyes upon her, he had recognised her.

These conversations, as a rule, covered only the years during which they had known each other. He recalled to her recollection insignificant details, the colour of her dress at a certain period, a person who had called on a certain day, what she had said on another occasion; and she replied, marvelling:

'Yes, I remember!'

Their tastes, their judgments, were the same. Often one of them, listening to the other, exclaimed:

'That's the way with me!'

And the other in turn replied:

'And with me!'

Then there were endless complaints about Providence:

'Why was it not the will of Heaven? If we had only met . . . !'
'Ah! If I had been younger!' she sighed.
'No, but if I had been a little older.'

And they pictured to themselves a life entirely given up to love, sufficiently rich to fill up the vastest solitudes, surpassing all other joys, defying all forms of wretchedness, in which the hours would have slipped away in a continual outpouring of their own emotions, and which would have created something as bright and glorious as the palpitating splendour of the stars.

They were nearly always at the top of the steps in the open air; treetops yellowed by the autumn rose in uneven, softly swelling curves before them up to the edge of the pale sky; or else they walked to the end of the avenue into a summerhouse whose only furniture was a couch of grey canvas. Black specks stained the glass; the walls exhaled a mouldy smell – and they stayed there chatting about themselves, other people, anything, in a state of bliss. Sometimes the rays of the sun, passing through the Venetian blind, extended from the ceiling down to the flagstones like the strings of a lyre; particles of dust whirled amid these luminous bars. She amused herself by breaking them with her hand – Frédéric gently caught hold of it; and he gazed on the network of her veins, the grain of her skin, and the form of her fingers. Each of her fingers was for him more than a thing, almost a person.

She gave him her gloves, and, the week after, her handkerchief. She called him 'Frédéric', he called her 'Marie', adoring this name, which, as he said, was made to be uttered with a sigh of ecstasy, and which seemed to contain clouds of incense and scattered heaps of roses.

They soon came to an understanding as to the days on which he would call to see her; and, leaving the house as if by chance, she would walk along the road to meet him.

She did nothing to stimulate his love, lost in that carefree state which is characteristic of intense happiness. During the whole season she wore a brown silk dressing-gown with velvet borders of the same colour, a loose garment suited to the indolence of her attitudes and her grave physiognomy. Besides, she was reaching the late summer period of a woman's life, in which reflection is combined with tenderness, in which the beginning of maturity colours the gaze with a more intense flame, when strength of feeling mingles with experience of life and when, reaching the fulfilment of its time of expansion, the entire being overflows with richness, in the harmony of its beauty. Never had she possessed more sweetness, more indulgence. Secure in the thought that she would not err, she abandoned herself to a sentiment which seemed to her to be a right, won by her sorrows. And, moreover, it was so good and so new! What an abyss lay between the coarseness of Arnoux and the adoration of Frédéric!

He trembled at the thought that by an imprudent word he might lose all that he thought he had gained, saying to himself that an opportunity might be found again, but that a foolish step could never be repaired. He wanted her to give herself, and not take her. The assurance of being loved by her delighted him like a foretaste of possession, and then the charm of her person troubled his heart more than his senses. It was an indefinable feeling of beatitude, an intoxication so intense that it made him lose sight of even the possibility of having his happiness complete. Away from her, he was consumed with raging desire.

Before long their conversations were interrupted by long spells of silence. Sometimes a kind of sexual reserve made them blush in each other's presence. All the precautions they took to hide their love only revealed it; the stronger it grew, the more constrained they became in manner. The effect of this dissimulation was to intensify their sensibility. They quivered deliciously at the odour of moist leaves, they could not endure the east wind, they got irritated without any apparent cause, and had melancholy forebodings; the sound of a footstep, the creaking of the wainscoting, filled them with as much terror as if they had been guilty; they felt as if they were being pushed towards the edge of an abyss; they were enveloped in a tempestuous atmosphere; and when complaints escaped Frédéric's lips, she made accusations against herself.

'Yes! I'm doing wrong! I'm acting like a coquette! Don't come any more!'

Then he would repeat the same oaths – to which on each occasion she listened with pleasure.

His return to Paris, and the complications occasioned by New Year's Day, interrupted their meetings briefly. When he returned, he had an air of greater boldness in his manners. She kept going out to give orders, and in spite of his entreaties she received every visitor that called. Then, they engaged in conversations about Léotade, M. Guizot, the Pope, the insurrection at Palermo, and the banquet of the Twelfth Arrondissement, which was causing some disquietude. Frédéric found relief in railing against Authority; for he longed, like Deslauriers, to turn the whole world upside down, so soured had he now become. Madame Arnoux, too, was becoming sombre.

Her husband, going from extravagance to extravagance, was keeping one of the girls in his factory, the one who was known as the Bordelaise. Madame Arnoux herself informed Frédéric about it. He wanted to make use of it as an argument, 'since she was being deceived'.

'Oh! I'm not very bothered by it!' she said.

This admission seemed to him absolutely to strengthen the intimacy between them. Did Arnoux suspect anything?

'No! Not now!'

She told him that, one evening, he had left them talking together, and had afterwards come back again and listened behind the door, and as they both were talking about matters of no consequence, he had lived since then in a state of complete security.

'With good reason, doesn't he?' said Frédéric bitterly.

'Yes, no doubt!'

It would have been better for her not to have given so risky an answer.

One day she was not at home at the hour when he usually called. It was, for him, a kind of betrayal.

Next, he was displeased at seeing the flowers which he brought always stuck into a glass of water.

'Wherever do you expect them to be?'

'Oh! Not there! Anyway, they're not so cold there as they would be over your heart!'

Not long afterwards he reproached her for having been to the Italian opera the night before without having told him. Others had seen, admired, fallen in love with her, perhaps; Frédéric fastened on these suspicions of his purely in order to pick a quarrel with her, to torment her; for he was beginning to hate her, and the very least he might expect was that she should share in his sufferings!

One afternoon (towards the middle of February) he surprised her in a state of great emotion. Eugène was complaining of a sore throat. But the doctor had said it was nothing, a bad cold, an attack of influenza. Frédéric was astonished at the child's delirious air. Nevertheless, he reassured the mother, and brought forward the cases of several children of the same age who had just been attacked with similar ailments, and had been speedily cured.

'Really?'

'Why, yes, of course!'

'Oh! How good you are!'

And she caught his hand. He clasped it tightly in his own.

'Oh! Let it go!'

'What does it matter, since you're offering it to me in the role of consoler . . . You place every confidence in me in that respect, but you doubt me . . . when I talk to you about my love!'

'I don't doubt your love, my poor dear!'

'Why this distrust, as if I were a wretch capable of abusing . . . '

'Oh, no! . . . '

'If I only had some proof . . . '

'What proof?'

'The proof that a person might give anyone, the proof that you have already granted to myself!'

And he reminded her how, on one occasion, they had gone out together, on a winter's twilight, when there was a fog. All that seemed a long time ago now! What, then, was to prevent her from showing herself on his arm before the whole world without any fear on her part, and without any ulterior motive on his, and with no one around to pester them?

'All right!' she said, with a promptness of decision that at first stunned Frédéric.

But he replied, swiftly:

'Would you like me to wait for you at the corner of the Rue Tronchet and the Rue de la Ferme?'

'Good heavens, my friend . . . ' faltered Madame Arnoux.

Without giving her time to reflect, he added:

'Next Tuesday, shall we say?'

'Tuesday?'

'Yes, between two and three o'clock.'

'I'll be there!'

And she turned away her face in a movement of shame. Frédéric placed his lips on the nape of her neck.

'Oh! That's not nice,' she said. 'You'll make me repent.'

He turned away, fearing the customary fickleness of women. Then, on the threshold, he murmured softly, as if it were a thing that was thoroughly understood:

'Till Tuesday!'

She lowered her beautiful eyes in a discreet and resigned fashion.

Frédéric had a plan.

He hoped that, owing to the rain or the sun, he might get her to stop under some doorway, and that, once under the doorway, she would go into the house. The difficulty was to find one that would suit.

So he made a search, and about the middle of the Rue Tronchet he read, at a distance on a signboard, 'Furnished apartments'.

The clerk, divining his intention, showed him immediately on the mezzanine a room and a closet with two exits. Frédéric took it for a month, and paid in advance.

Then he went into three shops to buy the rarest perfumery; he got a piece of imitation lace, to replace the horrible red cotton bedspread; he selected a pair of blue satin slippers. Only the fear of appearing vulgar checked him in his purchases; he came back with them − and more devoutly than those who erect processional altars, he altered the position of the furniture, arranged the curtains himself, put heather on the mantelpiece, and violets on the chest of drawers; he would have liked to pave the entire apartment with gold. 'It's tomorrow,' he said to himself, 'yes, tomorrow! I'm not dreaming.' And he felt his heart throbbing violently with the delirious excitement of his hopes; then, when everything was ready, he carried off the key in his pocket, as if the happiness which slept there might have flown away.

A letter from his mother was awaiting him when he got home:

Why such a long absence? Your conduct is beginning to look ridiculous. I understand your having more or less hesitated at first with regard to this union; but just think about it!

And she put the matter before him with the utmost clarity: an income of forty-five thousand francs. Moreover, 'people were talking' and M. Roque was waiting for a definite answer. As for the young girl, her position was really most embarrassing. 'She is deeply attached to you.'

Frédéric threw aside the letter before he had finished reading it, and opened another, a note from Deslauriers.

Dear Old Boy — The *pear* is ripe. In accordance with your promise, we are counting on you. We meet tomorrow at daybreak, Place du Panthéon. Come into the Café Soufflot. I have to talk to you before the demonstration.

'Oh! I know their demonstrations! No thank you very much! I have a more agreeable appointment.'

And on the following morning, at eleven o'clock, Frédéric had left the house. He wanted to give one last glance at the preparations; then, who knows, she might just happen to be early? As he emerged from the Rue Tronchet, he heard a great clamour behind the Madeleine; he pressed forward; and he saw at the far end of the square, on the left, a number of men in overalls and some well-dressed middle-class individuals.

In fact, a manifesto published in the newspapers had summoned all who had subscribed to the banquet of the Reform Party to meet in this spot. The Ministry had, almost immediately, posted up a proclamation prohibiting the banquet. The Parliamentary Opposition had, on the previous evening, disclaimed any connection with it; but the patriots, who were unaware of this resolution on the part of their leaders, had come to the meeting-place, followed by a great crowd of spectators. A deputation from the schools had made its way, a short time before, to the house of Odilon Barrot. It was now at the Ministry of Foreign Affairs; and nobody knew whether the banquet would take place, whether the Government would carry out its threat, and whether the National Guards would make their appearance. People were as angry with the deputies as with the authorities. The crowd was growing bigger and bigger, when suddenly the strains of the 'Marseillaise' rang through the air.

It was the students' column which had just arrived on the scene. They marched along at a walking pace, in double file and in good order, with angry faces, bare hands, and all exclaiming at intervals: 'Long live Reform! Down with Guizot!'

Frédéric's friends were there, for sure. They would see him and drag him along with them. He quickly sought refuge in the Rue de l'Arcade.

When the students had taken two turns round the Madeleine, they went down towards the Place de la Concorde. It was full of people; and, from a distance, the dense crowd looked like a field of dark ears of corn swaying to and fro.

At the same moment, some soldiers of the line ranged themselves in battle array at the left-hand side of the church.

The groups remained standing there, however. In order to put an end to this, some police officers in civilian dress seized the most aggressive of them, and carried them off in a brutal fashion to the guardhouse. Frédéric, in spite of his indignation, remained silent; he might have been arrested along with the others, and he would have missed Madame Arnoux.

A little while afterwards the helmets of the Municipal Guards appeared. They kept striking about them with the flat side of their sabres. A horse fell down; the people made a rush forward to save him; and as soon as the rider was in the saddle, they all ran away.

Then there was a great silence. The thin rain which had moistened the asphalt, was no longer falling. Clouds floated past, gently swept on by the west wind.

Frédéric began walking up and down the Rue Tronchet looking before and behind him.

At length it struck two o'clock.

'Ah! Now is the time!' he said to himself. 'She's leaving her house, she's coming nearer;' and a minute after: 'She'd have had the time to get here by now.' Until three o'clock he tried to keep calm. 'No, she's not late; have a little patience!'

And for want of something to do he examined the few shops that there were: a bookshop, a saddler's, a funeral parlour. Soon he knew the names of all the books, the various kinds of harness, and every sort of drape. Seeing him continually going backwards and forwards, the shopkeepers were at first surprised, then alarmed, and they closed up their shop-fronts.

No doubt she had met with some impediment, and she was suffering too. But what delight would be theirs, in a very short time! For she would come, that was certain! 'After all, she gave me her promise!' In the meantime an intolerable feeling of anxiety was gradually seizing hold of him.

On an absurd impulse, he returned to the hotel, as if he expected to find her there. At that very moment, she might be arriving in the street. He rushed out. No one! And he went on tramping up and down the pavement.

He stared at the gaps in the paving-stones, the mouths of the gutters, the street-lamps, and the numbers above the doors. The most trifling objects became for him companions, or rather, ironical spectators; and the regular fronts of the houses seemed to him to be pitiless. He was suffering from cold feet. He felt as if he were melting away with despair. The reverberation of his footsteps vibrated through his brain.

When he saw by his watch that it was four o'clock, he experienced a kind of vertigo, a feeling of terror. He tried to repeat lines of poetry to himself, to enter on a calculation of something or other, to invent some kind of story. Impossible! He was obsessed by the image of Madame Arnoux. He wanted to run to meet her. But which way should he go so as not to miss her?

He went up to a messenger, put five francs into his hand, and ordered him to go to the Rue Paradis to Jacques Arnoux's residence to enquire of the porter 'if Madame were at home'. Then he took up his position at the corner of the Rue de la Ferme and the Rue Tronchet, so as to be able to look down both of them at the same time. At the far end of his vista, on the boulevard, confused masses glided about. He could distinguish, every now and then, the aigrette of a dragoon or a woman's hat; and he strained his eyes in the effort to recognise the wearer. A child in rags, exhibiting a marmot in a cage, asked him, with a smile, for alms.

The man with the velvet jacket reappeared. 'The porter had not seen her going out.' What had kept her in? If she were ill he would have been told! Was it a visitor? Nothing was easier than to say that she was not at home. He struck his forehead.

'Ah! I'm stupid! Of course, it's the riot!' He was relieved by this obvious explanation. Then, suddenly: 'But her quarter of the city is quiet.' And a horrible doubt assailed him. 'What if she were not going to come? What if her promise was just a trick to get rid of me? No! No!' What was preventing her from coming, no doubt, was some extraordinary mischance, one of those occurrences that baffle all one's anticipations. In that case she would have written. And he sent the hotel errand-boy to his home in the Rue Rumfort to find out whether there happened to be a letter waiting for him there.

No letter had been brought. This absence of news reassured him.

He drew omens from the number of coins which he took up in his hand out of his pocket by chance, from the faces of the passers-by, and from the colour of different horses; and when the augury was unfavourable, he tried not to believe it. In his sudden out-bursts of rage against Madame Arnoux, he abused her in a low voice. Then came fits of weakness that nearly made him faint, followed, all of a sudden, by fresh surges of hope. She was about to appear. She was there, behind his back. He turned round: nothing! Once he perceived, about thirty paces away, a woman of the same height, with the same dress. He caught up with her; it was not she! It struck five! Half-past five! Six! The gas-lamps were lighted. Madame Arnoux had not come.

The night before, she had dreamed that she was on the pavement in the Rue Tronchet and had been for some time. She was waiting there for something indeterminate, but which, nevertheless, was of great importance, and, for some reason, she was afraid of being seen. But an annoying little dog wouldn't leave her alone and kept biting at the hem of her dress. He kept coming back, and barked louder and louder. Madame Arnoux woke up. The dog's barking continued. She strained her ears to listen. It came from her son's room. She rushed there in her bare feet. It was the child himself who was coughing. His hands were burning, his face flushed, and his voice singularly hoarse. Every minute he found it more and more difficult to breathe freely. She waited there till daybreak, bent over the coverlet watching him.

At eight o'clock the drum of the National Guard gave warning to M. Arnoux that his comrades were expecting him. He dressed quickly and went away, promising that he would call straight away on their doctor, M. Colot. At ten o'clock, when M. Colot had not come, Madame Arnoux despatched her chambermaid. The doctor was away, in the country, and the young man who was taking his place had gone out on some business.

Eugène kept his head on one side on the bolster with contracted eyebrows and dilated nostrils; his poor little face had become whiter than the sheets; and there escaped from his larynx a wheezing sound with every intake of breath, which became ever shorter and dryer, and metallic-sounding. His cough was like the noise made by those barbarous mechanical inventions which make toy dogs bark.

Madame Arnoux was seized with terror. She rang the bells violently, calling out for help, and exclaiming:

'A doctor! A doctor!'

Ten minutes later came an elderly gentleman in a white cravat, and well trimmed grey whiskers. He put several questions as to the habits, the age, and the constitution of the young patient, then examined his throat, pressed his ear to his back and wrote out a prescription. The calm manner of this old man was intolerable. He smelt of embalming fluid. She would have liked to beat him. He said he would come back in the evening.

The horrible coughing soon began again. Sometimes the child suddenly sat up. Convulsions shook the muscles of his chest, and in his efforts to breathe his stomach shrank in as if he were out of breath from running. Then he sank down, with his head thrown back and his mouth wide open. With infinite pains, Madame Arnoux tried to make him swallow the contents of the phials, some ipecacuana syrup and a potion containing antimony. But he pushed away the spoon, groaning in a feeble voice. He seemed to be blowing out his words.

From time to time she reread the prescription. The observations on the form frightened her; perhaps the apothecary had made some mistake! Her powerlessness filled her with despair. M. Colot's pupil arrived.

He was a young man of modest demeanour, new to the profession, and he made no attempt to disguise his opinion. He was at first undecided, for fear of compromising himself, and finally he ordered pieces of ice to be applied. It took a long time to get ice. The bag containing the ice-cubes burst. His nightgown had to be changed. All this disturbance brought on a new and even more dreadful attack.

The child began tearing off the bandages round his neck, as if he had wanted to remove the obstacle that was choking him, and he scratched the walls and seized the curtains of his cot, trying to get a point of support to help him to breathe. His face was now of a bluish hue, and his entire body, bathed in a cold sweat, appeared to be growing lean. His haggard eyes were fixed in terror on his mother. He threw his arms round her neck, and hung there in a desperate fashion; repressing her rising sobs, she gave utterance in a broken voice to loving words:

'Yes, my pet, my angel, my treasure!'

Then came intervals of calm.

She went to look for playthings, a puppet, a collection of images, and spread them out on his bed in order to amuse him. She even tried to sing.

She began a song which she used to sing years before, when she was nursing him wrapped up in swaddling-clothes in this same little upholstered chair. But a shiver ran through the entire length of his body, as when a wave is agitated by a gust of wind; the balls of his eyes protruded; she thought he was going to die, and turned away so as not to see him.

The next moment she had the strength to look at him. He was still alive. The hours succeeded each other, heavy, dull, interminable, despair-making; and she no longer counted the minutes save by the progress of his dying. The spasms in his chest threw him forward as if to shatter his body; finally, he vomited something strange, which was like a parchment tube. What was it? She fancied that he had evacuated part of his entrails. But he was breathing freely and regularly. This appearance of wellbeing frightened her more than all the rest; she was sitting like one petrified, her arms hanging by her sides, her eyes fixed, when M. Colot suddenly made his appearance. The child, in his opinion, was saved.

She did not realise what he meant at first, and made him repeat the words. Was not this one of those consoling phrases used by doctors? The doctor went away with an air of tranquillity. Then it seemed as if the cords that pressed round her heart had been loosened.

'Saved! Is this possible!'

Suddenly the thought of Frédéric presented itself to her mind in a clear and inexorable fashion. It was a warning sent to her by Providence. But the Lord in His mercy had not wished to complete her punishment! What an expiation hereafter if she were to persevere in this love affair! No doubt insults would be flung at her son's head on her account; and Madame Arnoux saw him a young man, wounded in a duel, brought home on a stretcher, dying. She leapt up and threw herself onto the little chair; and, sending up her soul towards the heights of heaven with all her strength, she offered up to God, as a holocaust, the sacrifice of her first passion, her only weakness.

Frédéric had returned home. He remained in his armchair, without even the energy to curse her. A sort of slumber fell upon him; and, in the midst of his nightmare, he could hear the rain falling, still under the impression that he was there outside on the pavement.

Next morning, yielding to one last access of weakness, he again sent a messenger to Madame Arnoux's house.

Whether the man failed to deliver the message, or whether she had too many things to say to explain herself in a word or two, the same answer was brought back. This insolence was too much! A feeling of angry pride took possession of him. He swore to himself that he would never again cherish even a desire; and, like the leaves of a tree carried away by a hurricane, his love disappeared. He experienced a sense of relief, a feeling of stoical joy, then a need of violent action; and he walked at random through the streets.

Men from the suburbs were marching past armed with guns and old swords, some of them wearing red caps, and all singing the 'Marseillaise' or the 'Girondins'. Here and there a National Guard was hurrying to join his mayoral department. Drums could be heard rolling in the distance. A conflict was going on at the Porte Saint-Martin. There was something lively and warlike in the air. Frédéric kept on walking. The excitement of the great city made him gay.

When he got up as far as Frascati's, he got a glimpse of the Maréchale's windows; a wild idea occurred to him, a reaction of youthfulness. He crossed the boulevard.

The carriage gate was just being closed; and Delphine, the chambermaid, who was in the act of writing on it with a piece of charcoal, 'Arms given', said to him hurriedly:

'Ah! Madame is in a nice state! She dismissed a groom who insulted her this morning. She thinks there's going to be pillage everywhere! She's frightened to death! And the more so as Monsieur has gone!'

'What Monsieur?'

'The Prince!'

Frédéric entered the boudoir. The Maréchale appeared in her petticoat, and her hair hanging down her back, beside herself.

'Ah! Thank you, you've come to save me! That's the second time! *You* never ask for anything in return!'

'A thousand pardons!' said Frédéric, catching her round the waist with both hands.

'What? What are you doing?' stammered the Maréchale, both surprised and cheered up by this behaviour.

He replied:

'I'm following the fashion, I'm reformed.'

She let herself fall back on the divan, and continued laughing under his kisses.

They spent the afternoon looking out through their window at the people in the street. Then he took her to dinner at the Trois-Frères-Provençaux. The meal was a long and dainty one. They came back on foot for want of a vehicle.

At the announcement of a change of Ministry, Paris had changed. Everyone was in a state of delight; people were promenading about the streets, and every floor was illuminated with lamps, so that it seemed as if it were broad daylight. The soldiers were making their way slowly back to their barracks, worn out and looking depressed. The people saluted them with exclamations of 'Long live the Line!' They went on without making any response. Among the National Guard, on the other hand, the officers, flushed with enthusiasm, brandished their sabres, bellowing: 'Long live Reform!' And every time the two lovers heard this word they laughed. Frédéric made jokes, and was very gay.

Making their way through the Rue Duphot, they reached the boulevards. Venetian lanterns hanging from the houses formed garlands of light. Underneath was a seething, shadowy mass; in the midst of those moving shadows could be seen, here and there, the steely glitter of bayonets. There arose a great uproar. The crowd was too compact, it was impossible to go straight back; and they were entering the Rue Caumartin, when suddenly there burst forth behind them a noise like the crackling made by an immense piece of silk being torn across. It was the shooting on the Boulevard des Capucines.

'Ah! A few citizens are getting a crack,' said Frédéric calmly, for there are situations in which a man of the least cruel disposition is so detached from his fellow-men that he would see the entire human race perish without a single throb of the heart.

The Maréchale was clinging to his arm, her teeth chattering. She declared that she could not walk another twenty steps. So, in a refinement of hatred, in order the better to insult Madame Arnoux in his own soul, he took her to the hotel in the Rue Tronchet, to the room he had prepared for the other.

The flowers were not withered. The lace was spread out on the bed. He took the little slippers out of the wardrobe. Rosanette considered these little attentions very delicate.

About one o'clock she was awakened by distant rumbling sounds; and she saw him sobbing with his head buried in the pillow.

'Whatever is the matter with you, my love?'

'It's excess of happiness,' said Frédéric. 'I'd been wanting you for too long!'

SENTIMENTAL
EDUCATION

PART THREE

He was abruptly roused from sleep by the sound of shooting; and, in spite of Rosanette's entreaties, Frédéric was fully determined to go and see what was happening. He hurried down towards the Champs-Elysées, from which the shots had been fired. At the corner of the Rue Saint-Honoré some men in overalls ran past him, exclaiming:

'No! Not that way! To the Palais-Royal!'

Frédéric followed them. The railings of the Convent of the Assumption had been torn away. A little further on he noticed three paving-stones in the middle of the street, the beginning of a barricade no doubt, then fragments of bottles and coils of wire, to obstruct the cavalry; and, at the same moment, there rushed suddenly out of an alley, a tall, pale young man, with his black hair flowing over his shoulders, and wearing a sort of jersey with coloured dots. In his hand he held a long military musket, and he ran along on the tips of his slippers with the air of a sleepwalker and swift as a tiger. At intervals a detonation could be heard.

On the evening of the day before, the sight of the wagon containing five corpses picked up from amongst those that had been on the Boulevard des Capucines had changed the disposition of the people; and, while at the Tuileries the aides-de-camp succeeded each other, and M. Molé, having set about the composition of a new Cabinet, did not come back, and M. Thiers was trying to constitute another, and the King was cavilling and hesitating, and finally assigned the post of commander-in-chief to Bugeaud in order to prevent him from making use of it, the insurrection was organising itself in a formidable manner, as if it were directed by a single arm. Men endowed with a kind of frenetic eloquence were haranguing the populace at street corners; others were in the churches ringing the tocsin as loudly as ever they could; lead was being cast for bullets, cartridges were being rolled; the trees on the boulevards, urinals, benches, railings, gas-burners, everything was torn off and thrown down; Paris, that morning, was covered with barricades. The resistance which was offered was of short duration; the National Guard was everywhere – so that at eight o'clock the people, by voluntary surrender or by force, had got possession of five barracks, nearly all the town halls, the most favourable strategic points. Of its own accord, without any effort, the Monarchy was melting away in rapid dissolution; and an attack was being made at this moment on the guardhouse of the Château-d'Eau, in order to liberate fifty prisoners, who were not there.

Frédéric was forced to stop at the entrance to the square. It was filled with groups of armed men. The Rue Saint-Thomas and the Rue Fromanteau were occupied by companies of the Line. The Rue de Valois was blocked by an enormous barricade. The smoke which hovered at the top of it thinned a little, men ran about over it, making violent gestures, then vanished from sight; then the firing began again. It was answered from the guardhouse, though no one was visible inside; its windows, protected by oaken shutters, were pierced with loopholes; and the monument with its two storeys, its two wings, its fountain on the first floor and its little door in the centre, was beginning to be speckled with white spots under the shock of the bullets. The three steps in front of it remained unoccupied.

At Frédéric's side a man in a Phrygian cap, with a cartridge-box over his knitted jacket, was arguing with a woman with a cotton kerchief on her head. She said to him:

'Come back now! Come back!'

'Leave me alone!' replied the husband. 'You can easily mind the lodge by yourself. Citizen, I ask you, is this fair? I've done my duty on every occasion, in 1830, in '32, in '34, and in '39! Today they're fighting: I must fight! Go away!'

And the porter's wife ended by yielding to his remonstrances and to those of a National Guard near them, a man in his forties, whose simple face was adorned with a circle of blonde beard. He was loading his gun and firing while talking to Frédéric, as cool in the midst of the disturbance as a horticulturist in his garden. A young lad in a tradesman's apron was trying to coax this man to give him a few capsules, so that he might make use of his gun, a fine fowling piece which a 'gentleman' had given to him.

'Take some from behind my back,' said the good man, 'and take cover! You'll get yourself killed!'

The drums were beating for the charge. Sharp cries, hurrahs of triumph, rose into the air. The crowd swayed backwards and forwards in one continuous movement. Frédéric, caught between two thick masses of people, did not move, indeed he was fascinated and enjoying himself enormously. The wounded who fell, the dead lying on the ground, did not seem like real wounded or real dead. It was like being at a show.

In the midst of the surging throng, above the sea of heads, could be seen an old man in a black coat, mounted on a white horse with a velvet saddle. He held in one hand a green branch, in the other a paper, and he kept shaking them persistently. At length, giving up all hope of obtaining a hearing, he withdrew.

The soldiers of the Line had gone, and only the municipal troops remained to defend the guardhouse. A wave of dauntless spirits dashed up the steps; they were flung down, others came on to replace them; and the gate shook and resounded under blows from iron bars; the municipal guards did not give way. But a wagon, stuffed full of hay, and burning like a gigantic torch, was dragged against the walls. Faggots were speedily brought, then straw, and a barrel of spirits of wine. The fire climbed up along the stones; the building began to smoke on all sides like a collection of sulphur springs; and at its summit, between the balustrades of the terrace, huge flames leapt up with a strident roar. The first storey of the Palais-Royal was occupied by National Guards. People were firing through every window in the square; the bullets whistled past, the water of the fountain, which had burst, was mingled with blood, forming little pools on the ground; people slipped in the mud over clothes, shakos, and weapons; Frédéric felt something soft under his foot; it was the hand of a sergeant in a grey greatcoat, lying on his face in the gutter. Fresh bands of people were continually coming up, driving the combatants towards the guardhouse. The firing became more intense. The wine-shops were open; people would go into them from time to time to smoke a pipe and drink a glass of beer, and then come back again to fight. A lost dog was howling. This made the people laugh.

Frédéric was jolted by the impact of a man falling on his shoulder with a bullet through his back and the death-rattle in his throat. At this shot, perhaps directed against himself, he felt furious; and he was plunging forward when a National Guard stopped him.

'No point – the King has just gone. Ah! If you don't believe me, go and see for yourself!'

This assurance calmed Frédéric. The Place du Carrousel had a tranquil aspect. The Hôtel de Nantes stood there as solitary as ever; and the houses in the rear, the dome of the Louvre in front, the long wooden gallery on the right, and the waste plot of ground that ran unevenly as far as the sheds of the stall-keepers, were as if drowned in the grey colour of the air, where distant murmurs seemed to mingle with the mist – while, at the other end of the square, a harsh light, falling through the parting of the clouds on to the façade of the Tuileries, cut out all its windows into white patches. Near the Arc de Triomphe a dead horse lay stretched on the ground. Behind the railings groups of five or six persons were chatting. The doors leading into the château were open; the servants on the threshold were allowing people to enter.

Below stairs, in a little room, bowls of *café au lait* were being served. A few of those who had come to look sat down at the table jokingly; others remained standing, and amongst them was a cab-driver. He snatched up with both hands a glass jar full of powdered sugar, cast an anxious glance right and left, and then began to eat voraciously, with his nose stuck into the neck of the jar. At the bottom of the great staircase a man was writing his name in a register. Frédéric recognised him from behind.

'Why, it's Hussonnet!'

'Of course,' replied the Bohemian. 'I'm introducing myself at court. This is a good joke, isn't it?'

'Suppose we go upstairs?'

And they went up to the Salle des Maréchaux. The portraits of those illustrious generals, save that of Bugeaud, which had been pierced through the stomach, were all intact. They were represented leaning on their sabres with a gun-carriage behind them, and in formidable attitudes unsuited to the occasion. A large timepiece proclaimed that it was twenty minutes past one.

Suddenly the 'Marseillaise' resounded. Hussonnet and Frédéric bent over the balusters. It was the people. They rushed up the stairs, shaking in a dizzying, wave-like motion bare heads, helmets, red caps, bayonets and shoulders with such impetuosity that some individuals disappeared every now and then in this swarming mass, which kept on rising, like a river pushed back by a spring tide, with a continuous roar, under an irresistible impulse. When they got to the top, they scattered, and the song died away.

All that could be heard now was the tramp of all their shoes intermingled with the babble of voices. The crowd not being in a mischievous mood, contented themselves with looking. But, from time to time, an elbow, for lack of room, broke through a pane of glass; or else a vase or a statuette rolled from a table down onto the floor. The wainscotings cracked under the pressure of people. Every face was flushed; sweat rolled down them in large beads; Hussonnet made this remark:

'Our heroes don't smell very nice!'

'Ah! You are provoking,' returned Frédéric.

And, pushed forward in spite of themselves, they entered an apartment in which a daïs of red velvet was stretched across the ceiling. On the throne below sat a representative of the proletariat with a black beard, his shirt gaping open, and looking as jolly and stupid as a potbellied figurine. Others climbed up onto the platform to sit in his place.

'What a myth!' said Hussonnet. 'There you see the sovereign people!'

The armchair was lifted up on the hands of a number of persons and passed across the hall, swaying from side to side.

'By Jove! How she sways! The Ship of State is tossed about in a stormy sea! See it cancan! See it cancan!'

They had drawn it towards a window, and in the midst of hisses, they pushed it out.

'Poor old chap!' said Hussonnet, as he saw it fall into the garden, where it was speedily picked up in order to be afterwards carried to the Bastille and burned.

Then a frenetic joy burst forth, as if, in the place of the throne, a future of boundless happiness had appeared; and the people, less through a spirit of vindictiveness than to assert their right of possession, broke or ripped the mirrors, the curtains, the chandeliers, the torch-holders, the tables, the chairs, the stools, all the furniture, including albums of drawings and needlework-baskets. Since they had triumphed, they must needs amuse themselves! The mob ironically decked themselves out in laces and cashmeres. Gold fringes were rolled round the sleeves of working men's shirts, hats with ostrich feathers adorned blacksmiths' heads, and ribbons of the Legion of Honour supplied waistbands for prostitutes. Each person satisfied his or her caprice; some danced, others drank. In the queen's apartment a woman was giving a gloss to her hair with pomade; behind a screen two amateurs were playing cards; Hussonnet pointed out to Frédéric an individual who was smoking his old pipe with his elbows resting on a balcony; and the frenzy redoubled with a continuous crashing of broken china and pieces of crystal, which rang, as they bounced, like the strips of a harmonica.

Then their rage took on a darker note. An obscene curiosity made them rummage through all the dressing-rooms, all the recesses, open all the drawers. Convicts thrust their arms into the beds in which princesses had slept, and rolled on top of them, as a consolation for not being able to rape them. Others, with more sinister faces, roamed about silently, looking for something to steal; but too great a multitude was there. Through the open doors nothing could be seen in the suite of apartments but the dark mass of the people amongst the gilt, in a cloud of dust. Every breast was panting; the heat became more and more suffocating; the two friends, afraid of being stifled, went out.

In the antechamber, standing on a heap of garments, stood a whore as a statue of Liberty − motionless, her eyes wide open, a fearful sight.

They had taken three steps outside when a company of municipal guards, in greatcoats, advanced towards them, and taking off their police hats, and at the same time, uncovering their balding skulls, bowed very low to the people. At this testimony of respect, the ragged victors swelled with pride. Hussonnet and Frédéric were not without experiencing a certain pleasure from it too.

They were in exultant mood. They went back to the Palais-Royal. In front of the Rue Fromanteau, soldiers' corpses were heaped up on straw. They passed by without a quiver of emotion, even feeling a certain pride in being able to keep their countenance.

The Palais overflowed with people. In the inner courtyard seven bonfires were burning. Pianos, chests of drawers and clocks were being hurled out through the windows. Fire-engines spat streams of water up to the roofs. Some hooligans were trying to cut some of the hoses with their sabres. Frédéric urged a pupil of the Polytechnic School to interfere. The latter did not understand him, and, moreover, appeared to be an idiot. All around, in the two galleries, the populace, having got possession of the cellars, were indulging in a horrible carouse. The wine flowed in streams and wetted people's feet, louts were drinking out of the tail-ends of bottles, and bellowed as they staggered about.

'Let's get out of here,' said Hussonnet; 'the people disgusts me.'

All along the Galerie d'Orléans the wounded lay on mattresses on the ground, with scarlet curtains for blankets; and local housewives brought them broth and linen.

'No matter!' said Frédéric; '*I* find the people sublime.'

The great vestibule was filled with a whirlwind of furious individuals; men tried to ascend to the upper storeys in order to put the finishing touches to the work of wholesale destruction; National Guards, on the steps, strove to restrain them. The most intrepid was a bareheaded rifleman, his hair bristling, and his straps in pieces. His shirt bulged out between his trousers and his coat, and he was struggling desperately in the midst of the others. Hussonnet, who had sharp sight, recognised Arnoux from a distance.

Then they went into the Tuileries garden, so as to be able to breathe more freely. They sat down on a bench; and they remained for some minutes with their eyes closed, so stunned that they had not the energy to speak. Passers-by struck up conversations around them. The Duchesse d'Orléans had been appointed Regent; it was all over; and they were all experiencing that kind of wellbeing which follows speedy conclusions, when at each of the windows of the attics in the château appeared menservants tearing their liveries to pieces. They flung them into the garden, as a mark of renunciation. The people booed. They retired.

The attention of Frédéric and Hussonnet was distracted by a tall fellow who was striding along among the trees with a rifle on his shoulder. A cartridge-belt was strapped around the waist of his red tunic, a handkerchief was wound round his forehead under his cap. He turned his head. It was Dussardier; and throwing himself into their arms:

'Ah! What a wonderful day, my dear old friends!' without being able to say another word, so much out of breath was he with joy and fatigue.

He had been on his legs for the last forty-eight hours. He had worked on the barricades of the Latin Quarter, had fought in the

Rue Rambuteau, had saved three dragoons, had entered the
Tuileries with the Dunoyer column, and then had repaired to the
Chamber, and next to the Hôtel de Ville.

'That's where I've just been! All goes well! The people are
victorious! Workmen and employers are embracing! Ah, if you
knew what I've seen! What excellent people! How marvellous it is!'

And without noticing that they had no arms:

'I was quite certain I'd find you here! It was a bit rough for a
while, no matter!'

A drop of blood ran down his cheek, and in answer to the
questions put to him by the two others:

'Oh, nothing! A slight scratch from a bayonet!'

'You ought to have it looked at, though.'

'Pooh! I'm tough! What does it matter? The Republic has been
proclaimed! We'll be happy now! Some journalists, who were
talking just now in front of me, were saying that we're going to
liberate Poland and Italy! No more kings, you understand? All the
world free! All the world free!'

And with one comprehensive glance at the horizon, he spread
out his arms in a triumphant attitude. But a long line of men was
rushing over the terrace along the water's edge.

'Ah, my goodness! I was forgetting! The forts have been captured.
I must be off! Goodbye!'

He turned round to cry out to them, brandishing his rifle:

'Long live the Republic!'

The chimneys of the château sent out enormous whirlwinds of
black smoke, carrying sparks. The ringing of the bells seemed, in the
distance, like terrified bleating. Right and left, in every direction,
the conquerors discharged their weapons. Frédéric, though he
was not a warrior, felt the Gallic blood leaping in his veins. He had
been caught by the magnetism of the public enthusiasm. With
voluptuous delight, he breathed in the stormy atmosphere, filled
with the odour of gunpowder; and yet he quivered with the waves
of an immense love, a supreme and universal tenderness, as if the
heart of all humanity were throbbing in his breast.

Hussonnet said with a yawn:

'I suppose it's time for me to go and instruct the populace!'

Frédéric followed him to his correspondence office in the Place
de la Bourse; and he began to compose for the Troyes newspaper

an account of recent events in a lyrical style, a real masterpiece, which he signed. Then they dined together in a tavern. Hussonnet was pensive; the eccentricities of the Revolution exceeded his own.

After leaving the café, when they repaired to the Hôtel de Ville to learn the news, the boyish impulses which were natural to him had got the upper hand once more. He scaled the barricades like a goat, and answered the sentinels with broad patriotic jokes.

They heard the Provisional Government being proclaimed by torchlight. At last, Frédéric got back to his house at midnight, dropping with exhaustion.

'Well,' said he to his manservant, while the latter was undressing him, 'are you pleased?'

'Yes, of course, Monsieur! But what I don't like to see is the people jittering about!'

Next morning, when he awoke, Frédéric thought of Deslauriers. He hurried round to see him. The lawyer had just left Paris, having been appointed a provincial commissioner. The evening before, he had managed to gain access to Ledru-Rollin, and laying siege to him in the name of the Écoles, had got out of him a post, a mission. Anyway, the doorkeeper explained, he was going to write and give his address in the following week.

After which, Frédéric went to see the Maréchale. She gave him a chilling reception, for she resented his desertion of her. Her rancour disappeared when he had given her repeated assurances that peace was restored. All was quiet now, there was no reason to be afraid; he kissed her; and she declared herself in favour of the Republic – as his lordship the Archbishop of Paris had already done, and as were about to do with a marvellous celerity: the magistrature, the Council of State, the Institut, the marshals of France, Changarnier, M. de Falloux, all the Bonapartists, all the Legitimists, and a considerable number of Orleanists.

The fall of the Monarchy had been so rapid that, as soon as the first feeling of stupefaction had passed away, there was a feeling of astonishment amongst the middle class at the fact that they were still alive. The summary execution of a few thieves, who were shot without trial, was regarded as an act of signal justice. For a month people repeated to each other Lamartine's phrase on the red flag, 'which had only gone the round of the Champ de Mars, while the tricoloured flag' etc.; and all ranged themselves under its shade, each party seeing amongst the three colours only its own – and firmly determined, as soon as it was the most powerful, to tear away the two others.

As business was suspended, anxiety and curiosity drove everyone outdoors. The careless style of costume generally adopted attenuated differences of social position, hatred concealed itself, hope was to the fore, the crowd seemed full of good nature. The pride of having gained their rights shone in people's faces. They were in carnival mood, behaved as in a bivouac; nothing could be more amusing than the aspect of Paris during the first days.

Frédéric gave the Maréchale his arm; and they strolled along through the streets together. She was highly diverted by the display of rosettes in every buttonhole, the banners hung from every window, and the posters of every colour that were stuck upon the walls, and threw some money here and there into the collection-boxes for the wounded, which were placed on chairs in the middle of the pathway. Then she stopped before caricatures representing Louis–Philippe as a pastrycook, as a mountebank, as a dog, or as a leech. But she was a little frightened by Caussidière's men with their sabres and scarfs. At other times it was a tree of Liberty that was being planted. The clergy joined in the ceremony, blessing the Republic, escorted by gold-braided acolytes; and the populace thought this very fine. The most frequent spectacle was that of deputations from no matter what, going to demand something at the Hôtel de Ville – for every trade, every industry, was looking to the Government to put a complete end to its wretchedness. Some of them, it is true, went to offer it advice or to congratulate it, or merely to pay it a little visit, and to see the machine at work.

One day, about the middle of March, as he was crossing the Pont d'Arcole, having to do an errand for Rosanette in the Latin Quarter, Frédéric saw approaching a column of individuals with strange hats and long beards. At its head, beating a drum, walked a negro who had formerly been an artist's model, and the man who bore the banner, on which this inscription floated in the wind, 'Artist-Painters', was no other than Pellerin.

He made a sign to Frédéric to wait for him, and then reappeared five minutes afterwards, having some time before him, for the

Government was, at that moment, receiving the stonecutters. He was going with his colleagues to ask for the creation of a Forum of Art, a kind of Exchange where the interests of Aesthetics would be discussed; sublime masterpieces would be produced, because the workers would pool their genius. Before long Paris would be covered with gigantic monuments; he would decorate them; he had even begun a figure of the Republic. One of his comrades came to fetch him, for they were closely pursued by the deputation of poulterers.

'What nonsense!' growled a voice in the crowd. 'Always some humbug! No real action!'

It was Regimbart. He did not greet Frédéric, but took advantage of the occasion to vent his spleen.

The Citizen spent his days wandering about the streets, pulling his moustache, rolling his eyes about, accepting and imparting dismal news; and he had only two phrases: 'Take care, we're going to be outflanked!' or else: 'Why, confound it! They're pinching our Republic!' He was discontented with everything, and especially with the fact that we had not taken back our natural frontiers. The very name of Lamartine made him shrug his shoulders. He did not consider Ledru-Rollin 'adequate for the problem', referred to Dupont (of the Eure) as an old numbskull; Albert as an idiot; Louis Blanc as an Utopist; Blanqui as an exceedingly dangerous man; and when Frédéric asked him what would be the best thing to do, he replied, squeezing his arm in a vice-like grip:

'Take the Rhine, I tell you, take the Rhine, damn it!'

Then he blamed the forces of reaction.

It was raising its head. The sack of the châteaux of Neuilly and Suresne, the fire in the Batignolles, the troubles at Lyons, all the excesses and all the grievances, were now being exaggerated and taken in conjunction with Ledru-Rollin's circular, the forced issue of banknotes, the fall of state funds to sixty francs, and, to crown all, as the supreme iniquity, a final blow, a culminating horror, the forty-five centimes tax! And over and above all these things there was Socialism as well! Although these theories, as new as the invention of the wheel, had been discussed sufficiently for the last forty years to fill a number of libraries, they terrified the wealthier citizens, as if they had been a shower of meteorites; and they were indignant, by virtue of that hatred which the advent of every idea provokes, simply because it is an idea, an odium from which it subsequently derives its glory, and which means that its enemies are always inferior to it, however mediocre it may be.

Then Property rose in their regard to the level of Religion, and was confounded with God. The attacks made on it appeared to them a sacrilege, almost a form of cannibalism. In spite of the most humane legislation that ever existed, the spectre of '93 reappeared, and the blade of the guillotine vibrated in every syllable of the word 'Republic' – which did not prevent them from despising it for its weakness. France, missing a master, began to cry with terror, like a blind man without his stick or an infant that has lost its nurse.

Of all Frenchmen, M. Dambreuse was the one who trembled the most. The new state of affairs threatened his fortune, but, more than that, it made a mockery of his experience. A system so good, a king so wise! Was it possible? The world would crumble! The very next day, he dismissed three servants, sold his horses, bought a soft hat to go out into the streets, thought even of letting his beard grow; and he remained at home, prostrated, gloomily digesting the newspapers which were the most hostile to his own ideas, and becoming so gloomy that even the jokes about Flocon's pipe had not the power to make him smile.

As a supporter of the previous reign, he was dreading the vengeance of the people on his estates in Champagne, when Frédéric's journalistic effusion fell into his hands. Then it occurred to him that his young friend was a very influential personage, and that he might be able, if not to serve him, at least to protect him; so that, one morning, M. Dambreuse presented himself at Frédéric's residence, accompanied by Martinon.

This visit, he said, had no object save that of seeing him for a little while, and having a chat with him. All in all, he rejoiced at recent events, and adopted wholeheartedly 'our sublime motto, *Liberty, Equality, and Fraternity*, having always been a Republican, at heart'. If he voted under the other *régime* with the Ministry, it was simply in order to accelerate an inevitable downfall. He even inveighed against M. Guizot, 'who has got us into a nice hobble, we must admit!' On the other hand, he greatly admired Lamartine, who had shown himself to be 'magnificent, upon my word of honour, when, with reference to the red flag . . . '

'Yes! I know,' said Frédéric.

After which, he declared that his sympathies were with the workers.

'For, after all, we are all, more or less, working men!' And he carried his impartiality so far as to acknowledge that Proudhon had a certain amount of logic in his views. 'Oh, a great deal of logic, my word yes!' Then, with the disinterestedness of a superior intellect, he chatted about the exhibition of painting, where he had seen Pellerin's picture. He considered it original and well put together.

Martinon backed up all he said with expressions of approval; he too was of the opinion that it was necessary 'to rally boldly to the side of the Republic', and he talked about his ploughman father, playing the peasant, the man of the people. They soon came to the question of the elections for the National Assembly, and the candidates in the arrondissement of La Fortelle. The Opposition candidate had no chance.

'You should take his place!' said M. Dambreuse.

Frédéric protested.

'But why not?' For he would obtain the votes of the Extremists owing to his personal opinions, and that of the Conservatives on account of his family. 'And perhaps also,' added the banker, with a smile, 'thanks to my influence, in some measure.'

Frédéric objected that he would not know how to set about it. There was nothing easier, if he only got himself recommended to the patriots of the Aube by one of the clubs of the capital. All he had to do was to read out, not a profession of faith such as might be seen every day, but a serious statement of principles.

'Bring it to me; I know what goes down well locally! And you could, I say again, render great services to the country, to us all, to myself.'

In such times as this, people ought to help each other, and, if Frédéric had need of anything, he or his friends . . .

'Oh, a thousand thanks, my dear Monsieur!'

'And, naturally, you'll do as much for me in return!'

The banker was really a decent man.

Frédéric could not refrain from pondering his advice; and soon he was dazzled by a dizzying prospect.

The great figures of the Convention passed before his eyes. It seemed to him that a splendid dawn was about to rise. Rome,

Vienna and Berlin were in a state of insurrection, and the Austrians had been driven out of Venice; the whole of Europe was in turmoil. Now was the time to make a plunge into the movement, and perhaps to accelerate it; and then he was attracted by the costume which it was said the deputies would wear. Already he saw himself in a waistcoat with lapels and a tricoloured sash; and this longing, this hallucination, became so powerful that he confided in Dussardier.

The honest fellow's enthusiasm was as strong as ever.

'Certainly, of course! Stand!'

Frédéric, nevertheless, consulted Deslauriers. The idiotic opposition which trammelled the commissioner in his province had strengthened his Liberalism. He at once replied, exhorting Frédéric with the utmost vehemence to put himself forward.

However, Frédéric needed the approval of a greater number of persons; and he raised the subject with Rosanette, one day when Mademoiselle Vatnaz happened to be present.

She was one of those Parisian spinsters who, every evening when they have given their lessons or tried to sell little sketches, or to place poor manuscripts, come home with mud on their petticoats, make their dinner, eat it alone, and then, with their feet resting on a footwarmer, by the light of a grubby lamp, dream of love, a family, a home, wealth, of all that they lack. So it was that, like many others, she had hailed in the Revolution the advent of vengeance – and she gave herself up to Socialist propaganda of the most unbridled description.

The enfranchisement of the proletariat, according to Vatnaz, was only possible by the enfranchisement of woman. She wished her own sex to be eligible for every kind of employment, to create paternity orders, a different code, the abolition, or at least 'a more intelligent regulation', of marriage. Then every Frenchwoman would be bound to marry a Frenchman, or to adopt an old man. Nurses and midwives should be public servants, salaried by the State; there should be a jury to examine works created by women, special editors for women, a polytechnic school for women, a National Guard for women, everything for women! And, since the Government ignored their rights, they ought to overcome force with force. Ten thousand citizenesses with good guns could make the Hotel de Ville shiver in its shoes!

Frédéric's candidature appeared to her to be favourable to her ideas. She encouraged him, showing him fame on the horizon. Rosanette was delighted at having a man who would make speeches in the Chamber.

'And then, perhaps, they'll give you a good job.'

Frédéric, a man prone to every kind of weakness, was infected by the universal mania. He wrote a speech and went to show it to M. Dambreuse.

At the sound made by the main door closing, a curtain gaped open a little behind a window; a woman appeared at it. He had not the time to find out who she was; but, in the anteroom, a picture arrested his attention, Pellerin's picture, which lay on a chair, temporarily, no doubt.

It represented the Republic, or Progress, or Civilisation, in the form of Jesus Christ driving a locomotive, which was passing through a virgin forest. Frédéric, after a minute's contemplation, exclaimed:

'How dreadful!'

'Isn't it just?' said M. Dambreuse, coming in unexpectedly just at the moment when the other said this, and fancying that it referred not to the painting but to the doctrine glorified by the picture. Martinon arrived at the same time. They went into the study; and Frédéric was drawing a paper out of his pocket, when Mademoiselle Cécile, entering suddenly, said, articulating her words in an ingenuous fashion:

'Is my aunt here?'

'You know perfectly well she isn't,' replied the banker. 'Never mind! Make yourself at home, Mademoiselle.'

'Oh! No thank you! I'm going.'

Scarcely had she left when Martinon seemed to be searching for his handkerchief.

'I left it in my coat, excuse me!'

'All right!' said M. Dambreuse.

Evidently he was not deceived by this manœuvre, and even seemed to regard it with favour. Why? But Martinon soon reappeared, and Frédéric began reading his speech. Even by the second page, which deplored the preponderance of financial interests, the banker pulled a face. Then, turning to the question of reforms, Frédéric demanded free trade.

'What . . . ? Allow me, now!'

The other did not hear, and went on. He called for a tax on yearly incomes, a progressive tax, a European federation, and the education of the people, and encouragement of the fine arts on the most liberal scale.

'If the country provided men like Delacroix or Hugo with incomes of a hundred thousand francs, where would be the harm?'

The address ended with some advice to the upper classes.

'Spare nothing, O ye rich! Give! And give again!'

He stopped, and remained standing. His two listeners sat on and did not speak; Martinon was goggling, M. Dambreuse was quite pale. At last, concealing his emotion under a sour smile:

'It's perfect, your speech!' And he praised the style exceedingly in order to avoid having to give an opinion as to the content.

This virulence on the part of an inoffensive young man frightened him, above all insofar as it was symptomatic of the times. Martinon tried to reassure him. The Conservative party would very soon take its revenge, without a doubt; in several cities the commissioners of the provisional government had been driven away: the elections were not to occur till the twenty-third of April, there was plenty of time; in short, M. Dambreuse must present himself personally in the Aube; and from that time forth, Martinon no longer left his side, became his secretary, and was as attentive to him as any son.

Frédéric arrived at Rosanette's house very pleased with himself. Delmar was there, and told him of his intention 'definitely' to stand as a candidate at the Seine elections. In a placard addressed 'to the People', in which he called them 'tu', the actor boasted that *he* was able to understand them, and of having, in order to save them, got himself 'crucified by Art', so that he was the incarnation, the ideal of the popular spirit – believing that be had, in fact, such enormous power over the masses that later, in the office of some ministry, he proposed to quell an outbreak by himself alone; and, as to the means he would employ, he gave this reply:

'Never fear! I'll show them my head!'

Frédéric, in order to mortify him, informed him of his own candidature. The actor, from the moment that his future colleague aspired to represent the province, declared himself his servant, and offered to be his guide to the various clubs.

They visited them all, or nearly all, the red and the blue, the ravers and the tranquil, the puritanical, the licentious, the mystical and the intemperate, those that advocated regicide, and those which denounced frauds in the grocery trade; and everywhere the tenants cursed the landlords, the workman attacked the bourgeois, and the rich conspired against the poor. Many wanted indemnities on the ground that they had been martyrs of the police, others appealed for money in order to carry out certain inventions, or else there were plans of phalansteria, projects for cantonal bazaars, schemes for public felicity – then, here and there a flash of intelligence amid these clouds of stupidity, declarations spurting up suddenly from nowhere, a point of law formulated by an oath, and flowers of eloquence on the lips of some ruffian with a sword-belt strapped over his bare, shirtless chest. Sometimes, too, a gentleman made his appearance, an aristocrat of humble de-meanour, speaking like a plebeian, and with his hands unwashed, to make them look hard. A patriot would recognise him, the most virtuous among those present would mob him; and he went off with rage in his soul. On the pretext of common sense, the rule was to be always disparaging lawyers, and to make use as often as possible of these expressions: 'to contribute one's stone to the building', 'social problem', 'workshop'.

Delmar did not miss the opportunities afforded him for taking the floor; and when he could no longer think of anything to say, his solution was to plant himself with one hand on his hip and the other in his waistcoat, turning himself round abruptly in profile, so as to give a good view of his head. Then there were bursts of applause, which came from Mademoiselle Vatnaz at the back of the hall.

Frédéric, in spite of the weakness of the orators, did not dare to risk speaking. All these people seemed to him too rough or too hostile.

But Dussardier made enquiries, and informed him that there existed in the Rue Saint-Jacques a club called the 'Club of the Intellect'. Such a name augured well. Besides, he would bring some friends along.

He brought those whom he had invited to take punch with him: the bookkeeper, the traveller in wines, and the architect; even Pellerin had come, and Hussonnet might come; and on the pavement before the door stood Regimbart, with two individuals, the first of whom was his faithful Compain, a rather thickset man marked with smallpox and with bloodshot eyes; and the second, a kind of negro apeman, exceedingly hairy, and whom he knew only as 'a patriot from Barcelona'.

They passed through a passage, and were then introduced into a large room, no doubt used by a joiner, with walls still fresh and smelling of plaster. Four oil lamps hung in a row shed an unpleasant light. On a platform, at the far end of the room, there was a desk with a bell; underneath it was a table, representing the rostrum, and on each side two others, somewhat lower, for the secretaries. The audience occupying the benches consisted of old hack painters, assistant school teachers, and literary men who had never been published. In the midst of these lines of overcoats with greasy collars could be seen here and there the bonnet of a woman or a workman's overall. The back of the hall was indeed full of work-men, who had probably come because they had nothing to do, or who had been introduced by some of the speakers in order that they might applaud.

Frédéric took care to place himself between Dussardier and Regimbart, who had scarcely sat down when he leaned both hands on his walking-stick and his chin on his hands and shut his eyes, while at the other end of the room Delmar stood and dominated the assembly.

Sénécal appeared at the president's desk.

The kind-hearted clerk had thought Frédéric would be pleased at this surprise. It annoyed him.

The meeting exhibited great respect for its president. He was one of those who, on the twenty-fifth of February, had desired an immediate organisation of labour; on the following day, at the Prado, he had declared himself in favour of attacking the Hôtel de Ville; and, as every person at that period took some model for imitation, one copying Saint-Just, another Danton, another Marat, he tried to look like Blanqui, who imitated Robespierre. His black gloves, and his cropped hair, gave him a rigid appearance, which was exceedingly respectable.

He opened the proceedings with the declaration of the Rights of Man and of the Citizen, a customary act of faith. Then, a vigorous voice struck up Béranger's 'Souvenirs du Peuple'.

Other voices were raised:

'No! No! Not that!'

' "La Casquette!" ' was the cry from the patriots at the back.
And they sang in chorus the favourite lines of the period:

> 'Doff your hat before my cap,
> Kneel before the working man!'

At a word from the president the audience became silent. One of the secretaries proceeded to inspect the letters.

'Some young men inform us that they burn a number of the *Assemblée Nationale* every evening in front of the Panthéon, and they urge all patriots to follow their example.'

'Bravo! Adopted!' replied the audience.

'The Citizen Jean-Jacques Langreneux, a printer in the Rue Dauphine, would like to raise a monument to the memory of the martyrs of Thermidor.'

'Michel-Evariste-Népomucène Vincent, ex-professor, expresses the wish that the European democracy should adopt unity of language. A dead language might be used for that purpose, as, for instance, improved Latin.'

'No! No Latin!' exclaimed the architect.

'Why?' replied a teacher.

And these two gentlemen engaged in a discussion, in which others also took part, each one speaking for effect, and this soon became so tedious that many went away.

But a little old man, who wore a pair of green spectacles at the lower end of his prodigiously high forehead, asked permission to speak in order to make an important communication.

It was a memorandum on the assessment of taxes. The figures flowed on in a continuous stream, as if they were never going to end! The impatience of the audience expressed itself at first in murmurs, in whispered talk; he allowed nothing to put him out. Then they began hissing and called him 'Fido'. Sénécal called the public to order; the speaker went on like a machine. It was necessary to catch him by the elbow in order to stop him. The old fellow looked as if he were waking out of a dream, and, placidly lifting his spectacles, said:

'I'm so sorry, citizens! I'm so sorry! I'm going! Do excuse me!'

Frédéric was disconcerted with the failure of the old man's attempts to read this written statement. He had his own address in his pocket, but an extemporaneous speech would have been better.

Finally the president announced that they were about to pass on to the main item, the electoral question. They would not discuss the big Republican lists. However, the 'Club of the Intellect' had every right, like any other, to form one of its own, 'with all respect for the noble pachas of the Hôtel de Ville', and the citizens who wished to solicit the popular mandate might set forth their claims.

'Go on, now!' said Dussardier.

A man in a cassock, with woolly hair and a petulant expression on his face, had already raised his hand. He declared, with a stutter, that his name was Ducretot, priest and agriculturist, and that he was the author of a work entitled *Manures*. He was told to try a horticultural club.

Then a patriot in overalls climbed up onto the rostrum. He was a working man, with broad shoulders, a big, very mild-looking face, and long black hair. He cast over the assembly an almost voluptuous glance, flung back his head, and, finally, spreading out his arms:

'You have repelled Ducretot, O my brothers! And you have done right, but it was not through irreligion, for we are all religious.'

Many of those present listened open-mouthed, with the air of neophytes and in ecstatic attitudes.

'It is not, either, because he is a priest, for we, too, are priests! The workman is a priest, just as the founder of Socialism was, the Master of us all, Jesus Christ!'

The time had arrived to inaugurate the Kingdom of God! The Gospel led directly to '89! After the abolition of slavery, the abolition of the proletariat. We had had the age of hate – the age of love was about to begin.

'Christianity is the keystone and the foundation of the new edifice . . .'

'Are you making a monkey of us?' exclaimed the traveller in wines. 'Where did you dig out this bible-thumper?'

This interruption gave great offence. Nearly all the audience climbed on to the benches, and, shaking their fists, shouted: 'Atheist! Aristocrat! Rascal!' whilst the president's bell rang without ceasing, and the cries of 'Order! Order!' redoubled. But, undaunted and, moreover, fortified by 'three coffees' which he had swallowed before coming to the meeting, he struggled in the midst of the others:

'What, me! An aristocrat? Don't be so silly!'

When, at length, he was permitted to explain himself, he declared that there would never be any peace while there were priests, and, since something had just been said about economy, it would be a splendid one to suppress the churches, the sacred vessels, and eventually all religions.

Somebody raised the objection that he was going very far.

'Yes! I am going very far! But, when a vessel is caught suddenly in a storm . . .'

Without waiting for the conclusion of this metaphor someone else replied:

'Granted! But this is to demolish at a single stroke, like an undiscerning mason . . .'

'You're insulting masons!' yelled a citizen covered with plaster; and persisting in the belief that he had been provoked, he hurled insults, and wanted to fight, clinging tightly to the bench whereon he sat. It took no less than three men to put him out.

Meanwhile the workman still remained on the rostrum. The two secretaries intimated that he should come down. He protested against the injustice done to him.

'You shall not prevent me from crying out, "Eternal love to our dear France! Eternal love also to the Republic!"'

'Citizens!' said Compain, at this point, 'Citizens!'

And, by dint of repeating 'Citizens', having obtained a little silence, he leaned on the rostrum with his two red hands, which looked like stumps, bent his body forward, and blinking his eyes:

'I believe that we should give a larger extension to the calf's head.'

All were silent, thinking they had misunderstood.

'Yes! The calf's head!'

Three hundred laughs burst forth at the same time. The ceiling shook. At the sight of all these faces convulsed with mirth, Compain shrank back. He continued in an angry tone:

'What! Don't you know about the calf's head!'

It was a paroxysm, delirium. They held their sides. Some of them even tumbled onto the ground, under the benches. Compain, not being able to stand it any longer, took refuge beside Regimbart, and tried to drag him away.

'No! I'm staying till the end!' said the Citizen.

This reply caused Frédéric to make up his mind; and, as he was looking about to the right and the left to see that his friends were ready to support him, he saw Pellerin on the rostrum in front of him. The artist assumed a haughty tone in addressing the meeting.

'I would like to get some notion as to who is the candidate for Art in all this? For my part, I have painted a picture . . . '

'We don't want anything to do with pictures!' was the brutal response of a thin man with red spots on his cheekbones.

Pellerin protested against this interruption

But the other, in a tragic tone:

'Ought not the Government already to have made an ordinance abolishing prostitution and want?'

And this phrase having at once won to his side the popular acclaim, he thundered against the corruption of great cities.

'Shame and infamy! We ought to catch hold of wealthy citizens on their way out of the Maison-d'Or and spit in their faces! If only, at least, the Government didn't encourage debauchery! But the collectors of the city dues exhibit towards our daughters and our sisters such indecency . . . '

A voice exclaimed, some distance away:

'That's a good one!'

'Throw him out!'

'They extract taxes from us to pay for licentiousness! Thus, the high salaries paid to actors . . . '

'My turn!' cried Delmar.

He leaped onto the rostrum, pushed everybody aside, took up his position; and declaring that he regarded such stupid accusations with scorn, expatiated on the civilising mission of the actor. Inasmuch as the theatre was the seat of the education of the nation, he would record his vote for the reform of the theatre; and to begin with, no more managements, no more privileges!'

'Yes! Of any sort!'

The actor's performance excited the audience, and subversive proposals came from all sides.

'No more academies! Down with the Institut!'

'No missions!'

'No more school-leaving exams!

'Down with University degrees!'

'Let us preserve them,' said Sénécal, 'but let them be conferred by universal suffrage, by the People, the only true judge!'

Besides, these things were not the most useful. The first thing was to cut the rich down to size! And he represented them as gorging themselves with crimes under their gilded ceilings, while the poor, writhing with hunger in their slums, cultivated all the virtues. The applause became so vehement that he interrupted his discourse. For several minutes he remained with his eyes closed, his head thrown back, and, as it were, rocking himself to sleep on the anger he had aroused.

Then he began to talk in a dogmatic fashion, in phrases as imperious as laws. The State should take possession of the Bank and of Insurance offices. Inheritances should be abolished. A social fund should be established for the workers. Many other measures were desirable in the future. For the time being, these would suffice; and, returning to the question of the elections:

'We want citizens who are pure, men who are entirely fresh! Would anyone like to present himself?'

Frédéric got up. There was a buzz of approval made by his friends. But Sénécal put on a Fouquier-Tinville face, and began to ask questions as to his surname, forenames, antecedents, life and morals.

Frédéric answered succinctly, and bit his lip. Sénécal asked whether anyone saw any impediment to this candidature.

'No! No!'

But *he* saw some. All bent forward and strained their ears. The citizen who was seeking their support had not delivered a certain sum of money which he had promised for the foundation of a democratic journal. Moreover, on the twenty-second of February, though he had had sufficient notice, he had failed to be at the meeting-place in the Place du Panthéon.

'I swear that he was at the Tuileries!' exclaimed Dussardier.

'Can you swear that you saw him at the Panthéon?'

Dussardier hung down his head; Frédéric was silent; his friends, scandalised, looked at him anxiously.

'At least,' Sénécal went on, 'do you know a patriot who will answer to us for your principles?'

'I will!' said Dussardier.

'Oh! That's not enough! Someone else!'

Frédéric turned towards Pellerin. The artist replied to him with an abundance of gestures, signifying:

'Ah! My dear boy, they've rejected me! The deuce! What can I do!'

Thereupon Frédéric nudged Regimbart.

'Yes all right! It's time for me to speak, I'm going!'

And Regimbart stepped upon the platform; then, pointing towards the Spaniard, who had followed him:

'Allow me, citizens, to present to you a patriot from Barcelona!'

The patriot made a low bow, rolled his silvery eyes about like a mechanical doll, and with his hand on his heart:

'Ciudadanos! Mucho aprecio el honor que me dispensáis, y si grande es vuestra bondad mayor es vuestra atención.'

'I claim the right to speak!' cried Frédéric.

'Desde que se proclamó la constitución de Cadiz, ese pacto fundamental de las libertades españolas; hasta la última revolución, nuestra patria cuenta numerosos y heróicos mártires.'

Frédéric once more tried to make himself heard:

'But, citizens . . . '

The Spaniard went on:

'El martes próximo tendrá lugar en la iglesia de la Magdelena un servicio fúnebre.'

'This is absolutely ridiculous! Nobody understands him!'

This observation exasperated the audience.

'Turn him out! Turn him out!'

'Who? Me?' asked Frédéric.

'Yourself!' said Sénécal, majestically. 'Out with you!'

He rose to leave; and the voice of the Iberian pursued him:

'Y todos los Españoles desearían ver allí reunidas las deputaciones de los clubs y de la milicia nacional. Una oración fúnebre, en honor de la libertad española y del mundo entero, será pronunciada por un miembro del clero de Paris en la sala Bonne-Nouvelle. Honor al pueblo francés, que llamaría yo el primero pueblo del mundo, si no fuese ciudadano de otra nación!'

'Aristo!' yelled one lout, shaking his fist at Frédéric, as the latter, boiling with indignation, rushed out into the courtyard.

He reproached himself for his devotion, without reflecting that, after all, the accusations brought against him were just. What a fatal idea was this candidature! But what asses, what cretins! He drew comparisons between himself and these men, and soothed his wounded pride with the thought of their stupidity.

Then he felt the need to see Rosanette. After so much ugliness and magniloquence, her dainty person would be refreshing. She was aware that he had intended to present himself at a club that evening. However, she did not ask him a single question when he came in.

She was sitting near the fire, unpicking the lining of a dress. He was surprised to find her thus occupied.

'Hallo! What are you doing?'

'You can see for yourself,' she said, curtly. 'I'm mending my clothes! So much for this Republic of yours.'

'Why do you call it mine?'

'Perhaps you want to make out that it's mine?'

And she began to reproach him for everything that had happened in France for the last two months, accusing him of having brought about the Revolution, blaming him for the fact that everybody was ruined, that all the rich people were leaving Paris, and that she would end up dying in the workhouse.

'It's easy for you to talk, with your yearly income! Though, at the rate at which things are going, you won't have your precious yearly income long.'

'That may be,' said Frédéric. 'The most devoted are always misunderstood; and if one were not sustained by one's conscience, the brutes with whom one is forced to compromise oneself would put you off self-denial for life!'

Rosanette gazed at him with half-closed eyes.

'Hey? What? What self-denial? Monsieur wasn't successful, it would seem? So much the better! That will teach you to make patriotic donations. Oh, don't lie! I know you've given them three hundred francs, for this Republic of yours has to be kept like a woman! Well, enjoy yourself with her, my lad!'

Under this avalanche of stupidity, Frédéric passed from his former disappointment to a more painful disillusion.

He had withdrawn to the back of the room. She came to him.

'Look! Think about it! In a country as in a house, there must be a master; otherwise, everyone will be out for himself. In the first place, everybody knows that Ledru-Rollin is head over ears in debt! As for Lamartine, how can you expect a poet to understand politics? Ah! It's all very well for you to shake your head and to think you've got more brains than everybody else; what I say is true! But you're always on your high horse; there's no saying anything to you! For instance, look at Fournier-Fontaine, of the Saint-Roch stores: do you know how much he's lost? Eight hundred thousand francs! And Gomer, the packer opposite, another Republican, that one, he smashed the tongs on his wife's head, and drank so much absinthe that they're going to put him into an asylum. That's what they're all like, Republicans! A Republic at twenty-five per cent! Ah, yes! That's something to be proud of!'

Frédéric took himself off. He was disgusted at the fatuousness of this girl, revealing itself suddenly in the language of the gutter. He even felt himself becoming the slightest bit patriotic once more.

The ill-temper of Rosanette only increased. Mademoiselle Vatnaz irritated her with her enthusiasm. Believing that she had a mission, she insisted on making speeches and laying down the law, and, sharper than Rosanette in matters of this sort, overwhelmed her with arguments.

One day she made her appearance burning with indignation against Hussonnet, who had just indulged in some ribald remarks at the Women's Club. Rosanette approved of this conduct, declaring even that she would take men's clothes to go and 'give them a bit of her mind, the entire lot of them, and whip them.' Frédéric entered at the same moment.

'You'll go with me, won't you?'

And, in spite of his presence, they started quarrelling, one playing the part of the respectable citizen's wife and the other the philosopher.

According to Rosanette, women were born exclusively for love, or in order to bring up children and keep house.

According to Mademoiselle Vatnaz, women ought to have a position in the State. Historically, Gaulish women, and Anglo-Saxon women too, took part in the legislative, the squaws of the Hurons were part of the Council. The work of civilisation was common to all. All should contribute towards it, and fraternity should at last be substituted for egoism, association for individualism, and cultivation on a large scale for minute subdivision of land.

'Come, that's good! You're an expert on agriculture now!'

'Why not? Besides, it's a question of humanity, of its future!'

'Mind your own business!'

'This is my business!'

They got into a passion. Frédéric intervened. Vatnaz became very heated, and went so far as to uphold Communism.

'What nonsense!' said Rosanette. 'How could such a thing ever come to pass?'

The other brought forward in support of her theory the examples of the Essenes, the Moravian Brethren, the Jesuits of Paraguay, the family of the Pingons near Thiers in Auvergne; and, as she gesticulated a great deal, her gold chain got entangled, among her bundle of trinkets, with a little gold sheep which hung from it.

Suddenly, Rosanette turned exceedingly pale.

Mademoiselle Vatnaz went on extricating her trinket.

'Don't give yourself so much trouble,' said Rosanette. 'Now I know your political opinions.'

'What?' replied Vatnaz, blushing like a virgin.

'Oh! Oh, you understand me!'

Frédéric did not understand. Something had come up between them which was obviously more fundamental and intimate than socialism.

'And so what?' said Vatnaz in reply, rising up undaunted. 'It's a loan, my dear, set off one debt against the other!'

'Goodness, I don't deny my debts! For a few thousand francs, that's a nice story! I borrow, at least; I don't rob anyone!'

Mademoiselle Vatnaz made an effort to laugh.

'Oh! I'd put my hand in the fire to prove it.'

'Take care! It's dry enough to burn.'

The old maid held out her right hand to her, and keeping it raised just in front of her:

'But there are friends of yours who find it suits them!'

'Andalusians, I suppose? As castanets!'

'You slut!'

The Maréchale made her a low bow:

'Charming!'

Mademoiselle Vatnaz made no reply. Beads of sweat appeared on her temples. Her eyes were fixed on the carpet. She panted for breath. At last she made for the door, and slamming it vigorously:

'Good night! You'll hear from me!'

'Delighted, I'm sure!' said Rosanette.

The effort of self-restraint had shattered her nerves. She sank down onto the divan, shaking all over, stammering out words of abuse, shedding tears. Was it this threat from Vatnaz that was tormenting her? Oh, no! She couldn't care less! All things considered, the other probably owed her money! It was the golden sheep, a present; and in the midst of her tears the name of Delmar escaped her lips. So, then, she was in love with the actor!

'In that case, why did she take up with me?' Frédéric asked himself. 'How is it that he's come back again? What compels her to keep me? What is the meaning of all this?'

Rosanette was still sobbing quietly . She was still on the edge of the divan, lying sidewards, with her right cheek resting on her two hands – and she seemed such a delicate little being, so unselfconscious, and so sorely troubled, that he drew closer to her and gently kissed her on the forehead.

Thereupon she gave him assurances of her affection for him; the Prince had just left, they would be free. But she was for the time being . . . short of money. 'You saw it yourself, the other day, when I was trying to turn my old linings to use.' No more carriages-and-pair now! And that was not all; the upholsterers were threatening to resume possession of the furniture in the bedroom and the large drawing-room. She did not know what to do.

Frédéric had a mind to answer: 'Don't worry about it! I'll pay!' But the lady could be lying. Experience had taught him. He confined himself to mere expressions of sympathy.

Rosanette's fears were not vain; she had to give up the furniture and quit the handsome apartment in the Rue Drouot. She took another on the Boulevard Poissonnière, on the fourth floor. The curiosities of her old boudoir were sufficient to make the three rooms look pretty. There were Chinese blinds, an awning on the terrace, and in the drawing-room a secondhand carpet still perfectly new, with pink silk pouffes. Frédéric had contributed largely to these purchases; he experienced the pleasure felt by a newly-married man who at last owns a house of his own, a wife of his own; and, being much pleased with the place, he would sleep there nearly every night.

One morning, as he was coming out of the anteroom, he saw, on the third floor, on the stairs, the shako of a National Guard coming up. Where in the world was he going? Frédéric waited. The man kept on up, with his head slightly bent: he raised his eyes. It was our friend Arnoux. The situation was clear. They both reddened simultaneously, overcome by the same feeling of embarrassment.

Arnoux was the first to find a way out of the difficulty.

'She's better, isn't that so?' As if Rosanette were ill, and he had come to learn how she was.

Frédéric took advantage of this opening.

'Yes, indeed! At least, so I was told by her maid,' wishing to convey that he had not been allowed to see her.

Then they stood facing each other, both undecided, and eyeing one another intently. The question now was, which of the two was going to remain. Arnoux once more settled the question.

'Ah! Pshaw! I'll come back later! Where were you going? I'll come with you!'

And, when they were in the street, he chatted as naturally as usual. Unquestionably he was not of a jealous disposition, or else he was too goodnatured to get angry.

Besides, his time was devoted to serving his country. He never left off his uniform now. On the twenty-ninth of March he had defended the offices of the *Presse*. When the Chamber was invaded, he distinguished himself by his courage, and he took part in the banquet given to the National Guard of Amiens.

Hussonnet, who was always on duty with him, profited, more than anyone, from his flask and his cigars; but, irreverent by nature, he delighted in contradicting him, denigrating the inaccurate style of the decrees, the Luxembourg conferences, the 'Vésuviennes', the 'Tyroliens', everything, down to the Chariot of Agriculture, drawn by horses instead of oxen and escorted by ugly girls. Arnoux, on the other hand, was the upholder of Authority, and dreamed of uniting the different parties. However, his affairs were taking an unfavourable turn. He was not greatly troubled.

Frédéric's relations with the Maréchale had not upset him; for this discovery made him feel justified (in his conscience) in withdrawing the allowance which he had renewed since the Prince had left her. He pleaded by way of excuse the embarrassed condition in which he found himself, complained a great deal, and Rosanette was generous. The result was that M. Arnoux regarded himself as the lover who appealed entirely to the heart – which raised him in his own estimation and made him feel young again. Having no doubt that Frédéric was paying the Maréchale, he fancied that he was 'playing a nice trick' on the young man, even managed to conceal his tracks, and when they happened to meet, left the coast clear for him.

Frédéric was not pleased with having to share; and his rival's courtesies seemed a joke that had gone on too long. But by taking offence, he would have removed from his path every opportunity of ever finding his way back to Madame Arnoux, and then, this was the only means whereby he could hear about her. The ceramics-dealer, in accordance with his usual practice, or perhaps with malice aforethought, recalled her readily in the course of conversation, and even asked him why he no longer came to see her.

Frédéric, having exhausted every excuse, assured him that he had called several times to see Madame Arnoux, but without success. Arnoux was convinced that this was so, for he often marvelled in her presence at the absence of their friend, and she invariably replied that she was out when he called; so that these two lies, in place of contradicting, corroborated each other.

The young man's gentle ways and the pleasure of finding a dupe in him made Arnoux all the fonder of him. He carried familiarity to its extreme limits not through disdain, but through assurance. One day he wrote saying that urgent business compelled him to be away in the country for twenty-four hours; he begged him to mount guard in his stead. Frédéric dared not refuse, and repaired to the guardhouse in the Place du Carrousel.

He had to endure the society of the National Guards! And, with the exception of a refiner, a facetious man who drank to an inordinate extent, they all appeared to him more stupid than their knapsacks. The principal subject of conversation was the substitution of leather cross-belts by ordinary ones. Others declaimed against the national workshops. 'Where will it end?' they asked. The man to whom the words had been addressed opened his eyes as if he were standing on the verge of an abyss, and replied: 'Where will it end?' Then, one who was more daring than the rest exclaimed: 'It can't go on! We must put a stop to it!' And as the same kind of talk went on till night, Frédéric was bored to death.

Great was his surprise when, at eleven o'clock, he suddenly beheld Arnoux, who immediately explained that he had hurried back to set him at liberty, having disposed of his business.

He had had no business. The whole thing was an invention to enable him to spend twenty-four hours alone with Rosanette. But the worthy Arnoux had placed too much confidence in his own powers, so that now, in the state of lassitude which was the result, he had been seized with remorse. He came to thank Frédéric, and to invite him to supper.

'No, thank you very much! I'm not hungry! All I want is to go to bed!'

'All the more reason for us to have breakfast together, later! How feeble you are! You can't go home at this hour! It's too late! It'd be dangerous!'

Frédéric gave in once again. Arnoux, whose appearance had not been expected, was a favourite with his brothers in arms, especially the refiner. They all loved him; and he was such a good fellow that he was sorry Hussonnet was not there. But he wanted to shut his eyes for one minute, no longer.

'Put yourself next to me,' he said to Frédéric, stretching himself out on the camp bed without taking off his belt and straps.

Through fear of an alert, in spite of the regulation, he even kept his gun; then stammered out a few words: 'My darling! My little angel!' and was soon fast asleep.

Those who had been talking became silent; and gradually there was a deep silence in the guardhouse. Frédéric, tormented by the fleas, went on staring about him. The wall, painted yellow, had, halfway up, a long shelf, on which the knapsacks formed a succession of little humps, while underneath lead-coloured rifles stood up in a row; and there was the sound of snoring, produced by the National Guards, whose stomachs were visible, outlined in the darkness in a confused fashion. On the top of the stove stood an empty bottle and some plates. Three straw chairs were drawn around the table, on which a pack of cards was spread out. A drum, in the middle of the bench, had its strap hanging down. The warm wind, making its way through the door, caused the lamp to smoke. Arnoux was asleep, with his two arms wide apart; and, as his gun was placed in a slightly crooked position, with the butt downwards, the mouth of the barrel came up right under his arm. Frédéric noticed this, and was alarmed.

'But no! I'm wrong! There's nothing to be afraid of! And yet, what if he died . . . !'

And immediately pictures unrolled themselves before his mind in endless succession. He saw himself with Her at night in a post-chaise; then on a river's bank on a summer evening, and in the light of a lamp at home in their house. He even planned their household budget and domestic arrangements, contemplating, feeling already his happiness between his hands – and in order to realise it, all that was needed was that the cock of the gun should rise! It could be pushed with one's toe; the gun would go off, it would be an accident, no more!

Frédéric brooded over this idea like a dramatist writing a play. Suddenly it seemed to him that it was on the point of being carried into practical operation, and that he was going to contribute, that he wanted to; and then a great fear took possession of him. In the midst of this distress he felt a sense of pleasure, and he allowed himself to sink deeper and deeper into it, with a dreadful awareness that his scruples were vanishing; in the wildness of his reverie the rest of the world faded away; and his only consciousness of himself was through an intolerable oppression of the chest.

'Shall we have some white wine?' said the refiner, as he awoke.

Arnoux sprang to his feet; and, as soon as the white wine had been taken, he wanted to relieve Frédéric of his sentry duty.

Then he took him to have breakfast in the Rue de Chartres, at Parly's; and as he needed to recuperate, he ordered himself two dishes of meat, a lobster, an omelette with rum, a salad, etc., all washed down with an 1819 Sauterne and a '42 Romanée, not forgetting the champagne at dessert and the liqueurs.

Frédéric did not in any way gainsay him. He was disturbed, as if the other might have been able to decipher on his countenance the traces of his thoughts.

With both elbows on the table and leaning over very low, so that he wearied Frédéric by his fixed stare, Arnoux confided some of his projects to the young man.

He wanted to take for farming purposes all the embankments on the Northern line, in order to plant potatoes there, or else to organise on the boulevards a monster cavalcade in which the 'celebrities of the day' would figure. He would hire out all the windows, which would, at the rate of three francs each, on average, produce a handsome profit. In short, he dreamed of a great stroke of fortune by means of acquiring some monopoly.

He assumed a moral tone, nevertheless, criticised excess and misconduct, spoke about his 'poor father', and every evening, as he said, examined his conscience before offering his soul to God.

'A little curaçao, eh?'

'Just as you please.'

As for the Republic, things would right themselves; in fact, he looked on himself as the happiest man on earth; and forgetting himself, he praised Rosanette's attractive qualities, and even compared her with his wife. That was quite a different thing! You couldn't imagine lovelier thighs.

'Your health!'

Frédéric touched glasses with him. He had, to be civil, drunk a little too much; besides, the strong sunlight dazzled him; and when they went back up the Rue Vivienne together, their epaulettes touched each other in a fraternal fashion.

When he got home, Frédéric slept till seven o'clock. After that he called on the Maréchale. She had gone out with somebody. With Arnoux, perhaps? Not knowing what to do, he continued his promenade along the boulevard, but could not get past the Porte Saint-Martin, owing to the great crowd that blocked the way.

Poverty had abandoned to their own resources a considerable number of workmen; and they used to come there every evening, no doubt for the purpose of taking stock and awaiting a signal. In spite of the law against public gatherings, these *clubs of despair* were increasing to a frightful extent; and many middle-class citizens repaired every day to the spot through bravado, and because it was the fashion.

All of a sudden Frédéric caught a glimpse, three paces away, of M. Dambreuse with Martinon; he turned his head away, for M. Dambreuse having got himself nominated as a representative of the people, he resented him for this. But the capitalist stopped him.

'One word, my dear Monsieur! I have some explanations to make to you.'

'I'm not asking for any.'

'Pray listen to me!'

It was not his fault in any way. People had begged him, even forced him, in a way. Martinon immediately endorsed all that he had said: some of the electors of Nogent had presented themselves in a deputation at his house.

'Besides, I thought I was free, since . . . '

A crush of people on the pavement forced M. Dambreuse to move away. A minute after he reappeared, saying to Martinon:

'That was a genuine service, really! You won't regret it . . . '

All three stood with their backs to a shop in order to be able to chat more at their ease.

From time to time there was a cry of 'Long live Napoleon! Long live Barbès! Down with Marie!' The countless throng was talking very loudly – and all these voices, echoing around the houses, made a sound like the continuous rippling of waves in a harbour. At intervals they ceased; and then could be heard voices singing the 'Marseillaise'. Under the carriage-gates, men of mysterious aspect offered swordsticks to passers-by. Sometimes two individuals, passing each other, would wink, and then quickly hurry away. The footpaths were full of groups of staring idlers; a dense crowd swarmed about on the pavement. Entire bands of police officers, emerging from the alleys, had scarcely made their way into the crowd when they were swallowed up in it. Little red flags here and there looked like flames; coachmen, from their high seats, gesticulated energetically, and then turned to go back. All this movement and spectacle were very droll.

'How all this,' said Martinon, 'would have amused Mademoiselle Cécile!'

'My wife, as you are aware, does not like my niece to come with us,' returned M. Dambreuse with a smile.

One would scarcely have recognised him. For the past three months he had been crying 'Long live the Republic!' and he had even voted in favour of the banishment of the d'Orléans. But there had to be an end to concessions. He was so angry that he carried a cosh in his pocket.

Martinon had one, too. The magistrature having ceased to offer permanent appointments, he had withdrawn from the Bar, so that he surpassed M. Dambreuse in his display of violence.

The banker particularly loathed Lamartine (for having supported Ledru-Rollin) and also Pierre Leroux, Proudhon, Considérant, Lamennais, all the hotheads, all the socialists.

'For, after all, what is it that they want? The duty on meat and arrest for debt have been abolished; now the project of a bank for mortgages is under consideration; the other day it was a national bank! And now there are five millions in the Budget for the workers! But luckily it's over, thanks to Monsieur de Falloux. Goodbye to them! Let them go!'

Indeed, not knowing how to feed the hundred and thirty thousand men in the national workshops, the Minister of Public Works had that very day signed an order inviting all citizens between the ages of eighteen and twenty to take service as soldiers, or else to leave for the provinces to till the soil.

They were indignant at the alternative thus put before them, convinced that the object was to destroy the Republic. Life away from the capital distressed them as if it were a kind of exile; they saw themselves dying of fevers in desolate regions. To many of them, moreover, who had been accustomed to delicate work, agriculture seemed a degradation; it was, in short, a snare, a mockery, a tangible denial of all the promises which had been made to them. If they offered any resistance, force would be employed against them; they had no doubt of it, and were taking steps to forestall it.

About nine o'clock the crowds which had formed at the Bastille and at the Châtelet ebbed back towards the boulevard. From the Porte Saint-Denis to the Porte Saint-Martin nothing could be seen save an enormous swarm of people, a single mass of a dark blue, almost black. The men one glimpsed all had glowing eyes, pale complexions, faces emaciated with hunger and exalted with a sense of injustice. Meanwhile clouds were gathering; the stormy sky roused the electricity that was in the people, and they whirled about uncertainly, with the great swaying movements of a swelling sea; and one felt that there was an incalculable force in their depths, and some elemental force. Then they all began to chant: 'Lamps! Lamps!' Many windows did not light up; stones were flung at their panes. M. Dambreuse deemed it prudent to withdraw. The two young men accompanied him home.

He predicted great disasters. The people might once more invade the Chamber; and on this point he told them how he would have been killed on the fifteenth of May had it not been for the devotion of a National Guard.

'But I'd forgotten! He's your friend, your friend the ceramics manufacturer, Jacques Arnoux!' The rioters were suffocating him, when that brave citizen had caught him in his arms and put him safely to one side. So it was that, since then, there had been a kind of intimacy between them. 'We must dine together one of these days, and, since you see him often, give him the assurance that I like him very much. He is an excellent man, and has, in my opinion, been slandered; and he has his wits about him, the rascal! My compliments once more! A very good evening!'

Frédéric, after having left M. Dambreuse, went back to the Maréchale; and, with a very sombre air, said that she must choose between him and Arnoux. She replied gently that she had no idea what he meant with 'such tittle-tattle', that she did not love Arnoux, and was not at all attached to him. Frédéric was dying to get away from Paris. She did not offer any opposition to this whim, and next morning they set out for Fontainebleau.

The hotel at which they stayed could be distinguished from the others by a fountain that splashed in the middle of the courtyard. The doors of the rooms opened out onto a corridor, as in monasteries. The one assigned to them was large, well-furnished, hung with chintz, and silent, owing to the scarcity of tourists. Alongside the houses, people passed by with nothing to do; then, under their windows, when the day was declining, children in the street would play a game of base – and this tranquillity, following the tumult they had witnessed in Paris, surprised and soothed them.

In the morning, early, they went to visit the château. As they passed in through the gate, they had a view of its entire front, with the five pavilions and their sharp-pointed roofs, and its staircase of horseshoe shape opening out at the far end of the courtyard, which is hemmed in, to right and left, by two lower buildings. On the paved ground lichens blend at a distance with the tawny hue of the bricks; and the entire appearance of the palace, rust-coloured like an old suit of armour, had about it something regally impassive, a sort of warlike melancholy grandeur.

At last, a manservant made his appearance with a bunch of keys in his hand. He first showed them the apartments of the queens, the Pope's oratory, the gallery of Francis I, the little mahogany table on which the Emperor signed his abdication and, in one of the rooms which cut in two the old Galerie des Cerfs, the place where Christine had Monaldeschi assassinated. Rosanette listened to this narrative attentively; then, turning towards Frédéric:

'No doubt it was out of jealousy! You be careful!'

After this they passed through the Council Chamber, the Guards' Room, the Throne Room, and the drawing-room of Louis XIII. The tall, uncurtained windows sent forth a white light; the handles of the window-fastenings and the brass feet of the side-tables were slightly tarnished with dust; the armchairs were everywhere hidden under coarse linen covers; above the doors could be seen hunting scenes of Louis XIV, and here and there tapestries representing the gods of Olympus, Psyche, or the battles of Alexander.

When she passed in front of the mirrors, Rosanette would stop for a moment to smooth her hair.

After passing through the courtyard of the keep and the Saint-Saturnin Chapel, they reached the Banquet Hall.

They were dazzled by the magnificence of the ceiling, which was divided into octagonal compartments set off with gold and silver, more finely chiselled than a jewel, and by the vast number of paintings covering the walls, from the immense chimney-piece, where the arms of France were surrounded by crescents and quivers, down to the musicians' gallery, which was constructed at the other end along the entire width of the hall. The ten arched windows were wide open; the sun threw its lustre onto the paintings, the blue sky continued in an endless curve the ultra-marine of the arches; and from the depths of the woods, where the misty summits of the trees filled the horizon, there seemed to come an echo of flourishes blown by ivory horns, and mythological ballets, gathering together under the foliage princesses and nobles disguised as nymphs and fauns – an age of innocent science, of violent passions and sumptuous art, when the ideal was to sweep away the world in a vision of the Hesperides, and when the mistresses of kings mingled their glory with the stars. There was a portrait of one of the most beautiful of these celebrated women on the right in the form of Diana the huntress, and even the Infernal Diana, no doubt in order to indicate the power which she possessed even beyond the limits of the tomb. All these symbols confirm her glory; and there remains about the spot something of her, an indistinct voice, a radiance whose glow stretches out indefinitely.

Frédéric was seized with a mysterious feeling of retrospective desire. In order to divert these passionate longings into another channel, he began to gaze tenderly on Rosanette, and asked her whether she would not have liked to be this woman.

'What woman?'

'Diane de Poitiers!'

He repeated:

'Diane de Poitiers, the mistress of Henry II.'

She gave utterance to a little 'Ah!' That was all.

Her silence clearly demonstrated that she knew nothing, understood nothing, so that out of kindness he said to her:

'Perhaps you're getting tired of this?'

'No, no, quite the reverse!'

And lifting up her chin, and casting around her a glance of the vaguest description, Rosanette let fall these words:

'It brings back memories!'

Yet her face showed that she was making an effort, showed a respectful intent; and, as this air of gravity made her look prettier, Frédéric excused her.

The carps' pond amused her more. For a quarter of an hour she threw pieces of bread into the water to see the fishes leap.

Frédéric had seated himself by her side under the lime trees. He thought of all the personages who had haunted these walls, Charles V, the Valois kings, Henry IV, Peter the Great, Jean-Jacques Rousseau, and 'the fair mourners of the stage boxes', Voltaire, Napoleon, Pius VII, and Louis-Philippe; he felt himself surrounded, elbowed, by the tumultuous dead; he was stunned by such a confusion of images, even though he found a certain fascination in contemplating them.

At length they descended into the flower-garden.

It is a vast rectangle, which gives an overall view of its wide yellow walks, its square grass-plots, its ribbons of boxwood, its yew trees shaped like pyramids, its low-lying greenery and its narrow borders, in which thinly-sown flowers make patches on the grey soil. At the end of the garden may be seen a park through whose entire length runs a long canal.

Royal residences have about them a peculiar kind of melancholy, due, no doubt, to their dimensions being far too large for the limited number of their occupants, to the silence which one is surprised to find in them after so many fanfares, to the immobility of their richness, which attests by its age the transitory character of dynasties, the eternal wretchedness of all things – and this exhalation of the centuries, enervating and funereal, like the perfume of a mummy, makes itself felt even in untutored brains. Rosanette was yawning immoderately. They went back to the hotel.

After their breakfast an open carriage came round for them. They left Fontainebleau by a large roundabout, then climbed at a walking pace up a sandy road in a wood of little pines. The trees became larger; and, from time to time, the driver would say, 'These are the Frères Siamois, this is the Pharamond, the Bouquet-du-Roi . . .' not forgetting any of the famous sites, sometimes even drawing up to enable them to admire them.

They entered the forest of Franchard. The carriage glided over the grass like a sledge; pigeons which they could not see were cooing; suddenly, the waiter of a café appeared; and they alighted before the gate of a garden in which a number of round tables were placed. Then, passing on the left by the walls of a ruined abbey, they made their way over great rocks, and soon reached the bottom of the gorge.

It is covered on one side with a mixture of sandstone and juniper trees, while on the other side the ground, almost quite bare, slopes towards the hollow of the valley, where a foot-track makes a pale line through the colour of the heather; and far in the distance one sees a flattened cone-shaped summit with a telegraph-tower behind it.

Half an hour later they stepped out of the cab once more, in order to climb the heights of Aspremont.

The road forms zigzags between the stocky pine trees, beneath rocks with angular profiles; all this part of the forest has a sort of stifled air, rather wild and contemplative. One thinks of hermits, companions of the great stags with fiery crosses between their horns, who were wont to welcome with paternal smiles the good kings of France when they knelt before their grottoes. The warm air was filled with the odour of resin, and roots of trees crossed one another at ground level like veins. Rosanette tripped over them, grew dejected, and wanted to cry.

But, at the very top, she became joyous once more on finding, under a roof made of branches, a sort of tavern, with carved wood for sale. She drank a bottle of lemonade, and bought herself a stick made of holly wood; and, without one glance towards the landscape which can be seen from the plateau, she entered the Brigands' Cave, preceded by a lad carrying a torch.

Their carriage was awaiting them in the Bas-Bréau.

A painter in a blue smock was working at the foot of an oak tree with his box of colours on his knees. He raised his head and watched them as they passed.

In the middle of the hill of Chailly, the sudden breaking of a cloud made them lower the hood. Almost immediately the rain stopped; and the paving-stones of the streets glistened in the sun when they drove back into the town.

Some travellers, who had recently arrived, informed them that a terrible battle was making a bloodbath of Paris. Rosanette and her lover were not surprised. Then everybody left, the hotel became quiet again, the gas was put out, and they fell asleep to the murmur of the fountain in the courtyard.

On the following day they went to see the Wolf's Gorge, the Fairies' Pool, the Long Rock, and the Marlotte; the day after that, they began again at random, wherever their coachman thought fit, without asking where they were, and often even neglecting the famous sites.

They were so comfortable in their old landau, which was as low as a sofa, and upholstered in a cloth with faded stripes! The ditches full of scrub passed along before their eyes, with a gentle, continuous movement. White rays shot like arrows through the tall ferns; sometimes, a track which was no longer used presented itself to them, in a straight line; and grass grew, softly, here and there. In the centre of the crossroads, a cross extended its four arms; elsewhere, posts leaned over sideways like dead trees, and little winding paths, disappearing into the foliage, offered themselves temptingly; at the same moment, the horse changed course and they turned into them, sinking into the mud; further along, moss had grown on the edges of the deep ruts.

They thought they were far away from other people, quite alone. But suddenly a gamekeeper passed with his gun, or a band of women in rags dragging long bundles of faggots along on their backs.

When the carriage stopped, there was a universal silence; the only sounds that reached them were the blowing of the horse in the shafts, with the faint cry of a bird, repeated.

The light at certain points illuminating the fringes of the wood, left the interior in deep shadow; or else, attenuated in the foreground by a sort of twilight, it flooded the background with violet vapours, a white radiance. The midday sun, falling directly on wide tracts of greenery, made splashes of light over them, hung gleaming drops of silver from the ends of the branches, streaked the grass with long lines of emeralds, and flung gold patches onto the beds of dead leaves; when they let their heads fall back, they could see the sky through the tops of the trees. Some of them, which were enormously high, looked like patriarchs and emperors, or, touching one another at their extremities, formed with their long shafts, as it were, triumphal arches; others, sprouting forth obliquely from below, seemed like columns ready to fall.

This mass of great vertical lines gaped open slightly. Then, enormous green billows unfurled in irregular curves as far as the surface of the valleys, towards which advanced the brows of other hills looking down on white plains, which ended by losing themselves in a vague paleness.

Standing side by side, on some rising ground, they felt, as they drank in the air, something like the pride of a freer life penetrating the depths of their souls, with a superabundance of energy, a joy without cause.

The diversity of the trees provided a constantly changing spectacle. The beeches with their smooth white bark twisted their tops together; ash trees softly curved their sea-blue branches; in the hornbeam coppices were bristling holly trees, looking like bronze; then came a row of slender birches, bent over into elegiac attitudes; and the pine trees, symmetrical as organ pipes, seemed to sing as they swayed to and fro. There were gigantic, knotted oaks, which writhed as they stretched themselves out from the earth, embraced each other, and with their firm trunks, which were like torsos, hurled despairing appeals to each other with their bare arms, and furious threats, like a group of Titans struck motionless in the midst of their rage. A heavier atmosphere, a feverish languor, brooded over the pools, whose sheets of water were etched in between bushes of thorn; the lichens on their banks, where the wolves come to drink, are of the colour of sulphur, burnt as if by the footprints of witches, and the incessant croaking of the frogs responds to the cawing of the crows as they wheel through the air. Then they passed through monotonous clearings, planted here and there with a sapling. The sound of iron, a succession of sharp, rapid blows, could be heard: on the side of a hill, a group of quarrymen were breaking the rocks. These became more and more numerous, and ended by filling the entire landscape, cube-shaped like houses, flat like flagstones, propping each other up, overhanging each other, intermingling with each other, as if they were the ruins, unrecognisable and monstrous, of some vanished city. But the wild chaos they exhibit makes one dream rather of volcanoes, of deluges, of great unknown cataclysms. Frédéric said they had been there since the beginning of the world and would remain so till the end; Rosanette turned aside her head, declaring that 'this would drive her mad', and went off to collect sweet heather. Their little violet blossoms, growing close together, formed unequal patches, and the soil, which trickled out from underneath, placed dark fringes on the edge of the sand, which was spangled with mica.

One day they reached a point halfway up a hill made entirely of sand. Its surface, untrodden till now, was streaked in symmetrical undulations; here and there, like promontories on the dry bed of an ocean, rose rocks with the vague outlines of animals, tortoises thrusting forward their heads, crawling seals, hippopotami, and bears. Not a soul. No sound. The sand was dazzling in the sun – and all at once in this vibration of light, the animals seemed to move. They hurried away, flying from their feeling of vertigo, almost terrified.

The gravity of the forest communicated itself to them; and hours passed in silence, during which, yielding to the rocking motion of the springs, they remained as if sunk in the torpor of a calm intoxication. With his arm around her waist, he listened to her talking while the birds twittered, took in with almost the same glance the black grapes on her bonnet and the juniper berries, the draperies of her veil, and the spirals of the clouds; and, when he bent towards her, the freshness of her skin mingled with the heavy perfume of the woods. They found amusement in everything; they showed one another, as a curiosity, gossamer threads hanging from the bushes, holes full of water in the middle of stones, a squirrel on the branches, the way in which two butterflies fluttered after them; or else, at twenty paces from them, under the trees, a doe strode on peacefully, with an air of gentle nobility, its fawn walking by its side. Rosanette would have liked to run after it to embrace it.

She got very much alarmed once, when a man suddenly appeared and showed her three vipers in a box. She flung herself wildly onto Frédéric's breast – he felt happy at the thought that she was weak and that he was strong enough to defend her.

That evening they dined at an inn on the banks of the Seine. The table was near the window, Rosanette sitting opposite him; and he gazed at her little fine white nose, her turned-up lips, her bright eyes, the swelling bands of her nutbrown hair, and her pretty oval face. Her dress of raw silk clung to her somewhat drooping shoulders; and her two hands, emerging from their plain cuffs, carved, poured out wine, moved over the tablecloth. They were served with a chicken with its four limbs stretched out, a stew of eels in a dish of pipeclay, rough wine, bread that was too hard, and knives with notches in them. All these things added to their pleasure and strengthened the illusion. They almost fancied they were on a journey, in Italy, on their honeymoon.

Before leaving, they went for a walk along the bank.

The soft blue sky, rounded like a dome, touched the horizon on the jagged edge of the woods. Opposite, at the end of the meadow, there was a village steeple; and further away, on the left, the roof of a house made a red patch on the river, which seemed immobile in all its sinuous length. Some rushes bent over it, however, and the water lightly shook some poles fixed at its edge in order to hold nets; a wicker eel-pot and two or three old fishing-boats were there. Near the inn a girl in a straw hat was drawing buckets out of a well; every time they came up, Frédéric heard the grating sound of the chain with a feeling of inexpressible delight.

He had no doubt that he would be happy till the end of his days, so natural did his felicity appear to him, so much a part of his life, and so intimately associated with the person of this woman. He was irresistibly impelled to address her with words of endearment. She answered him with pretty little speeches, light taps on the shoulder, displays of tenderness that charmed him by their unexpectedness. He discovered in her an entirely new sort of beauty, in fact, which was perhaps only the reflection of the surrounding things, unless it was their hidden potentialities that brought it to fruition.

When they were resting in the middle of the country fields, he would stretch himself out with his head on her lap, under the shelter of her parasol; or else, lying on their stomachs in the grass they stayed still, face to face, looking at each other, gazing into each other's eyes, thirsting for one another and ever satiating their thirst, and then with half-closed eyelids ceasing to speak.

Now and then the distant rolling of a drum reached their ears. It was the general alert which was being beaten in the different villages, calling on people to go and defend Paris.

'Ah, goodness! The riots!' said Frédéric, with a disdainful pity, all that agitation seeming pitiful to him compared with their love and eternal nature.

And they talked about whatever happened to come into their heads, things that were perfectly familiar to them, persons in whom they took no interest, a thousand trifles. She chatted with him about her chambermaid and her hairdresser. One day she forgot herself sufficiently to tell him her age: twenty-nine; she was getting old.

On several occasions, without intending it, she gave him details about herself. She had been a 'shop girl', had taken a trip to England, had begun studying for the stage; all this without transition, and he found it impossible to reconstruct an entire picture. She went into more detail one day when they were sitting under a plane tree at the edge of a meadow. At the roadside, further down, a little girl, barefoot in the dust, was grazing a cow. As soon as she caught sight of them, she came up to beg; and while with one hand she held her tattered petticoat, she kept scratching with the other at her black hair, which, like a wig of Louis XIV's time, curled round her dark face, which was lighted by a magnificent pair of eyes.

'She'll be very pretty by and by,' said Frédéric.

'How lucky she is, if she has no mother!' remarked Rosanette.

'Eh? How is that?'

'Oh yes; I, if it weren't for mine . . . '

She sighed, and began to speak about her childhood. Her parents were silk-weavers in the Croix-Rousse. She acted as an apprentice to her father. In vain did the poor man wear himself out with hard work, his wife was continually abusing him and sold everything for drink. Rosanette could see their room, with the looms ranged lengthwise against the windows, the stockpot on the stove, the bed painted like mahogany, a cupboard facing it, and the dark loft where she had slept till she was fifteen. At length a gentleman had come, a fat man with a face of the colour of boxwood, a sanctimonious manner and dressed in black. Her mother and he had a conversation together, with the result that three days afterwards . . . Rosanette stopped, and with a look as bitter as it was brazen:

'The job was done!'

Then, in response to a gesture of Frédéric's:

'As he was married (he would have been afraid of compromising himself in his own house), I was taken to a private room in a restaurant, and told that I would be happy, that I would get a lovely present.

'At the door, the first thing that struck me was a silver-gilt candelabra on a table, on which there were two covers. A mirror on the ceiling showed their reflections, and the blue silk hangings on the walls made the whole apartment look like an alcove. I was seized with astonishment. You understand, a poor creature who has never seen anything before! In spite of being dazzled, I was frightened. I wanted to go away. But I stayed.

'The only seat in the room was a sofa close beside the table. It was soft and gave way under me; the mouth of the hot-air vent in the carpet breathed warm air at me, and there I sat without taking anything. The waiter, who was standing near me, urged me to eat. He poured out for me immediately a large glass of wine; my head was swimming, I wanted to open the window. He said to me: "No, Mademoiselle! That is forbidden." And he left me. The table was covered with a heap of things that I had never seen before. Nothing seemed nice to me. So I fell back on a pot of jam, and kept on waiting. Something was keeping him. It was very late, midnight at least, I was tired out; pushing aside one of the pillows, in order to lie down more comfortably, I found under my hand a kind of album or notebook; they were obscene pictures . . . I was sleeping on top of it when he came in.'

She hung down her head and remained pensive.

The leaves rustled around them; in the tangled grass a great foxglove was swaying to and fro, the light flowed like a wave over the grass; and the silence was interrupted at rapid intervals by the browsing of the cow, which they could no longer see.

Rosanette kept her eyes fixed on a spot on the ground three paces away from her, her nostrils quivering, absorbed in thought. Frédéric caught hold of her hand.

'How you've suffered, poor darling!'

'Yes,' she said, 'more than you imagine! . . . So much so that I wanted to make an end of it; they fished me out.'

'What?'

'Ah! Think no more about it! . . . I love you, I am happy! Kiss me.'

And she picked off, one by one, the sprigs of the thistles which had stuck to the hem of her gown.

Frédéric was thinking more about what she had not told him. By what stages had she been able to emerge from poverty? To which of her lovers did she owe her education? What had occurred in her life down to the day when he had first come to her house? Her final avowal forbade these questions. All he asked her was how she had made Arnoux's acquaintance.

'Through Vatnaz.'

'Wasn't it you that I once saw with both of them at the Palais-Royal?'

He referred to the exact date. Rosanette made an effort to remember.

'Yes, it was! . . . I wasn't very happy at that time!'

But Arnoux had proved himself a very good fellow. Frédéric had no doubt of it; their friend was a queer character, though, full of faults; he took care to recall them. She agreed.

'Never mind! . . . He's very lovable, all the same, the old rascal!'

'Still – even now?' said Frédéric.

She began to blush, half smiling, half angry.

'Oh, no! That's ancient history. I don't keep anything hidden from you. Even if it were so, with him it's different! Besides, I don't think you're being very nice towards your victim.'

'My victim?'

Rosanette caught hold of his chin.

'Of course!'

And, dropping into baby-talk:

'We haven't always been a good boy! Went bye-byes with his wife!'

'I! Absolutely not!'

Rosanette smiled. He felt hurt by her smile, which seemed to him a proof of indifference. But she went on gently, and with one of those looks which seem to appeal for a denial of the truth:

'Honestly?'

'Absolutely!'

Frédéric declared on his word of honour that he had never bestowed a thought on Madame Arnoux, as he was too much in love with another.

'And who was that?'

'Why, you, my beautiful one!'

'Ah, don't laugh at me! You're making me cross!'

He thought it prudent to invent a story, some passion. He manufactured some circumstantial details. This woman, anyway, had made him very unhappy

'You really haven't had any luck!' said Rosanette.

'Oh! Oh! I may have had!' wishing to convey in this way that he had had several love affairs, so that she might have a better opinion of him, just as Rosanette did not tell him about all her lovers, in order that he might have more respect for her – for there are always restrictions in the midst of the most intimate confidences, through false shame, delicacy, or pity. You uncover either in the other or in yourself precipices or morasses which prevent you from going on; you feel, anyway, that you will not be understood; it is hard to express accurately anything at all; and so perfect unions are rare.

The poor Maréchale had never known one any better than this. Often, when she gazed at Frédéric, tears came into her eyes; then she would look up or cast a glance towards the horizon, as if she had glimpsed some bright dawn, perspectives of boundless felicity. At last, she confessed to him one day that she wished to have a mass said, 'so that it might bring good luck to our love'.

How was it, then, that she had resisted him so long? She could not tell herself. He repeated his question several times; and she replied, as she clasped him in her arms:

'It was because I was afraid of loving you too well, my darling!'

On Sunday morning, Frédéric read, amongst the list of the wounded in a newspaper, the name of Dussardier. He uttered a cry, and showing the paper to Rosanette, declared that he was going to start at once for Paris.

'To do what?'

'To see him, to look after him!'

'You're not going to leave me by myself, I hope?'

'Come with me.'

'Ha! To poke my nose into that mayhem! No thanks!'

'But I can't . . .'

'Ta! Ta! Ta! As if they were short of nurses in the hospitals!' And then, what business was it of his, what happened to Dussardier? Everyone for himself!

He was roused to indignation by this egoism; and he reproached himself for not being in the capital with the others. Such indifference to the misfortunes of the nation had in it something shabby and bourgeois. His love suddenly weighed on him as if it were a crime. For an hour they were cool towards each other.

Then she begged him to wait, not to expose himself to danger.

'Suppose you happen to be killed?'

'Well, I should only have done my duty!'

Rosanette gave a jump. His first duty was to love her. But no doubt he did not want anything more to do with her! There was no sense in it! Good heavens! What an idea!

Frédéric rang for the bill. But to get back to Paris was not easy. The Leloir stage coach had just left, the Lecomte berlins would not be leaving, the Bourbonnais coach would not be passing till late that night, and would perhaps be full; it was impossible to say. When he had lost a great deal of time in making these enquiries, the idea occurred to him to travel post. The master of the posthouse refused to supply him with horses, as Frédéric had no passport. Finally, he hired an open carriage (the same one in which they had driven about the country) and at about five o'clock they arrived at the Hôtel du Commerce at Melun.

The marketplace was covered with piles of arms. The prefect had forbidden the National Guards to proceed towards Paris. Those who did not belong to his department wished to go on. There was a great deal of shouting. The inn was in an uproar.

Rosanette, seized with fear, declared that she would not go on, and once more begged him to stay. The innkeeper and his wife joined in her entreaties. A decent sort of man who was dining there interposed, and assured them that the fighting would soon be over; besides, one ought to do one's duty. Thereupon the Maréchale sobbed more than ever. Frédéric got exasperated. He handed her his purse, kissed her quickly, and disappeared.

On reaching Corbeil, he learned at the station that the insurgents had cut the rails at various points and the coachman refused to drive him any farther; he said that his horses were 'done in'.

Through his influence, however, Frédéric managed to procure an indifferent cabriolet, which, for the sum of sixty francs, without counting the tip, agreed to convey him as far as the Barrière d'Italie. But at a hundred paces from the barrier his driver made him get out and turned round. Frédéric was walking along the road, when suddenly a sentinel thrust out his bayonet. Four men seized him, yelling:

'This is one of them! Look out! Search him! Brigand! Scoundrel!'

And he was so thoroughly amazed that he let himself be dragged to the guardhouse at the barrier, at the roundabout where the Boulevards des Gobelins and de l'Hôpital and the Rues Godefroy and Mouffetard converge.

Four barricades formed at the ends of the four ways enormous sloping ramparts of paving-stones; torches were spluttering here and there; in spite of the rising clouds of dust, he could make out footsoldiers of the Line and National Guards, all with their faces blackened, dishevelled, and wild-looking. They had just captured the square, and had shot a number of men; their rage had not yet cooled. Frédéric said he had come from Fontainebleau to help a wounded comrade who lodged in the Rue Bellefond; no one would believe him at first; they examined his hands, they even put their noses to his ear to make sure that he did not smell of powder.

However, by dint of repeating the same thing, he managed finally to convince a captain, who directed two fusiliers to conduct him to the guardhouse of the Jardin des Plantes.

They descended the Boulevard de l'Hôpital. A strong wind was blowing. It refreshed him.

After this they turned up the Rue du Marché-aux-Chevaux. The Jardin des Plantes on the right formed a large black mass, while on the left the entire front of the Pitié, illuminated at every window, blazed like a conflagration, and shadows passed rapidly over the windowpanes.

The two men in charge of Frédéric went away. Another accompanied him as far as the École Polytechnique.

The Rue Saint-Victor was quite dark, without a gas-lamp or a light at any window. Every ten minutes could be heard the words: 'Sentinels! On guard!' And this cry, cast into the midst of the silence, echoed like the repercussions of a stone falling into a pit.

Every now and then the stamp of heavy footsteps could be heard approaching. This was a patrol consisting of at least a hundred men; from this confused mass could be heard whisperings and a vague clinking of metal; and, moving away with a rhythmic swing, it melted into the darkness.

In the middle of the crossroads, a dragoon sat motionless on his horse. From time to time an express rider passed at a swift gallop, then all was silence once more. Cannons, moving along, made a heavy rolling sound on the paving that seemed full of menace; these sounds, so different from ordinary sounds, oppressed the heart. They seemed even to intensify the silence, which was profound, absolute – a black silence. Men in white overalls accosted the soldiers, spoke one or two words to them, and vanished like phantoms.

The guardhouse of the École Polytechnique overflowed with people. The threshold was blocked with women, asking to see their sons or their husbands. They were sent on to the Panthéon, which had been transformed into a morgue – and nobody listened to Frédéric. He persisted, swearing that his friend Dussardier was waiting for him, that he was at death's door. At last they sent a corporal to accompany him to the top of the Rue Saint-Jacques, to the town hall of the twelfth arrondissement.

The Place du Panthéon was full of soldiers lying on straw. The day was breaking. The bivouac-fires were going out.

The insurrection had left terrible traces in this area. The surface of the streets, from one end to the other, was covered with irregular bumps. Omnibuses, gas-pipes, and cartwheels remained on the wrecked barricades; little dark puddles, here and there, must have been blood. The houses were riddled with holes from missiles, and their framework showed under the shreds of plaster. Window-blinds, attached only by a nail, hung like rags. The staircases having fallen in, doors opened onto nothing. The interiors of rooms were plainly visible, with their wallpaper in shreds;

in some instances dainty objects had remained in them quite intact. Frédéric noticed a clock, a parrot's perch, and some engravings.

When he entered the town hall, the National Guards were chattering incessantly about the deaths of Bréa and Négrier, about the deputy Charbonnel, and about the Archbishop of Paris. He heard them say that the Duc d'Aumale had landed at Boulogne, that Barbès had fled from Vincennes, that the artillery were coming up from Bourges, and that abundant aid was arriving from the provinces. About three o'clock someone brought some good news; truce-bearers from the insurgents were in conference with the President of the Assembly.

Thereupon there was general rejoicing; and as he had a dozen francs left, Frédéric sent for a dozen bottles of wine, hoping by this means to hasten his deliverance. Suddenly they thought they heard shooting. The drinking stopped; they peered at the stranger with distrustful eyes; he might be Henry V.

In order to get rid of the responsibility, they took Frédéric to the town hall of the eleventh arrondissement, which he was not permitted to leave till nine o'clock in the morning.

He ran as far as the Quai Voltaire. At an open window an old man in his shirtsleeves was crying, with his eyes raised. The Seine glided peacefully along. There was a clear blue sky; and in the trees in the Tuileries birds were singing.

Frédéric was crossing the Place du Carrousel when a litter happened to pass by. The soldiers at the guardhouse immediately presented arms, and the officer, putting his hand to his shako, said: 'All honour to the gallant dead!' This phrase seemed to be almost obligatory; the person who pronounced it always seemed to be filled with a profound emotion. A group of people in a state of fierce excitement followed the litter, shouting:

'We will avenge you! We will avenge you!'

Carriages were driving about on the boulevard, and women were making lint in front of their doors. Meanwhile, the rising had been quelled, or very nearly so; a proclamation from Cavaignac, just posted up, announced the fact. At the top of the Rue Vivienne, a company of the Mobile Guards appeared. Then the bourgeois uttered cries of enthusiasm; they raised their hats, applauded, danced, wanted to embrace them, and to offer them a drink – and flowers, flung by ladies, fell from the balconies.

At last, at ten o'clock, at the moment when the cannon was booming in order to capture the Faubourg Saint-Antoine, Frédéric arrived at Dussardier's house. He found him in his garret, lying asleep on his back. From the adjoining room a woman came out with silent tread — Mademoiselle Vatnaz.

She led Frédéric aside and explained to him how Dussardier had got wounded.

On Saturday, on the top of a barricade in the Rue Lafayette, a young lad wrapped in a tricolore was calling out to the National Guards: 'Are you going to fire on your brothers!' As they were advancing, Dussardier had thrown down his gun, pushed the others away, leaped onto the barricade, and, with a well-directed kick, had knocked down the insurgent, from whom he tore the flag. He had been found under the rubble with a slug of copper in his thigh. It had been necessary to make an incision in the wound in order to extract the projectile. Mademoiselle Vatnaz had arrived the same evening, and since then had not left his side.

She skilfully prepared everything necessary for the dressings, helped him to drink, attended to his slightest wishes, came and went with footsteps lighter than a fly's, and gazed at him with eyes full of tenderness.

Frédéric, for two weeks, did not fail to come back every morning. One day while he was speaking about Vatnaz's devotion, Dussardier shrugged his shoulders.

'Oh, no! She does it out of self-interest!'

'Do you think so?'

He replied: 'I'm sure of it!' without committing himself to any further explanation.

She showered him with kindnesses, even bringing him the newspapers in which his gallant action was extolled. These praises seemed to embarrass him. He even confessed to Frédéric that he felt uneasy in his conscience.

Perhaps he ought to have put himself on the other side, with the workers; for, after all, they had been promised a heap of things which had not been carried out. Those who had vanquished them hated the Republic; and then they had been treated very harshly! No doubt they were in the wrong, but not entirely; and the honest fellow was tormented by the thought that he might have fought against the just cause.

Sénécal, who was immured in the Tuileries, under the terrace at the water's edge, had none of this mental anguish.

There they were, nine hundred men, herded together pell-mell, in the filth, their faces blackened with gunpowder and clotted blood, shivering with fever and uttering cries of rage; and those who happened to die were left there with the others. Sometimes, on hearing the sudden sound of a detonation, they thought they were all going to be shot; so they rushed to take shelter against the walls, then fell back again into their places, so stupefied by suffering that it seemed to them that they were living in a nightmare, a deathly hallucination. The lamp which hung from the arched roof looked like a stain of blood; and little green and yellow flames fluttered about, caused by the noxious gases rising from the cavern. Through fear of epidemics, a commission was appointed. Hardly had he taken a few steps, when the President recoiled, horrified by the stench of excrement and corpses. As soon as the prisoners drew near a vent-hole, the National Guards on duty – to stop them shaking the bars – thrust in their bayonets, stabbing at random into the heap of human flesh.

They were, generally, pitiless. Those who had not fought wished to acquire some distinction. There was an explosion of fear. They avenged themselves on everything at once, on the newspapers, the clubs, the gatherings, the doctrines, on everything that had exasperated them during the last three months; and in spite of the victory that had been gained, equality (as if to punish its defenders and expose its enemies to ridicule) manifested itself in a triumphal fashion as an equality of brute beasts, a dead level of bloody turpitude; for the fanaticism of self-interest balanced the madness of need, aristocracy was as rabid as the mob, and the cotton nightcap showed itself as no less hideous than the red cap. The public mind was disturbed as it is after great convulsions of nature. Men of wit and imagination were turned into idiots for the rest of their lives.

Père Roque had become very courageous, almost foolhardy. Having arrived in Paris on the 26th with the rest of the Nogent contingent, instead of going back at the same time as them, he had gone to give his assistance to the National Guard encamped in the Tuileries; and he was very pleased to be placed on guard in front of the terrace at the water's edge. There, at any rate, he had these brigands under his feet! He rejoiced in their defeat, in their humiliation, and could not resist uttering invectives against them.

One of them, a young lad with long fair hair, put his face to the bars, and asked for bread. M. Roque ordered him to hold his tongue. But the young man repeated in a mournful tone:

'Bread!'

'I haven't got any bread!'

Other prisoners appeared at the vent-hole, with their bristling beards, their burning eyes, all pushing forward, and yelling:

'Bread!'

Père Roque was indignant at seeing his authority flouted. In order to frighten them he took aim at them; and, carried up to the roof by the crush that nearly suffocated him, the young man, with his head thrown back, exclaimed once more:

'Bread!'

'Hold on! Here's some!' said Père Roque, firing a shot from his gun.

There was a fearful howl, then silence. On the edge of the bucket, something white was left lying.

After which, M. Roque went home; for he had a house in the Rue Saint-Martin, in which he had reserved a temporary residence for himself; and the injury done to the front of his building by the uprising had contributed in no slight degree to excite his rage. It seemed to him, when he next saw it, that he had exaggerated the amount of damage. His recent action had a soothing effect on him, as if it indemnified him for his loss.

It was his daughter herself who opened the door for him. She immediately told him that she had felt uneasy at his prolonged absence; she had been afraid that he had met with some misfortune, that he had been wounded.

This manifestation of filial love touched Père Roque. He was astonished that she should have set out on a journey without Catherine.

'I've sent her out on an errand,' was Louise's reply.

And she asked about his health, about one thing or another; then, with an air of indifference, she asked him whether he had chanced to come across Frédéric:

'No! No sign of him!'

It was on his account alone that she had come up from the country.

They heard a step in the passage.

'Oh! Excuse me . . . '

And she disappeared.

Catherine had not found Frédéric. He had been away for several days, and his intimate friend, M. Deslauriers, was now living in the provinces.

Louise came back shaking all over, without being able to speak. She leaned against the furniture.

'What's the matter? Tell me, what's the matter?' exclaimed her father.

She indicated by a wave of her hand that it was nothing, and with a great effort of will she regained her composure.

The caterer across the street brought their soup. But Père Roque had experienced too violent an emotion. 'It stuck in his throat' and at dessert he had a sort of fainting fit. A doctor was at once sent for, and he prescribed a potion. Then, when M. Roque was in bed, he asked to be as well wrapped up as possible in order to make him sweat. He sighed, he moaned.

'Thanks, my good Catherine! Kiss your poor father, my chicken! Ah, these revolutions!'

And, when his daughter scolded him for having made himself ill by tormenting his mind on her account, he replied:

'Yes! You're right! But I can't help it! I'm too sensitive!'

Madame Dambreuse, in her boudoir, between her niece and Miss Johnson, was listening to M. Roque as he described the severe military duties he had been forced to perform.

She was biting her lips, and appeared to be in pain.

'Oh! It's nothing! It will pass!'

And, with a gracious air:

'We are going to have an acquaintance of yours at dinner – Monsieur Moreau.'

Louise gave a start.

'Then just a few intimate friends, Alfred de Cisy, among others.'

And she praised his manners, his personal appearance, and especially his moral character.

Madame Dambreuse was lying less than she thought; the Vicomte was contemplating marriage. He had said so to Martinon, adding that Mademoiselle Cécile was certain to like him, and that her parents would accept him.

To risk such a confidence, he must have satisfactory information with regard to her dowry. Now, Martinon suspected Cécile of being M. Dambreuse's natural daughter; and it would have been, probably, a very good move on his part to ask for her hand on the off-chance. Such audacity, of course, was not unaccompanied by dangers; and for this reason Martinon had, up to the present, acted in a way that could not compromise him; besides, he did not see how to get rid of the aunt. Cisy's confidence decided him; and he had made his proposal to the banker, who, seeing no objection, had just informed Madame Dambreuse about the matter.

Cisy appeared. She arose and said:

'You have been neglecting us . . . Cécile, shake hands!'

At the same moment Frédéric came in.

Ah! At last! We've found you again!' exclaimed Père Roque. 'I called on you three times this week, with Louise!'

Frédéric had carefully avoided them. He pleaded by way of excuse that he spent all his days with a wounded comrade. For a long time, anyway, he had been tied up with various matters; and he tried to concoct some plausible narrative. Luckily the guests arrived; first M. Paul de Grémonville, the diplomat whom he had met briefly at the ball; then Fumichon, the manufacturer whose conservative zeal had scandalised him one evening; after them came the old Duchesse de Montreuil-Nantua.

But two voices were raised in the anteroom.

'I'm certain of it,' said one.

'Dear lady! Dear lady!' replied the other, 'please, calm yourself!'

The voices belong to M. de Nonancourt, an old beau who looked like a mummy preserved in cold cream, and Madame de Larsillois, the wife of a prefect of Louis-Philippe. She was terribly frightened, for she had just heard an organ playing a polka which was a signal amongst the insurgents. Many of the wealthy class of citizens had similar apprehensions; they thought that men in the catacombs were going to blow up the Faubourg Saint-Germain; noises were heard, escaping from cellars; strange things happened at windows.

Everyone in the meantime tried to calm Madame de Larsillois. Order was re-established. There was no longer anything to fear. 'Cavaignac has saved us!' As if the horrors of the insurrection had not been sufficiently numerous, they exaggerated them. There had been twenty-three thousand convicts on the side of the socialists – no less!

They had no doubt whatever that food had been poisoned, that Mobile Guards had been sawn between two planks, and that there had been inscriptions on flags inciting the people to pillage and arson.

'And something more!' added the ex-prefect's wife.

'Oh, my dear!' said Madame Dambreuse out of propriety, with a meaningful glance towards the three young girls.

M. Dambreuse came out of his study with Martinon. She turned her head away and responded to a bow from Pellerin, who was advancing towards her. The artist was gazing anxiously at the walls. The banker took him aside, and conveyed to him that he had had, for the present, to conceal his revolutionary picture.

'Of course!' said Pellerin, the rebuff which he had received at the Club of the Intellect having modified his opinions.

M. Dambreuse let slip very politely that he would give him orders for other works.

'But excuse me! . . . Ah! My dear friend! What a pleasure!'

Arnoux and Madame Arnoux stood before Frédéric.

His head spun. Rosanette had been irritating him all afternoon with her display of admiration for the soldiers; and the old love revived.

The butler came to announce that madam was served. With a look she directed the Vicomte to take Cécile's arm, said in a low tone to Martinon, 'You wretch!' and they passed into the dining-room.

Under the green leaves of a pineapple, in the middle of the tablecloth, a John Dory was lying, with its snout reaching towards a haunch of venison and its tail just grazing a heap of crayfish. Figs, huge cherries, pears and grapes (the first fruits of Parisian culti-vation) rose in pyramids in baskets of old Dresden china; here and there a bunch of flowers could be seen among the shining silver plate; the white silk blinds, drawn down in front of the windows, filled the apartment with a mellow light; it was cooled by two fountains, in which were pieces of ice; and tall menservants, in short breeches, waited on them. All these luxuries seemed more precious after the emotion of recent events. They were enjoying once more the things which they had been afraid of losing; and Nonancourt expressed the general sentiment when he said:

'Ah! Let us hope that these Republican gentlemen will allow us to dine!'

'In spite of their fraternity!' Père Roque added, wittily.

These two honourable personages were placed respectively to the right and left of Madame Dambreuse, who had her husband opposite, between Madame de Larsillois, at whose side was the diplomat, and the old Duchesse, who was elbow to elbow with Fumichon. Then came the painter, the ceramics dealer, and Mademoiselle Louise, and thanks to Martinon, who had taken his place in order to sit beside Cécile, Frédéric found himself next to Madame Arnoux.

She wore a black barège gown, a gold hoop on her wrist, and, as on the first day that he had dined at her house, something red in her hair, a branch of fuchsia twisted round her chignon. He could not help saying:

'It's a long time since we met!'

'Ah!' she returned coldly.

He went on, with a tenderness in his voice which mitigated the impertinence of his question:

'Have you thought of me sometimes?'

'Why should I think of you?'

Frédéric was hurt by these words.

'Perhaps you're right, after all.'

But very soon, regretting what he had said, he swore that he had not lived a single day without being ravaged by her memory.

'I don't believe a word of it, Monsieur.'

'But you know I love you.'

Madame Arnoux made no reply.

'You know I love you.'

She still kept silent.

'Well, then, go be hanged!' said Frédéric to himself.

And, as he raised his eyes, he noticed Mademoiselle Roque at the other end of the table.

She had thought she would look nice dressed entirely in green, a colour which swore horribly with her red hair. The buckle of her belt was too large and her collar cramped her neck; this lack of elegance had, no doubt, contributed to the coldness with which Frédéric had greeted her. She watched him intently from afar; and Arnoux, by her side, in vain lavished his gallantries – he could not get her to utter three words, so that, finally abandoning all hope of making himself agreeable to her, he listened to the conversation. It was concerned at present with the pineapple purees served at the Luxembourg.

Louis Blanc, according to Fumichon, owned a large house in the Rue Saint-Dominique, which he refused to let to workmen.

'For my part, what I find funny,' said Nonancourt, 'is Ledru-Rollin hunting over the Crown lands!'

'He owes twenty thousand francs to a goldsmith!' Cisy added; 'and it is even maintained . . . '

Madame Dambreuse stopped him.

'Ah! How nasty it is to be getting hot about politics! And for such a young man, too, fie, fie! Pay attention rather to your fair neighbour!'

After this, those who were of a serious turn of mind attacked the newspapers.

Arnoux defended them; Frédéric joined the discussion, describing them as commercial establishments just like any other. Those who wrote for them were, as a rule, idiots or humbugs; he gave his listeners to understand that he was acquainted with them, and combated with sarcasms the generous sentiments of his friend. Madame Arnoux did not notice that this was a revenge against her.

Meanwhile, the Vicomte was torturing his brain in the attempt to make a conquest of Mademoiselle Cécile. He began by demonstrating his artistic tastes, finding fault with the shape of the decanters and the engraving on the knives. Then he talked about his stable, his tailor and his shirtmaker; finally, he broached the subject of religion, and found a way of letting her know that he fulfilled all his duties.

Martinon showed greater finesse. With his eyes fixed on her continually, he praised, in a monotonous fashion, her birdlike profile, her dull fair hair, and her hands, which were too short. The plain-looking young girl revelled in this shower of compliments.

It was impossible to hear anything, as all present were talking at the tops of their voices. M. Roque wanted 'an iron hand' to govern France. Nonancourt even regretted that the death penalty for political crimes had been abolished. All those scoundrels ought to have been put to death in a body!

'And they're cowards,' said Fumichon. 'I can't see anything brave in skulking behind barricades!'

'Speaking of which, do tell us about Dussardier!' said M. Dambreuse, turning towards Frédéric.

The worthy clerk was now a hero, like Sallesse, the Jeanson brothers, the Péquillet woman, etc.

Nothing loth, Frédéric related his friend's story; it gave him some reflected glory.

Then they came quite naturally to recount different traits of courage. According to the diplomat, it was not hard to face death, witness the case of men who fight duels.

'We could take the Vicomte's testimony on that point,' said Martinon.

The Vicomte turned very red.

The guests stared at him; and Louise, more astonished than the rest, murmured:

'Whatever is it?'

'He *got cold feet* before Frédéric,' returned Arnoux, in a low voice.

'Do you know anything about this, Mademoiselle?' asked Nonancourt immediately; and he repeated her answer to Madame Dambreuse, who, bending forward a little, began to look at Frédéric.

Martinon did not wait for Cécile's questions. He informed her that this affair had reference to a woman of improper character. The young girl drew back slightly in her chair, as if to shun all contact with this libertine.

Conversation had begun once more. The great wines of Bordeaux were circulating, and the guests became animated; Pellerin had a grudge against the Revolution because of the Spanish Museum, now lost for good. That was what grieved him most, as a painter. At this M. Roque addressed him:

'Are you by any chance the painter of a very notable picture?'

'Perhaps! Which one?'

'It represents a lady in a costume . . . my word! . . . A little . . . scanty, with a purse, and a peacock behind.'

Frédéric, in his turn, reddened. Pellerin pretended that he had not heard.

'But it's definitely by you! For your name is written at the bottom, and there's a line on the frame stating that it belongs to Monsieur Moreau.'

One day, when Père Roque and his daughter were waiting at his residence to see him, they had seen the Maréchale's portrait. The old gentleman had even taken it for 'a Gothic painting'.

'No!' said Pellerin roughly; 'it's the portrait of a woman.'

Martinon added:

'And a woman who's very much alive! Isn't that so, Cisy?'

'Oh! I know nothing about it.'

'I thought you knew her. But, if it upsets you, I do beg your pardon!'

Cisy lowered his eyes, proving by his embarrassment that he must have played a pitiable part in connection with this portrait. As for Frédéric, the model could only be his mistress. It was one of those inferences which are immediately drawn, and the faces of the assembly revealed it with the utmost clarity.

'How he lied to me!' said Madame Arnoux to herself.

'That explains why he left me!' thought Louise.

Frédéric had an idea that these two stories might compromise him; and when they were in the garden, he uttered reproaches to Martinon on the subject.

Mademoiselle Cécile's wooer burst out laughing in his face.

'Oh, not at all! It'll be a help! Press on!'

What did he mean? Besides, what was the cause of this good nature, so contrary to his usual conduct? Without giving any explanation, he proceeded towards the lower end of the garden, where the ladies were seated. The men were standing, and, in their midst, Pellerin was holding forth. The form of government most favourable for the arts was an enlightened monarchy. He was disgusted with the modern world, 'if only on account of the National Guard', he regretted the Middle Ages and the days of Louis XIV; M. Roque congratulated him on his opinions, confessing, even, that they confounded all his prejudices against artists. But he moved away almost immediately, drawn by the voice of Fumichon. Arnoux was trying to establish that there are two socialisms, a good one and a bad one. The manufacturer saw no difference between them, his head becoming dizzy with rage at the word 'property'.

'It's a law written on the face of nature! Children cling to their toys; all peoples, all animals are of my opinion; the lion even, if he could speak, would declare himself a property-owner! Thus I myself, messieurs, began with a capital of fifteen thousand francs! For thirty years , you know, I used to get up at four o'clock every morning. I've had the absolute devil of a job to make my fortune! And you'll come and tell me I'm not the master of it, that my money is not my money, in short, that property is theft!'

'But Proudhon . . . '

'Leave me in peace with your Proudhon! If he were here I think I'd strangle him!'

He would have strangled him. Especially after liqueurs, Fumichon lost all control; and his apoplectic face was on the point of bursting like a bombshell.

'Good day, Arnoux,' said Hussonnet, who was walking briskly over the grass.

Our Bohemian was bringing M. Dambreuse the first leaf of a pamphlet entitled 'The Hydra', since he now defended the interests of a reactionary club, and in that capacity he was introduced by the banker to his guests.

Hussonnet amused them, first by relating how the dealers in tallow hired three hundred and ninety-two boys to bawl out every evening 'Lamps!', and then mocking the principles of '89, the emancipation of the negroes, and the orators of the Left; he even went so far as to do 'Prudhomme on a Barricade', perhaps under the influence of a naïve jealousy of these rich bourgeois who had enjoyed a good dinner. The caricature did not please them over-much. Their faces grew long.

This, moreover, was no time for joking; so Nonancourt said, as he recalled the death of Monseigneur Affre and that of General Bréa. These deaths were on everyone's lips; they were constantly cited as proofs. M. Roque declared the Archbishop's demise 'The epitome of the sublime'. Fumichon gave the palm to the soldier; and instead of simply deploring these two murders, they argued over which should excite the greatest indignation. A second comparison followed, between Lamoricière and Cavaignac, M. Dambreuse praising Cavaignac, and Nonancourt Lamoricière. Not one of the persons present, with the exception of Arnoux, had ever seen either of them engaged in action. None the less they all formulated an irrevocable judgment with reference to their operations. Frédéric had declined to give an opinion, confessing that he had not fought. The diplomat and M. Dambreuse gave him an approving nod of the head. Indeed, to have fought against the insurrection was to have defended the Republic. The result, although favourable, consolidated it; and now that they had got rid of the vanquished, they wanted to be rid of the victors.

Hardly had they got out into the garden when Madame Dambreuse, taking Cisy aside, had chided him for his clumsiness; when she caught sight of Martinon, she sent Cisy away, and then tried to learn from her future nephew the reason for his jokes at the Vicomte's expense.

'There is no reason.'

'And all this as if for the greater glory of M. Moreau! To what end?'

'None. Frédéric is a charming fellow. I'm very fond of him.'

'And so am I! Let him come here! Go and get him!'

After two or three commonplace phrases, she began by lightly disparaging her guests, which was to place him on a higher level than them. He did not fail to denigrate the rest of the ladies a little, which was an ingenious way of paying her compliments. But she left him from time to time, as it was a reception night, and ladies were arriving; then she returned to her seat, and the entirely fortuitous arrangement of the chairs enabled them to avoid being overheard.

She showed herself playful and yet grave, melancholy and yet reasonable. The problems of the day interested her very little; there was a whole order of sentiments of a less transitory kind. She complained of the poets who misrepresent truth, then raised her eyes towards heaven, asking him the name of a star.

Two or three Chinese lanterns had been suspended from the trees; the wind shook them, and lines of coloured light quivered over her white dress. She sat, after her usual fashion, a little back in her armchair, with a footstool in front of her; the tip of a black satin shoe was visible; and at intervals Madame Dambreuse allowed a louder word than usual, and sometimes even a laugh, to escape her.

These coquetries did not impinge on Martinon, who was occupied with Cécile; but they did strike M. Roque's daughter, who was chatting with Madame Arnoux. She was the only one, among all these women, whose manners did not seem to her disdainful. Louise had come and sat beside her; then, yielding to the desire to confide:

'Doesn't he speak well, Frédéric Moreau?'

'Do you know him?'

'Oh! Very well! We're neighbours – he used to play with me when I was a little girl.'

Madame Arnoux cast her a long look which signified:

'You're not in love with him, I suppose?'

The young girl's eyes replied with an untroubled 'Yes'.

'You see him often, then?'

'Oh, no! Only when he comes to stay with his mother. It's ten months now since he came! Yet he promised to be more particular.'

'The promises of men are not to be too much relied on, my child.'

'But he hasn't deceived me!'

'As he did others!'

Louise shivered: 'Can it be by any chance that he promised something to her?' and her features became contorted with distrust and hatred.

Madame Arnoux was almost afraid of her; she would have gladly withdrawn what she said. Then both became silent.

As Frédéric was sitting opposite them on a folding stool, they observed him, the one with propriety, out of the corner of her eye, the other frankly, with open mouth, so that Madame Dambreuse said to him:

'Come, now, turn round, so she can see you!'

'Whom do you mean?'

'Why, Monsieur Roque's daughter!'

And she laughed at him for having won the heart of this young provincial. He denied it, and tried to make light of it.

'Is it credible, I ask you! Such a plain Jane!'

Nevertheless, he experienced an intense feeling of gratified vanity. He recalled to mind the other party, the one he had left with his heart filled with bitter humiliation; and he drew a deep breath; it seemed to him that he was now in the environment that really suited him, almost his own domain, as if all these things, including the Dambreuse mansion, had belonged to himself. The ladies formed a semicircle around him while they listened to him, and in order to shine, he declared that he was in favour of the re-establishment of divorce, which should be easy enough for people to be able to leave each other and come back to one another indefinitely, as often as they liked. They uttered loud protests; a few of them began to whisper; there were little exclamations in the shadows, at the foot of the wall covered with aristolochia. It was like the cackle of happy hens; and he developed his theory with that aplomb which is generated by the consciousness of success. A manservant brought into the arbour a tray laden with ices. The gentlemen joined them. They were talking about the arrests.

Thereupon Frédéric revenged himself on the Vicomte by making him believe that he might be prosecuted as a Legitimist. The other objected that he had not stirred from his room; his adversary enumerated all the possible mischances; even M. Dambreuse and M. de Grémonville were amused. Then they paid Frédéric compliments, while expressing regret at the same time that he did not employ his abilities in the defence of order; and they shook his hand with the utmost warmth; he might for the future count on them. At last, as everyone was leaving, the Vicomte made a low bow to Cécile.

'Mademoiselle, I have the honour of wishing you a very good evening.'

She replied coldly:

'Good evening!' But she gave Martinon a smile.

Père Roque, in order to continue his discussion with Arnoux, offered to see him home, 'as well as Madame', since they were going the same way. Louise and Frédéric walked in front. She had caught hold of his arm; and, when she was some distance away from the others:

'Ah! At last! At last! What an awful time I've had all evening! How nasty those women are! What haughty airs they give themselves!'

He made an effort to defend them.

'For a start, you might have spoken to me when you came in, after being away a whole year!'

'It isn't a year,' said Frédéric, glad to be able to take her up on this point in order to avoid the others.

'All right! The time appeared very long to me, that's all! But, during this dreadful dinner, it was as if you felt ashamed of me! Ah! I understand, I haven't got what it takes to please as they do.'

'You're wrong,' said Frédéric.

'Really! Swear to me that you don't love any of them?'

He swore.

'And it's only me that you love?'

'Naturally!'

This assurance filled her with delight. She would have liked to get lost in the streets, so that they might walk about together the whole night.

'I've been so worried at home! All everybody talked about was barricades! I imagined I saw you falling on your back covered with blood! Your mother was in bed with rheumatism. She knew nothing about what was happening. I had to hold my tongue! I could stand it no longer! So I took Catherine with me.'

And she told him all about her departure, all the details of her journey, and the lie she had told her father.

'He's taking me home in two days. Come tomorrow evening, as if you were just dropping in, and take advantage of the opportunity to ask for my hand in marriage.'

Never had Frédéric been further from the idea of marriage. Anyway, Mademoiselle Roque appeared to him a rather absurd little person. How different she was from a woman like Madame

Dambreuse! A very different future was in store for him! He was sure of it today; and, therefore, this was not the time to involve himself, from mere sentimental motives, in a step of such momentous importance. It was necessary now to be positive about things – and then he had seen Madame Arnoux again. Nevertheless he was rather embarrassed by Louise's candour. He replied:

'Have you carefully considered this matter?'

'What!' she exclaimed, frozen with surprise and indignation.

He said that to marry at such a time as this would be folly.

'So you don't want to have me?'

'But, you don't understand what I'm saying!'

And he plunged into a confused mass of verbiage in order to impress upon her the fact that he was kept back by serious considerations, that he had huge amounts of business to attend to, that even his inheritance had been placed in jeopardy (Louise cut all this explanation short with one plain word), that, last of all, the present political situation made the thing undesirable. So, then, the most reasonable course was to be patient for a while. Matters would, no doubt, right themselves; at least, he hoped so; and, as he had run out of reasons, he pretended to have suddenly remembered that he should have been with Dussardier two hours ago.

Then, having said goodbye to the others, he darted down the Rue Hauteville, took a turn round the Gymnase, returned to the boulevard, and ran up Rosanette's four flights.

M. and Madame Arnoux left Père Roque and his daughter at the entrance to the Rue Saint-Denis. They returned home in silence; he worn out from all his talking, she feeling a great weariness; she even leaned against his shoulder. He was the only man who had displayed any honourable sentiments during the evening. She felt full of indulgence towards him. However, he still felt rather aggrieved towards Frédéric.

'Did you see his face when they were talking about the portrait? Didn't I tell you that he is her lover? You wouldn't believe me!'

'Oh, yes! I was wrong!'

Arnoux, gratified with his triumph, pressed the matter further.

'I'd even bet that when he left us, a little while ago, it was to go and see her! He's with her at this moment, you may be sure! He's spending the night with her.'

Madame Arnoux had pulled down her hood very low.

'Why, you're shaking!'

'That's because I'm cold!' was her reply.

As soon as her father was asleep, Louise made her way into Catherine's room, and, shaking her by the shoulder:

'Get up! Quick! As quick as ever you can! Go and fetch me a cab.'

Catherine replied that there was not one to be had at this hour.

'You take me there yourself, then!'

'But where?'

'To Frédéric's house!'

'You can't be serious! What do you want to go there for?'

It was to have a talk with him. She could not wait. She must see him immediately.

'What an idea! Turning up like that at a house in the middle of the night! Anyway, he'll be asleep by this time!'

'I'll wake him up!'

'But this is not a proper thing for a young girl!'

'I'm not a young girl! I'm his wife! I love him! Come on, put your shawl on.'

Catherine, standing at the side of the bed, was trying to make up her mind. She said at last:

'No! I won't!'

'Well, stay here then! I'm going!'

Louise slid like a snake towards the staircase. Catherine rushed after her, and came up with her on the pavement. Her remonstrances were fruitless; and she followed the girl, still fastening her dressing-jacket. The walk appeared to her very long. She complained about her old legs.

'After all, I haven't got the same thing as you to drive me on, for goodness' sake!'

Then she softened.

'Poor soul! Your old Katy is still your best friend, you see.'

From time to time she was visited by scruples.

'Ah, this is a nice thing you're making me do! Suppose your father woke up! Dear Lord! Let's hope no misfortune will happen!'

In front of the Théâtre des Variétés, a patrol of National Guards stopped them. Louise immediately explained that she was going with her servant to look for a doctor in the Rue Rumfort. The patrol allowed them to pass on.

At the corner of the Madeleine they came across a second patrol, and, Louise having given the same explanation, one of the citizens asked in return:

'Is it for a nine months' ailment, ducky?'

'Gougibaud!' cried the captain. 'No smut in the ranks! Pass on, ladies!'

In spite of the captain's orders, they still kept up their witticisms.

'Have a lovely time!'

'My respects to the doctor!'

'Beware of the wolf!'

'They like to have a joke,' Catherine remarked aloud. 'That's what it is to be young!'

At length they reached Frédéric's house. Louise gave the bell a vigorous pull, which she repeated several times. The door opened slightly, and, in answer to her inquiry, the porter said:

'No!'

'But he must be in bed?'

'I tell you he's not! It's now nearly three months that he hasn't slept at home!'

And the little window of the lodge fell down sharply, like the blade of a guillotine. They remained in the darkness under the archway. An angry voice cried out to them:

'Be off then!'

The door opened; they went out.

Louise had to sit down on a boundary-stone; and clasping her face with her hands, she wept copious tears, with all her full heart. The day was breaking, and carts were passing.

Catherine took her home, holding her up, kissing her, and offering her every sort of consolation that she could extract from her own experience. She mustn't take on so about a lover. If this one failed her, she could find others.

CHAPTER THREE

When Rosanette's enthusiasm for the Mobile Guards had calmed down, she became more charming than ever, and Frédéric insensibly glided into the habit of living with her.

The best part of the day was the morning on their terrace. In a light cambric dress, and with her stockingless feet thrust into slippers, she came and went around him, cleaned her canaries' cage, gave her goldfishes some water, and with a fire-shovel did a little gardening in the box filled with earth, from which rose a trellis of nasturtiums which grew over the wall. Then, leaning on their balcony, they stood side by side, gazing at the carriages and the passers-by; and they warmed themselves in the sun, and made plans for the evening. He absented himself for two hours at most; after that, they would go to some theatre, where they would get seats in the stage boxes; and Rosanette, with a large bouquet of flowers in her hand, would listen to the instruments, while Frédéric, leaning close to her ear, would tell her funny or affectionate things. At other times, they took an open carriage to drive to the Bois de Boulogne; they would stay out late, until the middle of the night. At last they would come back through the Arc de Triomphe and the main avenue, drinking in the air, with the stars above their heads, and with all the gas-lamps ranged as far as the eye could see like a double string of luminous pearls.

Frédéric always waited for her when they were going out; she was a very long time fastening the two ribbons of her bonnet around her chin; and she smiled at herself in the wardrobe mirror. Then she would tuck her arm in his, and, making him look at himself in the glass beside her:

'We look well like this, the two of us side by side! Ah! My poor darling, I could eat you!'

He was now her chattel, her property. She wore on her face a continuous radiance, while at the same time she appeared more languorous in manner, rounder in her figure; and, without being able to explain in what way, he found her altered, nevertheless.

One day she informed him, as if it were a very important bit of news, that friend Arnoux had lately set up a linen-draper's shop for a woman who used to be employed in his factory; he went there every evening, 'spent a great deal, only a week ago he had even given her a set of rosewood furniture'.

'How do you know?' said Frédéric.

'Oh! I'm sure of it!'

Delphine, carrying out her orders, had made enquiries. She must, then, be much attached to Arnoux, to take such a deep interest in his movements! He contented himself with saying to her in reply:

'What does that matter to you?'

Rosanette looked surprised at this question.

'Why, the rascal owes me money! Isn't it atrocious to see him keeping tarts!'

Then, with an expression of triumphant hatred in her face:

'Besides, she's having a nice laugh at him! She has three others on hand. So much the better! And I'll be glad if she eats him up, even to the last farthing!'

Arnoux was, in fact, letting himself be exploited by the Bordelaise with the indulgence which characterises senile attachments.

His factory was no longer operating; the entire state of his affairs was pitiable; so that, in order to set them afloat again, he thought at first of creating a *café chantant*, at which only patriotic pieces would be sung; with a grant from the Minister, this establishment would have become at the same time a focus for the purpose of propaganda and a source of profit. Now that power had been directed into a different channel, the thing was impossible. Now, his idea was a big military hat-making business. He lacked capital, however, to give it a start.

He was no more fortunate in his domestic life. Madame Arnoux was less agreeable in manner towards him, sometimes even a little rough. Marthe always took her father's part. This increased the discord, and the house was becoming intolerable. He often left it in the morning, passed his day making long excursions out of the city, in order to divert his thoughts, then dined at a rustic tavern, abandoning himself to his reflections.

The prolonged absence of Frédéric disturbed his habits. So he turned up one afternoon, begged of him to come and see him as he used to, and obtained from him a promise to do so.

Frédéric did not dare go back to see Madame Arnoux. It seemed to him as if he had betrayed her. But this conduct was very pusillanimous. He could think of no excuses. He would have to come to it in the end! And so, one evening, he set out on his way.

As the rain was falling, he had just turned into the Passage Jouffroy, when, in the light from the shop-windows, a fat little man in a cap accosted him.

Frédéric had no difficulty in recognising Compain, that orator whose proposal had excited so much laughter at the club. He was leaning on the arm of an individual whose head was muffled in a zouave's red cap, with a very long upper lip, a complexion as yellow as an orange, a tuft of beard over his chin, and who gazed at him with big staring eyes glistening with admiration.

Compain was, no doubt, proud of him, for he said:

'Let me introduce you to this jolly dog! He's a bootmaker, one of my friends, a patriot! Shall we have a drink?'

Frédéric having declined, he immediately thundered against the Rateau proposition, a manoeuvre of the aristocrats. They'd have to start '93 over again, to put an end to this sort of thing! Then he enquired about Regimbart and a few others who were equally well known, such as Masselin, Sanson, Lecornu, Maréchal, and a certain Deslauriers, who had been implicated in the case of the carbines lately intercepted in Troyes.

All this was new to Frédéric. Compain knew nothing more about the subject. He left him with these words:

'We'll meet again soon, won't we? For you belong to it.'

'To what?'

'The calf's head!'

'What calf's head?'

'Ha, you rogue!' returned Compain, giving him a tap in the stomach.

And the two terrorists plunged into a café.

Ten minutes later Frédéric was no longer thinking of Deslauriers. He was on the footpath of the Rue Paradis in front of a house; and he was staring at the light which came from a lamp on the second floor behind some curtains.

At length he climbed the stairs.

'Is Arnoux there?'

The chambermaid answered:

'No! But come in all the same.'

And, abruptly opening a door:

'Madame, it is Monsieur Moreau!'

She arose, whiter than the collar round her neck. She was trembling.

To what do I owe the honour . . . of a visit . . . so unexpected?'

'Nothing! The pleasure of seeing old friends again!'

And as he took a seat:

'How is dear Arnoux?'

'Very well! He has gone out.'

'Ah! I understand! Still following his old nightly practices; a little distraction!'

'And why not? After a day spent in making calculations, the head needs a rest!'

She even praised her husband as a hardworking man. Frédéric was irritated at hearing this eulogy; and pointing towards a piece of black cloth with blue braids which lay on her lap:

'What is it you're doing there?'

'It's a jacket which I'm trimming for my daughter.'

'Now that you remind me of it, I don't see her. Where is she, pray?'

'At a boarding-school,' was Madame Arnoux's reply

Tears came into her eyes; she held them back, while she rapidly plied her needle. To keep himself in countenance, he had taken up a number of *L'Illustration* which lay on the table close to where she sat.

'These caricatures of Cham are very funny, aren't they?'

'Yes.'

Then they relapsed into their silence.

All of a sudden, a fierce gust of wind shook the windowpanes.

'What weather!' said Frédéric.

'It was very good of you, indeed, to have come here in the midst of this dreadful rain!'

'Oh! What do I care about that! I'm not like those whom it prevents, no doubt, from going to keep their appointments!'

'What appointments?' she asked, innocently.

'Don't you remember?'

A shudder ran through her frame and she lowered her head.

He gently laid his hand on her arm.

'I assure you that you caused me great suffering!'

She replied, with a sort of wail in her voice:

'But I was frightened for my child!'

She told him about little Eugène's illness, and all the tortures of that day.

'Thank you! Thank you! I doubt you no longer! I love you as much as ever!'

'Ah no! That's not true!'

'Why?'

She looked at him coldly.

'You forget the other! The one you take to the races with you! The woman whose portrait you have, your mistress!'

'Well, yes!' exclaimed Frédéric, 'I don't deny anything! I'm a wretch! Listen to me!' If he had taken her, it was through despair, as one commits suicide. Anyway, he had made her very unhappy in order to avenge himself on her for his own shame. 'What torment! Don't you understand?'

Madame Arnoux turned her beautiful face while she held out her hand to him; and they closed their eyes, absorbed in a kind of intoxication that was like being cradled sweetly and forever. Then they stayed face to face, gazing at one another, side by side.

'Could you believe that I no longer loved you?'

She replied in a low voice, full of caressing tenderness:

'No! In spite of everything, I felt at the bottom of my heart that that was impossible, and that one day the obstacle between us two would disappear!'

'So did I! And I yearned so to see you again, I could have died!'

'Once', she said, 'I passed close to you in the Palais-Royal!'

'Did you really?'

And he spoke to her of the happiness he had experienced at finding her again at the Dambreuses' house.

'But how I hated you that evening as I was leaving the place!'

'Poor boy!'

'My life is so sad!'

'And mine, too! . . . If it were only the vexations, the anxieties, the humiliations, all that I endure as wife and as mother, seeing that one must die, I wouldn't complain; the frightful part of it is my solitude, without anyone . . . '

'But I'm here!'

'Oh! Yes!'

A sob of deep emotion had brought her to her feet. She spread out her arms; and they stood embracing, while their lips met in a long kiss.

A floorboard creaked. A woman stood near them, Rosanette. Madame Arnoux had recognised her; her eyes, opened to their widest, scanned this woman, full of surprise and indignation. At length Rosanette said to her:

'I've come to see Monsieur Arnoux about a matter of business.'

'He isn't here, as you see.'

'Ah! That's true!' returned the Maréchale. 'Your maid was right! I do apologize!'

And turning towards Frédéric:

'What are you doing here, sweetie?'

The familiar tone in which she addressed him, and in her own presence, too, made Madame Arnoux flush as if she had received a slap right across the face

'I tell you again, he is not here!'

Then the Maréchale, who was looking about her, said coolly:

'She we go home? I've got a cab waiting below.'

He pretended not to hear.

'Come on, let's go!'

'Ah, yes! It's a good opportunity! Go! Go!' said Madame Arnoux. They went out. She leaned over the banisters to see them once more; and a laugh, piercing, heart-rending, reached them from the top of the stairs. Frédéric pushed Rosanette into the cab, sat down opposite her, and during the entire drive did not utter a word

This disgraceful incident, with its appalling consequences for him, had been brought about by himself alone. He felt both the shame of a crushing humiliation and regret for the loss of his happiness; just when he was at last about to grasp it, it had become irrevocably impossible – and that through the fault of this tart, this whore. He would have liked to strangle her; he was choking with rage. When they had got into the house, he flung his hat on a piece of furniture and tore off his cravat.

'Ha! You've just done a nice thing, admit it!'

She planted herself defiantly in front of him.

'Well, and so what? Where's the harm?'

'What! You're spying on me?'

'Is that my fault? Why do you go and amuse yourself with virtuous women?'

'Never mind! I don't wish you to insult them.'

'How have I insulted her?'

He had no answer to make to this; and in a more spiteful tone:

'But that other time, at the Champ de Mars . . . '

'Ah! You're so boring, you and your old flames!'

'Bitch!'

He raised his fist.

'Don't kill me! I'm pregnant!'

Frédéric staggered back.

'You're lying!'

'Well, look at me!'

She seized a candlestick, and pointing at her face:

'You know the signs?'

Little yellow spots dotted her skin, which was strangely puffy. Frédéric did not deny the evidence. He went to open the window, took a few steps up and down the room, then sank into an armchair.

This event was a calamity which, in the first place, postponed their rupture – and, in the next place, upset all his plans. The notion of being a father, moreover, appeared to him grotesque, inadmissible. But why? If, in place of the Maréchale . . . ? And he fell into a reverie so deep that he had a kind of hallucination. He saw there, on the carpet, in front of the chimney-piece, a little girl. She looked like Madame Arnoux and himself, a little – dark, and yet fair, with black eyes, very large eyebrows, and a pink ribbon in her curling hair! (Oh, how he would have loved her!) And he seemed to hear her voice: 'Papa! Papa!'

Rosanette, who had just undressed, came across to him, saw a tear on his eyelids, and kissed him gravely on the forehead. He got up, saying:

'Damn it! We won't kill this little chap!'

Then she talked a lot. To be sure it would be a boy! His name would be Frédéric. She would have to begin making his clothes; and, seeing her so happy, a feeling of pity took possession of him. As he no longer felt any anger against her, he wanted to know the reason for her recent behaviour.

It was because Mademoiselle Vatnaz had sent her that very day a bill which had been protested for some time past; and she had hastened to Arnoux to get the money from him.

'I'd have given you some!' said Frédéric.

'It was simpler to go there and take what's mine, and to pay her back her thousand francs.'

'Is that all you owe her, at least?'

She answered:

'Of course!'

On the following day, at nine o'clock in the evening (the hour specified by the doorkeeper), Frédéric called on Mademoiselle Vatnaz.

In the anteroom, he bumped into piles of furniture. But the sound of voices and music guided him. He opened a door, and tumbled into the middle of a party. Standing by the piano, which a young lady in spectacles was playing, Delmar, as serious as a pontiff, was declaiming a humanitarian poem on prostitution; and his hollow voice boomed out, to the accompaniment of the chords which she struck. A row of women sat along the wall, dressed mostly in dark colours without collars or cuffs. Five or six men, all intellectuals, occupied seats here and there. In an armchair was seated a former writer of fables, a wreck now – and the pungent odour of two lamps mingled with the aroma of the chocolate which filled a number of bowls placed on the card-table.

Mademoiselle Vatnaz, with an Oriental shawl around her hips, was sat at one side of the chimney-piece. Dussardier was at the other side facing her; he seemed rather embarrassed at his position. Besides, he was intimidated by this artistic milieu.

Had Vatnaz broken off with Delmar? Perhaps not. However, she seemed jealous of the kind-hearted clerk; and, Frédéric having asked if he might have a word with her, she made a sign to him to go with them into her room. When the thousand francs were set down before her, she asked, in addition, for interest.

'Don't bother with that!' said Dussardier.

'You just be quiet!'

This want of moral courage on the part of so brave a man was agreeable to Frédéric as a justification of his own. He took the bill away with him, and never again referred to the scandal at Madame Arnoux's house. But from that time forth he saw clearly all the defects in the Maréchale's character.

She possessed incurable bad taste, was unimaginably lazy, as ignorant as a savage, so much so that she regarded Doctor Desrogis as a very famous person; and she was proud to receive him and his wife, because they were 'a married couple'. She lectured with a pedantic air on life and its problems to Mademoiselle Irma, a poor little creature endowed with a tiny voice, who had as a protector a 'very respectable' gentleman, an ex-customs-officer, who had a rare talent for card tricks; Rosanette used to call him 'My big Loulou'. Frédéric could also not bear the repetition of her stupid expressions, such as 'Pull the other one! Get lost! It's a mystery, etc.' And she persisted in dusting her trinkets in the morning with a pair of old white gloves! He was above all disgusted by her treatment of her servant − whose wages were constantly in arrears, and who even lent her money. On the days when they settled their accounts, they used to wrangle like two fishwives, and then made up, falling into each other's arms. Being alone together was becoming dreary. It was a relief to him when Madame Dambreuse's evening parties began again.

She, at least, amused him! She knew all about the intrigues of society, the changes of ambassadors, the personnel of the dressmakers; and, if commonplaces escaped her lips, they did so with such conventional phrasing that her phrase could pass as politeness or irony. You had to see her in the midst of twenty persons all talking, not overlooking any of them, bringing about the answers she desired and avoiding those that were dangerous! Things of a very simple nature, when related by her, seemed like confidences; her slightest smile could set you dreaming; in short, her charm, like the exquisite scent which she usually wore, was complex and indefinable. When he was with her, Frédéric experienced on each occasion the pleasure of a new discovery; and yet the next time they met he always found her with the same serenity, which was like the sheen of limpid waters. But why was there such coldness in her manner towards her niece? At times she even darted some very strange looks at her.

As soon as the question of marriage arose, she had urged as an objection to it, when discussing the matter with M. Dambreuse, the state of 'the dear child's' health, and had at once taken her off to the baths of Balaruc. On her return fresh pretexts had materialised: the young man was not in a good position, this ardent passion

did not appear to be a serious attachment, there was no harm in
waiting. Martinon had replied that he would wait. His conduct
was sublime. He praised Frédéric. He did more: he enlightened
him as to the best means of pleasing Madame Dambreuse, even
giving him to understand that he had ascertained from the niece
the feelings of her aunt.

As for M. Dambreuse, far from exhibiting any jealousy, he
treated his young friend with the utmost attention, consulted him
about different things, and even showed anxiety about his future,
so that one day, when they were talking about Père Roque, he
whispered to him with a very meaningful air:

'You did the right thing.'

And Cécile, Miss Johnson, the servants and the porter, no one
who was not charming to him in this house. He came there every
evening, leaving Rosanette for that purpose. Her approaching
maternity made her more serious, even a little melancholy, as if she
were tortured by anxieties. To every question put to her she
replied:

'You're wrong! I'm quite well!'

She had, as a matter of fact, signed five bills in her previous
transactions; and not having the courage to tell Frédéric after the
first had been paid, she had gone back to Arnoux, who had
promised her, in writing, the third part of his profits in the lighting
of the towns of the Languedoc by gas (a marvellous enterprise!),
while requesting her not to make use of this letter before the
meeting of shareholders; the meeting was put off from week to
week.

Meanwhile the Maréchale needed money. She would have died
sooner than ask Frédéric for any. She did not wish to take any from
him. It would have spoiled their love. He certainly contributed to
the household expenses; but a little carriage, hired by the month,
and other sacrifices, which were indispensable since he had begun
to frequent the Dambreuses, prevented him from doing any more
for his mistress. On two or three occasions, when he came home at
a different hour from his usual time, he fancied he could see men's
backs disappearing behind the door; and she often went out
without wishing to say where she was going. Frédéric did not
attempt to enquire minutely into these matters. One of these days
he would make up his mind to some definite course of action. He

dreamed of another life which would be more amusing and more noble. It was this ideal that rendered him indulgent towards the Dambreuse household.

It was a private annexe to the Rue de Poitiers. There he met the great M. A., the illustrious B., the profound C., the eloquent Z., the stupendous Y., the old stars of the Centre Left, the knights of the Right, the burgraves of the centrist party, the stock characters of the old comedy. He was astonished at their abominable way of talking, their meannesses, their rancours, their dishonesty – all these people who had voted for the Constitution, now striving to destroy it – and they were all very active, and launched manifestoes, pamphlets, and biographies; Hussonnet's biography of Fumichon was a masterpiece. Nonancourt devoted himself to the work of propagandism in the country districts, M. de Grémonville worked up the clergy, and Martinon brought together the young men of the middle class. Each exerted himself according to his resources, including even Cisy. With his thoughts now all day long absorbed in matters of grave moment, he ran errands in a cab, in the interests of the party.

M. Dambreuse, like a barometer, constantly reflected its latest variation. Lamartine could not be mentioned without his citing the famous phrase of a man of the people: 'Enough of poetry!' Cavaignac was, in his eyes, nothing now but a traitor. The President, whom he had admired for a period of three months, was beginning to sink in his esteem (as he did not appear to exhibit the 'necessary energy'); and, as he always needed a saviour, his gratitude, since the affair of the Conservatoire, went to Changarnier: 'Thank God, Changarnier. . . Let's hope that Changarnier. . . Oh, there's nothing to fear as long as Changarnier . . . '

Above all, M. Thiers was praised for his volume against Socialism, in which he had shown himself to be as much of a thinker as a writer. They laughed uproariously at Pierre Leroux, who quoted passages from the *philosophes* in the Chamber. Jokes were made about the phalansterian tail. They applauded the *Foire aux Idées*, and its authors were compared to Aristophanes. Frédéric went to see it, like everybody else.

Political verbiage and good living blunted his moral sense. Mediocre as these persons appeared to him, he was proud to know them, and inwardly longed for bourgeois respectability. A mistress like Madame Dambreuse would give him status.

He set about taking the necessary steps.

He turned up in her path when she was out walking, did not fail to go and greet her with a bow in her box at the theatre; and, knowing the hours at which she went to church, he would plant himself behind a pillar in a melancholy attitude. There was a continual interchange of little notes between them with regard to curiosities to which they drew each other's attention, information about a concert, or the borrowing of books or reviews. In addition to his evening visit, he sometimes made another towards the end of the day; and his pleasure became progressively more intense, as he passed successively through the large front entrance, through the courtyard, through the anteroom and through the two reception-rooms; finally, he reached her boudoir, which was as quiet as a tomb, as warm as an alcove, and in which one bumped against the upholstered padding of the furniture in the midst of all sorts of objects placed here and there: chiffoniers, screens, bowls, and trays made of lacquer, or shell, or ivory, or malachite, expensive trifles, to which fresh additions were frequently made. There were simple ones: three Etretat pebbles used as paperweights, a Frisian cap hanging from a Chinese screen; nevertheless, there was a harmony between all these things; one was even impressed by the noble aspect of the whole, which was perhaps due to the loftiness of the ceiling, the richness of the door-curtains, and the long silk fringes hanging over the gold legs of the stools.

She nearly always sat on a little sofa, near the flower-stand, which garnished the recess of the window. Frédéric, seating himself on the edge of a large wheeled pouffe, addressed to her compliments of the most appropriate kind that he could conceive; and she looked at him, with her head a little on one side, and a smile playing round her mouth.

He read her pages of poetry, into which he threw his whole soul in order to move her and excite her admiration. She would interrupt him with a disparaging remark or a practical observation; and their conversation would relapse incessantly into the eternal question of Love! They wondered what caused it, whether women felt it better than men, and what were the differences between them on that point. Frédéric tried to express his opinion, and, at the same time, avoid anything like coarseness or insipidity.

This became at length a species of contest between them, some-times agreeable and at other times tedious.

Whilst at her side, he did not experience that ravishment of his entire being which drew him towards Madame Arnoux, nor the happy excitement with which Rosanette had, at first, inspired him. But he desired her as a thing that was both abnormal and difficult of attainment, because she was an aristocrat, because she was wealthy, because she was devout – imagining that she had a delicacy of feeling as rare as the lace she wore, with amulets on her skin and modesty in the midst of depravity.

He made use of his old love. He retailed to her, as if she had been the cause, all that Mme Arnoux had made him feel in the past, his languors, his fears and dreams. She received these avowals like one accustomed to such things, and, without giving him a formal repulse, did not yield in the slightest degree; and he came no nearer to seducing her than Martinon did to getting married. In order finally to get rid of her niece's suitor, she even accused him of having money for his object, and asked her husband to put the matter to the test. So M. Dambreuse declared to the young man that Cécile, being the orphan child of poor parents, had neither 'expectations' nor a dowry.

Martinon, not believing that this was true, or too deeply com-mitted to draw back, or through one of those acts of obstinacy to which idiots are prone and which are acts of genius, replied that his patrimony, amounting to fifteen thousand francs a year, would be sufficient for them. The banker was touched by this unexpected display of disinterestedness. He promised the young man a tax-collectorship, undertaking to obtain the post for him; and in the month of May, 1850, Martinon married Mademoiselle Cécile. There was no ball. The young people started the same evening for Italy. Frédéric came next day to pay a visit to Madame Dambreuse. She appeared to him paler than usual. She sharply contradicted him about two or three matters of no importance. All men were egoists anyway.

There were, however, some devoted men, if only himself.

'Ah! Pooh! Just like the rest!'

Her eyelids were red; she was weeping. Then, forcing a smile:

'I'm sorry! I'm in the wrong! I just had a sad thought!'

He had not a clue what she meant.

'No matter! She's not so tough as I imagined,' he thought.

She rang for a glass of water, drank a mouthful of it, sent it away again, and then began to complain of the wretched way in which her servants attended on her. In order to amuse her, he offered to become her servant himself, pretending that he knew how to hand round plates, dust furniture, and announce visitors, in fact, to do the duties of a manservant, or, rather, of a running-footman, although the latter was now out of fashion. He would have liked to cling on behind her carriage with a hat adorned with cock's feathers.

'And how I would follow you with majestic stride, carrying your little dog on my arm!'

'You're in a good mood,' said Madame Dambreuse

Was it not folly, he returned, to take everything seriously? There were enough miseries in the world without creating fresh ones. Nothing was worth the cost of a single pang. Madame Dambreuse raised her eyebrows with a sort of vague approval.

This agreement in their views impelled Frédéric to take a bolder course. His former miscalculations now gave him insight. He went on:

'Our grandfathers lived better. Why not obey the impulse that urges us onward?' After all, love was not in itself a thing of such importance.

'But what you've just said is immoral!'

She had resumed her seat on the little sofa. He sat down on the edge of it, near her feet.

'Don't you see that I'm lying? For in order to please women, one must exhibit the thoughtlessness of a buffoon or all the wild passion of tragedy! They laugh at us when we simply tell them that we love them! For my part, I consider those hyperbolical phrases which appeal to them to be a profanation of true love; so that one is at a loss as to how to give expression to it, especially when addressing women . . . who possess . . . more than ordinary intelligence.'

She observed him through lowered lashes. He dropped his voice, leaning towards her face.

'Yes! You frighten me! Perhaps I'm offending you? . . . Forgive me! . . . I didn't intend to say all that ! It's not my fault! You are so beautiful!'

Madame Dambreuse closed her eyes, and he was astonished at the ease of his victory. The tall trees in the garden stopped their gentle quivering. Motionless clouds streaked the sky with long strips of red, and everything seemed to hang suspended. Then he recalled to mind, in a confused sort of way, evenings just the same as this, filled with the same silence. Where was it . . . ?

He sank upon his knees, seized her hand, and swore that he would love her for ever. Then, as he was leaving, she beckoned him back, and said to him in a low tone:

'Come back to dinner! We'll be alone!'

It seemed to Frédéric, as he descended the stairs, that he had become a different man, that he was surrounded by the balmy temperature of a hothouse, and that he was beyond all question entering into the higher sphere of patrician adulteries and upper-class intrigues. In order to occupy the first rank there all he required was a woman like that. Greedy, no doubt, for power and action, and married to a man of inferior calibre, for whom she had done prodigious services, she longed for someone strong in order to be his guide. Nothing was impossible now! He felt himself capable of riding two hundred leagues on horseback, of travelling for several nights in succession without fatigue; his heart over-flowed with pride.

Just in front of him, on the pavement, a man wrapped in an old overcoat was walking along with his head bowed, and with such an air of dejection that Frédéric turned round to have a better look at him. The other lifted his face. It was Deslauriers. He hesitated. Frédéric fell upon his neck.

'Ah! My poor old friend! What! It's you!'

And he dragged Deslauriers towards his house, asking him a lot of questions at once.

The ex-commissioner of Ledru-Rollin began by describing the tortures he had undergone. As he preached fraternity to the Conservatives, and respect for the laws to the socialists, the former had shot at him, and the latter brought a rope to hang him with. After June he had been brutally dismissed. He had thrown himself into a conspiracy, that which was connected with the seizure of arms at Troyes. He had been released for want of evidence. Then the acting committee had sent him to London, where he'd been in a brawl with his brothers, in the middle of a banquet. On his return to Paris . . .

'Why didn't you come to me?'

'You were always away. Your porter put on mysterious airs, I didn't know what to think; and then I didn't want to reappear as a loser.'

He had knocked at the portals of Democracy, offering to serve it with his pen, with his tongue, with his energies; he had been everywhere repelled: they mistrusted him; and he had sold his watch, his library, and even his linen.

'It would be better to be breaking one's back on the pontoons of Belle-Isle with Sénécal!'

Frédéric, who was fastening his cravat, did not appear to be much affected by this news

'Ah! So he's been deported, has he, old Sénécal?'

Deslauriers replied, surveying the walls with an envious air:

'Not everybody has your luck!'

'Excuse me,' said Frédéric, without picking up the allusion, 'but I'm dining out. Someone will get you something to eat; order whatever you like! You can even take my bed.

This unstinting generosity dissipated Deslauriers' bitterness.

'Your bed? But . . . that would inconvenience you . . . !'

'Oh, no! I have others!'

'Oh, all right!' returned the lawyer, with a laugh. 'Where are you dining then?'

'At Madame Dambreuse's.'

'Can it be that . . . you are . . . perhaps . . . ?'

'You're too inquisitive,' said Frédéric, with a smile which confirmed this hypothesis.

Then, after a glance at the clock, he sat down again.

'That's how it is! And we mustn't despair, old defender of the people!'

'Oh, pardon me! Let others have a go at it!'

The lawyer detested the workers, because he had suffered so much on their account in his province, a coalmining district. Every pit had appointed a provisional government, from which he received orders.

'Besides, their conduct has been charming everywhere: in Lyons, Lille, Le Havre, Paris! For, in imitation of the manufacturers, who would like to exclude foreign goods, these gentlemen demand a ban on English, German, Belgian, and Savoyard workers! As for their intelligence, what good was their famous guild system during the Restoration? In 1830 they joined the National Guard, without even having the sense to dominate it! Is it not a fact that, as soon as we'd had '48, the corporations reappeared with their banners? They even demanded popular representatives for themselves, who would have spoken only for them! Just as the deputies who represent sugarbeet concern themselves with nothing but sugarbeet! Ah! I've had enough of these characters, in turn grovelling before the scaffold of Robespierre, the boots of the Emperor, and the umbrella of Louis-Philippe, just scum, always ready to serve whoever flings bread into their gobs! People always cry out against the venality of Talleyrand and Mirabeau; but the messenger downstairs would sell his country for fifty centimes, if they'd only promise to fix a tariff of three francs an errand! Ah, what a fiasco! We ought to have set the four corners of Europe on fire!'

Frédéric said in reply:

'The spark was lacking! You were simply a lot of little shopkeepers at heart, and even the best of you were just pedants! As for the workers, they may well complain; for, if you except a million taken out of the civil list, and which you granted to them with the most grovelling flattery, all you've given them is phrases! The workman's certificate remains in the hands of the employer, and the employee remains (even in the eyes of the law) the inferior of his master, because his word is not believed. In short, the Republic seems to me to have had its day. Who knows? Perhaps Progress can be realised only through an aristocracy or through one single man? The initiative always comes from the top! The people has the status of a minor, whatever they say!'

'That may be true,' said Deslauriers.

According to Frédéric, the vast majority of citizens aimed only at a life of peace and quiet (he had learned by his visits to the Dambreuse mansion), and the chances were all on the side of the Conservatives. That party, however, lacked new men.

'If you came forward, I'm sure . . . '

He did not finish. Deslauriers understood, and passed his two hands over his forehead; then, all of a sudden:

'But what about you? Is there anything to stop you? Why should you not be a deputy?' In consequence of a double election, there was in the Aube a vacancy for a candidate. M. Dambreuse, who had been re-elected as a member of the Legislative Assembly, belonged to a different arrondissement. 'Would you like me to see to it?' He knew a lot of publicans, schoolmasters, doctors, notaries' clerks and their masters. 'Besides, you can make the peasants believe anything you like!'

Frédéric felt his ambition rekindling.

Deslauriers added:

'You ought to find me a situation in Paris.'

'Oh, it won't be hard to manage through Monsieur Dambreuse.'

'Since we were talking about coalmines,' the lawyer went on, 'what has become of his great company? That's the sort of employment that would suit me! And I could make myself useful to them while preserving my own independence.'

Frédéric promised that he would introduce him to the banker in the next three days.

The dinner, which he enjoyed alone with Madame Dambreuse, was an exquisite affair. She sat smiling across at him on the other side of the table, over a basket of flowers, in the light of the hanging lamp; and, as the window was open, they could see the stars. They talked very little, distrusting themselves, no doubt; but, the moment the servants's backs were turned, they blew kisses to each other from the tips of their lips. He told her about his idea of becoming a candidate. She approved of the project, promising even to get M. Dambreuse to work on it.

As the evening advanced, some of her friends presented themselves to congratulate her, and to sympathize: she must be so sad at the loss of her niece? It was a very good idea, however, for young newlyweds to travel; later, there would be encumbrances, children. But Italy did not match up to one's expectations. However, they were at the age of illusions! And then being on one's honeymoon made everything wonderful! The last two to remain were M. de Grémonville and Frédéric. The diplomat would not go. At last he rose, at midnight. Madame Dambreuse signalled to Frédéric to go with him, and thanked him for this compliance with her wishes by giving him a gentle pressure with her hand, more delightful than anything that had gone before.

The Maréchale uttered a cry of joy on seeing him again. She had been waiting for him for five hours. He gave as an excuse some urgent business on Deslaurier's behalf. His face wore a look of triumph, a positive halo, which dazzled Rosanette.

'It's perhaps because of your black coat, which suits you; but I've never seen you look so handsome! How handsome you are!'

In a transport of tenderness, she vowed to herself never again to belong to any other man, no matter what might be the consequence, even if she were to die of want!

Her pretty bright eyes sparkled with such intense passion that Frédéric took her upon his knees and said to himself: 'What a rascal I am!' while admiring his own perversity.

M. Dambreuse, when Deslauriers came to see him, was thinking of reviving his great coalmining speculation. But this fusion of all the companies into one was looked upon unfavourably; there was an outcry against monopolies, as if immense capital were not needed for carrying out enterprises of this kind!

Deslauriers, who had just read for the purpose the work by Gobet and the articles of M. Chappe in the *Journal des Mines*, understood the question perfectly. He demonstrated that the law of 1810 established for the benefit of the grantee an inalienable right. Besides, one could give a democratic colour to the undertaking: to interfere with the formation of coalmining companies was an attack against the very principle of association.

M. Dambreuse entrusted to him some notes for the purpose of drawing up a memorandum. As for the way in which he meant to pay for the work, his promises were all the better for not being precise.

Deslauriers came back to Frédéric's house, and gave him an account of the interview. Moreover, he had caught a glimpse of Madame Dambreuse at the bottom of the stairs, just as he was going out.

'I congratulate you, my word!'

Then they talked about the election. They would have to draw up a plan.

Three days later, Deslauriers reappeared with a manuscript intended for the newspapers, and which was a friendly letter from M. Dambreuse, expressing approval of their friend's candidature. Supported by a Conservative and praised by a Red, it ought to succeed. How was it that the capitalist had put his signature to such an elucubration? The lawyer had, of his own accord, and without the slightest embarrassment, gone and shown it to Madame Dambreuse, who, thinking it quite appropriate, had taken the rest of the business on her own shoulders.

Frédéric was astonished at this proceeding. Nevertheless, he approved of it; then, as Deslauriers was to have an interview with M. Roque, his friend explained to him how he stood with regard to Louise.

'Tell them anything you like, that my affairs are in an unsettled state; I'll sort them out; she's young enough to wait!'

Deslauriers left; and Frédéric looked upon himself as a very able man. He experienced, moreover, a feeling of gratification, a profound satisfaction. His delight at being the possessor of a rich woman was not spoiled by any contrast; sentiment harmonised with surroundings. His life now was full of joy in every way.

Perhaps the most delicious sensation of all was to gaze at Madame Dambreuse in the midst of a number of other ladies in her drawing-room. The propriety of her manners made him dream of other attitudes; while she was talking in a tone of coldness, he remembered stammered words of passion; all the respect shown for her virtue gave him a thrill of pleasure, as if it were a homage which was reflected back on himself; and at times he felt a longing to cry out: 'But I know her better than you! She's mine!'

It was not long before their liaison came to be socially recognised and accepted. Madame Dambreuse, during the whole winter, took Frédéric along with her into fashionable society

He nearly always arrived before her; and he watched her as she came in with bare arms, a fan in her hand, and pearls in her hair. She would pause on the threshold (the lintel of the door formed a frame around her), and she would make a slight gesture of indecision, blinking a little, in order to see whether he was there. She drove him back in her carriage; the rain lashed the windows; the passers-by seemed merely shadows struggling along in the mud; and, pressed close to each other, they observed all these things vaguely with a calm disdain. Under various pretexts, he would stay on for another hour in her room.

It was chiefly through a feeling of ennui that Madame Dambreuse had yielded. But this latest experience was not to be wasted. She wanted a consuming passion, and she began to shower him with adulation and caresses.

She sent him flowers; she had an upholstered chair made for him; she gave him a cigar-holder, a writing desk, a thousand little things for daily use, so that every act of his life should recall her to his memory. These kind attentions charmed him at first, and then in a little while he took them for granted.

She would step into a cab, get rid of it at the opening into an alley, and come out at the other end; and then, gliding along by the walls, with a double veil on her face, she would reach the street where Frédéric, who had been keeping watch, would take her arm quickly to take her to his house. His two menservants were out, the door-keeper would be doing some errand; she would throw a glance around her; nothing to fear! And she would breathe the sigh of an exile who beholds his country once more. Their good fortune emboldened them. Their appointments became more frequent. One evening, she even presented herself, all of a sudden, in full ball-dress. These surprises might have perilous consequences; he reproached her for her lack of prudence; besides, he was not taken with her appearance. The low bodice of her dress exposed her flat chest too much.

It was then that he discovered what he had been hiding from himself, the disillusion of his senses. This did not stop him feigning great desire; but in order to feel it he had to evoke the images of Rosanette or Madame Arnoux.

This sentimental atrophy left his intellect entirely untrammelled, and he was more ambitious than ever of attaining a high position in society. Since he had such a stepping-stone, the very least he could do was to use it.

One morning, about the middle of January, Sénécal came into his study; and in response to his exclamation of astonishment, announced that he was Deslauriers' secretary. He even brought Frédéric a letter. It contained good news, and yet took him to task for his negligence; he must come down at once.

The future deputy said he would set out in two days' time.

Sénécal gave no opinion on this candidature. He spoke about his own concerns and about the affairs of the country.

Miserable as the state of things was, it gave him pleasure; for they were advancing in the direction of communism. In the first place, the Administration was heading towards it of its own accord, since every day a greater number of things were control-led by the Government. As for Property, the Constitution of '48, in spite of its weaknesses, had not spared it; the State might, in the name of public utility, henceforth take whatever it thought would suit it. Sénécal declared himself in favour of Authority; and

Frédéric noticed in his remarks the exaggeration of his own words to Deslauriers. The Republican even inveighed against the inadequacy of the masses.

'Robespierre, by upholding the right of the minority, brought Louis XVI before the National Convention, and saved the people. The end justifies the means. A dictatorship is sometimes indispensable. Long live tyranny, provided that the tyrant promotes the public welfare!'

Their discussion lasted a long time, and, as he was taking his leave, Sénécal confessed (perhaps it was the real object of his visit) that Deslauriers was getting very impatient at M. Dambreuse's silence.

But M. Dambreuse was ill. Frédéric saw him every day, his character of an intimate friend enabling him to obtain access to him.

General Changarnier's dismissal had powerfully affected the capitalist. That same evening, he was seized with a burning sensation in his chest, together with an oppression that prevented him from lying down. The application of leeches gave him immediate relief. The dry cough disappeared, his breathing became more easy; and, a week later, he said, while swallowing some broth:

'Ah! That's better! But I was near going on the last long journey!'

'Not without me!' cried Madame Dambreuse, intending by this remark to convey that she would not have been able to survive his death.

Instead of replying, he cast upon her and her lover a singular smile, in which there was at the same time resignation, indulgence, irony, and even, as it were, a touch of humour, a hint almost of gaiety.

Frédéric wanted to start for Nogent. Madame Dambreuse objected to this; and he unpacked and repacked his luggage by turns according to the changes in the invalid's condition.

Suddenly M. Dambreuse coughed up a great deal of blood. The 'princes of medical science', on being consulted, had nothing new to recommend. His legs swelled, and his weakness increased. He had several times evinced the desire to see Cécile, who was at the other end of France with her husband, now a collector of taxes, a position to which he had been appointed a month ago. He gave express orders to send for her. Madame Dambreuse wrote three letters, which she showed him.

Without trusting him even to the care of the nursing sister, she would not leave him for one second, and no longer went to bed. The people who came to register their visits at the lodge asked about her with admiration; and the passers-by were filled with respect on seeing the quantity of straw which was placed in the street under the windows.

On the 12th of February, at five o'clock, a frightful haemoptysis came on. The doctor on duty explained that the case had assumed a dangerous aspect. They sent in hot haste for a priest.

While M. Dambreuse was making his confession, Madame kept gazing curiously at him from a distance. After this, the young doctor applied a blister and waited.

The lights of the lamps, obscured by the furniture, lighted up the apartment in an irregular fashion. Frédéric and Madame Dambreuse, at the foot of the bed, watched the dying man. In the recess of a window, the priest and the doctor chatted in low tones; the nun on her knees was mumbling prayers.

At last came a rattling in the throat. The hands grew cold, the face began to turn white. Sometimes he would suddenly draw a huge breath; these became rarer and rarer; two or three confused words escaped him; he let out a short breath, at the same time as his eyes turned upwards, and his head sank down sidewards onto the pillow.

For a minute, all remained motionless.

Madame Dambreuse approached the bed, and, with no effort, with the unaffectedness of one simply discharging a duty, she closed his eyelids.

Then she spread out her two arms, her figure twisting as if in a spasm of repressed despair, and left the room, supported by the physician and the nun. A quarter of an hour afterwards, Frédéric went up to her room.

There was in it an indefinable perfume, emanating from the delicate objects with which it was filled. In the middle of the bed lay a black dress, which formed a glaring contrast with the pink coverlet.

Madame Dambreuse was standing at the corner of the mantel-piece. Without attributing to her any passionate regrets, he thought she was a little sad; and, in a mournful voice, he said:

'Are you unhappy?'

'I? No, not in the least.'

As she turned around, her eyes fell on the dress, which she inspected; then she told him not to stand on ceremony.

'Smoke, if you like! You can make yourself at home with me!' And, with a great sigh:

'Ah! Blessed Virgin! What a good riddance!'

Frédéric was astonished at this exclamation. He replied, as he kissed her hand:

'All the same, he left us free!'

This allusion to the ease with which their affair had been conducted seemed to offend Madame Dambreuse.

'Ah! You don't know all I did for him, or the anxiety in which I lived!'

'What?'

'Why, of course! Was it security to have always near one that bastard, a child introduced into the house after five years of married life, and who, were it not for me of course, might have led him into some act of folly?'

Then she explained how her affairs stood. The arrangement on the occasion of her marriage was that the property of each party should be separate. The amount of her inheritance was three hundred thousand francs. M. Dambreuse had guaranteed by the marriage contract that in the event of her surviving him, she should have an income of fifteen thousand francs a year, together with the ownership of the mansion. But a short time afterwards he had made a will by which he gave her all he possessed; and this she estimated, so far as it was possible to ascertain just at present, at over three millions.

Frédéric opened his eyes wide.

'It was worth the trouble, wasn't it? However, I contributed to it! It was my own property I was protecting; Cécile would have robbed me unjustly.'

'Why did she not come to see her father?' said Frédéric.

As he asked her this question, Madame Dambreuse eyed him attentively; then, in a dry tone:

'I haven't the least idea! Want of heart, probably! Oh! I know her! And she won't get a farthing from me!'

She had not been very troublesome, at any rate since her marriage.

'Ha! Her marriage!' said Madame Dambreuse, with a sneer.

And she blamed herself for having treated only too well that stuck-up creature, who was jealous, self-interested, and hypo-critical. 'All the faults of her father!' She denigrated him more and more. There was never a person of such profound duplicity, and with such a merciless disposition into the bargain, as hard as a stone – 'a bad man, a bad man!'

Even the wisest people fall into errors. Madame Dambreuse had just made one through this overflow of hatred on her part. Frédéric, sitting opposite her in an easy chair, was reflecting deeply, scandalised.

She arose and tenderly sat on his lap.

'You alone are good! You are the only one I love!'

While she gazed at him her heart softened, a nervous reaction brought tears into her eyes, and she murmured:

'Will you marry me?'

He thought at first he had not understood. He was stunned by all this wealth. She repeated in a louder tone:

'Will you marry me?'

At last he said with a smile:

'Have you any doubt?'

Then a sense of decency came over him, and in order to make a kind of amends to the dead man, he offered to watch by his side himself. But, feeling ashamed of this pious sentiment, he added, in a flippant tone:

'It would be perhaps more seemly.'

'Perhaps so, indeed,' she said, 'on account of the servants!'

The bed had been drawn completely out of the alcove. The nun was at the foot of it; and at the head of it sat a priest, a different one, a tall, spare man, with the look of a Spaniard and a fanatic. On the night-table, covered with a white cloth, three candles were burning.

Frédéric took a chair, and looked at the corpse.

The face was as yellow as straw; at the corners of the mouth there were traces of bloodstained foam. A silk handkerchief was tied around the skull, he wore a knitted waistcoat, and on the breast lay a silver crucifix between his two crossed arms.

It was over, this life full of agitation! How many journeys had he not made to various offices? How many rows of figures had he not recorded? How many speculations had he not hatched? How many reports had he not heard? What quackeries, smiles and bows! For he had acclaimed Napoleon, the Cossacks, Louis XVIII, 1830, the workers, every regime, loving Power so passionately that he would have paid in order to sell himself.

But he had left behind him the estate of La Fortelle, three factories in Picardy, the woods of Crancé in the Yonne, a farm near Orléans, and a fortune in stocks and shares.

Frédéric thus made a mental calculation of his fortune; and it would soon, nevertheless, belong to him! First of all, he thought of 'what people would say', then of a present for his mother, of the carriages he would have, of an old coachman belonging to his family whom he would employ as doorkeeper. Of course, the livery would not stay the same. He would convert the large reception-room into a study. There was nothing to prevent him, by knocking down three walls, from setting up a picture-gallery on the second floor. There might be an opportunity for introducing into the lower portion of the house a room for Turkish baths. As for M. Dambreuse's office, a disagreeable spot, what use could be made of that?

These reflections were rudely interrupted from time to time by the sounds made by the priest blowing his nose, or by the nun settling the fire. But reality confirmed them; the corpse was still there. Its eyelids had reopened; and the pupils, although sunk in viscous darkness, had an enigmatic, intolerable expression. Frédéric fancied that he saw there a sort of judgment directed against himself; and he almost felt some remorse, for he had never had any reason to complain of this man, who, on the contrary . . . 'Come, now! He was an old wretch!'; and he looked at him more closely, in order to strengthen his spirit, mentally addressing him thus:

'Well, what? Did I kill you?'

Meanwhile, the priest read his breviary; the nun, motionless, was dozing; the wicks of the three tapers were growing longer.

For two hours could be heard the heavy rolling of carts making their way to the Halles. The windowpanes began to lighten, a cab passed, then a group of donkeys went trotting over the pavement, and then came sounds of hammering, cries of itinerant vendors and blasts of horns; everything already was merging into the great voice of Paris, awakening once more.

Frédéric set out on his errands. He first repaired to the town hall to make the necessary declaration; then, when the medical officer had given him a death certificate, he called a second time at the town hall to name the cemetery which the family had selected, and to make arrangements with the undertaker.

The clerk in the office showed him a plan and a programme, the first indicating the different classes of interment, the second giving full particulars with regard to the spectacular portion of the funeral. Would one like an open funeral-car or a hearse with plumes, plaits on the horses, aigrettes on the footmen, initials or a coat-of-arms, funeral-lamps, a man to display the family distinctions, and how many carriages? Frédéric was generous; Madame Dambreuse was determined to spare no expense.

After this he made his way to the church.

The curate who had charge of burials began by finding fault with the waste of money on funeral pomps; for instance, the officer for the display of armorial distinctions was really unnecessary; it would be far better to have plenty of candles! They agreed on a low mass accompanied by music. Frédéric signed the written agreement, with the binding obligation to defray all the expenses.

He went next to the Hôtel de Ville to purchase a piece of ground. A grant of a piece which was two metres long and one wide cost five hundred francs. Did he want a grant for fifty years or forever?

'Oh, forever!' said Frédéric.

He took the whole thing seriously and a great deal of trouble. In the courtyard of the mansion a marble-cutter was waiting to show him estimates and plans of Greek, Egyptian, and Moorish tombs; but the family architect had already been in consultation with Madame; and on the table in the vestibule there were all sorts of prospectuses with reference to the cleaning of mattresses, the disinfection of rooms, and the various processes of embalming.

After dining, he went back to the tailor's shop to order mourning for the servants; and he had still to run one other errand, for the gloves that he had ordered were of beaver, whereas the right kind for a funeral were floss-silk.

When he arrived next morning, at ten o'clock, the large reception-room was filled with people, and nearly everyone said, on encountering the others with a melancholy air:

'To think it's only a month since I saw him! Good heavens! We all come to this!'

'Yes; but let's try to make it as late as possible!'

Then they would give a little chuckle of satisfaction, and would even engage in conversations which were entirely unconnected with the occasion. At length, the master of ceremonies, in a traditional black coat and short breeches, with a cloak, cambric mourning-bands, a long sword by his side, and a three-cornered hat under his arm, gave utterance, with a bow, to the customary words: 'Messieurs, when it shall be your pleasure.' They set off.

It was the market-day for flowers on the Place de la Madeleine. The weather was bright and mild; and the breeze, which shook the canvas stalls a little, swelled at the edges the enormous black cloth which was hung over the church door. The escutcheon of M. Dambreuse, which covered a square piece of velvet, was repeated three times. It was *sable, with an arm sinister or and a clenched hand with a glove argent*, with the coronet of a count, and this device: *By every path*.

The bearers lifted the heavy coffin to the top of the staircase, and the mourners entered the building.

The six chapels, the chancel, and the seats were hung with black. The catafalque at the bottom of the choir formed, with its great candles, a single focus of yellow lights. At the two corners, on candelabra, flames of spirits of wine were burning.

The most important mourners took up their position in the sanctuary, and the rest in the nave; and the Office for the Dead began.

With the exception of a few, the religious ignorance of all was so profound that the master of the ceremonies, from time to time, made signs to them to rise, to kneel, or to resume their seats. The organ and two double-basses alternated with the voices; in the intervals of silence, the mumblings of the priest at the altar could be heard; then the music and the chanting began again.

The light of day shone dimly through the three cupolas; but the open door let in a kind of river of white light, which, entering horizontally, fell on every uncovered head; and in the air, halfway towards the roof of the church, floated a shadow, which was penetrated by the reflection of the gildings that decorated the ribbing of the pendentives and the foliage of the capitals.

Frédéric, in order to distract his attention, listened to the *Dies irae*; he gazed at those around him, or tried to catch a glimpse of the paintings too far above his head which represent the life of Mary Magdalen. Luckily, Pellerin came to sit down beside him, and immediately plunged into a long dissertation on the subject of frescoes. The bell began to toll. They came out of the church.

The hearse, adorned with hanging draperies and tall plumes, set out towards Père-Lachaise, drawn by four black horses, with their manes plaited, their heads decked with tufts of feathers, and enveloped down to their hooves in large caparisons embroidered with silver. Their driver, in riding-boots, wore a three-cornered hat with a long piece of crape falling down from it. The ropes were held by four people: a treasurer of the Chamber of Deputies, a member of the General Council of the Aube, a delegate from the coalmining company – and Fumichon, as a friend. The carriage of the deceased and a dozen mourning-coaches followed. The guests came in the rear, filling up the middle of the boulevard.

The passers-by stopped to see all this; women, with their children in their arms, got up on chairs, and people drinking glasses of beer in the cafés presented themselves at the windows with billiard cues in their hands.

The way was long; and – as at formal meals at which people are at first reserved and then expansive – the general deportment soon relaxed. They talked of nothing but the refusal of an allowance by the Chamber to the President. M. Piscatory had behaved too harshly, Montalembert had been 'magnificent, as usual', and M. Chamballe, M. Pidoux, M. Creton, in fact the entire committee, should perhaps have followed the advice of M. Quentin-Bauchard and M. Dufour.

These conversations continued as they passed through the Rue de la Roquette, with shops on each side, in which could be seen nothing but chains of coloured glass and black circular tablets covered with drawings and letters of gold – which makes them look like caves full of stalactites and crockery-ware shops. But, when they had reached the cemetery gate, everyone immediately fell silent.

The tombs rose up among the trees: broken columns, pyramids, temples, dolmens, obelisks, and Etruscan vaults with doors of bronze. In some of them could be seen what might be called

funereal boudoirs, with rustic armchairs and folding stools. Spiders'
webs hung like rags from the little chains of the urns; and the
bouquets with their satin ribbons and the crucifixes were covered
with dust. Everywhere, between the balustrades on the tombstones, were wreaths of immortelles and chandeliers, vases, flowers,
black discs set off with gold letters, and plaster statuettes: little boys
and little girls, or little angels held in the air by brass wires: several
of them have even a roof of zinc over their heads. Huge cables
made of spun glass, black, white, and azure, descend from the tops
of the steles to the foot of the tombstones, with long folds, like
boas. The rays of the sun, striking on them, made them sparkle
among the black wooden crosses – and the hearse advanced along
the broad paths, which are paved like the streets of a city. From
time to time the axles cracked. Women, kneeling down, with their
dresses trailing in the grass, spoke softly to the dead. Little white
fumes of smoke arose from the green masses of the yew trees. These
came from offerings that had been left behind, debris that was being
burnt.

M. Dambreuse's grave was close to the graves of Manuel and
Benjamin Constant. The earth here slopes with an abrupt decline.
One has beneath one's feet the tops of green trees; further down,
the funnels of fire-pumps, then the entire great city.

Frédéric found an opportunity of admiring the view while the
speeches were being delivered.

The first was in the name of the Chamber of Deputies, the
second in the name of the General Council of the Aube, the third
in the name of the Coalmining Company of Saône-et-Loire, the
fourth in the name of the Agricultural Society of the Yonne; and
there was another in the name of a Philanthropic Society. Finally,
just as everyone was going away, a stranger began reading a sixth
address, in the name of the Amiens Society of Antiquaries.

And they all took advantage of the occasion to denounce
Socialism, of which M. Dambreuse had died a victim. It was the
spectacle of anarchy and his devotion to order that had shortened
his days. They praised his intellectual powers, his integrity, his
generosity, and even his silence as a representative of the people,
for, if he was not an orator, he possessed instead those solid
qualities a thousand times more useful, etc. – with all the requisite
phrases: 'Premature end – eternal regrets – better land – farewell,

or rather no, *au revoir!*'

Earth, mingled with stones, fell onto the coffin; and the world would never mention him again.

There were still a few allusions to him as people came down through the cemetery; and they were blunt in their appreciations of him. Hussonnet, who had to give an account of the burial in the newspapers, even parodied all the addresses; for, after all, old Dambreuse had been one of the most distinguished 'palm-greasers' of the last reign. Then the worthy citizens were driven in the mourning-coaches to their various places of business; the ceremony had not lasted too long; they congratulated themselves on the circumstance.

Frédéric, tired, went home.

When he presented himself next day at the Dambreuse residence, he was informed that Madame was working downstairs in the office. The boxfiles, the drawers had been opened pell-mell, and the account books had been flung about right and left; a roll of papers on which were endorsed the words 'bad debts' lay on the floor; he was near falling over it, and picked it up. Madame Dambreuse had sunk back in the great armchair, so that he did not see her.

'Well? Where have you got to? What is the matter?'

She sprang to her feet with a bound.

'What's the matter? I'm ruined, ruined! Do you understand?'

M. Adolphe Langlois, the notary, had asked her to call at his office, and had informed her about the contents of a will made by her husband before their marriage. He had bequeathed everything to Cécile; and the other will was lost. Frédéric turned very pale. No doubt she had not made sufficient search?

'Well, then, look for yourself!' said Madame Dambreuse, pointing around the room.

The two strongboxes were gaping wide, having been broken open with blows of a cleaver, and she had turned the desk inside out, rummaged in the cupboards, and shaken the doormats, when, all of a sudden, uttering a piercing cry, she dashed into a corner where she had just noticed a little box with a brass lock; she opened it – nothing!

'Ah! The wretch! I, who took such devoted care of him!'

Then she burst into sobs.

'Perhaps it is somewhere else?' said Frédéric.

'Oh no! It was there! In that strongbox. I saw it there recently. It's been burned! I'm certain of it!'

One day, in the early stage of his illness, M. Dambreuse had come down to sign some documents.

'It's then he must have done it!'

And she fell back on a chair, crushed. A mother grieving beside an empty cradle is not a more lamentable sight than Madame Dambreuse was over the gaping strongboxes. Indeed, her sorrow – in spite of the baseness of the motive which inspired it – seemed so deep that he tried to console her by reminding her that, after all, she was not reduced to destitution.

'It is destitution, when I'm not in a position to offer you a large fortune!'

All she had left was thirty thousand livres a year, without taking into account the mansion, which was worth from eighteen to twenty thousand, perhaps.

Although to Frédéric this was opulence, he felt, none the less, disappointed. Farewell to his dreams and to all the grand life he would have led! Honour compelled him to marry Madame Dambreuse. For a minute he reflected; then, in a tone of tenderness:

'I'll still have you!'

She threw herself into his arms; and he clasped her to his breast with a tenderness in which there was a slight element of admiration for himself. Madame Dambreuse, whose tears had ceased to flow, raised her face, radiant with happiness, and, seizing his hand:

'Ah! I never doubted you! I knew I could count on you!'

The young man did not like this tone of anticipated certainty concerning what he regarded as a noble action.

Then she took him into her room, and they made plans. Frédéric should now consider the best way of advancing himself. She even gave him some excellent advice with reference to his candidature.

The first point was to be familiar with two or three phrases borrowed from political economy. He should take up a speciality, such as horse-breeding, for example, should write a number of notes on questions of local interest, have always at his disposal post offices or tobacconists' shops, and render a heap of little services. In this respect M. Dambreuse had shown himself a true model. Thus, on one occasion, in the country, he had drawn up his wagonette,

full of friends, in front of a cobbler's stall, and had bought a dozen
pairs of shoes for his guests, and a dreadful pair of boots for himself
– which he even had the courage to wear for an entire fortnight.
This anecdote put them into a good humour. She related others,
and that with a renewal of grace, youthfulness, and wit.

She approved of his notion of taking a trip immediately to
Nogent. Their parting was an affectionate one; then, on the
threshold, she murmured once more:

'You do love me, don't you?'

'Eternally!' was his reply.

A messenger was waiting for him at home with a note written in
pencil informing him that Rosanette was about to be confined. He
had been so preoccupied for the past few days that he had forgotten
all about it. She had put herself into a special establishment in
Chaillot.

Frédéric took a cab and set out.

At the corner of the Rue de Marbeuf he read on a board in big
letters: 'Nursing Home and Lying-in Hospital, kept by Madame
Alessandri, first-class midwife, ex-pupil of the Maternity, author of
diverse works, etc.' Then, in the middle of the street, over the
door, a little side-door, there was a signboard which repeated
(without the words 'lying-in'): 'Nursing Home of Madame
Alessandri', with all her titles.

Frédéric knocked at the door.

A chambermaid, with the figure of a soubrette, introduced him
into the reception-room, which was adorned with a mahogany
table and armchairs of red velvet, and a clock under a globe.

Almost immediately Madame appeared. She was a tall brunette
of forty, with a slender waist, fine eyes, and the manners of good
society. She apprised Frédéric of the mother's happy delivery, and
took him up to her room.

Rosanette broke into a smile of unutterable bliss; and, as if
drowned in the floods of love that were suffocating her, she said in
a low tone:

'A boy, there, there!' pointing towards a cradle close to her bed.

He opened the curtains, and saw, wrapped up in linen, a
yellowish-red object, exceedingly wrinkled, which had a bad
smell, and was wailing.

'Kiss him!'

He replied, in order to hide his repugnance:

'But I'm afraid of hurting him.'

'No, no!'

So, with the tips of his lips, he kissed his child.

'How like you he is!'

And with her two weak arms, she clung to his neck with an outburst of feeling such as he had never seen.

The memory of Madame Dambreuse came back to him. He reproached himself as a monster for deceiving this poor creature, who loved and suffered with all the sincerity of her nature. For several days he kept her company till the evening.

She felt happy in this discreet house; even the window shutters in front of it remained constantly closed; her room, hung with bright chintz, looked out onto a large garden; Madame Alessandri, whose only shortcoming was to talk about eminent physicians as her friends, showed her the utmost attention; her companions, nearly all young ladies from the provinces, were exceedingly bored, as they had nobody to come to see them; Rosanette saw that they regarded her with envy, and told this to Frédéric with pride. They had to speak quietly, nevertheless; the partitions were thin and everyone eavesdropped, in spite of the constant thrumming of the pianos.

He was at last about to take his departure for Nogent, when he got a letter from Deslauriers.

Two new candidates had offered themselves, one a Conservative, the other a Red; a third, whatever he might be, would have no chance. It was all Frédéric's fault; he had let the right moment pass by. He should have come sooner and stirred himself. 'You weren't even seen at the agricultural fair!' The lawyer blamed him for not having any newspaper connection. 'Ah! If you'd followed my advice long ago! If only we had a journal of our own!' He laid special stress on this point. Besides, many people who would have voted for him out of consideration for M. Dambreuse, would abandon him now. Deslauriers was one of the number. Not having anything more to expect from the capitalist, he dropped his *protégé*.

Frédéric took the letter to show it to Madame Dambreuse.

'You've not been to Nogent, then?' she said.

'Why do you ask?'

'Because I saw Deslauriers three days ago'

Having learned that her husband was dead, the lawyer had come to make a report about the coalmines, and to offer his services to her as business adviser. This seemed strange to Frédéric; and what was his friend doing in Nogent?

Madame Dambreuse wanted to know how he had spent his time since they had parted.

'I've been ill,' he replied.

'You ought at least to have told me.'

'Oh! It wasn't worth it'; besides, he had had to settle a heap of things, to keep appointments and to pay visits.

From that time forth he led a double life, sleeping religiously at the Maréchale's abode and passing the afternoon with Madame Dambreuse, so that there was scarcely a single hour of freedom left to him in the middle of the day.

The child was in the country at Andilly. They went to see it every week.

The wetnurse's house was in the upper part of the village, at the back of a little yard as dark as a pit, with straw on the ground, hens here and there, and a vegetable-cart in the shed. Rosanette would begin by frantically kissing her baby; and, seized with a kind of delirium, would keep moving to and fro, trying to milk the goat, eating rough bread, and inhaling the smell of the manure; she wanted to put a little of it into her handkerchief.

Then they went for long walks; she went into the nurseries, tore off branches from the lilac trees which hung down over the walls, exclaimed, 'Gee up, neddy!' to the donkeys drawing a cart, and stopped to gaze through the gate into the interior of beautiful gardens; or else the wetnurse would take the child, they would place it in the shade of a walnut tree; and for hours the two women would talk the most tiresome nonsense.

Frédéric, not far away from them, gazed at the square patches of vines on the slopes, with here and there the bushy shape of a tree, at the dusty paths like strips of greyish ribbon, at the houses, which showed as white and red patches in the midst of the green; and sometimes the smoke of a locomotive stretched out horizontally, at the foot of the hills covered with foliage, like a gigantic ostrich feather, of which the slender tip trailed away.

Then his eyes would once more rest on his son. He imagined him as a young man, he would make a companion of him; but he would perhaps be a blockhead, and certainly wretched. The illegality of his birth would weigh on him forever; it would have been better for him if he had never been born, and Frédéric murmured, 'Poor child!' his heart swelling with an incomprehensible sadness.

They often missed the last train. Then Madame Dambreuse would scold him for his want of punctuality. He would make up some story.

He had to make up stories for Rosanette too. She could not understand how he spent all his evenings; and when she sent a messenger to his house, he was never there! One day when he chanced to be at home, the two women made their appearance almost at the same time. He got rid of the Maréchale, and concealed Madame Dambreuse, pretending that his mother was about to arrive.

Before long, he found these lies amusing; he would repeat to one the oath which he had just sworn to the other, send them two bouquets of the same sort, write to them at the same time, and then would institute comparisons between them; there was a third always present in his thoughts. The impossibility of having her justified his perfidies, which intensified his pleasure by the fact that he had to practise them alternately; and the more he had deceived one or other of the two, the fonder of him she grew, as if the love of one of them added heat to that of the other, and as if, by a sort of emulation, each of them had been seeking to make him forget the other.

'Admire my trust in you!' said Madame Dambreuse one day to him, opening a sheet of paper, in which she was informed that M. Moreau and a certain Rose Bron were living together as husband and wife.

'Can it be that this is the lady of the races?'

'How absurd!' he returned. 'Let me have a look at it.'

The letter, written in Roman characters, was not signed. Madame Dambreuse, in the beginning, had tolerated this mistress, who furnished a cloak for their adultery. But, as her passion became stronger, she had insisted on a rupture, a thing which had been effected long since, according to Frédéric; and when he had ceased to protest, she replied, blinking her eyes, in which shone a look like the point of a stiletto through muslin:

'Well, and what about the other one?'

'What other one?'

'The ceramics-dealer's wife!'

He shrugged his shoulders disdainfully. She did not press the matter.

But, a month later, while they were talking about honour and loyalty, and he was boasting about his own (in a casual sort of way, for the sake of precaution), she said to him:

'It's true, you are honest, you don't go there any more.'

Frédéric, who was thinking of the Maréchale, stammered:

'Where do you mean?'

'To Madame Arnoux's.'

He begged her to tell him from whom she got this information. It was through her second dressmaker, Madame Regimbart.

So, she knew all about his life, and he knew nothing about hers!

But he had found in her dressing-room the miniature of a gentleman with long moustaches: was this the same person about whom a vague story had been told him at one time to do with suicide? But there was no way of finding out any more! What was the point, anyway? The hearts of women are like those little pieces of furniture with secret hiding-places, full of drawers fitted into each other; you go to a lot of trouble, break your nails, and in the bottom find some withered flower, a few grains of dust − or emptiness! And then perhaps he was afraid of learning too much.

She made him refuse invitations where she was unable to accompany him, kept him close by her side, was afraid of losing him; and, in spite of this union which was every day becoming stronger, all of a sudden abysses would open between them about the most trifling questions, the appreciation of an individual or a work of art.

She had a style of playing on the piano which was correct and hard. Her spiritualism (Madame Dambreuse believed in the transmigration of souls into the stars) did not prevent her from taking the utmost care of her cashbox. She was haughty towards her servants; her eyes remained dry at the sight of the poor in their rags. In her favourite expressions, a candid egoism revealed itself: 'What concern is that of mine? I should be so silly! Why should I?' − and a thousand little acts incapable of analysis and hateful. She would have listened behind doors; she must have lied to her confessor. Out of a spirit of despotism, she insisted on Frédéric going to church with her on Sunday. He obeyed, and carried her prayer book.

The loss of her inheritance had changed her considerably. These marks of grief which people attributed to the death of M. Dambreuse made her an object of interest; and, as in former times, she had a great number of visitors. Since Frédéric's lack of electoral success, she was ambitious of obtaining for both of them an embassy in Germany; so the first thing they had to do was to submit to the ideas currently in favour.

Some people wanted the Empire, others the Orléans, others the Comte de Chambord; but they were all of one opinion as to the urgency of decentralisation, and several expedients were proposed with that view, such as: to cut up Paris into a great number of high streets in order to turn it into villages, to transfer the seat of government to Versailles, to have the schools in Bourges, to suppress the libraries, and to entrust everything to major-generals – and they praised country life on the assumption that the uneducated man had naturally more sense than the others! Hatreds were legion: hatred of primary teachers and wine-merchants, philosophy classes, history lessons, novels, red waistcoats, long beards, independence in any shape, or any manifestation of individuality; for it was necessary 'to restore the principle of authority', let it be exercised in the name of no matter whom, let it come from no matter where, as long as it was Power, Authority! The Conservatives now talked like Sénécal. Frédéric was puzzled; and when he went to see his former mistress, he found the same remarks uttered by the same men!

The salons of the prostitutes (it was from this period that their importance dates) were a neutral ground where reactionaries of different kinds met. Hussonnet, who had a habit of denigrating the great names of the time (excellent for the restoration of Order), inspired Rosanette with a longing to have evening parties too, like anybody else; he undertook to publish accounts of them; and first of all he brought a man of grave deportment, Fumichon; then came Nonancourt, M. de Grémonville, our friend de Larsillois, ex-prefect, and Cisy, who was now an agriculturist in Lower Brittany, and more Christian than ever.

They were joined, in addition, by men who had at one time been the Maréchale's lovers, such as the Baron de Comaing, the Comte de Jumillac and others, and Frédéric was annoyed by their free and easy behaviour.

In order to assert himself as the master, he increased the rate of expenditure in the house. Then they took on a groom, moved house, and got a fresh supply of furniture. These displays of extravagance were useful for the purpose of making his marriage appear less disproportionate to his fortune. So his means became terribly reduced – and Rosanette had no inkling of all that!

By origin from the lower middle-class, she adored a domestic life, a quiet little home. However, she was pleased to have an 'at home'; she said, 'Women like that!' about women like herself; she wanted to be 'a society lady', and believed herself to be one. She begged him not to smoke in the drawing-room any more, and for the sake of good form tried to make him observe fast-days.

She played her part badly, after all, for she grew serious, and even, before going to bed, always displayed a little melancholy, just as there are cypress trees at the door of a tavern.

He discovered the cause: she was dreaming of marriage – she, too! Frédéric was exasperated. Besides, he remembered her appearance at Madame Arnoux's house, and then he cherished a grudge against her for having held out against him so long.

He made enquiries none the less as to who her lovers had been. She denied having had any relations with any of them. A sort of jealousy took possession of him. He was annoyed at the presents she had received, did still receive – and the more he was irritated by her basic personality, the more he was drawn to her by a harsh, bestial sensuality, illusions of a moment, which ended in hate.

Her words, her voice, her smile, all began to displease him, and especially her glances, that woman's eye forever limpid and inept. Sometimes he felt so sick of her that he would have seen her die without any emotion. But how could he get cross with her? She was so mild that there was no hope of picking a quarrel with her.

Deslauriers reappeared, and explained his stay in Nogent by saying that he was making arrangements to buy a lawyer's practice. Frédéric was glad to see him again; it was somebody to talk to! He included him as a third person in everything they did.

The lawyer dined with them from time to time, and whenever any little disputes arose, always took Rosanette's side, so that Frédéric, on one occasion, said to him:

'Oh! Sleep with her, if it amuses you!' So much did he long for some chance of getting rid of her.

About the middle of the month of June, she was served with an order by which Maître Athanase Gautherot, sheriff's officer, enjoined her to pay four thousand francs due to Mademoiselle Clémence Vatnaz; if not, he would come the next day to seize her effects.

Indeed, of the four bills which she had previously signed, only one had been paid – the money which she had happened to get since then having been spent on fulfilling other needs.

She rushed off to see Arnoux. He lived in the Faubourg Saint-Germain, and the porter did not know which street. She made her way next to the houses of several friends, could not find anyone in, and came back in a state of despair. She did not wish to tell Frédéric anything about it, fearing that this new occurrence might prejudice the chance of marriage between them.

On the following morning, Maître Athanase Gautherot appeared, flanked by two assistants, one of them sallow with a mean-looking face, who looked as if he were eaten up with envy, the other wearing a detachable collar and trouser-straps drawn very tightly, with a sort of thimble of black taffeta on his index-finger – and both ignobly dirty, with greasy collars, and the sleeves of their coats too short.

Their employer, on the other hand, a very good-looking man, began by apologising for the disagreeable duty he had to perform, while at the same time looking round the room, 'full of pretty things, my word!' He added, 'Not to speak of the things that can't be seized.' At a gesture the two bailiff's men disappeared.

Then his compliments redoubled. Could anyone believe that a lady so . . . charming would not have had a reliable friend! A sale of her goods under an order of the courts was a real misfortune! One never gets over a thing like that. He tried to frighten her; then, seeing that she was agitated, suddenly assumed a paternal tone. He knew the world, he had been brought into business relations with all these ladies; and as he mentioned their names, he examined the frames of the pictures on the walls. They were pictures that had belonged to dear Arnoux, sketches by Sombaz, watercolours by Burieu, and three landscapes by Dittmer. It was evident that Rosanette was ignorant of their value. Maître Gautherot turned round to her:

'Look here! To show you that I'm a decent fellow, let's do one thing: give me up those Dittmers and I'll pay the lot! Is it agreed?'

At that moment Frédéric, who had been informed about the matter by Delphine in the anteroom, and who had just seen the two assistants, came in with his hat on his head, in a brutal manner. Maître Gautherot resumed his dignity; and, as the door had been left open:

'Come on, gentlemen, take this down! In the second room, we have: one oak table with two leaves, two sideboards . . .'

Frédéric stopped him, asking whether there was not some way of preventing the seizure.

'Why, certainly! Who paid for the furniture?'

'I did.'

'Well, draw up a claim; at least it will give you some more time.'

Maître Gautherot quickly finished his inventory, and, in the report to the court, entered an injunction against Mademoiselle Bron, then withdrew.

Frédéric uttered no reproach. He gazed at the traces of mud left on the carpet by the bailiffs' shoes; and, speaking to himself:

'We will have to look for some money!'

'Ah! My God, how stupid I am!' said the Maréchale.

She rummaged in a drawer, took out a letter, and hurried off to the Languedoc Lighting Company, in order to get the transfer of her shares.

She came back an hour later. The shares had been sold to someone else! The clerk had said, in answer to her demand, while examining the sheet of paper containing Arnoux's written promise: 'This document in no way constitutes you the owner of the shares. The Company doesn't recognise it.' In short, he had sent her away unceremoniously, she was choking with rage; and Frédéric would have to go to Arnoux's house at once to have the matter cleared up.

But Arnoux would perhaps imagine that he had come to recover in an indirect fashion the fifteen thousand francs due on the mortgage which he had lost! And then this claim from a man who had been his mistress's lover seemed to him a piece of turpitude. Selecting a middle course, he went to the Dambreuse mansion to get Madame Regimbart's address, sent a messenger to her residence, and in this way ascertained the name of the café which the Citizen now frequented.

It was a little café on the Place de la Bastille, in which he sat all day in the right-hand back corner, never moving any more than if he had been built into the structure.

After having passed successively through the half-cup of coffee, the glass of grog, punch, mulled wine, and even red wine and water, he had fallen back again on beer; and every half hour he let fall the word, 'Beer!' having reduced his language to the basic minimum. Frédéric asked him if he saw Arnoux occasionally.

'No!'

'Oh, why?'

'An idiot!'

Politics, perhaps, kept them apart, and so Frédéric thought it might be diplomatic to enquire about Compain.

'What an oaf!' said Regimbart.

'How is that?'

'His calf's head!'

'Ah! Explain to me what the calf's head is!'

Regimbart's face wore a contemptuous smile.

'Rubbish!'

After a long silence, Frédéric went on to ask:

'So, has he moved?'

'Who?'

'Arnoux!'

'Yes: Rue de Fleurus!'

'What number?'

'Do I associate with Jesuits?'

'Jesuits!'

The Citizen replied angrily:

'With the money of a patriot whom I introduced to him, that pig has set up as a dealer in rosaries!'

'It can't be true!'

'Go and see for yourself!'

It was perfectly true; Arnoux, enfeebled by a fit of sickness, had turned to religion; besides, 'he had always been religious at heart', and (with that mixture of commercialism and ingenuity which was natural to him), in order to gain salvation and make his fortune, at the same time, he had begun to deal in religious objects.

Frédéric had no difficulty in discovering his establishment, on whose signboard appeared these words: '*Emporium of Gothic Art —*

Ecclesiastical restoration – Church ornaments – Polychrome sculpture – Frankincense of the Magi, etc., etc.'

At the two corners of the shop window rose two wooden statues, daubed with gold, vermilion and azure; a Saint John the Baptist with his sheepskin, and a Saint Genevieve with roses in her apron and a distaff under her arm; next, groups in plaster: a nun teaching a little girl, a mother on her knees beside a little bed, and three school boys before the holy table. The prettiest object was a kind of châlet representing the interior of the stable with the ass, the ox, and the baby Jesus lying on straw, real straw. From top to bottom of the shelves could be seen medals by the dozen, rosaries of every kind, fonts in the form of shells, and portraits of ecclesiastical dignitaries, amongst whom Monsignor Affre and our Holy Father shone forth with smiles on both their faces.

Arnoux sat dozing at his counter with his head down. He had aged terribly. He had even round his temples a crown of pink spots, and the reflection of the gold crosses touched by the rays of the sun fell onto it.

Frédéric was filled with sadness at this spectacle of decay. Out of devotion to the Maréchale he resigned himself, however, and stepped forward; at the back of the shop Madame Arnoux appeared; thereupon, he turned on his heel.

'I didn't find him,' he said, when he got home.

And in vain did he promise that he would write at once to his notary at Le Havre for some money. Rosanette flew into a rage. She had never seen a man so weak, so flabby; while she was enduring countless privations, other people lived like lords.

Frédéric was thinking about poor Madame Arnoux, and picturing the heart-rending mediocrity of her surroundings. He had seated himself at the writing-desk; and, as Rosanette's voice continued its bitter railing:

'Ah! In the name of Heaven, be quiet!

'You're not going to defend them, by any chance?'

'Well, yes!' he exclaimed, 'for what's the cause of this persecution?'

'But why is it that you don't want to make them pay up? It's for fear of vexing your old flame, confess it!'

He felt an inclination to smash her head with the clock; words failed him. He relapsed into silence. Rosanette, walking up and down the room, continued:

'I'm going to sue your precious Arnoux. Oh! I don't need you!' And pursing her lips: 'I'll get legal advice.'

Three days later, Delphine burst into the room.

'Madame, madame, there's a man here with a pot of paste who's given me a fright.'

Rosanette went into the kitchen, and saw a vagabond whose face was pitted with smallpox, who was paralysed in one arm, and was three fourths drunk and gibbering.

This was Maître Gautherot's bill-sticker. The objections raised against the seizure having been overruled, the sale followed as a matter of course.

For his trouble in having got up the stairs he demanded, in the first place, a half-glass of brandy – then he begged another favour, namely tickets for the theatre, assuming that the lady of the house was an actress. After this he spent several minutes winking in an incomprehensible manner; finally, he declared that for forty sous he would tear off the corners of the poster which he had already affixed to the door downstairs. Rosanette was there referred to by her name, a piece of unusual harshness which revealed all Vatnaz's spite.

She had at one time been of a softer disposition, and had even, while suffering from the effects of a heartache, written to Béranger for his advice. But under the ravages of life's storms, her spirit had become soured; for she had been forced, in turn, to give lessons on the piano, to run a boarding-house, collaborate on fashion journals, sublet apartments, and buy and sell lace to prostitutes – where her connections enabled her to oblige many persons, Arnoux among others. She had formerly been employed in a commercial establishment.

There it was one of her functions to pay the workwomen; and for each of them there were two account books, one of which always remained in her hands. Dussardier, who through kindness kept the account book of a girl named Hortense Baslin, presented himself one day at the cash office at the moment when Mademoiselle Vatnaz was presenting this girl's account, 1,682 francs, which the cashier paid her. Now, on the very day before this, Dussardier had entered down the sum as only 1,082 in the girl's book. He asked to have it back on some pretext; then, anxious to bury out of sight the story of this theft, he told her that he had lost it. The workwoman ingenuously repeated this lie to Mademoiselle Vatnaz; she, in order to satisfy her mind about the matter, came with a show of indifference to talk to the kindly clerk about it. He contented himself with the answer: 'I've burned it'; that was all. A little while afterwards she left the establishment, without believing that the book had been really destroyed, and believing that Dussardier was holding on to it.

On hearing that he had been wounded, she had rushed to his abode, with the object of getting it back. Then, having discovered nothing, in spite of the closest searches, she had been seized with respect, and soon with love, for this young man, so loyal, so gentle, so heroic and so strong! At her age such good fortune in an affair of the heart was a thing one would not have expected. She threw herself into it with the appetite of an ogress – and because of it she had given up literature, socialism, 'consoling doctrines and generous Utopias', the course of lectures which she gave on the 'Desubalternization of Woman', everything, even Delmar; finally she offered to unite herself to Dussardier in marriage.

Although she was his mistress, he was not at all in love with her. Besides, he had not forgotten her theft. Then she was too wealthy for him. He refused her offer. Thereupon, with tears in her eyes, she told him about what she had dreamed of: it was for them both to have a dress shop. She possessed the necessary basic capital, and next week this would be increased by another four thousand francs; and she told him the story of the proceedings she had taken against the Maréchale.

Dussardier was grieved on account of his friend. He recalled the cigar-holder that had been presented to him at the guardhouse, the evenings of the Quai Napoléon, so many pleasant conversations, books lent to him, the thousand acts of kindness which Frédéric had done on his behalf. He begged Vatnaz to desist.

She laughed at him for his good nature, while exhibiting a loathing of Rosanette which he could not understand; she longed for wealth, in fact, only in order to humiliate her, by and by, with her carriage.

Dussardier was horrified by such black abysses of hate; and when he ascertained what was the exact day fixed for the sale, he went out. On the following morning he made his appearance at Frédéric's house with an embarrassed countenance.

'I owe you an apology.'

'Whatever for?'

'You must think me very ungrateful, I, whom she is . . . ' He faltered. 'Oh! I'll see no more of her, I won't be her accomplice!' And as the other was gazing at him in astonishment: 'Isn't your mistress's furniture to be sold in three days' time?'

'Who told you that?'

'She did, Vatnaz! But I'm afraid of offending you . . . '

'You couldn't, my dear friend!'

'Ah! That's true, I'd forgotten how good you are!'

And he held out to him, discreetly, a little pocketbook made of leather.

It contained four thousand francs, all his savings.

'What! Oh, no! . . . No! . . . '

'I knew I would offend you,' returned Dussardier, with a tear in the corner of his eye.

Frédéric pressed his hand; and the honest fellow went on in a piteous tone:

'Take the money! Give me that much pleasure! I'm in such despair! Besides, isn't everything over now? I thought when the Revolution came we would be happy. Do you remember how fine it was? How freely we breathed! But now we've fallen back worse than ever.'

And, fixing his eyes on the ground:

'Now, they're killing our Republic, just as they killed the other one, the Roman one! And poor Venice, poor Poland, poor Hungary! What acts of abomination! First of all, they knocked down the trees of Liberty, then they restricted the right to vote, shut up the clubs, re-established censorship and surrendered education to the priests, until the Inquisition's ready. Why not? Some Conservatives would like the Cossacks in Paris! The newspapers are fined for speaking against the death penalty, Paris is bristling with bayonets, sixteen departments are in a state of siege; and the demand for amnesty has again been rejected!'

He placed both hands on his forehead; then, spreading out his arms as if he were in great distress:

'But if we only made an effort! If we were only sincere, we might get on together! But no! The workers are no better than the capitalists, you see! At Elboeuf recently they refused to help at a fire. There are wretches who profess to regard Barbès as an aristocrat! In order to make the people look ridiculous, they want to nominate for the presidency Nadaud, a mason, just imagine! And there's no way out of it! No remedy! Everybody is against us! For my part, I've never done anything wrong; and yet this is like a weight pressing down on my stomach. If this state of things continues, I'll go mad. I'd like to get myself killed. I tell you I don't need my money! Pay it back to me if you like, deuce take it! I'll lend it to you!'

Frédéric, who felt constrained by necessity, ended by taking his four thousand francs. And so they had no more anxiety so far as Vatnaz was concerned.

But it was not long before Rosanette lost her action against Arnoux, and through sheer obstinacy wished to appeal.

Deslauriers exhausted himself in trying to make her understand that Arnoux's promise constituted neither a gift nor a regular transfer; she did not even listen, her notion being that the law was unjust; it was because she was a woman, men stuck together! In the end, however, she followed his advice.

He made himself so much at home in the house, that on several occasions he brought Sénécal to dinner. Frédéric, who lent him money, and even got his own tailor to supply him with clothes, did not like this lack of ceremony; and the lawyer gave his old coats to the socialist, whose means of existence were unknown.

He was, however, anxious to be of service to Rosanette. One day, when she showed him a dozen shares in the Kaolin Company (that enterprise which had led to Arnoux being cast in damages to the extent of thirty thousand francs), he said to her:

'But this is a shady transaction! It's wonderful!'

She had the right to call on him for the reimbursement of her shares. In the first place, she could prove that he was jointly bound to pay all the Company's liabilities, then that he had certified personal debts as collective debts, in short, that he had embezzled sums which were payable only to the Company.

'All this renders him guilty of fraudulent bankruptcy under articles 586 and 587 of the Commercial Code; and you may be sure, my pet, we'll have his skin.'

Rosanette threw herself on his neck. He entrusted her case next day to his former master, not having time to devote attention to it himself, as he had business at Nogent; in case of any urgency, Sénécal would write to him.

His negotiations for the purchase of an office were a mere pretext. He spent his time at M. Roque's house, where he had begun not only by sounding the praises of their friend, but by imitating his manners and language as much as possible – and in this way he had gained Louise's confidence, while he won over that of her father by attacking Ledru-Rollin.

If Frédéric did not return, it was because he was mixing in aristocratic society; and gradually Deslauriers gave them to understand that he was in love with somebody, that he had a child, and that he was keeping a fallen creature.

The despair of Louise was intense, the indignation of Madame Moreau no less strong. She saw her son whirling towards the bottom of a vague abyss, was wounded in her religious sense of the conventions, and reacted as if her own honour were tainted, when all of a sudden her physiognomy underwent a change. To the questions which people put to her with regard to Frédéric, she replied in a sly fashion:

'He is well, very well.'

She had learned that he was about to be married to Madame Dambreuse.

The date of the event had been fixed; and he was even trying to think of some way of making Rosanette swallow it.

About the middle of autumn she won her action with reference to the kaolin shares. Frédéric found out about it through Sénécal, whom he met at his door, on his way back from the courts.

It had been held that M. Arnoux was privy to all the frauds; and the ex-tutor had such an air of delight that Frédéric prevented him from going any further, assuring him that he would convey the intelligence to Rosanette. He presented himself before her with a look of irritation on his face.

'Well, now you're satisfied!'

But, without minding what he said:

'Look here!'

And she pointed towards her child, who was lying in a cradle close to the fire. She had found him so sick at the house of the wetnurse that morning that she had brought him back to Paris.

All his limbs had grown exceedingly thin, and his lips were

covered with white specks, which in the interior of the mouth looked like clots of milk.

'What did the doctor say?'

'Oh, the doctor! He claims that the journey has increased his . . . I don't know what it is, some name ending in "ite" . . .anyway that he's got thrush. Do you know what that is?'

Frédéric replied without hesitation: 'Certainly', adding that it was nothing.

But that evening he was alarmed by the child's debilitated look and by the progress of these whitish spots, which looked like mould, as if life, already abandoning this poor little body, had left nothing but matter from which vegetation was sprouting. His hands were cold; he was no longer able to drink anything now; and the nurse, another woman, whom the porter had gone and taken on on chance at an employment office, kept repeating:

'It seems to me he's very low, very low!'

Rosanette was up all night.

In the morning she went to look for Frédéric.

'Just come and look at him. He's stopped moving.'

Indeed, he was dead. She took him up, shook him, clasped him in her arms, calling him the most tender names, covered him with kisses and sobs, twisted from one side to the other in a state of distraction, tore her hair, cried out – and then let herself sink onto the edge of the divan, where she stayed with her mouth open and a flood of tears running from her wildly-staring eyes. Then a torpor fell upon her, and all became still in the apartment. The furniture was overturned. Two or three napkins were lying about. It struck six. The night-light went out.

Frédéric, as he gazed at the scene, could almost believe that he was dreaming. His heart was oppressed with a feeling of anguish. It seemed to him that this death was only a beginning, and that behind it was a worse calamity, which was just about to arrive.

Suddenly, Rosanette said in a tender tone:

'We'll preserve him, won't we?'

She wished to have the dead child embalmed. There were many objections to this. The principal one, in Frédéric's opinion, was that the thing was impracticable in the case of children so young. A portrait would be better. She adopted this idea. He wrote a line to Pellerin, and Delphine hastened to deliver it.

Pellerin arrived speedily, anxious by this display of zeal to efface all recollection of his former conduct. The first thing he said was:

'Poor little angel! Ah, my goodness, what a misfortune!'

But gradually (the artist in him getting the upper hand), he declared that nothing could be done with those dark-smudged eyes, that livid face, that it was a real case of still-life, and would require very great talent to treat it effectively; and he murmured:

'Oh, not easy, not easy!'

'As long as it's lifelike,' objected Rosanette.

'Pooh! What do I care about a thing being lifelike! Down with Realism! It's the spirit you have to paint! Let me alone! I'm going to try to imagine how it should look!'

He reflected, with his left hand clasping his brow, and with his right hand clutching his elbow; then, all of a sudden:

'Ah, I have an idea! A pastel! With coloured mezzotints, almost spread out flat, you can get a lovely effect of relief, just along the edges!'

He sent the chambermaid to look for his box of colours; then, with a chair under his feet and another by his side, he began to throw out broad strokes, as calm as if he had drawn them from a bust. He praised the little Saint Johns of Correggio, the Infanta Rosa of Velasquez, the milk-white flesh-tints of Reynolds, the distinction of Lawrence, and especially the child with long hair that sits in Lady Gower's lap.

'Besides, could you find anything more charming than these little tots? The type of the sublime (Raphael proved it by his Madonnas) is probably a mother with her child.'

Rosanette, who was choking with emotion, left the room; and immediately Pellerin said:

'Well, about Arnoux! . . . You know what's happened?'

'No! What?'

'Well, it was bound to end that way!'

'What has happened? Tell me!'

'Perhaps by this time he's . . . Excuse me!'

The artist stood up in order to raise the head of the little corpse higher.

'You were saying . . . ?' Frédéric resumed.

And Pellerin, half-closing his eyes, in order to take his dimensions better:

'I was saying that our friend Arnoux is perhaps by this time locked up!'

Then, in a tone of satisfaction:

'Just look at that! Isn't that the thing?'

'Yes, very good! But what about Arnoux?'

Pellerin laid down his pencil.

'As far as I could understand, he's being sued by a chap called Mignot, a close friend of Regimbart – what a mug he is, isn't he? What an idiot! Just imagine! One day . . . '

'Oh! What's Regimbart got to do with it!'

'All right. Well, yesterday evening, Arnoux had to produce twelve thousand francs; if not, he was a ruined man.'

'Oh, that may be an exaggeration,' said Frédéric.

'Not a bit of it! It looked serious to me, very serious!'

At that moment Rosanette reappeared, with red patches under her eyes, which glowed like patches of make-up. She sat down near the drawing and gazed at it. Pellerin signalled to the other that he was holding his tongue on account of her. But Frédéric, ignoring this:

'But I can't believe . . . '

'I tell you I met him yesterday,' said the artist, 'at seven o'clock in the evening, in the Rue Jacob. He even had his passport, just in case; and he spoke about embarking from Le Havre, himself and the whole band.'

'What! With his wife?'

'Of course! He's too much of a family man to live all by himself.'

'And are you sure of this?'

'Come on! Where do you think he'd have found twelve thousand francs?'

Frédéric took two or three turns round the room. He was panting for breath, biting his lips, and then he snatched up his hat.

'Where are you going now?' said Rosanette.

He made no reply, and disappeared.

He needed twelve thousand francs, or he would never see Madame Arnoux again; and until now he had retained an invincible hope. Did she not constitute the very substance of his heart, the very essence of his life? For a few minutes he went staggering along the pavement, tortured with anxiety, and nevertheless happy that he was no longer with the other.

Where was he to get the money? Frédéric was well aware from his own experience how hard it is to lay hands on it immediately, at no matter what cost. There was only one person who could help him, Madame Dambreuse. She always kept several banknotes in her desk. He called at her house; and, in a bold tone:

'Have you twelve thousand francs to lend me?'

'What for?'

That was another person's secret. She wanted to know who this person was. He would not give way on this point. Both were equally determined not to yield. Finally, she declared that she would give nothing until she knew for what purpose. Frédéric turned very red. One of his comrades had committed a theft. The sum had to be returned this very day.

'What's his name? His name! Come! What's his name?'

'Dussardier!'

And he threw himself on his knees, begging her to say nothing about it.

'What do you think of me?' Madame Dambreuse replied. 'It's as if you are the guilty one. Please stop looking tragic! Look, here's the money, and much good may it do him!'

He hurried off to see Arnoux. The dealer was not in his shop. But he still lived in the Rue Paradis, for he had two domiciles.

In the Rue Paradis, the porter swore that M. Arnoux had been away since the evening before; as for Madame, he could not say; and Frédéric, having rushed like an arrow up the stairs, laid his ear against the keyhole. At length, the door was opened. Madame had gone away with Monsieur. The servant did not know when they would be back; her wages had been paid; and she was leaving herself.

Suddenly he heard the creaking of a door.

'But there's someone here?'

'Oh, no, Monsieur! It's the wind!'

Thereupon he withdrew. Nonetheless, there was something inexplicable in such a rapid disappearance.

Regimbart, being Mignot's intimate friend, could perhaps enlighten him? And Frédéric took a cab to that gentleman's house at Montmartre in the Rue de l'Empereur.

Attached to the house there was a small garden shut in by a railing which was stopped up with iron plates. A flight of three steps set off the white façade; and a passer-by on the pavement could see the two rooms on the ground floor, the first of which was a parlour with ladies' dresses lying all around on the furniture, and the second the workshop in which Madame Regimbart's female assistants were accustomed to sit.

They were all convinced that Monsieur had important occupations, distinguished connections, that he was a man altogether beyond comparison. When he passed along the corridor with his hat cocked up at the sides, his long grave face, and his green frock-coat, the girls stopped in the midst of their work. Besides, he never failed to address to them a few words of encouragement, some observation which showed his ceremonious courtesy – and afterwards, in their own homes, they felt unhappy, because they had kept him as their ideal.

No one, however, was so devoted to him as Madame Regimbart, an intelligent little woman, who supported him on the proceeds of her business.

As soon as M. Moreau had given his name, she came out quickly to receive him, knowing through the servants what his relations were with Madame Dambreuse. Her husband 'would be back in a moment'; and Frédéric, while he followed her, admired the appearance of the house and the profusion of oilcloth that was in it. Then he waited a few minutes in a kind of office, into which the Citizen was in the habit of retiring, in order to think.

Regimbart's reception of him was less surly than usual.

He related Arnoux's recent history. The ex-manufacturer of ceramics had spun a yarn to Mignot, a patriot who owned a hundred shares in the *Siècle*, professing to show that it was necessary from the democratic standpoint to change the management and the editorship of the newspaper; and under the pretext of making his views prevail in the next meeting of shareholders, he had asked the other for fifty shares, telling him that he would pass them on to reliable friends who would back up his vote; Mignot would have no personal responsibility, no trouble with anyone; then, when he had achieved success, he would secure him a good place in the administration, of at least five to six thousand francs. The shares had been delivered. But Arnoux had at once sold them, and with the money had entered into partnership with a dealer in religious articles. Thereupon came complaints from Mignot, evasive answers from Arnoux. At last the patriot had threatened to bring against him a charge of cheating if he did not restore his share certificates or pay an equivalent sum: fifty thousand francs.

Frédéric's face had an air of despair.

'That's not all,' said the Citizen. 'Mignot, who is an honest fellow, reduced his claim to one fourth. New promises on the part of the other, and, of course, new dodges. In short, on the morning of the day before yesterday, Mignot sent him a written application to pay up, within twenty four hours, twelve thousand francs, without prejudice to the balance.'

'But I have them!' said Frédéric.

The Citizen slowly turned round:

'You're joking!'

'Excuse me! They're in my pocket. I brought them with me.'

'How you do go at it! By Jove, you do! But it's too late; the complaint has been lodged, and Arnoux has gone.'

'Alone?'

'No! With his wife. They were seen at the Le Havre terminus.'

Frédéric grew exceedingly pale. Madame Regimbart thought he was going to faint. He retained his self-possession, and had even sufficient presence of mind to ask two or three questions about the occurrence. Regimbart was grieved, considering that it injured the cause of Democracy. Arnoux had always been lax in his conduct and with no sense of order.

'A regular harebrained fellow! He burned the candle at both ends! The skirt ruined him! It's not him I pity, but his poor wife!'

For the Citizen admired virtuous women, and had a great esteem for Madame Arnoux. 'She must have suffered a nice lot!'

Frédéric felt grateful to him for his sympathy; and, as if Regimbart had done him a service, he warmly pressed his hand.

'Have you done all that's required?' said Rosanette when she saw him again.

He had not had the heart, he answered, and had walked about the streets at random to take his mind off things.

At eight o'clock, they passed into the dining-room; but they sat face to face in silence, heaving a deep sigh every now and then, and pushing away their plates. Frédéric drank some brandy. He felt quite shattered, crushed, annihilated, no longer conscious of anything save a sensation of extreme fatigue.

She went to get the portrait. The red, the yellow, the green, and the indigo made glaring stains that jarred with each other, so that it looked a hideous thing, almost ridiculous.

Besides, the dead child was now unrecognisable. The purple hue of his lips intensified the whiteness of his skin; his nostrils were even more drawn, his eyes more hollow; and his head rested on a pillow of blue taffeta, surrounded by petals of camelias, autumn roses, and violets; this was an idea suggested by the chambermaid; and both of them had thus with pious care arranged the little corpse. On the mantelpiece, covered with a cloth of lace, were silver-gilt candlesticks with bunches of consecrated box in the spaces between them; at the corners there were a pair of vases in which oriental pastilles were burning; all these things, taken in with the cradle, formed a kind of altar; and Frédéric recalled the night he had watched beside M. Dambreuse's deathbed.

Nearly every quarter of an hour Rosanette drew aside the curtains in order to take a look at her child. She saw him, a few months hence, beginning to walk, then at school, in the courtyard, playing a game of base; then at twenty years old a full-grown young man; and all these pictures conjured up in her mind created for her, as it were, all the sons she would have lost – the excess of her grief making her many times a mother.

Frédéric, sitting motionless in the other armchair, was thinking of Madame Arnoux.

She was at that moment in a train, no doubt, with her face at a carriage window, while she watched the country disappearing behind her in the direction of Paris, or else on the deck of a steamboat, as when he had first met her; but this boat was carrying her away into countries from which she would never return. Then he saw her in a room at an inn, with trunks on the floor, the wallpaper hanging in shreds, and the door shaking in the wind. And after that? What would become of her? Would she become a schoolmistress, or a lady's companion, a chambermaid, perhaps? She was exposed to all the vicissitudes of poverty. His utter ignorance as to what her fate might be tortured him. He ought either to have opposed her departure or to have followed her. Was he not her real husband? And, as he thought that he would never see her again, that it was all over forever, that she was lost beyond recall, he felt something like a rending of his entire being; the tears that had been gathering since the morning overflowed.

Rosanette noticed.

'Ah! You're crying just like me! You're grieving, too?'

'Yes! Yes, I am! . . .'

He pressed her to his heart, and they both sobbed, locked in each other's arms.

Madame Dambreuse was weeping too, as she lay face downwards on her bed, with her head in her hands.

Olympe Regimbart having come that evening for her to try on her first coloured gown after mourning, had told her about Frédéric's visit, and even about the twelve thousand francs which he had ready to transfer to M. Arnoux.

So, then, this money, her money, was to be used to stop the other from leaving, to hold on to a mistress!

At first, she broke into a violent rage; and she had determined to drive him from her door, like a lackey. Floods of tears calmed her down. It was better to keep it all to herself, and say nothing.

Frédéric brought back the twelve thousand francs the next day.

She begged him to keep the money, in case of need, for his friend, and she asked a lot of questions about this gentleman. Whoever had tempted him to such a breach of trust? A woman, no doubt! Women drag you into every kind of crime.

This bantering tone put Frédéric out of countenance. He felt deep remorse for the calumny he had invented. He was reassured by the reflection that Madame Dambreuse could not be aware of the facts.

All the same, she was very persistent about the subject; for, two days later, she again made enquiries about his young friend, and, after that, about another, Deslauriers.

'Is this young man trustworthy and intelligent?'

Frédéric sang his praises.

'Ask him to call on me one of these mornings; I would like to consult him about a matter of business.'

She had found a roll of old papers in which there were some bills of Arnoux, which had been duly protested, and which had been signed by Madame Arnoux. It was about these very bills that Frédéric had called on M. Dambreuse on one occasion while the latter was having breakfast; and, although the capitalist had not sought to enforce repayment of this outstanding debt, he had got judgment from the Tribunal of Commerce not only against Arnoux, but also against his wife, who knew nothing about it, as her husband had not thought fit to warn her.

Here, now, was a weapon! Madame Dambreuse had no doubt about it. But her notary would advise her perhaps to abstain; she would have preferred to act through someone obscure; and she had remembered that big fellow with the impudent face, who had offered her his services.

Frédéric ingenuously performed this commission for her.

The lawyer was enchanted at the idea of having business relations with such an aristocratic lady.

He rushed to see her.

She informed him that the inheritance belonged to her niece, a further reason for liquidating those debts which she should repay, her object being to overwhelm the Martinon couple by a display of impeccable conduct.

Deslauriers guessed that there was some mystery behind all this; he looked at the bill and reflected. Madame Arnoux's name, traced by her own hand, brought once more before his eyes her entire person, and the insult which he had received at her hands. Since vengeance was offered to him, why not take it?

He accordingly advised Madame Dambreuse to have the bad debts which went with the inheritance sold by auction. A man of straw, whose name would not be divulged, would buy them up, and would exercise the legal rights thus given him to realise them. He would take it on himself to provide that man.

Towards the end of the month of November, Frédéric, happening to pass through the street in which Madame Arnoux lived, raised his eyes towards her windows, and saw posted on the door a placard on which was printed in large letters:

'Sale of valuable furniture, consisting of kitchen utensils, body and table linen, shirts and chemises, lace, petticoats, trousers, French and Indian cashmeres, an Erard piano, two Renaissance oak chests, Venetian mirrors, Chinese and Japanese pottery.'

'It's their furniture!' said Frédéric to himself; and his suspicions were confirmed by the doorkeeper.

As for the person who had given instructions for the sale, he did not know who it was. But perhaps the auctioneer, Maître Berthelmot, might be able to throw some light.

The functionary did not at first want to tell which creditor was having the sale carried out. Frédéric pressed him on the point. It was a gentleman named Sénécal, a business broker; and Maître Berthelmot was even kind enough to lend his own copy of the *Petites Affiches*.

Frédéric, on reaching Rosanette's house, flung down this paper on the table spread wide open.

'Read that!'

'Well, so what?' she said with a face so calm that he was revolted.

'Ah! Keep up that air of innocence!'

'I don't understand.'

'Are you the one selling out Madame Arnoux?'

She read over the announcement again.

'Where is her name?'

'Oh, it's her furniture! You know that better than I do!'

'What's it got to do with me?' said Rosanette, shrugging her shoulders.

'What it's got to do with you? But you're taking your revenge, that's all! This is the consequence of your persecutions! Haven't you insulted her so far as to call at her house! You, a worthless tart. And she the most saintly, the most charming, the best of women! Why are you set on ruining her?'

'I assure you, you're wrong!'

'Come on! As if you hadn't put Sénécal up to this!'

'What nonsense!'

Then he was carried away with rage.

'You lie! You lie, you wretch! You're jealous of her! You've got hold of a judgment against her husband! Sénécal has already been mixed up in your affairs! He detests Arnoux, your two hatreds are in league with each other. I saw how delighted he was when you won that action of yours about the kaolin shares. Are you going to deny *that*?'

'I give you my word . . .'

'Oh! I know what that's worth, your word!'

And Frédéric reminded her of her lovers, giving their names and circumstantial details. Rosanette drew back, all the colour fading from her face.

'That surprises you! You thought I was blind because I shut my eyes. I've finally had enough! One doesn't die through the treacheries of a woman of your sort. When they become too monstrous we leave them; to punish them would be only to degrade oneself!'

She twisted her arms about.

'My God, whatever has brought about this change in him?'

'Nobody but yourself!'

'And all this for Madame Arnoux!' exclaimed Rosanette, weeping.

He replied coldly:

'I have never loved any woman but her!'

At this insult her tears ceased to flow.

'That shows your good taste! A woman of mature years, with a complexion like liquorice, a thick waist, eyes as big as the vent-holes of a cellar, and just as empty! As you like her so much, go and join her!'

'That's what I was waiting for! Thank you!'

Rosanette remained motionless, thunderstruck by this extra-ordinary behaviour. She even allowed the door to shut; then, with a bound, she caught up with him in the anteroom, and flinging her arms around him:

'Why, you're mad! You're mad! This is absurd! I love you!' She pleaded with him: 'Good heavens! For the sake of our little child!'

'Admit that it was you who pulled off this trick!' said Frédéric.

She again protested that she was innocent.

'You won't admit?'

'No!'

'Well, then, farewell! And forever!'

'Listen to me!'

Frédéric turned round:

'If you knew me better, you would know that my decision is irrevocable!'

'Oh! Oh, you'll come back to me!'

'Never as long as I live!'

And he slammed the door behind him violently.

Rosanette wrote to Deslauriers saying that she needed to see him at once.

He called one evening, five days later; and, when she had told him about the rupture:

'Is that all! A nice piece of bad luck!'

She had thought at first that he would be able to bring Frédéric back to her; but now all was lost. She had learned from her doorkeeper that he was about to be married to Madame Dambreuse.

Deslauriers gave her a lecture, and showed himself even to be an exceedingly gay fellow, quite a jolly dog; and, as it was very late, asked permission to spend the night in an armchair. Then, next morning, he set out again for Nogent, informing her that he could not say when they would meet again; in a little while, there would perhaps be a great change in his life.

Two hours after his return, the town was in a state of revolution. The news was that M. Frédéric was going to marry Madame Dambreuse. At length the three Auger girls, unable to stand it any longer, went to see Madame Moreau, who confirmed this intelligence with pride. Père Roque became quite ill when he heard it. Louise locked herself up. It was even rumoured that she had gone mad.

Meanwhile, Frédéric was unable to hide his dejection. Madame Dambreuse, in order to distract him, no doubt, redoubled her attentions. Every afternoon she took him out for a drive in her carriage; and, on one occasion, as they were crossing the Place de la Bourse, she took the idea into her head to pay a visit to the public auction rooms for the sake of amusement.

It was the 1st of December, the very day on which the sale of Madame Arnoux's furniture was to take place. He remembered the date, and manifested his repugnance, declaring that this place was intolerable on account of the crush and the noise. She only wanted to have a peep at it. The brougham drew up. He had no alternative but to accompany her.

In the courtyard could be seen wash handstands without basins, the wooden portions of armchairs, old baskets, pieces of porcelain, empty bottles, mattresses; and men in overalls or in dirty frock-coats, all grey with dust, and with mean-looking faces, some with canvas sacks over their shoulders, were chatting in separate groups or hailing each other enthusiastically.

Frédéric urged that it was inconvenient to go on any further.

'Pooh!'

And they went up the stairs.

In the first room, on the right, gentlemen with catalogues in their hands were examining pictures; in another, a collection of Chinese weapons were being sold; Madame Dambreuse wanted to go downstairs again. She looked at the numbers over the doors, and led him to the end of the corridor, towards a room which was crowded with people.

He immediately recognised the two display-shelves belonging to the office of *L'Art Industriel*, her work-table, all her furniture! Heaped up at the far end of the room according to size, they formed a wide slope from the floor to the windows; and on the other sides of the apartment, the carpets and the curtains hung down straight along the walls. Underneath, there were steps occupied by old men half asleep. On the left rose a sort of counter at which the auctioneer, in a white cravat, was lightly swinging a little hammer. A young man by his side was writing; and below him stood a sturdy fellow, something between a commercial traveller and a tout, calling out the furniture for sale. Three attendants placed the articles on a table, at the sides of which sat a row of secondhand dealers and women who sold old clothes. The general public moved around behind them.

When Frédéric came in, petticoats, neckerchiefs, handkerchiefs and even chemises were being passed from hand to hand, and turned inside out; sometimes they were flung from a distance, and suddenly strips of whiteness went flying through the air. After that her gowns were sold, then one of her hats, with a broken feather hanging down, then her furs, then three pairs of boots – and the disposal of these relics, where he could recognize in a confused sort of way the outlines of her limbs, seemed to him an atrocity, as if he had seen crows tearing at her corpse. The atmosphere of the room, heavy with so many breaths, made him feel sick. Madame Dambreuse offered him her smelling-bottle; she was having a lovely time, she said.

The bedroom furniture was now exhibited.

Maître Berthelmot named a price. The crier immediately repeated it in a louder voice; and the three auctioneer's assistants waited quietly for the stroke of the hammer, and then carried the article away to an adjoining room. In this way disappeared, one after the other, the large blue carpet spangled with camellias, which her dainty feet used to touch so lightly as she advanced to meet him, the little upholstered easy-chair, in which he used to sit facing her when they were alone; the two fireside screens, the ivory of which had been rendered smoother by the touch of her hands; a velvet pincushion, which was still bristling with pins. It was as if parts of his heart were removed with these things; and the monotonous recurrence of the same voices and the same gestures numbed him with fatigue, and plunged him into a funereal torpor, a sensation like that of death itself.

There was a rustle of silk close to his ear; Rosanette touched him.

It was through Frédéric himself that she had learned about this auction. Once she had got over her grief, the idea of deriving some profit from it had occurred to her mind. She had come to see it in a white satin waistcoat with pearl buttons, a flounced gown, tightfitting gloves, and a look of triumph on her face.

He grew pale with anger. She stared at the woman by his side.

Madame Dambreuse had recognised her; and for a minute they looked each other up and down minutely, in order to discover the defect, the blemish – the one perhaps envying the other's youth, and the other riled by the extreme good form, the aristocratic simplicity of her rival.

At last Madame Dambreuse turned her head away, with a smile of inexpressible insolence.

The crier had opened a piano – her piano! He remained standing as he played a scale with his right hand, and put up the instrument at twelve hundred francs, then brought it down to one thousand, then to eight hundred, and finally to seven hundred.

Madame Dambreuse, in a playful tone, laughed at the old tin can.

Placed before the secondhand dealers was a little chest with medallions and silver corners and clasps, the same one which he had seen at the first dinner in the Rue de Choiseul, which had subsequently been in Rosanette's house, and had again returned to Madame Arnoux's; often during their conversations his eyes would wander towards it; it was bound to him by the dearest of memories, and his soul was melting with tenderness, when suddenly Madame Dambreuse said:

'Look here! I'm going to buy that.'

'But it's nothing special,' he returned.

She considered it, on the contrary, very pretty; and the crier commended its delicacy:

'A gem of the Renaissance! Eight hundred francs, gentlemen! Almost entirely of silver! With a little whiting you'll get a lovely shine!'

And, as she was pushing forward through the crush of people:

'What an odd idea!' said Frédéric.

'Does it annoy you?'

'No! But what is the use of a fancy article like that?'

'Who knows? You could keep love-letters in it, perhaps?'

She gave him a look which made the allusion very clear.

'All the more reason for not robbing the dead of their secrets.'

'I didn't imagine she was as dead as all that.' And then she added in a penetrating voice: 'Eight hundred and eighty francs!'

'What you're doing isn't right,' murmured Frédéric.

She began to laugh.

'But this is the first favour, dear, that I am asking from you.'

'Come, now! Doesn't it strike you that at this rate you won't be a very nice husband?'

Someone had just made a higher bid; she raised her hand:

'Nine hundred francs!'

'Nine hundred francs!' repeated Maître Berthelmot.

'Nine hundred and ten . . . fifteen . . . twenty . . . thirty!' squeaked the auctioneer's crier, with jerky nods of his head as he swept his eyes over those in the room.

'Prove to me that I'm going to have a wife who is amenable to reason,' said Frédéric.

He drew her gently towards the door.

The auctioneer continued:

'Come, come, gentlemen, nine hundred and thirty! Is there any bidder at nine hundred and thirty?'

Madame Dambreuse, who had reached the door, stopped; and, in a loud voice:

'One thousand francs!'

A thrill of astonishment ran around the room, and then there was a silence.

'A thousand francs, gentlemen, a thousand francs! Is there any advance? No? Very well, then, one thousand francs! Going! – Gone!'

And down came the ivory hammer.

She passed in her card, and the little chest was handed over to her.

She thrust it into her muff.

Frédéric felt a great chill penetrating his heart.

Madame Dambreuse had not let go of his arm; and she dared not look at his face until they were in the street, where her carriage was awaiting her.

She flung herself into it, like a thief escaping, and, once she was seated, she turned towards Frédéric. He had his hat in his hand.

'Aren't you coming?'

'No, Madame!'

And, bowing to her frigidly, he shut the carriage door, and then made a sign to the coachman to drive away.

His first feeling was one of joy at having regained his independence. He was proud of having avenged Madame Arnoux by sacrificing a fortune to her; then, he was amazed at what he had done, and overcome by a feeling of extreme physical exhaustion.

Next morning his manservant brought him the news. The city had been declared to be in a state of siege, the Assembly had been dissolved, and a number of the representatives of the people were in Mazas prison. Public affairs left him indifferent, so deeply preoccupied was he by his own.

He wrote to several tradesmen countermanding various orders which he had given for articles relative to his marriage, which now appeared to him in the light of a rather ignoble speculation; and he loathed Madame Dambreuse, because, owing to her, he had been very near committing an act of turpitude. He even forgot the Maréchale, and did not even bother about Madame Arnoux, thinking of himself, himself alone – lost amid the wreckage of his dreams, sick at heart, full of grief and disappointment; and in his hatred of the artificial atmosphere wherein he had suffered so much, he longed for the freshness of green fields, the repose of provincial life, a sleepy existence spent in the shade of his natal roof in the midst of ingenuous hearts. At last, when Wednesday evening arrived, he went out.

On the boulevard numerous groups had taken up their stand. From time to time a patrol came and dispersed them; they gathered together again behind it. They talked freely, and did nothing more than hurl jokes and insults at the soldiers.

'What! Aren't they going to fight?' said Frédéric to a workman. The man in overalls replied:

'We're not such fools as to get ourselves killed for the bourgeois! Let them take care of themselves!'

And a gentleman muttered, as he glanced sideways at this man of the people:

'Socialist rascals! If only we could wipe them out this time!'

Frédéric failed to understand the necessity for so much rancour and stupidity. His disgust for Paris intensified; and two days later he set out for Nogent by the first train.

The houses soon became lost to view, the country stretched out before his gaze. Alone in his carriage, with his feet on the seat in front of him, he pondered over the events of the last few days, and on his entire past. The memory of Louise came back to him.

'She really loved me! I was wrong not to snatch at that chance of happiness . . . Pooh! Let's forget it!'

Then, five minutes afterwards:

'Who knows, after all? . . . Later, why not?'

His reverie, like his eyes, wandered afar towards vague horizons.

'She was artless, a peasant girl, almost a savage, but so kind-hearted!'

In proportion as he drew nearer to Nogent, she drew closer to him. As they were passing through the meadows of Sourdun, he saw her under the poplar trees, as in the old days, cutting rushes on the edges of the pools; and now they had reached their destination; he stepped out of the train.

Then he leaned with his elbows on the bridge, to gaze again at the island and the garden where they had walked together one sunshiny day – and the dizzy sensation caused by travelling and the open air, together with the weakness engendered by his recent emotions, arousing in his breast a sort of exaltation, he said to himself:

'She's gone out, perhaps; suppose I went to meet her!'

The bell of Saint-Laurent was ringing; and in the square in front of the church there was a crowd of poor people around an open carriage, the only one in the district (the one which was used for weddings), when, all of a sudden, under the porch, accompanied by a number of well-dressed persons in white cravats, a newly-married couple appeared.

He thought it must be a hallucination. But no! It really was her, Louise! – covered with a white veil which fell from her red hair down to her heels; and it was really him, Deslauriers! – dressed in a blue coat embroidered with silver, the costume of a prefect. How was this?

Frédéric concealed himself behind the corner of a house to let the procession pass.

Shamefaced, vanquished, crushed, he retraced his steps to the railway station, and returned to Paris.

The cabman who drove him assured him that the barricades were erected from the Château-d'Eau to the Gymnase, and turned down the Faubourg Saint-Martin. At the corner of the Rue de Provence, Frédéric stepped out in order to reach the boulevards.

It was five o'clock, a fine rain was falling. A number of citizens blocked the pavement close to the Opéra. The houses opposite were closed. No one at any of the windows. All along the width of the boulevard, dragoons were galloping at breakneck speed, leaning with drawn swords over their horses; and the plumes of their helmets, and their great white cloaks, billowing up behind them, could be seen against the light of the gas-lamps, which guttered in the mist as the wind caught them. The crowd gazed at them mute with terror.

In the intervals between the cavalry charges, squads of police-men arrived on the scene to push the people back into the streets.

But on the steps of Tortoni, a man – Dussardier – who could be distinguished at a distance by his great height, remained standing as motionless as a caryatid.

One of the police officers, marching at the head of his men,

with his three-cornered hat drawn over his eyes, threatened him
with his sword.

The other thereupon took one step forward, and shouted:

'Long live the Republic!'

He fell on his back with his arms spread out.

A howl of horror arose from the crowd. The police officer
created a circle around himself through the power of his gaze; and
Frédéric, thunderstruck, recognised Sénécal.

He travelled. He learned about the melancholy of steamships, the cold awakenings in tents, the dizzying effect of landscapes and ruins, the bitterness of interrupted affections.

He came back.

He mingled in society, and he had other loves. But the constant recollection of the first love made these insipid to him; and besides the vehemence of desire, the bloom of the sensation had vanished. His intellectual ambitions had also grown weaker. Years passed, and he had grown to accept his mental stagnation and the inertia of his heart.

Towards the end of March, 1867, just as it was getting dark, he was alone in his study, when a woman came in.

'Madame Arnoux!'

'Frédéric!'

She caught hold of his hands, and drew him gently towards the window; and she gazed into his face, repeating:

'It's him! It's really him!'

In the shadows of the twilight, he could see only her eyes under the black lace veil that hid her face.

When she had laid down on the edge of the mantelpiece a little wallet of red velvet, she sat down. They both remained silent, unable to speak, smiling at one another.

At last he asked her a lot of questions about herself and her husband.

They had gone to live in a remote part of Brittany for the sake of economy, so as to be able to pay their debts. Arnoux, now almost always ill, seemed an old man now. Her daughter was married and living in Bordeaux, and her son was garrisoned at Mostaganem. Then she raised her head to look at him again:

'But I see you once more! I'm happy!'

He did not fail to let her know that, as soon as he heard of their misfortune, he had hastened to their house.

'I knew!'

'How?'

She had seen him in the courtyard, and had hidden.

'Why?'

Then, in a trembling voice, and with long pauses between her words:

'I was afraid! Yes . . . afraid of you . . . and of myself!'

This disclosure caused in him something like a shock of sensual desire. His heart was beating wildly. She went on:

'Excuse me for not having come sooner.' And, pointing towards the little red wallet covered with golden palms: 'I embroidered it on your account, just for you. It contains the amount for which the Belleville property was given as security.'

Frédéric thanked her for the present, while chiding her at the same time for having taken the trouble.

'No! It wasn't for that that I came! I was determined to pay you this visit, then I'll go back . . . there.'

And she spoke about the place where she lived.

It was a low-built house of only one storey, with a garden full of huge box trees, and a double avenue of chestnut trees, reaching up to the top of the hill, from which there was a view of the sea.

'I go and sit there on a bench, which I have called "Frédéric's bench." '

Then she proceeded to look at the furniture, the ornaments, the pictures, with eager intentness, so that she might carry them away in her memory. The Maréchale's portrait was half-hidden behind a curtain. But the golds and the whites, which stood out in the surrounding darkness, attracted her attention.

'It seems to me I know that woman?'

'Impossible!' said Frédéric. 'It's an old Italian painting.'

She confessed that she would like to take a walk through the streets on his arm.

They went out.

The light from the shop windows fell, every now and then, on her pale profile; then once more she was wrapped in shadow; and in the midst of the carriages, the crowd, and the din, they walked on without noticing anything but each other, without hearing anything, like those who walk together in the country on beds of dead leaves.

They talked about the old days, the dinners at the time of *L'Art*

Industriel, Arnoux's fads, the way he pulled at the ends of his collar and squeezed cosmetic over his moustache, other things more intimate and more profound. What delight he had experienced the first time he had heard her sing! How lovely she looked on her feast-day at Saint-Cloud! He reminded her of the little garden at Auteuil, of evenings at the theatre, a chance meeting on the boulevard, and some of her old servants, her negress.

She was astonished at his memory. However she said to him:

'Sometimes your words come back to me like a distant echo, like the sound of a bell carried by the wind; and it seems to me that you are there when I read passages about love in books.'

'All that people have criticized as exaggerated in fiction you have made me feel,' said Frédéric. 'I can understand characters like Werther, who felt no disgust at his Charlotte for cutting bread and butter.'

'Poor, dear friend!'

She heaved a sigh; and, after a prolonged silence:

'No matter; we shall have loved each other truly!'

'Without having ever belonged to each other, however!'

'That's perhaps all the better,' she replied.

'No, no! What happiness we would have had!'

'Oh, I am sure of it, with a love like yours!'

And it must have been very strong to endure after such a long separation!

Frédéric asked her how she had first discovered that he loved her.

'It was when you kissed my wrist one evening between the glove and the cuff. I said to myself, "Ah! He loves me . . . he loves me!" I was afraid of making sure of it, however. Your reserve was so charming, that I took pleasure in it as in an act of involuntary and continuous homage.'

He regretted nothing. He was compensated for all he had suffered in the past.

When they came back to the house, Madame Arnoux took off her hat. The lamp, placed on a side-table, threw its light onto her white hair. Frédéric felt as if someone had punched him in the middle of his chest.

In order to conceal this disappointment from her, he knelt down on the floor, and, seizing her hands, began to say to her words of tenderness:

'Your person, your slightest movements, seemed to me to have a more than human importance in the world. My heart, like dust, used to rise in your footsteps. You were to me like moonlight on a summer's night, when all is perfume, soft shadows, gleams of whiteness, infinity; and all the delights of the flesh and of the spirit were contained for me in your name, which I kept repeating to myself, trying to kiss it with my lips. I thought of nothing further. It was Madame Arnoux just as you were with her two children, tender, grave, dazzlingly beautiful, and so kind! This image effaced every other. Did I even think of any others? For I had always in the very depths of my soul the music of your voice and the splendour of your eyes!'

She accepted with rapture these tributes of adoration to the woman she no longer was. Frédéric, growing drunk with his own words, came to believe what he was saying. Madame Arnoux, with her back turned to the light, leaned towards him. He felt the caress of her breath on his forehead, and, through her clothes, the vague touch of her entire body. Their hands were clasped; the tip of her boot peeped out from beneath her gown, and he said to her, ready to faint:

'The sight of your foot disturbs me.'

An impulse of modesty made her rise. Then, without any further movement, and with the strange intonation of a sleepwalker:

'At my age! He! Frédéric! . . . No woman has ever been loved as I have been! No, no! What is the use of being young? What do I care about that! I despise them, all those women who come here!'

'Oh, very few women come here!' he returned, obligingly.

Her face lit up, and she asked him whether he meant to be married.

He swore that he never would.

'Are you perfectly sure? Why?'

'Because of you,' said Frédéric, clasping her in his arms.

She remained there, with her body leaning backwards, her lips parted, and her eyes raised. Suddenly she pushed him away with a look of despair; and when he begged her to say something to him in reply, she lowered her head and said:

'I would have liked to make you happy.'

Frédéric suspected Madame Arnoux of having come to offer herself to him; and once more he was seized with a desire to possess her stronger than ever, fierce, desperate. And yet he felt, also, something inexpressible, repugnance, and something like the dread of incest. Another fear, too, stopped him, the fear of being disgusted later. Besides, what a bother it would be! And partly through prudence, and partly so as not to degrade his ideal, he turned on his heel and began to roll a cigarette.

She watched him, seized with admiration.

'How delicate you are! There is no one like you! There is no one like you!

It struck eleven.

'Already!' she exclaimed; 'at a quarter-past I must go.'

She sat down again; but she kept looking at the clock, and he went on walking up and down the room, smoking. Neither of them could think of anything further to say to the other. There is a moment at the hour of parting when the person we love is already no longer with us.

At last, when the hands of the clock had got past the twenty-five minutes, she slowly took up her hat, holding it by the strings.

'Goodbye, my friend, my dear friend! I shall never see you again! This was my last act as a woman. My soul will never leave you. May all the blessings of Heaven be upon you!'

And she kissed him on the forehead, like a mother.

But she appeared to be looking for something, and asked him for a pair of scissors.

She unfastened her comb; all her white hair fell loose.

With a brutal movement of the scissors, she cut off a long lock from the roots.

'Keep it! Goodbye!'

When she had gone, Frédéric opened his window. Madame Arnoux, on the pavement, summoned a passing cab. She stepped into it. The vehicle disappeared.

And that was that.

CHAPTER SEVEN

About the beginning of this winter, Frédéric and Deslauriers were chatting by the fire, once more reconciled by the fatality of their nature, which made them always reunite and be friends again.

Frédéric briefly explained his quarrel with Madame Dambreuse, who had married again, to an Englishman.

Deslauriers, without saying how he had come to marry Mademoiselle Roque, told his friend how his wife had one fine day eloped with a singer. In order to wipe away to some extent the ridicule that this brought upon him, he had compromised himself by an excess of governmental zeal in the exercise of his functions as prefect. He had been dismissed. After that, he had been an agent for colonisation in Algeria, secretary to a pasha, editor of a newspaper, and a canvasser for advertisements, his latest employment being the office of settling disputed cases for a manufacturing company.

As for Frédéric, having squandered two thirds of his fortune, he was now living like a citizen of comparatively humble rank.

Then they questioned each other about their friends.

Martinon was now a member of the Senate.

Hussonnet occupied an important position, in which he had all the theatres and the entire press dependent upon him.

Cisy, given up to religion, and the father of eight children, was living in his ancestral home.

Pellerin, after having turned his hand to Fourierism, homoeopathy, table-turning, Gothic art, and humanitarian painting, had become a photographer; and he was to be seen on every wall in Paris, where he was represented in a black coat with a tiny body and a big head.

'And what about your chum Sénécal?' asked Frédéric.

'Disappeared! I don't know! And you! What about your great love, Madame Arnoux?'

'She's probably at Rome with her son, a cavalry lieutenant.'

'And her husband?'

'Died last year.'

'You don't say so!' exclaimed the lawyer.

Then, striking his forehead:

'Now that I think of it, the other day in a shop I ran into our good old Maréchale, holding by the hand a little boy whom she has adopted. She's the widow of a certain M. Oudry, and very fat now, enormous. What a comedown! She who used to have such a slender waist!'

Deslauriers did not deny that he had taken advantage of her despair to assure himself of that fact by personal experience.

'As you had given me permission to do, by the way.'

This avowal was a compensation for the silence he maintained with reference to his attempt with Madame Arnoux. Frédéric would have forgiven him for it, since it had not succeeded.

Although a little annoyed at the discovery, he pretended to laugh at it; and the idea of the Maréchale brought Vatnaz to his recollection.

Deslauriers had never seen her, any more than a lot of the others who used to come to visit Arnoux; but he remembered Regimbart perfectly.

'Is he still alive?'

'Hardly! Every evening regularly he drags himself past all the cafe's from the Rue de Grammont to the Rue Montmartre, enfeebled, bent in two, emaciated, a spectre!'

'Well, and what about Compain?'

Frédéric uttered a cry of joy, and begged the ex-delegate of the provisional government to explain to him the mystery of the calf's head.

'It's an English importation. In order to parody the ceremony which the Royalists used to celebrate on the thirtieth of January, some Independents founded an annual banquet, at which they ate calves' heads, and drank red wine out of calves' skulls while giving toasts in favour of the extermination of the Stuarts. After Thermidor, some Terrorists organised a brotherhood of a similar description, which just goes to show how fertile folly is.'

'You seem to me to have calmed down a lot about politics.'

'The effect of age,' said the lawyer.

And they resumed their lives.

They had both failed, the one who had dreamed only of love,

and the other who had dreamed of power. What was the reason for this?

'It was perhaps from not having followed a straight line,' said Frédéric.

'In your case that may be so. I, on the contrary, sinned through excess of rectitude, without taking into account a thousand secondary things more important than anything else. I had too much logic, and you too much sentiment.'

Then they blamed chance, circumstances, the time they were born.

Frédéric went on:

'That isn't what we thought we would become long ago in Sens, when you wanted to write a critical history of Philosophy and I a great medieval romance about Nogent, of which I'd found the subject in Froissart: "How Messire Brokars de Fénestranges and the Bishop of Troyes attacked Messire Eustache d'Ambrecicourt". Do you remember?'

And, exhuming their youth with every sentence, they said to each other:

'Do you remember?'

They saw once more the school playground, the chapel, the parlour, the fencing-school at the bottom of the staircase, faces of ushers and of pupils, a chap named Angelmarre, from Versailles, who used to make himself trouser-straps cut from old boots; M. Mirbal and his red whiskers; the two professors of linear drawing and freehand drawing, Varaud and Suriret, who were always wrangling, and the Pole, the compatriot of Copernicus, with his planetary system made of cardboard, an itinerant astronomer whose lecture had been paid for by a dinner in the refectory – then a terrible orgy while they were out on a walking excursion, the first pipes they had smoked, prize-days, and the joy of the holidays.

It was during the vacation of 1837 that they had been to see the Turkish woman.

This was the phrase used to designate a woman whose real name was Zoraïde Turc; and many believed her to be a Muslim, a Turk, which added to the poetic character of her establishment, situated at the water's edge behind the rampart; even in the middle of summer there was shade around her house, which could be recognised by a bowl of goldfish near a pot of mignonette at a window. Young ladies in white nightdresses, with painted cheeks and long earrings, used to tap at the panes as people passed by, and in the evening, on the doorstep, they would sing softly in a husky voice.

This place of perdition spread its fantastic reputation over the whole arrondissement. Allusions were made to it in a circumlocutory style: 'The place you know of – a certain street – below the Bridges.' It made the farmers' wives of the district tremble for their husbands, and the ladies grow apprehensive as to their servants' virtue, because the subprefect's cook had been caught there; and it was, of course, the secret obsession of all the young lads.

Now, one Sunday, during vespers, Frédéric and Deslauriers, having previously curled their hair, gathered some flowers in Madame Moreau's garden, then made their way out through the gate leading into the fields, and, after making a wide detour through the vines, came back through the Pêcherie and stole into the Turkish woman's house with their big bouquets still in their hands.

Frédéric presented his as a lover does to his betrothed. But the great heat, the fear of the unknown, a kind of remorse, and even the very pleasure of seeing at one glance so many women placed at his disposal, disturbed him so much that he turned exceedingly pale, and stood rooted to the spot, speechless. All the girls burst out laughing, delighted to see him so embarrassed; thinking that they were mocking him, he ran away; and, as Frédéric had the money, Deslauriers was naturally obliged to follow him.

They were seen leaving. The result was a story which had not been forgotten three years later.

They told it to each other at great length, each filling in the gaps in the other's memory; and, when they had finished:

'That was the best time of our lives!' said Frédéric.

'Yes, maybe it was. The best time of our lives!' said Deslauriers.

WORDSWORTH CLASSICS
OF WORLD LITERATURE

Requests for inspection copies – Lecturers wishing to obtain copies of Wordsworth Classics or Wordsworth Classics of World Literature titles on inspection are invited to contact: Clive Reynard, Sales Director, Wordsworth Editions Ltd, 6 London Street, London W2 1HL; E-mail CReynard@compuserve.com. Please quote the author, title and ISBN of the titles in which you are interested; together with your name, academic address, E-mail address, the course on which the books will be used and the expected enrolment.

Teachers wishing to inspect specific GCSE or A level course core titles are also invited to contact Wordsworth Editions at the above address.

Inspection copies are sent solely at the discretion of Wordsworth Editions Ltd

APULEIUS
The Golden Ass

LODOVICO ARIOSTO
Orlando Furioso

ARISTOTLE
The Nicomachean Ethics

MARCUS AURELIUS
Meditations

FRANCIS BACON
Essays

JEREMY BENTHAM
Utilitarianism

JAMES BOSWELL
The Life of Samuel Johnson
(UNABRIDGED)

JOHN BUNYAN
The Pilgrim's Progress

BALDASSARE CASTIGLIONE
The Book of the Courtier

CATULLUS
Poems

CERVANTES
Don Quixote

CARL VON CLAUSEWITZ
On War
(ABRIDGED)

CONFUCIUS
The Analects

CAPTAIN JAMES COOK
The Voyages of Captain Cook

DANTE
The Inferno

CHARLES DARWIN
The Origin of Species
The Voyage of the Beagle

RENÉ DESCARTES
Key Philosophical Writings

DOSTOEVSKY
The Brothers Karamazov

ERASMUS
Praise of Folly

SIGMUND FREUD
The Interpretation of Dreams

EDWARD GIBBON
The Decline and Fall of the Roman Empire
(ABRIDGED)

KAHLIL GIBRAN
The Prophet

JOHAN WOLFGANG VON GOETHE
Faust

HERODOTUS
Histories

THOMAS HOBBES
Leviathan

HOMER
The Iliad
The Odyssey

HORACE
The Odes